Dedicated to the memory of
— Glen R. Fitzpatrick —
fair winds and following seas, my friend

ALSO BY
ROBERT DAVIES

When the River Ran Dry

THE SPECIMEN CHRONICLES

Specimen 959
Echoes of Esharam

ROBERT DAVIES

THE SEVENTH LIFE OF ALINE LLOYD

A NOVEL

Livonia, Michigan

Editors: Chet Benson & Rebecca Rue

THE SEVENTH LIFE OF ALINE LLOYD
Copyright © 2019 Robert Davies

All rights reserved. No part of this publication may be reproduced, distributed, or transmitted in any form or by any means, including photocopying, recording, or other electronic or mechanical methods, without the prior written permission of the publisher, except in the case of brief quotations embodied in critical reviews and certain other noncommercial uses permitted by copyright law. For permission requests, please write to the publisher.

This book is a work of fiction. The characters, incidents, and dialogue are drawn from the author's imagination and are not to be construed as real. Any resemblance to actual events or persons, living or dead, is entirely coincidental.

Published by BHC Press

Library of Congress Control Number: 2018949513

ISBN: 978-1-948540-91-9 (Hardcover)
ISBN: 978-1-947727-93-9 (Softcover)
ISBN: 978-1-947727-94-6 (Ebook)

For information, write:
BHC Press
885 Penniman #5505
Plymouth, MI 48170

Visit the publisher:
www.bhcpress.com

"The Old Ones were, the Old Ones are, and the Old Ones shall be. Not in the spaces we know, but between them. They walk serene and primal, undimensioned and to us unseen."

~ H.P. Lovecraft ~

THE SEVENTH LIFE OF ALINE LLOYD

PRELUDE

SECRETS. My philosophy professor lectured about the nature of secrets and I can hear him still. Without a need to qualify his statement our ancient, slightly eccentric Austrian teacher insisted secrets were made by a mysterious behavioral instrument to shield weak and flawed humanity from the truth—to hide away from others those things we think or do but cannot justify. Sometimes, he said, the worst secrets become easier to conceal when there's too much to lose if the light is allowed to invade the darkness. I ignored his words as indecipherable, pre-Socratic nonsense threatening my final grade, but today they've become something more.

    I always hated secrets, even as a kid. Secrets were simply lies of omission by another name when I was young and hadn't kept enough of them to understand the distinction. I hated surprises, too. It was irrational, perhaps, but secrets and surprises somehow made me feel inadequate and the victim of a swindle. Today, I live with a secret like no other and I'll keep this one the rest of my life because it's in my interest; all things considered, it seems a small price to pay. Reviewers in a distant future might read and find this narrative an amazing discovery—earth-shattering, perhaps—but in the beginning, most of it just seemed like plain, shitty luck to me.

    At the end of it all, we waited for a decision from shadowy figures that hide within soundproof government agencies I once believed exist only in the minds of Hollywood screenwriters. They will make demands and we will either meet them or the conflict will escalate. I'm hopeful because I know they're unwilling to provoke a power and fury they were once determined to harness, if only for a need to keep unexplained and impossible events from public view. We, on the other hand, just want to be left alone.

When I met with them on an otherwise deserted airport ramp, Burke and Halliwell stood away at what probably seemed a reasonable distance, even if it wasn't. Their Minister wanted to think about it, they said, so we agreed and a sort of truce was struck with the memory of those horrific scenes still fresh in Burke's mind.

We didn't know it then but the faceless Minister had already agreed to a proposal drafted by Burke as a condition for a peaceful end. I was surprised when he finally told us but the plan was inspired, and I have to give him credit for that. And anyway, a bargain would mean the terrible effects of another confrontation could be avoided and the tragic events would drift from memory. Ordinary people beyond the fence will never know and that truth makes Burke feel better.

In exchange, they wanted a series of in-depth discussions plus blood and tissue samples for study so that science and technology might yet be brought to bear in a hunt to explain those things nothing else can. It's unlikely they needed "interviews" for anything beyond the purpose of demonstrating thorough adherence to procedure, in case anyone above them ever asks, but they demanded a chronology, too—a narrative—as accompanying documentation to those sessions.

Burke insisted the talks would be informal but men like him don't do anything that *isn't* formal. He wouldn't admit it openly but they're convinced the transcripts will never be seen outside their insular society. Perhaps they could broker some of the research findings to other agencies in Israel or Germany through the normal process of intelligence horse-trading, but I think they'll keep most of it for themselves. The deal was reasonable so we went along with it and a chronological text was the product of our bargain.

Debriefings would take barely a week, Halliwell said. I watched her as he spoke and it was easy to see the tedious negotiation was becoming intolerable. They were polite and overtly apologetic about the delay but only because they didn't want another look behind a curtain where cautious, rational people never go. Waiting in that curtain's shadow is a promise—a direct threat—the officials would rather not face again, and who could blame them? Despite a cool façade they're still afraid of her, and they should be, but it serves to remind them what will happen if they renege on our agreement. After it ends, solitude will be its own reward and the researchers will have plenty to study, so the purposeful, delicate truce is maintained; the mutual goals—ours *and* theirs—are still in harmony. In another month, Burke's laboratory people will have something interesting to hold them over until the next time (and more interviews) with other unique, gifted people who don't yet know what's coming at them.

It couldn't be said for all the moments on the road of this strange adventure but most of it I remember in fairly elaborate detail. Do I remember by my natural memory alone, you could reasonably wonder, or is it something more? I like to think it's the former but I couldn't swear to it at this point. The officials might ask if she influences my recall merely to enhance it, but they would rather know if she shapes and guides my thoughts to her own design with or without my approval. Either way, they expected a written record as one of the conditions for our freedom—for being left alone—so I filled the pages of an ordinary Word document with our absurd and unlikely story.

"Don't limit your account," they said. "Describe what happened—the events as they occurred—but tell us more than mere facts, Mr. Morgan; be creative and think of yourself as a storyteller!"

A storyteller, perhaps, but my task was typing out the procession of an impossible tale that may never be fully explained. The important people with secret titles the public never sees wanted me to "be comfortable with the process," Burke insisted, as though I was recounting the story aloud to an audience. They stared at us from across the table and said with straight faces, "You mustn't name *us*, of course—keep our involvement removed as you would actors in a stage production, but always remember to describe how it felt."

Yes—tell the story for their archives and future study but be sure to avoid connecting them to it. After all, we can't have this sort of thing getting out, can we? I could hear them muttering in the corner and worried something bad may yet happen before we're safely gone. I want them to read that damned narrative with expectations of a sanitary, linear account, only to see and understand in the end how lives can be turned upside down or even ended *because* of them and what they represent.

Halliwell and Burke won't mind seeing their names in my notes because they will simply delete the references they don't like and leave the ones that carry no risk of identification. They'll pick through word by word in one of their hidden, windowless enclaves where "insider" status and retinal scanning are required for access. Bland people with forgettable faces will match my words against the evidence they've collected if only to reassure themselves nothing sneaky and frightening waits for them in the dark. I gave them their narration and now we will leave others to prepare for an uncertain future; they will go down those paths without us because bargains and agreements cut both ways.

While we wait out the last details (and the reliable plod of all government bureaucracies) I have decided to edit my original notes and expand them into this private account. Hurd and his Minister would be furious if they found out but Burke is smarter than that and I'm sure he considered such a thing long ago; he knows any revelations I might make will be kept under wraps and made mostly for Vienne's benefit. When this last bit is finished I'll save the document to three or four external hard drives and squirrel them away where no one would think to look. If we are ever compelled to explain, this chronology will be my first stop.

Berezan, the anemic runt from Livermore Labs (*officially*, I should add because I am not certain he ever set foot in the place) asked me during our first interview for a point of origin to the experience. Halliwell wondered, too, and since I don't dislike him as much as Berezan I answered truthfully: it was a phone call from a London attorney to my sister, Vienne. I didn't get the relayed message until later but that's really where all this started and it's as good a place as any to begin.

1
DEATH IN THE FAMILY

ON that rainy October morning, I was en route to an investigation in southeast Tennessee where firefighters and rescue teams stepped carefully over twisted aluminum panels and what little else remained of a private airplane. As they usually do, the shreds and tatters of affluence scattered up a wooded hillside gave stark testimony to the suddenness and finality of most plane crashes. Hours later, details would emerge and the backstory local newsrooms were more than eager to run filtered out through televisions as families sat down to dinner.

A dental technologies vice president from Memphis was flying himself down to Chattanooga for a conference about expensive, 3D waterjet machines that create prosthetic teeth. When weather conditions and visibility he believed would improve had not, his single-engine Mooney went into the side of a mountain at 180 mph not far from Wauhatchie. On an instrument flight plan, the controllers in Atlanta would have guided him safely for a handoff to Chattanooga Approach and vectors for an eventless landing. Instead, he committed the sin of ignoring weather updates and zero visibility, a grave error committed by those pilots without instrument training who don't always come home alive. He made no calls to air traffic controllers—no urgent request for positional help. Judging by the impact point and angle of attack as his plane tore through the trees, Mr. Memphis was flying straight and level with no idea he was about to die.

Field reporters, suitably grim in North Face jackets with embroidered network logos, looked at the charred debris field and saw the arrogance of success.

They wouldn't say it directly but all of them recognized the signs: a well-heeled, corporate climber with more money than brains who ignored rules when they became inconvenient. The pilot was a prominent industry figure, equal parts "mover and shaker" they used to say. Fourteen hours earlier he became another who paid the price for pushing his luck in fog-bound, instrument conditions he wasn't trained to handle. In the hovering mist the reporters aimed their harsh camera lights at another statistic: a horrible mistake by an up-and-coming executive unaccustomed to making them. This one would be his last.

The preliminaries pointed to simple pilot error and interviews with the dead man's associates only confirmed what was already believed: he had gone beyond himself and his flying skills because no one was there to tell him he couldn't. In the previous year, I had worked the investigation of an identical machine that suffered fuel starvation, compelling its pilot to set down inconveniently early along the furrowed rows of a cornfield outside Indianapolis.

As my plane taxied to a stop, the ramp director signaled between two hangars for our van and I pulled my phone from a pocket to find a missed call. In the drizzle on a shimmering tarmac at Chattanooga Metro Airport, I listened in silence as Vienne's voice message told me Damon was gone.

When I called her, Vienne's voice was weak and distant. I struggled with sadness but also shock because his life had not been led in dangerous pursuits or filled with high-risk adventures that invite disaster and bring little surprise for survivors when the worst finally happens. Damon didn't climb mountains or scuba dive with sharks; he didn't know a wingsuit from a garden rake and zip lining that grandmothers routinely enjoy was at the top of his "never going to happen" list. I won't pretend we were ever close, not the way brothers usually are, but Vienne's disappointment made clear my muted reaction was something less than it should be. In truth, I found myself dwelling on the pathology of his death more than the meaning of it. Arrhythmia—sudden and unexpected—took him as he slept in the sweltering heat of a cheap Nairobi hotel room. He was fit and careful to maintain a proper diet but even that couldn't shield him from what waited inside a genetically flawed heart.

Our brother made his living as an archaeologist, dividing time between lectures for master's candidates and filthy dig sites that always seem to pop up in places where decent living conditions are rare and the fly population is heaviest. He had a remarkable knack for spotting and appraising exceptional pieces, which also kept him in the favor of wealthy collectors, and we later learned a prospective client's interest in Meru tribal art was his purpose for being in Kenya at all.

Archaeology was his passion and reason for living but brokers (and the money they represent) went far beyond compensation for his part-time job at the university in Reading a few miles west of London. I've never been to equatorial Africa but I know Damon wasn't overly fond of the place. I could see Vienne in my thoughts smiling sadly at the irony, insisting Damon would resent dying so far from the fragments of Phoenician pottery and erotic Hindu sculptures cluttering his strange, angular apartment in Spain.

They bought a nook for his ashes at the cemetery in a little town near Malaga because, Vienne said, it was the only place where Damon felt he belonged. She always waited at the halfway point between us, as middle siblings are often obliged to do, but I suspect her tolerance for his eccentricities was tested more often than she would admit. He had a girlfriend I never knew about, too—a primary school teacher he met in Alicante named Isolda Marquez. We met her at the funeral but she didn't say much. Vienne learned an estrangement between them wasn't reconciled before he died so we watched her for a while, knowing how the helplessness of regret could only have made things that much worse.

I remember when he moved there to do research for his doctoral dissertation, and in the photos he took near Gibraltar he was wearing khaki expedition shorts, a Syracuse University T-shirt, and utilitarian sandals with soles made of old tires. Damon was in his element, smiling into an Iberian afternoon behind mirrored sunglasses he was convinced made him appear hip and cosmopolitan. He told Vienne about northern Europeans who flocked there to bask on the Mediterranean shore in winter, pasty white and desperate to escape gray skies when the first storms of winter rolled in from the North Atlantic. She laughed when he complained about swarms of tour groups at the airport pouring out of chartered LTU widebodies from Germany in weekly waves to invade the beaches. They lounged and smiled for photos, tanning with overpriced drinks and the false hospitality of locals who despise them. Beyond the horizon, their envious and shivering neighbors in places like Düsseldorf, Helsinki, or Aalborg huddled against the cutting wind.

Damon believed the "holiday army" couldn't truly appreciate the ground beneath their feet and most, he insisted, walked upon it in ignorance. For him, it was a hallowed place where the ancient Arab world collided with the west in a distant past as Europe clawed its way out from the Dark Ages. Two realities blending on those bright shores, he said, long before the industrial power of one subsumed nomadic traditions of the other. Alhazen walked there, and before him, Roman legions and Berber kings in the shadow of the great rock. Damon loved all of it.

Weeks went by until at last a London attorney retained by the university was given the job of organizing those aspects of Damon's estate that applied to the institution. As executor, Vienne went to see after his will and complete the administrative tasks that so often make the mourning process a worse nightmare than it should be. At first, it seemed a simple process and she authorized the release of purpose-built containers with Damon's most valuable artifacts to be sorted, cataloged, and stored in one of the dimly lit basement rooms most college archaeology departments seem to maintain. Some artifacts were more prized than others, loaned or vended off to museums, and the curators at one of those museums—in Sendai, of all places—even ran a lovely show conducted in part as a memorial to Damon's globe-spanning career and his contributions to the discipline.

It seemed odd when we discovered the notoriety he enjoyed and how much his fellow archaeologists admired and appreciated his talents. I knew he had no trouble paying his bills, but a pile of trade publications ran stories about Damon's intuitive success and he became a celebrity in a world filled with the names of people few of us have ever heard. Vienne wondered if my surprise was a product of the temperamental distance between us or simply the different people we became. I knew of Damon's travels and various appraisal jobs for Australian or Saudi billionaires mostly from Vienne, but her perspective on our brother was always better than my own.

After the remaining bits in his apartment were packed and prepared for shipment to America, Vienne called from London to tell me it was time to meet and execute bequeathing tasks. What they found inside his will, she said at nearly a whisper, was not at all expected and she begged me to come at once. Vienne never begged anyone for any reason and when I asked her to explain she simply said, "Hurry" before hanging up. There were surprises left behind, she said, surprises that would alter our perception of Damon forever. I booked the flight arrangements then and there, concerned more for the tone in Vienne's voice than anything our elder brother wrote into his will.

    I MANAGED TO sleep for most of the flight from Dulles, finishing the last drops of morning coffee by the time we broke out of the cloud layer inbound for Heathrow. Vienne had flown in from Spain two days earlier and she was waiting as my taxi squeaked to a halt in front of an imposing hotel off Sloane Square—very British, very grand. Damon's solicitor, a tall, scarlet-faced man called Liam Fields-Donnelley, met us two hours later at his firm's offices on the east side of London near the boundary of Whitechapel. While we waited on a junior solicitor laying out documents in tidy groups on a splendid oak table, I reminded Vienne of the neighborhood's notorious past as Jack the Ripper's hunting grounds. I said so mostly to pass the time but she didn't seem to care. A moment later Donnelley arrived and with him was the first step of my sudden, bizarre odyssey.

    "Yes, well," he began as he traced a finger along the lines on a page of notes before him, "we have concluded most of your brother's affairs with his employer—the artifacts he left as legacies to the university."

    We waited again as he shifted his eyes between folders as though he needed to convince himself all was in order. On a wall behind us a massive clock the size of a stop sign—transparent to show off its polished brass gears—clunked and clicked the seconds away, and from it the only break from silence I knew was wearing thin on Vienne's patience. Donnelley seemed to know it, too.

    "Oh, and Damon's personal effects in Spain have been boxed by our Madrid representative's local agents as well; they were given access to his apartment by way of a surprisingly cooperative former girlfriend, I'm told."

    Vienne waited through a last pause as Donnelley shuffled the release papers she would be required to sign, until at last he drew from his folio the reason and purpose that brought us all the way to England.

    "Your sister saw the contents before you arrived, Mr. Morgan, but the bulk of his estate and its disposition, such that it is, can be finalized now that both of you are here. The document is rather crude by professional standards, of course, but British law recognizes and accepts its authenticity, regardless that he was not a subject of the Crown. You may review at your leisure and then provide signatures to indicate acceptance."

"It's only us," Vienne said softly, turning sideways in her chair toward me. "Except for the artifacts that went to that college, plus money and some jewelry for Isolda, everything he had passes to you and me."

I looked at her and shrugged but she leaned over and placed her hand on top of mine.

"This might be a bit of a shock, okay?"

Another surprise—another secret; I hate them still.

Donnelley took the silence as his cue.

"I should note the properties themselves carry current-market value, of course, but the bank accounts and precious metals are relatively static, provided you move them without long-term delay. We can recommend a well-regarded finance institution to guide you with these sorts of matters, Mr. Morgan."

"This is why you needed to be here," Vienne whispered as she slid the papers across the table.

I went down the handwritten list line by line and it seemed like a cruel, impossible joke. Had it been played on me by Vienne or on us both by a dead brother with a unique, misplaced sense of humor? It couldn't be real, I decided with a frown, as the contents stared back at me from the noticeably creased paper.

On the page, a single column of items paralleled a precise value in British pounds and US dollars that added to a subtotal before being divided, half to Vienne and half to me. I saw stock, annuities, and rotating investment accounts in Switzerland, Germany, and Belize. Further along, he listed locations of safe deposit boxes in several countries holding considerable gold, some silver, and cash in varying currencies that alone totaled to nearly $2.4 million. Damon gifted sole ownership of his Malaga apartment to Vienne (which I regarded as her reward for having kept in touch better and more frequently than I), but near the middle of the list there was something else: a simple line that described a clean deed for a private dwelling on eight acres in the Denbighshire countryside Damon left specifically to me. It was time to consider how little we knew about the life our elder brother led, and how it could be that so much had been acquired by one who once cared so little for material wealth. No matter the method or mechanism, Damon left this world a wealthy man.

I looked at Vienne and then to Donnelley but they said nothing. There was no mistake, hoax, or misapprehension; without others to whom he felt an obligation, and except for a handsome legacy of cash and the bits of jewelry he left to Isolda, Vienne and I were his sole beneficiaries. Because of Damon's relative youth and healthy condition, Donnelley noted, his risk of death by any means beyond unforeseen injury was low. The work was certainly benign, too; rummaging around in galleries, nodding at auctions, or brushing away the layers of dirt at an active dig site with a toothbrush could hardly be described as thrill-inspiring. However, Donnelley explained, the money Damon's exceedingly rare (and private) collection could bring was considerable and steps were taken. I wondered why he thought to create a will and testament at all, and when Donnelley continued the answer was easy to see.

Many of the pieces our brother gathered over the years, with the understanding he would gift them to the university, carried significant historic value, compelling his employers to ask for a valid will. They did so to avoid difficulty if Damon suddenly died in a car accident, for example, or by some other tragic event. Their own obligation to protect their interests was no less important than his, it would seem, and an understanding between them made a formal will and testament inescapable.

"You are now fully apprised of your brother's last wishes and those parts of his estate he wanted passed to you," he continued. "The documentation will be copied and sent along sometime next week. Are there any questions before we finalize the transfer authorizations?"

I looked on in silence to absorb the changes coming at both of us. The money, at least, was not entirely without explanation; collectors and brokers who take five-star hotels and private jets for granted know an expert eye is worth the trouble and expense, if only to help them establish a price when each piece is in turn sold to others. I admit the actual dollar amount was well beyond anything we imagined, but the fortune Damon amassed from doing for the wealthy what they couldn't do for themselves was at least understandable. I smiled and shook my head sadly at what I didn't know about my own brother's admirable financial condition, but it was the property that grabbed my attention.

"This place," I said, pointing to the words on Donnelley's paper. "It's in Wales, isn't it?"

"That is correct," he replied with a polite, automatic smile. "The property itself is located near Llangollen, which lies about fifty miles southwest from Liverpool; a bit touristy for my taste but quite lovely. Damon noted your fondness for the family's Welsh heritage, which may have compelled him to leave it with you."

I had been to Cardiff and Swansea on two brief occasions but my knowledge of our paternal ancestral home was sorely lacking. It didn't seem to bother Donnelley, so I asked for more detail, hoping he might know why Damon was interested in real estate. His answers didn't help explain Damon's idea of appropriate inheritances but another source, he insisted, *might*. Jeremy Collingwood, a local solicitor in Llangollen, was retained when Damon bought the land and that made him the logical person to assist should I decide to sell the property outright or hold it against market fluctuations for a better, more advantageous opportunity.

"Damon never mentioned owning property *anywhere*, let alone in Wales," I said, frowning.

Donnelley returned one of those sympathetic "sorry, but you're asking the wrong person" smiles as he handed me a business card.

"This is Mr. Collingwood's contact information. His firm was engaged as your brother's agency, so he would be far better suited to fill in the blanks."

I suddenly felt exposed and alone. Vienne only shrugged with raised eyebrows that signaled her agreement with Donnelley's suggestion. Time was no issue, since my boss insisted that I take as much of it for bereavement as needed, but a journey to look at a cramped little hut on a muddy field in Wales would require a better reason than Damon leaving it to me in his will.

"Look," I said at last, "can't we just put it up for sale right now and take the best offer?"

"Certainly," Donnelley replied. "What you do with your property is entirely your affair. Our part is ensuring you understand and take custody of those items in accordance with British law and your brother's wishes."

I looked at the card in a frantic search for an excuse not to go. I had no desire to fight with real estate people and I knew enough to know I was out of my depth in selling Damon's land on my own. I also knew what she was thinking before I asked and when I turned again to Vienne, the face of disappointment returned.

"You don't have to say anything," I mumbled.

"It's your call, Evan."

"But you obviously think I should go out there."

"He left the place to you; this is *your* decision."

Vienne watched my reaction with the same hint of betrayal I heard in her voice the day she called to tell me of his death. I didn't care about Damon's house, she would argue, simply because I didn't care enough about *him*. I felt trapped inside a problem for which the most acceptable solution was a forced march to Wales. In quiet frustration, I saw only the path I wanted most to avoid and one that led to a seasonal tourist trap in Denbighshire.

More secrets, I thought in silence; more surprises. In that same moment one of the forks in the road that confront us from time to time demanded an answer. I've thought of those seconds that tick-tocked away to the cadence of Liam Donnelley's expensive clock and the binary decision point that waited with the patience of a tax collector. I had a chance to go this way or that—to accept or turn away. Had I chosen otherwise and left instructions to sell Damon's property, the damage would likely have been confined to waiting Vienne out until she got over her disappointment

All of it was avoidable.

Instead, I nodded, and we signed the papers. Donnelley prepared for the transfer of Damon's UK funds into our accounts. The metals and bundles of cash, plus property holdings and stock options, remained where they were until we decided how and when to deal with them. The prospect of a road trip to Wales, however, went quickly from concept to reality and the logistics question needed an answer.

"I've never been up that far but I'm guessing they don't have much in the way of an airport?"

Fields-Donnelley had done his homework.

"Virgin has trains leaving from Euston Station up to Ruabon or Wrexham, so that option might be favorable to you. You will have to hire a car regardless but it's only a few miles farther on to Llangollen—less than twenty minutes, I should think."

Another pause and it was done. Vienne's flight from London City Airport to Malaga wasn't scheduled until later in the day so we lunched in Kensington and held onto each other through the awkward moments, trying our best to understand why Damon kept the gifts he left for us in the pages of his will a secret.

We felt gratitude, of course, and maybe some guilt for wrongly presuming his life's pursuits were more important to him than his own family. Through most of it we spoke about better times when we were young and when childhood memories were still under construction. Vienne wondered what our parents would think had they survived to see that moment, but the question was pointless. After my sister climbed in a taxi to Gatwick, I sat with a hotel concierge in grateful silence while she organized my reservations and mapped out the next day's adventure in a railway coach bound for Wales.

2
NO ORDINARY DAY

MINDFUL of the mysteries waiting in Llangollen, I suddenly welcomed a return trip to Wales, one that would take me beyond the borders of Cardiff and Swansea. I guess it's reasonable to say most people in America couldn't find Wales quickly on a globe, but once you've discovered and seen the country for yourself, it gets inside you and sticks. The place is mostly mountainous and vistas across green valleys are breathtaking in any season. The shoreline is often defined by severe cliffs but also broad, sandy beaches I never knew were there until I walked them. It rains a lot, but when the sun streaks through the gaps between clouds, you stop and watch a while because it's just that beautiful.

Wales is also an ancient land, inhabited since Neanderthals arrived over 200,000 years ago. Through the Copper, Bronze, and Iron Ages, tribes solidified their position and a distinct culture rose on the foundation of what would become a unique society. Only decades after the birth of Christ, the first Romans arrived and a conquest-turned-occupation continued for nearly 350 years. During this period, the enigmatic Druids were hunted, cornered and slaughtered by General Paulinus' legions on the island of Anglesey (Mona, in those days), the very soldier who ended the uprising of the fierce, woman-warrior Boudicca of the Iceni. Rome's dominance over Wales ended when the Empire's reach outstretched its ability to defend against mounting barbarian attacks at home and all of Britain was abandoned by the early 400s.

Welsh identity developed over a thousand years as the future country adjusted to its post-Roman division into distinct, competing kingdoms. From the Medieval period through the Middle Ages, attacks came from Normans, Picts, Irish, and Viking hordes but the Welsh survived. Despite the effective annexation in the mid-1500s by Henry VIII (whose uncle was Welsh, by the way), a unique culture emerged.

I read texts about Welsh history in college due mostly to a private feeling of distance from my heritage. Friends regarded their family ties to Italy, Ireland or any other country as a given and some had relatives in the "old country" they visited regularly. For me, there was no such experience. It seemed as though my identity as an American always allowed for, and even encouraged, a connection to ancestral beginnings, but I was unable to see it. When I climbed in a taxi for the ride to Euston Station, all of it changed.

THE JOURNEY UP was spent mostly in a rainy, gray blur but it went faster than I expected. I remembered hit-or-miss train schedules when I made my first excursions after college. Like many Americans standing at the chasm between youth and the rest of their lives, I wanted to see something of the world before jobs and responsibilities helped time erode the notion into an unfulfilled dream. My roommate's sister was studying at Christ's College and a chance to visit (not to mention our glaring lack of continental language skills) made England the obvious choice, so three of us boarded a flight to London. Only wide-eyed kids at that time, we watched the fields of East Anglia speed by, stopping in Bishop's Stortford and Cambridge to visit friends for a week. Life was a different proposition then but things change and time passes.

When my train eased to a stop at Ruabon, I felt rising loneliness and isolation, unsure if it was only the adjustment to Damon's death or something more. The leaves had abandoned their trees long before and the cold air hit me when I stepped slowly onto the narrow platform and stood stupidly alone to survey my surroundings and find a taxi without drawing too much attention.

I found my cabbie on the Station Road loop, a cheerful man called Eddie who replied to most sentences with, "Oh yeah?" Not the way we do in America—challenging and hostile—but with a polite acceptance tinged with just enough conversational indifference so that further discussion was clearly optional. After a short ride west along the banks of the River Dee, he dropped me at the Royal Hotel where, Liam Donnelley had insisted, it would be easier to let them arrange for a rental car.

The sunset was nearly finished beneath rolling, slate skies when I settled and unpacked. After dinner, I lounged in my room and a parade of television programs in Welsh only amplified my long-held resentment at not being taught the language as a kid. The conspicuous quiet of an off-season Denbighshire village at night made sleeping a nearly unattainable goal for one just in from a metropolis where noise is a constant. Without the mild sedatives I usually keep around to deal with strange hotel rooms I could rely only on fatigue to finally send me over.

IN THE MORNING I felt better. After breakfast a short walk in the cool, still air brought me to Jeremy Collingwood's office off Berwyn Street, and the answers I needed. We exchanged the usual pleasantries but he was profoundly different from the image I'd made in my mind on the ride up from London. In a splendid contradiction to my pre-conceived idea of a rural Welsh solicitor (bushy brows, ruddy complexion, and a heavy cardigan), Jeremy could portray a very convincing, if slightly graying, Omar Sharif.

"How long have you been here, Mr. Collingwood?"

"Almost thirty years now." He smiled. "I'm from Merthyr, but we came up in the mid-eighties."

"Just wanted to get away?" I asked.

"I met my wife in Swansea, but she was born and brought up in Ruthin. After our boys arrived, city life became more than she could tolerate so we settled here."

"It is a beautiful place," I added.

Jeremy grinned with a nod as an assistant moved deftly past us with a carafe of freshly brewed coffee. His office was a casual, welcoming place by comparison with Fields-Donnelley's modern corporate spaces filled with trendy Finnish spruce and stainless steel fixtures, but that quality operated against my plan. The moment wasn't what it was supposed to be and not the place my imagination had formed and nurtured. Jeremy was not what *he* was supposed to be, either. I needed him to be curt, distant, and suspicious of a clumsy foreigner invading places he didn't belong. I wanted him to dislike me for no apparent reason and do only what was necessary to conclude our business and then point the way out. If he eyed me with distaste and annoyance, leery of an American arriving with little warning and questionable intent, I would have a decent excuse for abandoning the idea for a fast retreat back to the States. Instead, he was (and still is) one of the easiest gentlemen I ever met.

Alerted by Donnelley, no doubt, Jeremy presented the paperwork from Damon's purchase and with it a detailed map showing its location nearer to Llantysilio village. He had aerial photos, too, circling with a capped ballpoint a solitary house positioned on a slight diagonal between two forested hills.

"That's it," he said. "Your very own Welsh estate."

I looked on, hoping he would notice my confusion.

"I presumed it was a farm," I offered. "The trees make it look more like a retreat in the woods than a place for growing crops."

"Oh, it *was* a farm," Jeremy said quickly. "Well, a long time ago, but still…"

"And the family?" I asked.

"The last ones went away south when they grew too old to tend the place. They sold up to some famous Argie poet in the early eighties, but she sped off home to Buenos Aires when the South Atlantic War made her somewhat of a pariah up here."

"Nobody else lived there since?"

"A few, but mostly it went vacant for quite a time—decades, actually."

"We never knew Damon had this place," I mumbled. "Did he spend a lot of time there?"

Jeremy replied with a slow shake of his head.

"He came 'round first about three years ago, asking after available properties, but the agent didn't have anything that suited. When this parcel came open again a year ago last spring, they sent notice. We made arrangements with the owner—an oral surgeon in Sheffield—and Damon flew up. He bought it next day and that was that."

I had the chronology, at least, but not the reason.

"He moved from Spain?"

"Not full time," Jeremy replied. "He had the carpenters do a proper renovation, and you'll see it's been upgraded to modern standards rather well, but he was in and out over the past year."

"Did he keep it for a vacation home?"

"Not really, no. After the renovation, Damon sort of disappeared for a while. He left instructions to contact him in the event anyone asked after the property and that was about it."

"I don't understand," I said. "Why go to those lengths if he didn't intend to live there?"

"We assumed it was for investment purposes," Jeremy replied. "They come up from London now and again looking for a nice spot without Tube stations and sirens—nouveau twits from Hampstead or Knightsbridge with Jags in the car park and sailing yachts down on the Channel."

"My brother was nothing like that, Mr. Collingwood."

"No indeed," Jeremy replied, "and it was clear he had no interest in selling after all."

I smiled and nodded at the idea. Nothing in Jeremy's description would have made sense only a day or two earlier, but that was before Vienne and I saw Damon's will. Something must've changed in his life to make him consider investment properties and deposit boxes full of gold and silver. Had a colleague at the university, perhaps, or an acquaintance who watches real estate trends put him onto the idea? At once, I imagined Vienne was going through a similar exercise that very moment in southern Spain and shaking her head sadly as the cleaners finished up in Damon's apartment. Jeremy leaned on his elbows, lowering his voice considerably as he spoke.

"If I might ask, Mr. Morgan, did you intend to sell off the property straight away or wait a while?"

I couldn't decide if the question was asked with specific intent or if he was only curious. The fees he charged for representing Damon's interests weren't modest but neither were they excessive, if that's where he was going. The suddenly hushed tone seemed odd, too, as if to suggest my answer was best kept between us.

"I'd like to see it, first," I replied. "This is all new to me, so I'd rather not make decisions until I understand how and why my brother came to be here in the first place."

"Yes, of course," Jeremy said, but it was clear he hoped for something more definitive. I waited another moment, looking over the paperwork to buy time while I considered my options.

"You said Damon left suddenly, Mr. Collingwood, but you're sure there was no particular reason?"

"I couldn't say with certainty. We were given to understand his work duties would keep him on the move for some time, but…"

"Why do *you* think he left in a hurry?"

Jeremy looked through the window for a moment and I saw at once the conversation had taken him to an uncomfortable place.

"Mr. Collingwood?"

He sipped at his coffee and held up a hand the way people do to insulate themselves from a question their words may invite or to convey a certain caution and distance so as not to be blamed.

"I don't have anything specific, but it's possible his neighbor may have become a bit much for Damon to handle."

"Oh? What's the neighbor's story, if you don't mind me asking?"

Jeremy's voice was deliberate and measured in spite of the privacy of his meeting room. It was unlikely anyone could overhear, even at a conversational level behind a closed door, yet his tone remained cautious.

"Aline Lloyd—she lives alone on the other side of the hill from your property. She's been up in the valley about four years now. Not a recluse or shut-in, certainly, but mostly she keeps herself to herself."

"Was there friction between them?" I asked. "Damon wasn't exactly the confrontational type."

"I wouldn't say it was *friction*, really, but there have been three separate owners of your property who sold up and moved on since Aline came down, and I think your brother was simply the most recent."

I wanted to avoid presumptions and judgment of others I hadn't met, especially as a foreign visitor in another land, but Jeremy's characterization of Damon's neighbor sounded like something more than a crotchety, intolerant old lady. I waited as he wiped the coffee droplets from a glazed, ceramic mug sculpted in the exaggerated likeness of a snake's head.

"Three owners in four years?"

"Yeah," he said, nodding, "and none of them lasted more than a few months. The house has been vacant most of the time and only got a decent wash and brush up when Damon was here. Aline can be a bit difficult, you see."

I smirked at him knowingly and with a nod at the image forming in my mind: a nasty-tempered spinster, calling the cops because the music is forever too loud.

"Mean old battleship, is she?" I grinned.

Jeremy's eyes went wide open.

"Oh no, Mr. Morgan, nothing like that. She's more your age, actually; mid-thirties, I'd say. Aline's a very pretty girl but not always easy to come at."

"Any particular reason?"

"Temperament, I suppose. She was a bit of a mystery when we first saw her. Aline came here from a transitional facility after some troubles up in Scotland—Glasgow, I believe it was—and the social services man advised she was best left alone, so we leave her alone."

"What does she do?" I wondered, suddenly more interested in the dynamic between Damon and an oddball hermit.

"She owns a fashion boutique up in Colwyn Bay; does very nicely from it, too. Most days she's pleasant enough, so long as you keep a distance and stick to the formalities."

"I remember Colwyn Bay from the travel pamphlets."

"It's a nice little seaside town, if you've never been—very quaint. The summer crowds are a bit thick, though…"

"Seems like a long way to go for a day job, doesn't it?"

"Aline makes her way about in an ancient Rover cast off from the Royal Marines. Knows how to look after it, too—not afraid of getting her hands dirty."

"But she settled all the way down here?" I asked. "Why not find something closer to her shop?"

"I couldn't say for sure, but I think she just prefers space around her—away from the crowds. She loves the trees, and anyway, she has a manager and two employees that see after things day to day. With all the laptop computers and telephones with cameras these days, it's not essential for her to pop in each morning, is it?"

"No, I guess not."

Another image began to form in my mind, but the description of the enigmatic Miss Lloyd only created more questions.

"You said she had trouble in Scotland?"

"That's what we were told," Jeremy replied, "and we tend to leave that part alone, if you take my meaning."

"That part?"

He leaned back with a nervous laugh, peering through the window and down to the street. I had struck a sour chord, and Jeremy's expression confirmed it, but knowing a notoriously aloof woman owned the adjacent parcel pushed me to want to understand what I was getting into.

"It's not entirely clear as to the circumstances, and I'm certainly not casting aspersions toward Aline, you understand, but…"

"Go on, Mr. Collingwood," I said, but his response came nearly under his breath.

"Emotional difficulties, apparently; they had her in a sort of ward for a brief time, you see. The government man explained her treatment was quite successful and we shouldn't regard Aline differently than any other."

"Did they elaborate on her condition or the nature of these difficulties?" I asked.

"Not a chance," he said, snorting. "They would never reveal such things, and I can't name all the violations if they divulged private medical information. They would only say she'd been discharged from hospital and was making a new start here in Denbighshire. Aline is from Cardiff, so it's not surprising she wanted to restart somewhere in Wales."

In the middle of our conversation, and for no reason I could think of, a new image came suddenly and clearly into my mind like a photo burned onto a glass transparency dangling in front of my eyes. I'd never experienced such a thing, but the picture was nearly alive with an image of a windswept neighborhood on an island. It was unrecognizable by any landmark I'd seen and nondescript to a stranger, yet somehow, I knew at once where it was. A figure walked alone in tall grass between six or seven stout houses. I could hear myself muttering the words but they came out on their own as if I was a puppet in the hands of a clever ventriloquist.

"Stornoway—Damon's neighbor came here from Stornoway."

Jeremy blinked a few times and it was clear my unexpected revelation took him off guard. I couldn't tell him how I knew where the neighbor girl came from because I had no idea. My surprise was no less than his but the words just came out and the awkward moment went on.

"They had her at a sort of halfway house for patients returning to society. Did Mr. Fields-Donnelley mention…"

"In the Hebrides," I added quickly.

"Yes, that's right. She was with them a few months before she was sent on her own again."

My ears clicked and began to ring in the high-pitched tone I experience from time to time. The condition started when I was young and never lasts for long, but it seemed louder than usual and with a mild sensation of pressure. I looked at Jeremy for a moment but was unable to make a sound. His eyebrows were up, waiting for me to speak, but I could only ride out the seconds and that piercing noise until it began to ease. I cleared my throat needlessly and returned to the map.

"No fence between the properties?"

He looked at the map mostly with relief and probably grateful for a change in topic.

"No, but that's not unusual here; why do you ask?"

"No reason," I said quickly, "just wondered, I guess. It would be handy to know the property line to avoid crossing over it by accident; I'd rather not disturb her while I explore the area."

"There are boundary poles on the corners you can see quite easily. The road forms the western side as well and that should help you find your bearings."

The ringing returned but this time it was much louder, shrill and with a discomfort Jeremy noticed.

"Are you well, Mr. Morgan? Can I get you a tablet—something for a headache, perhaps?"

"No, no," I replied, "it'll pass in a few moments. I get ringing in my ears once in a while—a sort of mild tinnitus—it's probably flaring up from all the travel, that's all."

Jeremy smiled, but his eyes shifted suddenly in a way that seemed to expect trouble to walk through his door.

"As you say, but do let me know if you'd like to rest or maybe have a short visit with the doctor."

"Thanks, but I'm fine," I answered.

As the sensation eased, I couldn't take my eyes from the map Jeremy laminated between sheets of cellophane. I felt stuck in a strange daydream, aware of it as though watching from outside my body. Only the map mattered and I could hear footfalls on the street clopping along like a hobnail boot on old paving stones. The sensation released its grip once more and I looked at Jeremy.

"Can I see the property now?"

"Yes of course," he replied. "I'll just grab my coat and we're off."

It shouldn't have been surprising but the ride up to my new acquisition went by quickly, reminding me of the close geography of a small town and my distance from the city streets of D.C. The road curved gently uphill as Jeremy leaned forward, craning his neck, nearly against the wheel so he wouldn't miss the gap between two hedgerows where a pebbled drive fell suddenly downward. The way was uneven and scattered with puddles, leveling where a very Welsh, two-story stone house waited in the clutches of untended shrubbery and groundcover advancing with each passing month.

Brand new, six-pane windows were set deep into place and a porch with a steep-pitched, narrow roof guarded a heavy wooden door painted in thick coats of dark green. Above, the slate roof I had noticed in Jeremy's photos was gone, replaced instead with utilitarian metal panels—ribbed and tightly fitting against the weather and likely changed out by Damon's renovation crew. I stood next to the car for a moment, smiling at a scene the manager of a Pier 1 Imports store might call "new rustic."

"Is everything in Wales made of stone?" I asked.

"Not quite," Jeremy said, grinning, "but stone doesn't rot and it doesn't burn so there is a wisdom to it."

He pulled the keys from his pocket and handed them over, nodding for me to lead. After the door moved silently on its hinges, absent the creaks and groans I was sure were waiting, a wide plank floor—smooth and blackened by a century of traffic—led through a foyer to an inviting living room. The white, lime-washed walls were blank and above them, a low ceiling of rough-hewn beams set in plaster separated the ground floor from upstairs bedrooms.

"We came up last night to check on things and air it out a bit," Jeremy began. "The electricity and water are back on and the television's connected as well."

The furniture was surprisingly modern and Damon's kitchen was fitted out with major appliances in brushed metal finish sitting neatly between fashionable brick arches. It was surprising to find the place so livable, despite the short time that had passed since work crews and carpenters finished up, but Jeremy anticipated my curiosity.

"You'll find most of the essentials except for linens and bathroom items. Kitchen's done up but I'm afraid the plates and cookware are rather gaudy. Damon bought them at a discount store but they work well enough, and he didn't seem to be the sort who's concerned for trends or fashion."

We walked through a narrow hallway where the stairs jutted upward on steep treads, opening to each of three bedrooms. I went slowly, inspecting the way people do when visiting a place for the first time and applying silent judgment of others and the styles they prefer. Damon had obviously left decorating in the hands of professionals and doing so made for a stark contradiction to his cluttered and confused apartment in Spain. Jeremy handed me a sheet of paper with names and addresses so I would have a starting point when searching out food stores and places to buy pillows or rugs.

"We have most of these things locally," he explained, "but a dash over to Wrexham or up to Liverpool will find the more specialized items; Chester has some good shops, too."

With the changing season, I decided, throw rugs would be needed on cold nights in bare feet padding to the kitchen, but I could feel Jeremy's eyes suddenly on me.

"Eventually, you will run into Aline," he said gently. "Maybe on the road or in town."

I waved his thought away and said, "I don't want to cause trouble for anyone and least of all a neighbor who has no patience for strangers."

"I understand, Mr. Morgan, and I'm glad of it, but Aline…she's not a *bad* person or a lunatic. The ones who sold the place to Damon were told about Aline's problems in Scotland and it made them a bit leery of her. They get odd ideas, especially when the others who came here before packed it in so suddenly; it's hard for them to not imagine Aline had anything to do with it, you understand."

"Something must've put them off," I said.

Had it been this way for Damon, I wondered? Jeremy nodded through the window where the hillside rose gently.

"She's a bit different and not…I just mean we've gotten used to her and she's gotten used to us. She doesn't like strangers and you're right about that, but all I'm saying is this: be patient—let some time pass, and she'll get used to you, too. You're an even-tempered lad and she'll see that."

He waited for me to speak, but I was suddenly lost in a strange void between decisions. It was clear he wondered if I was there to stay or if I meant to take the profit from selling off and return to America. I wondered, too. For most of the ride up from London, I'd spent the time reinforcing my carefully made intention only to look around, nod, and then make arrangements for the sale, but suddenly, standing in a house I didn't buy, the strange sensation of belonging began to invade my thoughts.

It was supposed to run only as a formality—a dutiful inspection tour for the sole purpose of warding off Vienne's disappointment by proclaiming the mission complete and unworthy of further effort. Having done so, I would be free and clear of the obligation and off for a late plane back to D.C., yet something held me in time and by a silent hand. I wondered in that moment if ownership of the farm was a compelling enough experience to withdraw my complaint and stick around. I could feel them coming on loud and clear—the justifications and rationalized arguments making the little house into more than a real estate transaction. Whether I liked it or not, my new place was beginning to feel like a home.

Jeremy's cell phone blared out a "Rule, Britannia!" ringtone with a confirmation from his assistant my rental car had been delivered and photocopies of my driving license and passport were sufficient. We walked a while on the overgrown weed field that once was Damon's front lawn. Jeremy insisted "a good going over with a sharpened mower would set it right in the spring," but I wasn't as confident.

At last, and with the keys safely in my coat pocket, we returned to town and one of the lengthy signature sessions I'd thought I left behind at Fields-Donnelley's law office in London. The deed was duly transferred and insurance certificates updated. My scrawl at the bottom of service contracts for utilities shifted responsibility from Damon to me. After a handful of ancillary arrangements, I shoehorned myself into a blue Vauxhall Astra that might fit easily in the bed of my F250 back in Virginia. Armed with Jeremy's roadmap and determined to adjust once more to driving in a passenger's seat, I went painfully slowly over the distance back to the little house in the valley.

THE AIR WAS quiet when I stood again on the gravel of my driveway, and it seemed like a good time to check in with Vienne. She told me a platoon of workmen had finished clearing out some repair tasks before she arrived from her hotel, but it felt strange and sad looking at boxes in Damon's guest room and the pieces of his relationship with Isolda that would be returned to her as an afterthought from strangers. I told her about Damon's time at the farm and his abrupt departure. I told her about "the neighbor girl," too, mostly because Jeremy's description didn't square with the previous owners' apparent belief she was still off in the head.

I walked with mild curiosity through the weeds angling for a depression that defined an informal line between my backyard and a wooded expanse rising up a hillside where the big trees stood like monuments. Beneath them, twisted growth appeared here or there across a thick carpet of brown leaves, and I smiled at the stark contrast between the place and my antiseptic, big-city condominium.

A solitary pair of ravens weaved their way gently through a stand of young birch, and I watched them for a while. They spun in a graceful arc to perch in a tangle of branches, but as they did, my eyes were drawn at once to something near the ground—obvious and impossible to miss. It was the first time I ever saw her and the moment still brings a tingle up my spine when I recall it today.

Amid the shades of brown and black through the branches of trees—barren and cold under a clouded, autumn sky—Aline Lloyd looked straight at me, unmoving and clearly unmoved. Her hair, long and blonde with columns of gentle curls, flared out against the gloom like a pyramid of gold in a black-and-white movie. Her eyes were barely visible in the fading light, but still she stood fast in a dark purple cloak that seemed too flimsy for the cool air.

Without thinking I waved in a half-hearted gesture that was more reflex than consideration, simply to break the awkward pause and let her know I was looking, too. Suddenly, and without a word, she turned and moved slowly up the hill, wandering gently through the ancient oaks. Even from that distance I could see she was barefoot, but it didn't seem to bother her. After a moment, she stopped and turned one last time before disappearing into the trees.

I stood for a while in silence with an expectation she would show again, but I abandoned the idea with Jeremy's words echoing in my mind: "She keeps herself to herself." At least, I thought with a smile, the mysterious girl from the farm next door came over the hill to have a look. A good sign, I wondered, or was she merely sizing me up for battle? He said Aline could be hard to get along with, but I was in no hurry to find out. Perhaps she just needed to look and listen, and I decided it was best to avoid the trees for a while.

At the back door to my garage, I stopped to inspect an iron mud scraper set into a crude concrete square beside the stone walkway. Surface rust and the absence of dirt around it suggested it hadn't been used much, but as I reached for the door, I could feel the sensation wash over me—singular and unmistakable. As if held by a memory brought back from a dream, I knew she was still watching. I spun quickly but nothing was there; no one was watching. My heart raced and both hands trembled at my side. A cat's tail puffs up and its back hunches under the same pressure, but it was only imagination taking me away.

"Goddamn jitters," I mumbled aloud to no one.

I stayed a while longer, knowing the farm had never been Damon's home. Was it becoming mine? I spent a last night at the Royal, and ordinary household items would be my target the following morning. Despite my resolve to guard against it, the process of acclimating was already underway.

A SHORT CIRCUIT around the narrow triangle made by my little farmhouse, Llangollen and Wrexham made for an interesting adventure in domestic shopping. I wandered through a Sainsbury's supermarket and smiled at both the familiar and utterly alien European branding, mostly grateful marketing philosophies aren't so different from ours in America. I filled my "carriage" with plenty of options to maximize my chances of avoiding death by starvation; dining at a London hotel is one thing, but working my way through a Welsh kitchen to create even a rough estimate of breakfast is quite another. Grinning involuntarily at the evidence of my shifting sense of place, I stepped slowly through the shops in a quest for items I buy at home without a thought. It was slow going, but I was at least slightly prepared for what was becoming a long-term proposition.

In town, I expected them to stare and whisper behind flattened hands, but the clerks and shop owners of Llangollen seemed not to notice. A few wondered why an American would come so far up for a Welsh "holiday" since the summer crowds and tour groups were gone. I guess they were typical of small-town people in a lot of places: courteous and genuine by force of their nature. There is a requirement among villagers the world over to look after neighbors and help when they should because they are their own best support mechanism; it's been that way for thousands of years and nothing's changing it now. I looked at them with envy and a growing sense of distance from the big city I'd left only days before. In the faces of those villagers was a reflection and measure of home, and I wondered for the first time in a long time what lured me out from my own little town so long ago.

When evening fell, my house was still alien the way all new places are, but the night passed easily and I woke only once to gleaming moonlight streaking in through the bedroom window like a silent and reassuring signal everything would work itself out in time.

AFTER BREAKFAST I was ready to renew my inspection tour. Out-of-date magazines with ads about travel to exotic destinations were fanned out like playing cards on a coffee table in my front room, and it made me wonder who had left them. Damon wouldn't have considered such a detail, which left his decorators as the most likely source.

When I stepped slowly across the yard still enveloped in a clinging fog, only the birds, awake and calling out from the hillside beyond, broke the quiet. An occasional car up on the road passed slowly through poor visibility, and I looked at their headlight beams with memories of the pilot in Tennessee who died so violently. I thought about other things, too; the path I followed to a quiet, Welsh farm seemed somehow more than a long road trip and an unwanted administrative burden. There was plenty of time to decide, but I could sense the answer to a question had already been made: I had less interest in leaving after all and changes would follow. Unsure of myself and what I wanted, I decided to give it another week.

ON THE FIFTH day, my inheritance was shifting from an impersonal real estate opportunity to a place that looked more familiar each time I returned from town. I was getting pretty good at right-side driving, too, although the habit of reaching for the shifter with my left hand was more difficult to acquire and getting honked at for wrong-way incursions became embarrassingly routine.

As I poured coffee, my phone vibrated on the tile counter; Vienne was waiting at Barajas Airport north of Madrid before her flight to New York and a connector to Montreal. I listened as she spoke, but her experience at Damon's apartment described a much different process than my first week in Denbighshire.

"Are you still in the UK?" she asked.

"Standing in my little country kitchen; I just conquered the new coffee machine."

"Wow! Are you moving in, or what?"

"I'm not sure yet. The place was already furnished so I didn't have much to buy, but it's very livable while I figure out what I'm going to do with it."

"Is it nice, or all messed up like Damon's apartment?"

"Very nice, actually," I replied. "It's still a little weird, and it felt like I was house-sitting for him when I first got here, but I'm getting more comfortable each day."

Vienne's surprise was understandable but it brought a note of relief. She made no secret of her hope I would retain ownership of the property instead of selling it off, at least for a while.

"How'd it go with Damon's lawyer?" she asked.

"He had everything ready and waiting," I replied. "Are you finished in Spain?"

When she told me of the awkward moments when Isolda collected her things, I listened and nodded at the image in my mind as she walked through Damon's empty apartment. Vienne hadn't made up her mind any faster than I, but the similar condition suddenly held little importance to me. I walked in a nervous circle as she described how precise and neat the painters had been, but she went on for a while and the words became irrelevant, as if I was in a hurry and she'd called to tell me the price of gasoline went up or a friend I never met had become engaged; no matter the subject, I had little interest in hearing about it.

The paperwork was forwarded from Fields-Donnelley to the authorities in Malaga, she said; there was nothing else to do except make her choice to keep it or sell. I nodded impatiently as I moved on a looping circuit around my house, wishing silently she would hang up. Just to break the routine, I detoured instead through my front room, stopping to peer out from a window and up the gentle rise where my driveway meets the road. I had no particular reason to look, but somehow, I needed to. It wasn't surprising when I saw a sand-colored Land Rover idling at my gate. Pale sunlight glaring against the driver's window prevented a decent view inside, yet I knew who was at the wheel just the same.

I knelt on a couch positioned near the window while bracing myself to get a better look. At once, the Rover turned and trundled up the road, and it made me smile with a satisfied nod. It took a few moments before I was able to beg off successfully from Vienne's call, and as the circuit went dead, I tapped in Jeremy's number. When he answered I was still watching the gate.

"Good morning, Evan," he began. "All settled?"

"It's getting there, but I'm looking at a mountain of work in the springtime."

He chuckled and said, "I know the lads who tidied up for Damon if you'd like their number?"

"Thanks; for the moment I'll leave nature alone."

"What can I do for you?" he asked.

"It's nothing important but didn't you say Aline Lloyd drives an old Land Rover?"

"Yes, that's right. She bought it at a military auction as I recall. Why?"

"What color is it just out of curiosity?"

"Lightish shade of tan. The Marines had them painted up in trop camouflage for desert operations in Iraq. See her on the road, did you?"

"Sort of," I replied. "She stopped at the end of my driveway just now—sat there for a few minutes until I looked out through the window."

"You've gotten her attention; that's clear enough."

"I hope I haven't pissed her off."

"Oh, she was bound to have a look at some point. I'd let her make contact first, Evan; the others went 'round to introduce themselves but that's not the way with Aline."

It seemed odd and a bit gossipy to mention my earlier "sighting" in the glen, but I worried the little wave toward her may have been enough to leave a bad impression.

"Damon included?"

"I think so, yeah," he replied. "Your brother was a very…*positive* sort of gent and I believe he regarded others likewise."

"He could rub feathers the wrong way sometimes but he didn't mean to."

"Possibly," Jeremy replied, "Aline thought of him as a bit of a wet puppy, so it follows she has concerns, especially as you're his brother."

"She knows who I am?"

"It's not surprising, really. I know she asked after you in the shops the day you arrived, and it is a very small community after all."

"I'm the new kid on the block, so I'll keep my mouth shut and stay on this side of the hill."

"Watch," he said. "She'll show again soon enough and probably with a few questions of her own."

"Thanks, Jeremy; that's all I needed."

"No problem, Evan. Cheers."

My new neighbor's interest was obvious, but not as clear was her goal. Vienne said it was terrible of me to say but I felt uneasy at the prospect of a mental patient lurking on the edges of my property. In simple terms, I wondered what the hell she wanted. "Treat her like any other," Jeremy had cautioned, but that's not so easily accomplished if she *isn't* like any other.

It seemed useless to worry about it, and I resumed my slow property walks, establishing from Jeremy's map the neighboring property line I was determined not to violate. Damon's investment was a rough, dogleg parcel matching the contours of our road on the western side and those of the hill separating it from Aline Lloyd's farm to the east. It was getting late in the day, but splendid sun breaks made for a nice stroll through the trees when I decided to aim downhill toward the southeastern corner and the limits of my modest domain.

The ground levels for a while with space between the groves where sunlight splashed across gathered leaves and twigs. I moved through them, dry and rustling with each plow of my boot, uncaring for the noise that echoed beyond. I remember being charmed at the notion of becoming a gentleman farmer until I saw in tangible terms what the process would demand. Taking out the underbrush alone would consume a summer, I reckoned, and that meant time I didn't want to spend. It wasn't long before my fanciful idea died out under the weight of cold reality, and standing on a decent-sized plot of land that was suddenly mine brought a strange calming effect I couldn't help but notice. I bathed in it for a while until the daydream changed abruptly when I could hear the thump of my own heartbeat.

There was no reason or cause; I was at peace, alone and content in that solitude. I didn't know why—not back then—but I turned left slowly and looked at a precise spot halfway up the hillside. Of course, she was there, motionless and watching me through the trees. She hadn't made a sound and my line of sight was focused in the opposite direction, but somehow, I knew just where to look.

There is an interesting effect that happens in the ocean when predators hunt the shallow waters of a reef. Sea animals make noise—clicks and pops, squeaks and gurgles—and it is unexpected if you've never heard it. I marveled at a sound, shouting out the power of life, while snorkeling ten feet deep along a cliff of coral in the tidal channels of Takaroa when suddenly the water around me changed and went quiet when a sleek, gray shark moved through, perhaps compelling the subordinate creatures to silence (and survival). In the sunlight that poured on an angle through the trees, I felt like that as I stood perfectly still, looking only at her. Was I predator or prey?

I decided to offer a test, an unexpected action that might provoke an interesting response. Instead of a shout or another idiotic wave, I knelt down in the leaves and leaned over a bit to prop myself up with an outstretched arm as one might in the park on a summer afternoon. Would she return a gesture of her own, I wondered, or move down the hillside at the very least? Instead, she did nothing. A test returned in a silent war of wills? It was childish, but I wanted to see how far she would go. Could she be spooked if I called the bluff?

I looked away, only for a second, and when I turned back she was gone. But as I grinned with a self-satisfied chuckle, a sudden, sharp noise like rocks being clapped together in a slow, deliberate cadence pulled me to my feet when I realized it came from the direction of my house. Without a thought, I sprinted across even ground and the spaces between trees, dodging them like a football player on a straight line for the opening to my weed-covered backyard. I could hear the clacking sound increase in its frequency, as though reacting to my pounding feet. Suddenly the direction changed, echoing down from the north through trees to my right. As I drew nearer, and the roof of my house came into view, the air went suddenly and deathly still.

I paused where the ground levels off to catch my breath beside the remains of an old, fallen tree rotting on its side among the ferns. The odd sounds seemed frantic and hurried to draw attention but were now only a slight rustle in the leaves as a soft breeze wandered through. I breathed with relief those strange noises had not been made by uninvited visitors at my house. By habit, or maybe instinct, my eyes wandered from left to right looking for something—*anything*—to account for the sounds. Only the oaks, still holding their brown leaves tightly, looked back at me. The answer would stay hidden, it would seem, but I decided to move up the hill on my next foray to look around and find the source. A mystery to be solved, I thought to myself, but only for the moment.

As I turned to go, she stood in the open a few yards away, and I felt the hair on my neck standing in the shock and wash of adrenaline sudden surprise always brings. It was impossible she could have closed the distance so silently in a tangle of branches and dead leaves, yet she faced me without the slightest sign of fatigue or breathlessness. For a moment there was only the quiet of undisturbed forest and an awkward pause until she spoke.

"Hello, Mr. Morgan," she said.

"Evan," I replied. "You must be Aline."

3
IT BEGINS

ALINE walked slowly toward me and her eyes—deep blue like an evening sky—never wavered. Instead, they remained fixed and purposeful as those of a hunter tracking elusive game, and I admired how calm and unaffected she seemed because I was anything but. I wanted to explain, at least to demonstrate a meaning beyond the random encounter of strangers, but my words sounded distant and impersonal for such a moment.

"Damon passed away suddenly and he left me this property."

Aline reached to draw back the hair that framed her face, slowly and without averting her gaze.

"Yes, I know," she replied evenly. "I was very sorry to hear it."

She moved to within a foot or two, and I wondered if she regarded me with only the mild interest of a new neighbor. A crocheted ivory shawl hung loosely around her shoulders and, unlike our first encounter, she wore ordinary blue jeans and ankle-high boots made of dark brown suede. A sweater in soft garnet material made for a simple but stylish look and nothing like the cloak and bare feet that had moved so effortlessly through the trees the day before. Had the townspeople told her of my intention to stay, at least for a while, as I sorted out what to do?

"You startled me there, and…"

"What do you do?" she asked abruptly.

"I'm sorry, what?"

"Your profession in America."

The interruption was so sudden and I fumbled with my answer.

"Oh…well, I'm an investigator; I work for an agency that looks into aviation accidents."

"It must be unpleasant to find the remains of those poor people in wreckage."

I remembered again the debris field in Tennessee and yellow cordon tape secured to the trees warning onlookers away.

"Sometimes it is, but the things we learn from our work help prevent other accidents."

Aline stood beside me shoulder to shoulder as dusk closed in. The light streaking through the trees wandered on angled shafts across her face—delicate and wispy—like the beams of tiny searchlights playing in the curls of her shining hair. She squinted beneath a hand to shade her eyes, and I saw at last the measure of her beauty. Her frame was average for a thirty-five-year-old woman, but its proportions were nearly ideal; neither too much nor too little and a shape that demands and holds attention. Thin, sculpted lips revealed a lovely smile that evaporated the mystery surrounding her, and I tried not to stare at smooth, unblemished skin—those piercing blue eyes. But for all her physical attributes, her manner and gentle style held me as if caught in time.

Another quiet moment passed, and then she turned to offer her hand. Her palm was noticeably warm and an interesting contradiction to the chill gathering around us.

"I live beyond the hill there," she said in a new, softer voice that seemed to signal the ice had been broken without disaster.

"Yes, I saw it on a map when I first arrived. I hope I haven't wandered across the property line?"

"It's all right," she said. "You haven't."

"My brother's solicitor told me you and Damon weren't exactly the best of friends, so…"

"Jeremy is a thoughtful man," she interrupted again, "but I think he may have made things sound worse than they were."

"Oh?"

"Damon could be a bit noisy sometimes, but I liked him and there was no animosity between us."

"I'm told he wasn't here for very long, and it seemed..."

"Did they warn you?" she asked suddenly. Once more, she shunted aside my words in mid-sentence and with a whisper that seemed distant as if she was thinking out loud. Although surprising, her question wasn't rude and I found it oddly endearing. I knew by a strange, hidden instinct she hadn't interrupted me out of impatience or thoughtless indifference.

"Warn me?"

She turned and nodded over my shoulder.

"When you came here, did Jeremy tell you to avoid me?"

I felt the uneasiness return and with it, a muffled sound growing in my ears like a lonely cat yowling in the distance. I know my face reddened because I could feel it go warm, but her expression was unchanged. The moment seemed to take forever as I searched frantically for an answer, guessing the question was more a test than an honest search for information. Her past had come up in spite of my determination to stay away from halfway houses or mental hospitals.

"No, not at all," I said quickly. "Jeremy only mentioned you're a very private person."

"That was all he said?"

Had she spoken with him, I wondered? Would she gauge my answer against a previous conversation between them? There was no point in pretending otherwise.

"He mentioned some troubles when you lived in Scotland, but..."

"Did he explain them to you?"

The moment was rushing suddenly beyond my grasp but I held on tight so she wouldn't see the flustered surprise on my face. I had to respond but it felt like tumbling down a slippery, oiled chute toward an obvious trap.

"Only that you were making a new start after some treatment you received in a hospital. It was none of my business so I didn't ask further. I'm sorry if I've offended you, or..."

"You haven't offended me, Mr. Morgan."

Aline's tone was steady and calm, and I envied her somehow. It was strange the way she first looked at me without a hint of emotion, and suddenly that changed. She nodded and smiled, looking again toward the hillside.

"Would you like to walk a while? I can show you 'round the property, if you have time."

Like a life preserver tossed to a drowning man, I grabbed at the offer with both hands.

"Lead the way."

Aline motioned me toward an open spot where barren trees stood like sentinels across the forest floor. No matter where she led, I decided to follow quietly; we were on decent terms to start and that was precisely where I aimed to stay. As we strolled, she moved her arm in a gentle arc, tracing the ridgeline above and to the east.

"If you follow the hill just there, it goes 'round to the edge of my field. Beyond, a footpath in the grass leads to my house; I'll show you."

The way was mostly level and sunlight creeping ever lower in the western sky made a bright orange swath across the leaves. I stayed beside her in the easy, unhurried pace people take as they chat on a relaxed stroll. It was delightful, and I felt as if I had been given extra time—a bonus to which I wasn't otherwise entitled—and I smiled because the encounter wasn't yet over. I tried not to be noticed but I know Aline caught me stealing glances from the corner of my eye. She didn't seem to mind.

Past the rise where I saw her that first day, I stopped and looked uphill toward the big oaks.

"After Jeremy brought me out the day I arrived, I came here to poke around and noticed you looking down from the trees."

She stopped and shaded her eyes from the sunlight once more.

"Yes."

"It was cold that day," I said, "but I saw you were barefoot."

"I like to walk without these shoes sometimes," she replied. "The way is soft and the leaves hide no dangers."

"Weren't you freezing?"

"Not here," she said with a smile.

I couldn't know what that meant as she led us deeper into the woods, and after a while she spoke again.

"Will you investigate air accidents in the UK now?"

"I'm not authorized, and they have plenty of very skilled people as it is; I'm just a visitor here."

"But you bought things for your house—the things people need when they're preparing to stay."

Had she spoken to the shopkeepers in town, I wondered? Perhaps she mentioned it merely out of curiosity, but the hidden message in her words suggested more than casual interest, and I waited a moment to consider my response carefully.

"To be honest," I began, "I wasn't wild about the idea of coming up here at all. I just wanted to look around and figure out the best way to sell it."

"And now?"

I stood at an invisible gate and one of the momentary pauses when preferences shape and fashion decisions we make that later become "life-changing." Her question was simple enough, but my answer labored against a wall of consequence. Had I gone too far? Was my growing fondness of the little house and forested hills surrounding it enough to compel so permanent a move? It seems silly describing the moment today as a thoughtful pause—a hold on time itself—when I already knew what I would say.

"Everything has changed; I don't need a job anymore, and this is a beautiful place, but I never really thought about staying on permanently."

Aline stuffed her hands inside the pockets of her jeans, nodding with an understanding expression as her gaze wandered through the trees. It wasn't simply to plan her response or prime it through the thin suggestion of indecision. She seemed to know without being told I had no intention of leaving.

"There are worse places than the hills and valleys of North Wales."

I nodded with Washington D.C. in mind and said, "Yes there are."

She squinted into the late-day sun, and I wondered again about her past and what brought her to a secluded Denbighshire farm. Aline came down from windswept islands that stand between Scotland and the Arctic, but her name, manner, and dialect were clearly Welsh. Was it too soon to inquire? I remember fumbling in silence, trying to decide, but the question forced its way out.

"How about you?" I asked. "I understand you were up in Stornoway for a few weeks to transition, but it sounds like you've settled here permanently."

"That discussion will take more time than we have today, Mr. Morgan."

I smiled so she would know I understood, but the signal to leave it alone was obvious. We moved past those first awkward moments, and I wanted to show her I could take a hint. It was also a chance to bridge the conversation elsewhere and to do it gracefully. I wanted Aline to see thoughtful deference; I needed her to know I was more than happy to take things slowly and without expectations. I suppose I had to show her I wasn't Damon.

"A topic for another day," I replied. "Jeremy tells me you have a shop on the coast?"

"A small clothing store for ladies," she replied. "We have a jewelry line and lots of swimwear for the beach in summer—those sorts of things."

"I've never been but they tell me Colwyn Bay is a nice place."

"Maybe you should come up with me one day," she said softly. I heard in her voice something more than a suggestion and it was a welcome sign I hadn't blundered too badly.

"I might do just that," I said with a smile and relief the formalities Jeremy warned about were becoming needless.

We walked through an opening in the trees where Aline pointed to a wide, grassy field. She told me previous owners had a local farmer plow it only days before she moved in, but there was no explanation why they thought to turn and disc the soil one last time. Now, it's just grass and patches of weeds, a forgotten field from an earlier time.

A gentle rise led us to the high side of a long meadow, and beyond, a house not unlike my own waited in the kidney-shaped clearing of a lawn dotted by a handful of dormant fruit trees. A heavy stone wall—ancient and weatherworn—defined the edge of her front yard, and within it carefully placed antique farm equipment rusted in silence atop raised garden beds.

The conversation while we walked was restrained but the stretches between words seemed natural and welcome. Most would find it impossible to wander around with a stranger and not search for something to say, but Aline was content in our silence until she stopped and regarded me for a moment. I was about to comment on the picturesque sylvan scene and offer a polite nod to the charming image her farm made, but she intercepted the thought.

"How long since your family moved away?"

My paternal ancestry was obvious, and predecessors called Morgan may have walked in that very place long before, but her question made me feel lacking when I couldn't answer with certainty. Had she expected better? I thought of countless souls who made their way across the ocean in search of a better life, clutching worn suitcases and the total of their worldly possessions on the decks of sailing ships in New York harbor. Some of them came from Wales in the final moments of a journey from which many never returned.

"I know the first ones arrived before the Civil War," I replied, "so it had to have been in the early or middle 1800s. My grandfather told us about distant cousins who fought at Cold Harbor and Antietam, and I saw their names on a memorial plaque when I was a kid. I think some of them may have been sappers at the Siege of Petersburg, fresh off the boat from collieries in South Wales, and…"

I stopped suddenly and looked at her. I had rambled on about places that likely meant nothing to her—foreign places where Americans killed each other by the thousand, sometimes in only minutes, to free people they would never meet from bondage. She was patient, letting me drift from the present to a distant past, but I smiled and shook my head to offer an apology or explanation, hoping she hadn't heard the voice of a clumsy expat.

"Sorry for the tangent," I offered.

I thought she would return an understanding smile and leave it at that. I was sure she had heard the names of faraway places and accepted the importance of their meaning as only my own. Instead, she surprised me again.

"I remember those battles," she said. "The towns and farms where your Republic became a nation. A headmaster told the children about it in a history class when I was at school—Gettysburg and Abraham Lincoln—but he didn't understand it the way you do. None of them understood that time and its terrible cost."

There was an odd note of melancholy in her voice and a distant expression that suggested meaning of events beyond an average person's experience.

"Are you a student of history?" I asked.

She smiled again and said, "I *am* history."

I had no idea what her answer meant in that odd moment, but now that I do, the mild embarrassment tugs at my elbow to remind me again how easily secrets can be missed. She looked upward through the trees.

"It's getting chilly."

I nodded in silence, and she pointed toward her house.

"I have tea inside, if you'd care for some?"

There was something different in her expression—something new. It's difficult to describe without the tactile indicators we notice in sudden, unexpected moments, but the strange sadness I had seen in her face was gone. Instead, she looked on with calmness and warmth that contradicted my impression of her only hours before. Once more, I fumbled badly in the wake of misperception, standing alone in a quiet and foreign place. She was nothing like the image my mind made—suspicious and wary. After a pleasant walk, Aline was signaling her approval at the prospect of a friendship in its earliest moments.

"Yes, please," I answered, and she motioned for me to follow.

ALINE'S HOUSE WAS similar to mine, mostly from the architectural standards in the days when they were first built. Inside I expected a haven of knickknacks and domestic accessories an uninitiated American's imagination paints as necessary in a quaint Welsh cottage. Instead, it was starkly utilitarian with few decorations, artwork, or personal photos. She had been there far longer than I, but deliberate minimalism was clearly her chosen style.

Her modest kitchen was warm and welcoming, and I sat at her table while she prepared a kettle on the smooth glass surface of a contemporary range that seemed out of place. A laptop stood open on the counter beside a toaster I judged to be older than both of us, and above, where copper anodized pots and pans dangled from their hooks attached to a circular wrought iron band that looked like the tread of a wagon wheel. In the air a faint aroma of pine incense lingered, but not so much that recent use was likely. Did she favor it for only the scent, I wondered, or was there a spiritual side she hadn't shown yet?

"This is a nice place," I said, feeling suddenly better about things for the first time since Vienne's phone message and the news of Damon's death. Traveling from one crash site to another, I was a faceless government official poking around the wreckage and its terrible human cost—a cold, seemingly indifferent presence at a place of profound tragedy. In Aline's house, I felt the tension release like a tourniquet around my head mercifully loosened.

"We can sit in the front when tea's up."

I looked through an archway from her kitchen into the living room, suddenly aware of a beautiful, crackling fire I'd missed when we walked in from her yard. It seemed strange and unlikely, but I didn't remember her building one or the curls of smoke rising up from her chimney as a signal when we finished our tour. I went toward it, expecting perhaps an artificial gas arrangement ignited with the flip of a wall switch. Instead, it *was* real, with licking tongues of orange flame through twisted logs. I remember that moment particularly well today, and it might've been a clue to a smarter man, but she cut short my thoughts when she asked if I took anything in my tea.

"Oh, uh, just cream, thank you," I replied automatically.

At last we settled on her couch, but the moment was not as I imagined. There was no awkward silence or pause while one waits for the other to begin in what my aunt referred to as "parlor paralysis." Aline reclined on an elbow and said, "Are you feeling comfortable in your new home?"

"Little by little," I replied. "I've been living for the past several years near a big city, so it's a bit of a challenge getting used to the country again."

"Which city?"

"Fairfax, Virginia, just outside Washington, D.C."

"I've never been," she said. "We see it at the cinema or on the television sometimes—all the statues."

"It's just another big city to me."

"It's not your hometown?"

"God no!" I said at once. "I was transferred there for my job."

"I take it you don't care for Washington?"

"People who haven't been there believe it's an amazing city made of marble and alabaster, but behind the statues, D.C. is mostly tribes of hypocrites, professional liars, and self-serving opportunists. They ride in limousines on filthy, violent streets where children get killed over basketball shoes…it's not my favorite place."

"Where *were* you born?" she asked.

"Western side of New York."

"Near Central Park?"

"No, not the city. I meant New York *state*; I'm from a small town called Batavia about 350 miles west and nearer to Buffalo."

"I see," she said with a nod. "My American geography is not as precise as I'd like."

I asked if she had been to the US.

"Occasionally," she answered, "but it's been a long time."

Aline turned on the couch to pull a leg beneath her, and I wondered if she would tell me something of her life—the past that Jeremy was careful and deliberate to discuss in only the broadest terms. Perhaps, I thought, she understood my brother's otherwise innocent social transgressions were not mine. She waited a while, and I wanted to tell her about the place where I grew up if only to continue the topic, but she suddenly looked at me with that funny, sideways glance I've since decided is charming and said, "The people you work for; do they understand your situation now?"

"No," I answered, "but I'll have to fill them in pretty soon."

"How will you tell them it's permanent?"

Her voice was different. Well, maybe not her *voice*, exactly, but certainly its tone and timbre: almost childlike with an odd inflection of innocence that caught me off guard.

"I'm sorry, but I'm not sure I understand the question."

She raised her cup, stopping short of her lips for a second to blow away the steam.

"What will you say to let them know you're staying in Wales from now on?"

Aline steadied the cup in the palm of her hand, looking away, and before I could reply, she continued quickly.

"I'm glad of it, though," she said softly. "This will be interesting, getting to know each other, and I'm looking forward to it." She leveled her eyes at mine, straight on and unwavering.

"Are you?"

The question wasn't delivered in a playful manner or precociously through the suggestive banter we sometimes use to signal our own desires—barely concealed declarations of hope and preference that are often disguised as questions. Instead, Aline spoke with a matter-of-fact quality and confidence that seemed to wash away any pretense of indecision. I didn't mind, but it was strangely satisfying she somehow understood what I hadn't told her, as if calling out to me from a future place where she waited. I inched closer but with only enough caution to show the contest was fully engaged.

"We'll have to see," I replied with a very small grin. "I haven't made up my mind yet."

I thought I was being clever in our playful volley, raising the ante as I waited for a coy response, but as she stood and took my cup to refill, Aline just smiled.

"Of course you have, Mr. Morgan."

Her words hovered in the air as I sat out the silent, thoughtful moment to consider their meaning. It made for a sudden sensation of relief, at least in my mind, that I wouldn't become an adversary or a bother living on the other side of the hill. Maybe I felt that way knowing she didn't look at me and see equivalent social challenges that made Damon who he was. As I watched her sipping tea, I wanted desperately to understand how that same moment played out inside *her* mind, but those answers would have to wait.

We sat a while longer, chatting about the ordinary parts of life that are common and of no particular importance: the places I had been and how it was I came to be an aviation accident investigator. Some of the discussion went to Damon but only at the surface. Throughout, the conversation was one-sided and she was careful to steer each topic away from herself. I saw it immediately, and yet I made no complaint. It was understandable, I thought, since my story was the foreign, untold tale, obliging me to it as a newcomer. The demand for proper etiquette was obvious, so I went along out of respect for a reasonable desire to leave her troubled past in the past.

Aline listened and asked the right questions, but she never revealed much. A coping mechanism, I thought silently, a planned and deliberate part of her recovery one of the faceless psychotherapists might have recommended as a condition of her release.

Laura Maitland, a pal from my childhood days in Batavia, became a clinical psychologist, and she treats those who've suffered when ordinary lives are turned to nightmares after the fragile, emotional buffers our minds construct to protect us ultimately fail. Sometimes, she told me, they end it of their own accord or try to, at least. Others descend even further into an irreversible free fall and wind up in locked wards where floor attendants patrol with an eye out for trouble. When it arrives, they call resident physicians who calm with sedatives and restraints, making notes on a clipboard that will guide interviews and therapists determined to reinforce sanity for those on the brink of losing it. I thought of Laura, and I admire her dedication, but it's not a career path I could endure.

Despite Jeremy's caution and the mysterious circumstances he wanted so clearly to avoid discussing, Aline didn't seem to be a person recovering from *anything*, let alone emotional collapse. Laura told me about the life of patients in her facility when I went home a few years ago: sometimes hopeful and calm this moment but carried to a different, confusing place the next. They're understandably vulnerable, watchful like cats in a new house, alert and scanning with dilated eyes for signs of trouble they know will undo everything and hurl them backward into an emotional no-man's-land. Aline was nothing like that, and by the time we finished it was nearly dark.

I was cautious of wearing out my welcome but as I stood to go, Aline asked me to wait a moment while she fetched a torch. A walk up the narrow lane to where it intersects with the road and back down the winding road to my driveway would take half an hour, she insisted, but the better option—a shortcut over the hill—would be made easier with a light to guide my way. I promised to return it the following day when I thanked her for tea and turned south along the footpath through her field.

I knew she stood at the edge of her yard for a while, watching as I made my way carefully down the gentle incline where it parallels the hillside, and it made me smile. It wasn't for any reason other than knowing we took the first steps without the combative skirmishes my imagination created after learning of the mysterious neighbor girl from Jeremy. Those worries were gone, and I felt closer to the place, no longer an unwanted invader. The experience (and a pleasant stroll through the trees with Aline) left me with a sudden confident sensation of belonging.

In my earliest hours in the valley, the thought of veering into the dark recess of the trees would surely have put me on edge, but somehow it seemed effortless. Retracing our earlier steps wasn't difficult or confusing, and I put the success down to my keen sense of direction. Was it so, or had I only been lifted by a pleasant visit and the warmth it created? I walked without fear—without concern. Even in the echoes of an otherwise eerie place it seemed strangely familiar, and when I reached my back door to switch on the lights, the feeling was immediate and unmistakable; I had come home.

4
TOOTHBRUSHES, SHOVELS, AND BOULLION

AFTER breakfast I turned into Aline's driveway in a light morning drizzle. We chatted a while and I returned Aline's flashlight in exchange for a cup of coffee and an orange-glazed scone. She was about to leave for Colwyn Bay because auditors, she explained, would arrive soon for an inspection of her books and she wanted to be there so the young girl who manages her shop wouldn't have to endure the grilling alone.

In that brief second meeting, the moments passed with ease and the comfort of familiarity I wouldn't have expected (but took with gratitude anyway). I said goodbye and made the short drive around our hill back to my house, and as I tossed my keys on the kitchen counter, my cell phone buzzed suddenly with the number of my supervisor, Tony Morales.

He wondered how I was doing and we talked about Damon for a while. I knew Tony would be able to backfill my position without difficulty, and there were certainly plenty of qualified candidates from which to choose, but resigning my position carried with it an explanation I couldn't make without the guilt of abandoning my post. I had no lucrative job offers or compelling prospects that made leaving the NTSB at least understandable. Instead, my choice was made by simple desire and I wasn't prepared to tell him.

Of course, a job as means for continued existence had been made irrelevant by the money delivered from Damon's will, but even drastic early retirement and an easy life as a modestly wealthy landowner seemed shallow and without purpose. More guilt and unresolved questions between brothers, you could argue? I wish it was so because it would be easy to defend, but in truth, it was only because I wanted nothing to do with crowing about my newly acquired resources like a lottery winner determined to show off in front of ex-colleagues. I knew the money surprise would surface at some point but that was a bridge best left for a future crossing. Rather than a lengthy explanation and a clean break, I decided to tell him a lie.

Damon's possessions, I insisted, had been meted out in haphazard ways that required full-time attention to sort through in order to avoid lengthy legal battles. Since Vienne moved to a new job herding fashion models at an agency in Montreal, the demands of her responsibilities made it difficult to get away and because of it, transatlantic trips to deal with administrative details fell to me. I tried my best to sound disgusted with it all if only to maintain believability, but I still felt like a heel for offering half-truths to an old friend.

Tony is a steady, patient man who trusts people, and I don't think it ever occurred to him I was making needless excuses. I did find enough courage to admit a chance existed I might not return for a while; I wanted him to understand there was no expectation he would hold my position. Tony said he would give me another two weeks, but unless I could wrap things up and get back to my caseload, he would be compelled to begin a search for my replacement. I heard a tone of sadness in his voice—the professional responsibilities as a manager overriding friendship because he had to. I didn't resent it, of course, but it only made worse the needling rub against my guilty conscience, knowing that very process was only a matter of time. It wasn't fair to him, I know, but at least he wouldn't be taken off guard when I called to say I was done at the NTSB. An hour later the phone went off again, but this time the number was Vienne's.

"Hey," she said with a voice that sounded low and muted by fatigue.

"You okay?" I asked, but she had other things on her mind.

"Did you speak with the money people yet?"

"No, but it sounds like you have."

On Liam Donnelley's recommendation, we retained a wealth management firm outside London charged with assessing the specifics of Damon's legacy beyond the cash transferred into our accounts in Montreal and the UK. They sent representatives to find and sort through the details, especially those hidden in almost a dozen banks all over the world. I knew their preliminary work was finished, making for an inevitable meeting—and another train ride south—at their offices in Guildford.

"They called about an hour ago," she said in a careful, hushed voice. "Evan, this is getting crazy now; when we gave them all the stuff from the will—the keys and custody documents—they sent their agents to bring back the valuables Damon had in those banks."

"What did they find?"

"They finished with the first phase, so I went online and looked at our joint account—the one I set up after my first meeting with Mr. Donnelley?"

"I remember."

"The bill for their services so far was almost twenty-five thousand and that's not even counting their management fees; it was mostly expenses for hotels and airline tickets!"

"Twenty-five grand for travel? Where were they going?"

"That's what I wanted to know, so I looked at the itemized invoice they sent to my e-mail and now I can see why."

The amounts seemed excessive, but Vienne's discovery was only the beginning.

"They had to fly to Tokyo, Hong Kong, then to Melbourne, and that's just the first wave. They came back to England for a day or two, then off to Pretoria, some place called Antananarivo, and then back up to Zurich. Yesterday, two of them came in to London after a final stop in Santiago. I knew Damon's job took him all over the place but this is ridiculous!"

"What the hell was he doing in Chile?"

"Looking at dead people," she mumbled. "He told me about freeze-dried mummies, or some weird shit like that—typical Damon stuff—but the dig was in a really remote desert, and…"

"The Atacama," I noted. "It's where those copper miners were stranded a few years ago, remember?"

"Yeah, that's it; Damon was so excited because he'd never been. He sent me a card right after he arrived in some town called Antofagasta. It's a beautiful city near the ocean with palm trees and beaches, but it's right on the edge of this huge desert wasteland. I always loved that name—Antofagasta. It sounds like a Mafia insult or something, right? Hey asshole, *Antofagasta!*"

"Vienne…"

"Okay, I'm sorry, Evan; this is just so strange and…"

"He had bank accounts in all these places?" I asked, as the details of Damon's secret life began to emerge.

"Yep, and we're not talking about some hole-in-the-wall credit union, either; these are places with armed guards in the lobby and customers who don't use drive-through ATM machines to grab a twenty."

"So where does that leave us?"

"There's a separate amount for handling fees," she continued. "Another fifteen thousand."

"What was there to handle," I demanded. "Isn't the currency safe where it is?"

"They left most of the currency; their handling fee was for the gold and silver—a lot of it."

"I thought it was just a few coins or Krugerrands."

She waited a moment and I heard her take in a full breath of air, exhaling slowly.

"You didn't see the full list. There are *thousands* of them, Evan. They had to be gathered and put into special locking containers accompanied by hired goons all the way back to London. Some of the little bars were minted over a century ago; they're worth more than the gold they're made of."

"Damon was always crawling around in the places where priceless stuff pops up, so I guess it makes sense he kept a few for himself, right?"

"He didn't find them," she said. "When I looked at copies of his invoices and transfer statements with his clients, I noticed a sudden uptick in his service fees and part of their payments started shifting to gold."

"I don't understand what that means."

"He started charging twice or even three times the amount for a standard appraisal than he did before," she replied. "This wasn't a random percentage increase here or there; it was applied across the board. I know those artifacts are high-end, but even still…"

It was my turn to pause, trying to envision what Vienne's words meant.

"What the hell was he into?"

"I don't know," she answered, "but whatever it was, he jacked the price for his services right out of the blue. Damon never gave a shit about the business side of appraisals; he did what he did because he enjoyed the work."

"What changed?" I asked.

"*He* changed," Vienne replied. "I checked around with some people in town who know a lot about the market for the shit Damon dug up or went to look at on his clients' behalf."

"And?"

"He was charging next to nothing for his services, but then almost two years ago he woke up and made huge adjustments to his price list."

"Wouldn't that hurt his business?"

"I guess not because none of his clients put up a fight; they kept going to him for appraisals."

"They must've done well following his advice," I added.

"I'm sure they did," she replied, "but it gets stranger still: last year, Damon's invoicing for services switched from electronic transfer of funds to equivalent amounts in precious metals and also for options in a bunch of companies."

"*Damon* did that?" I asked in disbelief.

"Yes, and it was so sudden; almost overnight."

"So, now what?"

"Hold on," she continued, "we're just getting started."

I smiled and shook my head in helpless disbelief as she read from a list.

"That little farm of yours and the apartment in Malaga weren't the only properties he owned, not by a long shot. The agents brought back letters of incorporation, or at least the local equivalent, from businesses in places I've never heard of, and all those documents showed partial interest or ownership in Damon's name."

"What kinds of businesses?"

"Well, for starters, a precision manufacturing shop in Linz, Austria—five percent. Here's an advertising and promotional studio, also in Austria, but this one is near Salzburg—eight percent. Almost *fifteen* percent in a farm that grows cash crops somewhere near Manaus, which I had to look up on the internet to find it's a city way the hell down in central Brazil. Damn it, Evan, this is like learning he was some sort of secret agent, or who knows what!"

"Was that it?"

"Nope. It looks like he was some kind of silent partner—had almost ten percent of an apartment complex in Ventura County and minor holdings at a fish processing plant in Norway. Here's a three percent stake from a company in Poland that builds control systems for those huge windmills to generate electricity. You need to see this stuff, Evan; he had interest in property from one end of the planet to the other!"

"Does any of the documentation point to a reason *why*? Nobody buys into a Norwegian fish plant as an investment!"

"Well, *Damon* did, or at least he assumed ownership of the stake, but that's where it gets fuzzy."

Vienne had been at it a while, and I heard the sound of a detective in her words: a path followed and lured by clues and a desire to understand no different than mine at a crash site.

"Fuzzy?"

"All this stuff was transferred from previous owners into Damon's name by somebody else; he didn't really do anything except sign the paperwork."

Our brother may have been fond of the unusual, but his behavior was always deliberate and cautious. People who profit from risk are more comfortable with it than Damon ever was. I listened to Vienne, but a conclusion was coming and I needed to know what transformed him from detached archaeology nerd into an investment razor.

"There's something else," she continued. "A lot of transactions went through a finance agency in Boston and *all* of those were handled by one person named Edward Vaughan."

"Have you talked to him?"

"For about twenty minutes but he either couldn't or wouldn't give me much detail; only that he was instructed by a client's representative in Sweden to make the necessary arrangements for the transfer of ownership percentages into Damon's name. I asked him about the others but he hadn't seen anything because his client wasn't part of those deals."

The scenarios were becoming muddled and confusing.

"What did the Boston guy have to do with it?"

"Apparently, interest in the businesses and properties Mr. Vaughan managed were acquired by his firm on the client's behalf much earlier; he was only shifting specific ownership percentages to Damon on his client's instructions."

"But he didn't say why?"

"No. Vaughan's client simply told him to transfer a specific percentage of title and interest each time and that was it."

"I don't suppose he told you who this client was?"

"Oddly enough, he did: a woman in Sweden named Birgit Nyström. He said she's a well-known art collector with deep pockets and nothing better to do. Apparently, she hired Damon on more than one occasion to find or appraise rare pieces and artifacts. I had to pour on the tears to convince him, but all he would say is that she lives on a secluded estate near Karlstad."

"Stockholm area?"

"Nowhere near; I checked, and Karlstad is almost two hundred miles west. It's actually closer to the Norwegian border than Stockholm, if that helps."

"It doesn't, but I'll go online and look at a map. I presume you were hoping I'd call this lady and see what she knows?"

"You can't; Mr. Vaughan wouldn't release anything more; no address or phone number."

"Then how do we find her?"

"I have no idea, Evan, but you're a lot closer to Sweden than *I* am."

I felt the uncomfortable push and circumstance urging me forward at just the moment I wished to be left alone. Another plane ride—another hotel.

"Let me know if you find anything," Vienne said before hanging up.

In the morning, merely by an impulse, I dialed Aline's number to let her know I'd be gone for a day or two. I was under no obligation, but it seemed like the right thing to do. She answered from the road to Colwyn Bay but we didn't stay on very long. Three hours later, I boarded a Scandinavian Air flight in Manchester.

5
JAMES BOND GOES TO SWEDEN

THE ride to Stockholm was a two-hour affair, plus two-and-a-half more on a train to reach Karlstad. The sudden trip was purposeful and nothing like my first, arguably reluctant, journey up from London. It felt like a scene in a cheap B movie as the elusive spy slips neatly past airport security checkpoints in enemy territory, and I smirked at myself for the absurd thought when I climbed into a taxi for a short ride to my hotel. It was still early, but I was determined to pull back the layers of a mystery that seemed to grow by the day. I found an exclusive gallery in town on a map the hotel clerk showed me; if Birgit Nyström was a heavy hitter in the art world, it stood to reason they'd know how to find her.

The gallery was spacious and well-lit with abbreviated panels jutting outward from the walls, and upon them the hopes and dreams of artists hung in staggered displays that seemed to echo the imperfect creative impulse. I wandered in the quiet across a gleaming hardwood floor, trying my best not to look ridiculous until a man approached and asked if I had any particular work in mind. I didn't, of course, and his disappointment with a lost sales opportunity was obvious when I asked about Birgit.

"Yes, we know Birgit," he said blandly.

"I'm trying to find her, but I only know she lives near here; I don't have an address or phone number."

He eyed me a moment before nodding his head with a smile that was only polite and not meant to infer he would help.

"She comes in from time to time, but we don't publish the personal information of our clients, sir."

"I understand, but if you happen to see her, would you tell Miss Nyström I stopped in?"

"I'm sorry, but that is not something we're in the habit of doing. Privacy regulations prevent it, and we are very sensitive to…"

"Just tell her I'm Damon Morgan's brother. He died unexpectedly and I was the beneficiary of properties he owned—some are connected to Birgit."

He stared at me for a moment, and I remember the expression vividly. It was the look of somebody with secrets, but as I turned to go, there was time to finish the point.

"I'm at the Drott."

I made the return walk quickly into a stiff breeze and a second line of showers threatening to get worse. I decided to move on to the next gallery on my list until the telephone rang and a girl at the reception desk told me I had a call. When I answered, a deep voice said, "I'm sorry to bother you, Mr. Morgan, but I'm calling for Birgit Nyström; she is ready to speak with you."

"Yes, of course," I replied, and he told me to be at the hotel's entrance in ten minutes. I expected a face-to-face conversation but the phone went dead and that was that.

I hurried to freshen up and pull on my shoes, patting at myself to ensure the key card for my room was safely in a pocket. It was irritating being hurried along by somebody I hadn't met, but speaking to Birgit was all that mattered. When I stepped outside, the cold air felt good on my face as I scanned the sidewalk with an expectation she would be there. Instead, a single figure in the heavy clothing one would expect from a construction supervisor walked quickly across the street toward me.

"Mr. Morgan?"

"Yes, that's me."

"Birgit is waiting; follow me, please."

On the far side of the street, a red Iveco 35 crew truck idled at the curbside. As we drew closer, the right-side passenger door opened and a younger man motioned for me to sit. Before I could ask he said, "Only twenty-minute ride, sir."

In that moment my imagination force-fed me an idiotic, sinister plot from an adventure novel—a tension-building scene when we know the poor slob who takes a ride with strangers always wakes up dead. I had no idea who they were and only that Birgit sent them. Should I have mentioned something to the hotel desk girl? If I never returned, where would the police begin a search? I thought furiously for an excuse to wait—a forgotten key, perhaps. They looked at me for a moment, and when the younger man mumbled something to the other in muted Swedish with a shrug and look of confusion, it was clear to them I didn't understand.

"We take you now to Birgit."

He spoke slow and loudly the way people do when languages are confused or misunderstood. I felt a sting of embarrassment at the idea, so I waved him away and climbed into the van as if to demonstrate I wasn't stupid after all.

"Twenty minutes?" I asked.

"Yes," the older one answered. "It's not so far, okay?"

I nodded and pulled my seatbelt, but the worry was still there and building to outright fear as we swung around and accelerated. At last the young one offered his hand and told me his name was Mats. As I shook it, the driver smiled through the rearview mirror and said he was called Daniel. Mats asked me where I came from, and it suddenly occurred to me there were two possible answers: Washington D.C. or Wales. I chose D.C.

"Caps!" he shouted. "Let's go, Ovi!"

"Yeah, Ovechkin plays for the Capitals," I said nearly under my breath, "but I'm a Sabres fan."

"Oh," Mats replied sadly, as if he was offering condolences. I smiled at the unintended insult and settled in for the ride.

Värmland County's hills and dense forests seemed endless, and my suddenly talkative companions wondered if I had family there; lone Americans roaming around western Sweden during the late days of autumn weren't abundant. They seemed to ask only for the customary reasons cabbies feel obliged to make conversation, but my purpose was hardly that of a tourist and I watched closely as we turned through the gap of a line made by old spruce along a grassy field. Beyond, a substantial house painted in a gentle shade of mustard yellow with black trim stood alone and apart from outbuildings more suited to an industrial farming operation. When Daniel eased to a stop on a circular gravel drive, Birgit was waiting inside her doorway.

"Miss Nyström," he said, nodding toward the entry beyond. "When you finish, we bring you back, okay?"

The van disappeared through the trees and Birgit gestured toward a modest porch.

"Please come inside, Mr. Morgan."

We moved past a silent woman in a plaid skirt and black sweater looking out from the hallway with a severe expression and folded arms. Judging by the size of the place, I took her to be an assistant or a housekeeper, but I followed Birgit to a sitting room made in an octagon of glass panels from floor to ceiling that was furnished in heavy rattan chairs and settees.

"May I offer you something?"

"Thank you, no," I replied, and Birgit nodded twice for her assistant to withdraw through ancient double doors.

"I was saddened by the news of Damon's death; it was quite sudden?"

"Heart attack," I answered.

"I see. But we now understand his estate has passed to you and Vienne."

"Most of it, yes."

She looked away for a moment, watching a gathering rainstorm make its way in from the northwest. In the dull light, I gauged her to be in her early seventies from the furrows and creases across her face and the waves of thin gray hair hanging carelessly around her shoulders. There was an odd calm about her, considering the news of Damon's death and my sudden arrival; others might regard my visit with suspicion, but Birgit's reaction was resignation—inevitability—though I had no idea why.

"I am impressed you found me so easily, Mr. Morgan; I don't pass out my address and telephone number very often and certainly not to strangers. It was clever of you to inquire at an art gallery."

"We spoke with your agent in Boston," I offered, hoping Edward Vaughan's help wouldn't end up costing him later for putting me on the path to Birgit's estate.

"Edward told you where to find me?" she asked, suddenly alert.

"He only told us you live near Karlstad, Miss Nyström; beyond that, he wouldn't say."

"Ah. Well, now you're here, so what can I do for you?"

I sat forward on the pillows of a long couch, surprised to find little in the way of artwork considering Birgit's passion for collecting.

"My sister was going through Damon's papers, and she discovered holdings for several commercial properties were transferred from your name into his and most of it within the last two years."

"Yes, that's correct," she replied with the odd combination of a smile and wrinkled brow, as if to suggest the root of my statement was somehow surprising to me when it should be obvious.

"We found Damon had been working for brokers and collectors and often in your employ. It was somewhat of a shock to find he had been given interest in a lot of disparate businesses; Damon wasn't known for being a skilled entrepreneur."

She smiled again and tilted her head to one side for just a second.

"Perhaps, but he was an astonishing and talented man who understood his work better than anyone I ever met; I was more than happy to return a significant reward in money for what he brought us in art."

"I understand, but we're trying to figure out why his fee payments would suddenly shift to property rights, cash, and precious metals instead of ordinary electronic bank transfers. We don't think that was something Damon thought of by himself."

Birgit's smile faded quickly and she stood, moving slowly behind the couch.

"Vienne suspects the decision to alter our agreement was mine?"

"She doesn't suspect anything, Miss Nyström; we're merely trying to understand why it changed so suddenly."

Birgit turned quickly and leaned both arms on the back of the couch, looking straight into my eyes.

"Damon's fees were unusually modest for an expert of his caliber until he notified us of his intent to raise them considerably."

"Did he give you a reason for the sudden increase?"

"Our arrangement was much closer to what you might consider industry standard, so they didn't apply to us in that degree. There was talk other collectors misled him, and he simply adjusted when he discovered the inequitable structure through discussions with a business analyst, perhaps."

"Some of these fee increases were fifty to sixty-five percent, Miss Nyström."

"Yes, I know," she said with a smile, "but he must have sorted it out and brought them in line with what he was entitled."

"I appreciate the point," I continued, "and I'm glad he did, but we're talking about millions of dollars in liquid and invested assets."

"You were obviously unaware of his successes; most collectors at my level regarded Damon's professional opinion as absolute, and his payments were always well-earned."

"I don't understand."

"Simply put, if you wanted an exceptional piece, it had to satisfy his evaluation or there was no transaction. In the past five or six years, even the biggest names engaged Damon for his services, and it should not be surprising he demanded and received appropriate compensation."

"I hadn't spoken with him in quite a while," I said. "He wasn't around much after leaving for Spain. The money he asked for in return for his services was startling, but the sudden switch from traditional bank transfers to only cash or equity interest is the part we found most confusing."

Birgit stopped near her wall of glass and surveyed the grounds as she spoke.

"We are trying to understand it as well, Mr. Morgan. Damon never complained about the payment methods but there must have been changes."

"He never gave you a reason why?"

"He simply wanted to move away from traditional finance practices and we agreed; he offered no particular reason and it was not for us to ask because we have always done exceptionally well from acting on his guidance and skill."

"When did this dramatic shift begin?" I asked.

"Damon identified and recommended a rather large private collection in Dubai last year, which we bought near the end of autumn; that was the first transaction paid for in property interests."

"But there was no explanation given for the change?"

"Nothing."

"We discovered most of the hard currency, plus a considerable amount of gold and silver were squirreled away in various banks all over the world."

"Damon's clientele was growing and we know he represented several international collectors who agreed to pay their fees into local accounts during that period. We were not among them, but we knew who they were."

"Any idea why he did that?"

"Not precisely, Mr. Morgan; Damon went to many places in the course of his work, so we presumed he was uncomfortable carrying large sums and preferred instead to secure them locally."

"Can you think of anything else that might help us?"

"I'm afraid that is all I can tell you."

A dead end. I felt suddenly embarrassed after wasting both my time and Birgit's, but there was nothing more to do. I thanked her and she sent for Daniel to drive me back to town. Waiting at her door, I wondered if a detailed study of the paperwork Vienne brought back from London would show something more—another clue or direction. I could hear the little van starting from around the corner of a brick garage across the compound as Birgit suddenly touched my arm.

"It may not be anything helpful, Mr. Morgan, but I remember Damon telling me about property he acquired last year—in England, I believe. It was months before he insisted on modifying our fee arrangement, but he seemed quite distracted by it for a while."

"An old farm in Wales, actually," I replied. "It was part of my inheritance from Damon; I've been staying there the last few weeks."

Birgit looked at me closely, and I felt her grip on my arm tighten.

"I asked him about it in casual conversation but he reacted rather badly and refused to discuss it."

"Why didn't he want to talk about it?"

"Damon would only say the experience was not what he hoped it would be," she replied. "I wondered if he had been cheated by agents, or the real value had been far less than he paid, but he said his problems were personal—that he would have to make changes regarding a woman."

"Isolda," I said with a nod.

Birgit paused for a moment as if I had gone too far. I couldn't decide if her expression was one of surprise or anger.

"I apologize, Mr. Morgan, I don't understand what that means."

"Isolda Marquez—Damon's girlfriend?"

"I see," Birgit replied, but the sad smile and a subtle shake of her head described something else.

"A school teacher," I continued. "There was a falling-out and they separated recently. He didn't mention her?"

"Not to me," she replied. "I didn't consider it carefully but it seemed very odd behavior."

I replayed in my mind our brief conversations at Damon's funeral. There had been loud disagreements between them in the months before his death, but Isolda insisted it was only her desire for him to stay closer to home. She urged him, we were told, to take a permanent local teaching job and settle down, but he refused and the rift was opened. It's not very nice to say but at that moment, on a remote Swedish estate amid swirling questions from a growing mystery, I didn't care what happened in Spain.

"Thank you for seeing me, Miss Nyström," I said at last. "I hope something will show in the paperwork to explain all this, but I do appreciate the time you've given me today."

"Not at all," she replied. "I hope you find what you're looking for, Mr. Morgan."

On an impulse, I paused for a second.

"If anything pops up, I wonder if I could call, just in case we need your perspective?"

"Of course," she said. "Wait a moment and I'll give you my number, but you must promise me you will keep it strictly confidential."

"I will and thank you again."

HALF AN HOUR later, Daniel and Mats waved goodbye at the curb outside my hotel, and I hurried to pack. When the door closed behind me, I was already dialing and Vienne answered after several rings.

"Did you find Birgit Nyström?" she asked immediately.

"I just left her house but she wasn't much help."

"You went to Sweden?"

"I had to; there was no number to call, so I flew into Stockholm this morning, then caught a train to Karlstad with the hope somebody in the local art community would know how to find her. I asked around at a gallery but the guy working the floor wouldn't give up anything directly. He knows her so

I told him who I am, and a couple of hours later they sent a van to take me up to her estate."

"That was easy!"

"She seemed nice enough. Amazing place, too—money is never going to be a problem for ol' lady Nyström."

"Okay," Vienne continued with clear excitement in her voice. "What did she say?"

"We chatted for a while, but she was just as surprised as we were about Damon's sudden switch from ordinary bank transfers to cash payments and then again to property rights. She didn't know about Isolda, by the way; he must've kept that detail from everyone except you."

"The switch wasn't Birgit's idea?"

"Funny you should ask because she wondered if you suspected her, but there's something else: just as I was leaving, she mentioned the farm in Wales, right out of the blue."

"What about it?"

"Nothing specific, but Birgit noticed Damon's behavior changed around that time, and she said he was having trouble with some woman. I thought she meant Isolda but when I asked, Birgit had no idea who I was talking about. If there was a connection, we need to know how and why."

"You're going back to Spain, aren't you?"

"Maybe. I'll call Isolda first and see how it goes, but there's still the weird timeline. Birgit saw and wondered about it the same as we did, but that's all she knows."

"I don't follow," Vienne said.

"She just meant the move away from bank transfers to cash and all the property rights stuff began shortly after Damon renovated the farm."

"Okay, but if it wasn't Isolda, then who is this woman Damon was talking about?"

"I can't be sure, but it might've been Aline."

"Who is Aline?"

"His neighbor; the lawyer in town said she and Damon weren't exactly close, so it's possible she's our mystery woman. Either way, there's a connection between

72

Damon's jackass behavior about money and the timeline when he acquired the old farm. Birgit knew it, and now it makes me wonder, too."

"If that's true, maybe we missed something in the paperwork," Vienne added. "Hold on a second while I look."

I paced in my room, waiting while she searched. I could hear rustling as she pawed through the papers until she spoke slowly and with a decidedly muted tone.

"Okay, I'm looking at the closure document Damon executed with Jeremy Collingwood; it shows a signature date from two years ago...August 22nd."

I nodded quickly and said, "Jeremy told me Damon left in October last year; does anything show when he made the switch to cash or property?"

Again, she flipped through the notes, whispering words from document titles in the odd habit people keep so that somebody listening on the other end of a phone conversation can follow along. Finally, she stopped.

"I'll be damned—right there."

"What are you seeing, Vienne?"

"A memo from Birgit to Edward Vaughan instructing him to begin the process of transfer in partial interest certain percentages of businesses she owned into Damon's name. It doesn't say anything about currency or gold, but the properties are listed on the last pages of the document."

She went silent and I thought the call had dropped.

"Vienne?"

"Evan, the date is the eleventh of October—just over a year ago and right around the same time he left Wales."

I went back in my mind to what Birgit had described, and the fleeting, wispy clues were beginning to gel.

"She told me they concluded a deal to buy a private collection in the UAE on Damon's recommendation eighteen months ago, and payment for those pieces was the first made under this new arrangement."

"What the hell happened?" Vienne asked suddenly.

"Something is screwy here," I said.

The matching dates were impossible to miss if you knew where to look, but with them, the mystery grew.

"I'm going to call Isolda when I get back, but also, I want to talk to Jeremy—see if he knows something he forgot to mention earlier."

"Are you saying he lied to you?" Vienne asked suddenly.

"I'm saying something happened to Damon in that place and time—something that suddenly turned him into a crafty businessman. Maybe Jeremy knows more than he let on, or maybe not, but something went sideways. Damon had trouble keeping his goddamn *checkbook* balanced, Vienne; how did he go from scatterbrain academic to hard-ass business fanatic almost overnight?"

She waited a moment and I know Vienne wished she couldn't say the words.

"I get the feeling you're not looking forward to the answer," she replied.

BY SATURDAY THE weather across most of Wales cleared. After several frustrating and unsuccessful tries, Isolda Marquez finally answered her phone, but she was in the process of relocating to her childhood home outside Barcelona. Damon had no trouble navigating between Spanish and Catalan, but English was all I could manage. Regardless, the conversation was brief and even terse.

We spoke about Damon for a while, and it surprised me to learn how close they were. Isolda still held obvious disappointment he never told me about her and the seriousness of their relationship. Inside her words, it was easy to detect the unmistakable tone of betrayal and injured feelings. I insisted my ignorance had nothing to do with her and more likely the product of our distance as brothers, but it was clear she didn't accept the idea.

I asked Isolda how much she knew of Damon's business arrangements with his clients, but she would only say he kept those details to himself. Was it only the aftermath of a love affair gone wrong, now made forever irreparable? She wouldn't say it outright, but I was left with a distinct impression their separation was never intended to be permanent (at least by Isolda). There were tears and awkward pauses and it was understandable so soon after Damon's passing. I was surprised to find they never traveled together outside continental Europe, and because of it, she had no knowledge of the farm in Wales or any other property.

When I asked about Birgit, the question was met with suspicion as though Isolda heard in error the name of a rival—a carefully hidden mistress, perhaps. I assured her Damon was interested in many things but an elderly Swedish woman wasn't one of them. It seemed to make her feel better to know their relationship was only business, but that didn't get me any closer to understanding Damon's sudden move with his finances.

After we hung up, I thought about the conversation for a while, hoping in retrospect a hidden clue might emerge not evident when we spoke. There was no signal or red flag to indicate Isolda was anything more than a grieving ex-girlfriend trying to make her way through the sadness and crushing feelings of loss. Our discussion by phone at least negated another plane ride and an uncomfortable meeting in Spain, but my report to Vienne left us both stopped at an invisible barrier; we were left to figure out Damon's strange behavior alone. I decided to leave it for a while and concentrate instead on my immediate problems, pushed mostly by the nagging and persistent reminders it was time to call Tony and officially resign my position.

When he answered I tried to ignore the guilt my conscience wouldn't let me forget, hoping he wouldn't hear it in my voice and know. There was too much to do, I told him. My responsibilities had shifted, and with them, an impossible scenario had formed that would oblige me to remain in the UK into the foreseeable future. I expected disappointment, but he only wished me luck and promised to stay in touch. I felt the binds loosen like mooring lines released from a ship moving slowly away from its dock. The path waiting for me was still unknown, but I made the choice and severed the link; it was time to get on with a new life.

6
DECENT CLUES EASILY MISSED

ALINE called to tell me her audit ordeal had ended without incident and to alert me she was on the highway headed south. I smiled and nodded as I listened and it occurred to me the otherwise innocent update was a signal the distance between us was narrowing. Not a ground-shaking event but it meant she would arrive home near dark and there would be another visit to the far side of the hill.

I invited her to join me and catch up or simply pass the time, and she stepped from her truck with a smile, giving my house a good once-over as she stood in the driveway. I wondered if she ever visited when Damon was there but she didn't mention it. A brief struggle with the fireplace flue finally ended in victory, and we sat together as she told me about nitpicking auditors who took entirely too long to find nothing out of the way with her shop's finances.

The conversation went to my decision to stay on and I wondered how she would react as I recounted my conversation with Tony Morales. It's obvious today, but Aline's reaction, knowing the outcome long before I told her, was strangely satisfying. I chose not to mention Karlstad and the previous week's detective work trying to make sense of Damon's strange behavior. It seemed out of context and awkward to bring it up until she walked to the hearth with her hands clasped behind her in the warmth of the fire.

"You went to Sweden, I see."

I remember the moment clearly: a sudden and stark surprise that left me without a response. Again, she held me in her palm, watching to gauge my reaction, and I fumbled with an answer to avoid appearing flustered or taken aback.

"Oh, uh…yeah, I flew to Stockholm a couple of days ago."

"How was it?"

"Rainy."

She smiled and moved again to the couch.

"I meant your trip."

I thought of Birgit's words as I was leaving and the presumption Isolda was somehow involved in Damon's odd financial decisions, only to land on a suspicion the woman he mentioned to Birgit may well have been Aline.

"Not as well as I had hoped, unfortunately."

She said nothing, perhaps waiting for me to explain further, and when I looked again her eyes were nearly closed. It seemed as if she was dozing off from boredom, but she nodded at last and said, "What did she tell you?"

"She?" I asked stupidly.

"Your travels took you to Karlstad."

"How did you know that?"

Aline nodded at the stub of my train ticket where it lay open on a lampstand near the front door. I hadn't noticed but her attention to detail was impressive.

"Ah," I said. Knowing where I had gone was not at all equivalent to understanding *why* and I hadn't spoken of it. I decided to play along and see where it led. She glanced at it for a moment, and as she replaced it, Aline smiled and said, "You went to see Birgit Nyström."

I could feel my heartbeat and hear its thump in both ears. In the silence, she looked into my eyes and hers never blinked, unwavering and fixed, just as they had the day we met. At once, I felt my face redden and at each fingertip felt an odd, prickly sensation like static electricity discharging from a wool sweater.

"As a matter of fact, I did. Do you know Birgit?"

It felt as if time slowed and the silence was interrupted only by the crackling fire. I stood alone and exposed but also unsure what she might say or do and I teetered on the edge of indecision.

At last, she nodded and said, "I never met her but I know who she is. Damon said she was an important client."

"Yes, she was," I answered but still I watched her. "We discovered irregularities in Damon's financial paperwork, and…"

"Irregularities?" she asked suddenly. Her expression changed abruptly, too: more serious and alert than before.

"It's probably nothing," I replied, "but he changed the way he did business with his clients abruptly last year."

"The irregularities," she continued suddenly, "were errors in the accounting numbers?"

"Well, no, not errors—it was just a sudden shift away from how Miss Nyström and the others among his clientele paid for his services, that's all."

"But you said the meeting was not successful."

"For every answer, we were left with more questions."

"We?"

"My sister, Vienne, and I; we're looking into Damon's business ventures together."

"I see."

Aline sat back on my couch, satisfied with what I had given her. It seemed strange, at first, but we left the subject and returned to other more customary topics for an informal chat. She told me a brief history of the place, having investigated it for herself in the days before she relocated from Scotland, and how long it had been since our two homes functioned as working farms. But then, and likely by an impulse, she turned to me with a new, almost precocious grin.

"Now that you're settled, perhaps you'll take some time and explore North Wales?"

I had thought of that very thing while looking out from my kitchen earlier, but her implied invitation was hard to miss.

"I'd like to," I replied. "Can you recommend a route for me to follow?"

She paused a moment and said, "We can go together if you like; it would give me a chance to show you my shop."

The idea was perfectly timed and welcome; a short road trip to Colwyn Bay and a ride together that might cement our friendship was suddenly obvious.

"Let's do it," I answered quickly.

"I'll be 'round to collect you in the morning. Nine o'clock?"

"It's a date," I said with a smile as she prepared to go.

I watched her amble up my driveway as the steam curled from her old Rover's exhaust pipe in puffs that hovered in the still air. As she went the sensation returned—expected and persistent—and I let it wash over me without a thought. It wasn't the usual gush of growing attachment, not like it often is when two people meet, and I felt a different, more familiar closeness. I grinned at the notion something beyond our fledgling friendship now seemed a possibility.

I thought about her, analyzing and determined to keep in perspective all that had happened. I was hardly an innocent schoolboy wallowing in a haze of hormone-driven desire or forming the lewd images in my mind we never talk about with others. I felt no compulsion, yet the certainty Aline was becoming more than just the girl on the other side of the hill was inescapable. Was it the same in *her* mind, I wondered? The excitement—and thrill of the unknown—had been muted by a calm, even soothing surety that all things *were* possible. Aline's powerful lure did its work.

OUR DAY TRIP to Colwyn Bay was a welcome diversion, although the weather turned again and the surf pounded ashore only blocks from her boutique where it waited between a home improvement store and a hairdresser's shop on Greenfield Road. I met Margaret Stiles, a wispy girl Aline had hired to look after day-to-day operations, and she showed me the racks and shelves where seasonal apparel took the place of summer wear. Above, stylish lighting hung from gleaming chrome bands suspended from the ceiling, aimed at precise places to lend a warm and sophisticated ambiance as holiday shoppers browsed in search of Christmas gifts.

I watched and listened quietly as she dealt with the logistics of a small business while Margaret described her frantic search for a specific sweater one of their customers was determined to find. Aline aimed short, reassuring glances in my direction, and it seemed as if she wanted to make sure I was still there, but an unsolicited smile or two made it clear there was something more. I tried my best to seem cool and unaffected—to pretend eye contact was nothing out of the ordinary—but Aline sharpened the effect when she steered me to a corner and announced we were leaving soon. It wouldn't have been anything special until she smiled and said it was "nicer when there's only the two of us."

I'm sure my expression was obvious, knowing we were moving in complementary directions. I wanted to believe it was simply a function of alignment—personalities attracted as powerfully as anything physical—but she was inside my head even then, probing and measuring the emotional markers I once believed hidden and safe. We describe those moments in silly hyperbolic phrases that lend legitimacy to the phenomenon of finding another who is just as interested and taken by fancy as we. As I did in that time, we all believe with steadfast assurance there is no such thing as mind reading, but now, I want to find dismissive naysayers and let them see for themselves how wrong those declarations can be.

Later, we walked arm in arm along the West Promenade and watched under a leaden sky as the breakers rolled in on a deserted beach. As we went, there was little conversation, and more than once I wondered if she was tiring of it all—growing weary of *me*. Sipping tea at a well-disguised café where locals go to avoid the weather seemed to liven her up when she described the comical circumstances by which she'd acquired the space for her boutique. I listened politely, but it was more her manner than the meaning that interested me. She took on a mildly animated tone in precise increments I found surprising, but the process only re-affirmed a sense of belonging and she noticed at last.

"So, what do you think of our shop?" she asked as we returned to her Rover for the drive back home.

"It's really very nice," I replied. "I imagine a little busier in July, though?"

"Much," she said with a smile, turning east along the coast highway for Abergele and a course change where the A55 veers southward. "We run at a faster pace in summer."

The ride went by in silence for a while as Aline raced blackened clouds I knew would intercept us long before we reached Llangollen. Aline kept her eyes forward, and then she finally spoke.

"Shall we have dinner together?"

The invitation was somehow unsurprising, and I agreed immediately, but then she went silent. I couldn't work out if it was simply a return to the quiet she seemed to favor instead of the often-forced conversation between people who feel obliged to talk in the car. Aline pulled suddenly into a narrow lay-by where Horseshoe Pass divides two mountains several miles north of Llangollen because, she said, "everyone stops here at some point to enjoy the view." The orange glow wandering up the slopes from the west at sunset emphasized her point, and we stood squinting against a blustery wind. After we returned to her truck, I thought we would be back on the road, but she turned to me and said, "Did Jeremy tell you what happened to me in Scotland?"

My pause was brief but it was necessary so that the answer wouldn't appear flippant or unconsidered.

"He told me you were there for treatment but nothing beyond that," I replied.

She heard the hesitation in my voice but I couldn't think of anything else to say.

"He didn't tell you why?"

"Only that you had some personal difficulties."

"You weren't concerned about it?"

"I just…well, now that I've gotten to know you better, I guess it makes me wonder why it was necessary in the first place."

"Why do you wonder?" she asked.

I fumbled in silence, trying desperately to avoid a misstep or blunder on a topic so profoundly personal.

"I don't know, really. You don't seem…"

She finished my thought for me.

"Crazy?"

I couldn't answer. I know she understood my dilemma but the effect was powerful and immediate. I had never been overly sensitive about the word because no one I considered close was treated for a mental disorder. It was sudden and unexpected, but I hated hearing that term when it applied to Aline. The air inside her truck was noticeably cooler, and I must've hunched over automatically because she flicked the heater switch and opened the vents to a warming rush from a bland and otherwise featureless dashboard. I wished in silence she hadn't brought up the subject but once broached, her stay in a psychiatric ward, and the questions I was determined not to ask, was dragged into view.

"I don't know why you were in that place but Jeremy didn't say and it's none of my business anyway."

"It's all right, Evan," she said softly. "I don't mind talking about it."

Without direct declarations we were suddenly on a first-name basis, I noticed, but another thought intruded. Was she testing me? Had Aline decided to expose and study my response or gauge the uncomfortable assumptions so many others hold when confronted with the subject of emotional problems? I decided to remain neutral.

"I presumed you'd get to it when and if you were ready; I wasn't looking for an explanation, Aline."

She only nodded and I moved quickly to close the awkward topic.

"I'm just glad we came up here today; this was a good idea."

She smiled again and looked at me. I couldn't make out if the expression was one of gratitude or if she saw only a naïve and sentimental man wishing to avoid a touchy subject on a lengthy ride home. I remembered worrying about Aline's hidden past on the phone with Vienne only days earlier, but I did so with prefabricated bias I shouldn't have held. It didn't seem to bother Aline, and we continued in the hum of her truck's tires along a wetted highway as the late-day sun disappeared beneath a shelf of gathering clouds.

It was an important moment, although I was too busy living within it to notice, mostly because it was a time when innocence I carried with me still mattered; when the future was an untouched canvas both inviting and full of promise. No matter her ability to see and understand without words, I went along in my ignorance, expecting at any moment to watch the wreckage of her time in Scotland pour out in an avalanche of tears. She was in no such state and it makes me feel better today knowing she simply waited for me to walk that path on my own. I had to, of course, and Aline knew that truth far better than I.

We spent a pleasant evening together dining and sipping a few pints at a raucous pub she seemed to prefer over others. The lively crowd didn't bother her and I wondered if Aline's mysterious past, and demand for solitude, had been oversold. She smiled and chatted with a few of the regulars and it was clear they accepted her as one of their own. If she had come to the valley for a new start, Llangollen was a great place to do it and her plan was obviously working.

7
"O CANADA"

FRIENDSHIPS develop and progress along mostly predictable lines, and ours wasn't meaningfully different. Once made, my decision to stay in Wales seemed more acceptable as the days settled into winter and I began to feel the comfort of permanence. In town I met and enjoyed the company of others, many due to introductions by Jeremy, but the faces became familiar so that first names were common. In the shops they called me Evan instead of "Mr. Morgan" and I found the distinction delightful.

On the far side of our hill, Aline was different, too; almost three months beyond our first encounter, the impressions formed in my mind during those earliest moments were fading. In precise and careful increments, even the invisible border surrounding secrets of her past began to fall as she came to regard me less and less as an object to be kept at a distance. On our walks through the trees, now a regular practice despite the worsening weather, her backstory began to emerge. I discovered she was an only child, born in Cardiff. Her mom and dad were college professors—math and geology, respectively—but her father's considerable experience with the influence of loading on subsurface rock was in demand. I spent an hour on the internet trying to figure out what that meant in layman's terms and it translated into gobs of consultancy fees when bridge builders called for his expertise.

After he took a job as a geotechnical analyst for a London-based firm, some of Aline's formative years were spent on the move as her dad's survey work obliged frequent relocations. She allowed only glimpses at details of her childhood in those first talks, and I wondered if that was a product of her difficulties in Scotland or if something worse happened she simply wished to avoid in conversation. Instead, hers was a happy, if slightly unorthodox, upbringing.

Visits with her parents had become biannual events at best since they moved away in 2005 to begin their retirement by exchanging land-bound property for a thirty-meter yawl. They tried life in Bermuda for a few years, she explained, but hurricanes that threaten sailboats like theirs, plus the necessary borders of an island overrun by tourists, demanded a change. Now, they keep a slip at a marina in Trieste as their home base on the northern shore of the Adriatic, not far from Venice. When I asked why they chose Trieste, Aline smiled and told me her mom and dad spent their honeymoon in a villa overlooking nearby Gorizia.

I remember she paused suddenly as though the history of her family should not have been revealed. It was an awkward moment as we stood out a drizzle beneath an overhang at her back door, and I worried the pace of getting to know one another might have exceeded its limits, at least in Aline's mind. It wasn't surprising but she asked about my parents and I told her Vienne and I don't see our extended family as much as we once did. Of course, she wondered why and I explained the sudden and tragic deaths of our parents when they were on holiday in Europe.

It was an honest and understandable question, but I think Aline felt worse about asking than I did by explaining the accident that took them when a German passenger train they were riding collided with another at speed outside the station in Rüsselsheim. Her expression changed just a little, enough to see evidence of her empathy and warmth that contradicted my early perceptions of an aloof, difficult hermit with emotional scars.

Contact with her relatives remained an unknown and she never spoke in those first days of aunts, uncles, or cousins. The distance from family made me wonder if Aline's solitude was an unavoidable product or a deliberate choice? I could only determine she was alone and had been for years, but that truth also suggested the Christmas season might be an unwelcome annual misery. In the quiet of that moment, I thought again of Damon and Vienne.

Jeremy called a few days later to catch up, excited at the prospect of his boys arriving with their own families for a holiday visit. He sounded like the grandfatherly ideal, doting on his children's children at every opportunity, and I smiled at the picture his description made. I wondered if he would ask and it wasn't a surprise when he brought up my plans for the upcoming season as my own path—and another fork in the road—still loomed.

Vienne expected me in Montreal through New Year's Day, but I think she extended the invitation from a mistaken belief I needed rescue from solitude and the remote hills of North Wales. I made up the excuse an electrician was due to inspect my circuit breakers a few days after Christmas, obliging me to fly back early. Knowing the tedious society parties Vienne would force me to attend in one or two of Montreal's elite havens made my decision for a shortened stay all the more attractive.

I did a decent job of ignoring the impending trip until Vienne's e-mail reminded me parking at Trudeau Airport wasn't the best option because of ongoing construction, forcing her to wait at the curb as I cleared Customs and baggage claim on my own. Suddenly, I just wanted it to be over. A genie, released from its bottle and ready to grant any wish, would laugh at my request to transport me forward in time and any day would do so long as it was in January. I'm certain no amount of prodding would have made me admit it then, but my hesitation was built mostly on a hope (or need) to stay close and within easy reach of Aline's house.

THE CHRISTMAS RUSH was accelerating and I wondered how Aline kept it or if she bothered at all. Aside from small bunches of mistletoe that seemed to be in every room, there was scant evidence of Yuletide trappings in her house and she hadn't made any special mention of the season. Of course, I missed the Celtic significance of the plant entirely, but I couldn't help wondering and it stung to think of her enduring Christmas alone. I took the opportunity to investigate during one of the now-regular Friday morning breakfast dates with Jeremy.

"Just out of curiosity, does Aline usually stay in town over Christmas, or does she go to visit relatives somewhere?"

"Has she said something to you about it?" he asked warily.

"She hasn't," I answered, "but knowing about her folks' distance and being an only child, I just wondered how it goes for her this time of year."

He waited a moment, likely gathering his thoughts before speaking, and I thought for a moment I'd asked the wrong question until he continued.

"It's obvious you and Aline are getting on rather well."

"No problems so far," I answered. "She's quiet but actually very nice and not at all what I expected."

"There, you see?" he said. "All that was needed was a bit of time for her to get used to things."

I said nothing about my Swedish adventure and he continued.

 "She goes up to Colwyn to celebrate the season with her shop manager's family; Margaret's mum and dad live close by."

"Ah. Well, that's good to know, and at least I won't feel weird about bringing it up next time I see her."

He waited again, and I know he was hoping I'd elaborate, but when I didn't, Jeremy went on.

"At the risk of sounding like an old hen with nothing better to do, they tell me you and Aline have been spending a lot of time together."

"Who's 'they'?"

"In the shops—they notice things like that, especially in small towns."

"Gossip is a way of life all over the world, apparently."

"They don't mean anything ill by it, Evan; it's just that Aline hasn't kept company with a gentleman caller since she's been down from Scotland; they would like to see things running normal for her again, that's all."

I laughed out loud at the notion and said, "I'll take that as encouragement."

"And you should," he replied. "Aline may be a different sort, reserved and sometimes at a bit of a distance, but she's still just a girl. She fancies you, and that's a very good sign."

I thought of a hospital psychiatric ward and how it must've been for her.

"She hasn't knocked me down and stomped on my head, so…"

"I had my doubts, to be honest," he continued. "When they called to tell us you were coming up from London, we worried she might take it badly, but you've gotten through and much further than any others."

We chatted a while longer, agreeing to meet the following Monday for tea. It was always nice spending time with Jeremy and yapping about sports or politics, but it was his place as both an anchor and social compass in a new community I valued most. Hearing my friendship with Aline drew attention in town was hardly surprising, but it forced me to confront my growing interest in her and the truth it was no longer a matter of simple acquaintance. I found something different in her company and a quality that went far beyond animal magnetism. It felt good to know she might have reached a similar conclusion.

Near dusk, I called Aline for the outward reason of telling her I would be leaving for Canada soon but mostly it was a need to hear her voice again. She reacted mildly to the news and I felt a bit cheated when she seemed not to care at all. Instead of disappointment, knowing I would be gone for the Christmas week, she was more interested in learning about Vienne—what she did and where she lived. It was clear Damon hadn't spent much time telling her about Vienne *or* me, and it seemed strange when she probed for more, ignoring the itinerary details in favor of my big sister's history, but I told her the story.

Vienne studied veterinary medicine at Colorado State, but after our parents died, she left school in the middle of her junior year when a former classmate offered her a city job in Van Nuys as a coordinator in the fashion industry. She made the shift and moved to California, aiming young models dutifully toward their dreams of fame and public adoration, only because she had a knack for the work (and an appreciation of the salary it brought).

A better offer came her way from Québec, but the luster wore off quickly for the simple reason, she insisted, the runways of Montreal were not wildly different from those in Los Angeles, New York, Paris, or London. She was in no particular hurry but there was little doubt my sister had decided to revive and complete her veterinary studies, and our sudden financial windfall would eventually shorten her stay in Montreal. When Vienne hinted at the prospect, I didn't pay much attention because a future move didn't carry immediate obligations, but Aline found it interesting.

I went to visit at the boutique, but our time was spent mostly on ordinary topics and adjustments Margaret was making to seasonal decorations and displays. Aline's house remained as it was and I wondered again if Christmas held a negative meaning for her. There was no evidence she carried hostile, atheist dislike for religious holidays, yet it seemed an afterthought or something she went along with in polite ambivalence the way people genuflect on cue at Catholic weddings in deference to traditions practiced by others.

I wanted to ask but it was bad timing, and there were moments in the quiet of her kitchen she seemed to drift away, distant and startled suddenly when I called her name. The glaring absence of conversation I once found unsettling had become routine and she was content for us only to sit and enjoy one another's company without a word. It might seem odd to others, I suppose, but we didn't always need words to fill the spaces and silence. After a while, it became our way and that was good enough for me.

For most of those hours I worked hard to complete the transition from my old life to the new. There would be no finish line through which I could surge or celebrate, and I understood the unpredictable nature of my place and condition demanded a week-to-week plan at best. I had no job or purpose beyond assimilation into a rural Welsh setting, and for the first time in a very long time I felt useless, with nothing better to do than exist.

The nagging question of Damon's fortune and the weird behavior we'd found in the transactions exposed by his will would resurface soon enough, but I simply didn't have the patience to continue until after the holidays. Vienne made it clear the leg work was mine alone, since I no longer had a day job, and that meant more travel and the emotional bribery of strangers as each clue pulled away the weeds hiding still more. Regardless, there were loose ends and unwelcome tasks I had to attend and waiting further would only make matters worse.

It was a drudgery I agonized over during quiet moments in bed at night, but once complete the process of closing out my administrative duties would be liberating. I had to find a buyer for my condominium, a home for my truck, but also a place to store my things, and as I packed for Canada, I felt like a stranger at the prospect of returning to North America. In a bizarre moment, I realized my next transatlantic flight heading west would no longer be the process of going home.

I stopped in to spend an hour with Aline, and she promised to drive by now and then to keep an eye on the place while I was gone. Her manner shifted back to one of distance and caution; again, she seemed more acquaintance than friend and the difference bothered me until she dropped me at the railway station in Ruabon and said, "I wish you were staying, but please be careful and hurry back."

By the time I walked along a concourse at Heathrow hours later, my mind had drifted to other things and most of them were questions I knew Vienne would ask about my brief mission to Sweden and my conversation with Birgit Nyström. I wondered if she would ask about Aline, and I rehearsed in my mind suitable answers that would give enough detail to satisfy her curiosity but not so much that would invite closer scrutiny. It seemed a juvenile indulgence, but a part of me *wanted* Vienne to ask so I could describe for her those things about Aline I found most compelling. I needed her to hear more than comfort with my new surroundings and to understand the girl across the hill was no longer a mere acquaintance.

MY WEEK WITH Vienne went along much better than I expected if only for an agreed moratorium prohibiting discussion of all that had happened since Damon's death. We spent our time enjoying the season and recounting fond remembrances the way all families do when one of their own has passed on. We went down the St. Lawrence River to Québec City to let the charms of a place in harmony with winter wash over us. The experience transported me back to a time when we threw snowballs and pounded on the hill behind our childhood home with sleds, toboggans, inner tubes, and the occasional hood of a destroyed car—anything would work, so long as it was fast and reasonably comfortable. Each evening, I dressed up in the uniform of stylish urban success and went along without complaint (relatively speaking) when Vienne insisted on introducing me to every unattached woman in eastern Canada because that is what big sisters do.

Christmas morning found us late to rise and the gift exchange process took a while because Vienne's fondness for mimosas kept us in her kitchen. It was nice, and a wonderful throwback to our childhood, observing family traditions all by ourselves. Stories rolled out amid laughter and a few tears, but mostly it reminded us neither was alone in the world.

She had visitors through the day, and when her neighbors dropped in, I took a moment to inspect my phone for messages. Inside one of them, a single line from Aline made me smile broadly: "Happy Christmas, Evan—thinking of you!" I returned the simple text with one of my own and the moment eased a feeling of isolation made by the distance between us; another connection reaffirmed. I didn't tell Vienne because doing so invited merciless teasing, but rereading Aline's simple note three more times made me feel better.

On my final night in Montreal, we arrived at an exclusive, invitation-only event and sipped disgusting pomegranate margaritas with fashion designers and models pretending to be sober until the buffet's ice sculpture melted away and with it, their inhibitions. According to the engraved invitation, the evening was supposed to be a "deliciously wicked" affair. Instead, I saw an expensive audition for a deliberately vulgar, R-rated reality show. I watched them from a safe corner of the room—pretty boys and prettier girls—trolling like pimps in a bus station with selfish, pornographic intent, and when we made our way at last to Vienne's car, the evening had taken its toll. We stepped carefully over channels of slush made by tires earlier in the day, now hardened by single-digit temperatures into slippery granite, but it didn't seem to matter; I just wanted to go home.

AS A LATE-DAY blizzard steamrolled the city, Vienne dropped me at the airport facing a two-hour wait before my flight to London. With nothing better to do, I sat at the gate thumbing through messages in my phone from former colleagues wondering how I was doing. Some asked when I intended a return to Virginia, and I answered them with a standard description of obligations in the wake of Damon's death that would keep me in the UK for a while.

From my position near the boarding gate, I watched deicing trucks descend on our plane and smiled my approval as clouds of steam and sickly yellow glycol solution billowed around the big Boeing. A man sat nearby with a woman half his age, and I turned away to hide my smile as his companion recalled a road trip to Las Vegas where "it never gets cold and the cops are really nice."

In the valley at that moment it was well after midnight, and my mind wandered for a while to thoughts of Aline. I looked at her message for the twentieth time and cursed myself for failing to book an earlier flight. In a moment of absurd impulse, I fought a powerful temptation to place the call, but the thought passed. It seemed much more than an idea or innocent gamble and I felt compelled to it—driven, perhaps—until a sobering flush of embarrassment shocked me back to reality. Was her hold on me so powerful even then? I turned the phone off and stuffed it into my bag in disgust, suddenly disappointed with myself for considering such a thing. I imagined how it would be and a confused, disapproving scowl on Aline's face for being pulled from her sleep by a call from across the Atlantic.

There was still an hour before boarding, so I went for a walk along the concourse to stretch my legs and enjoy another aimless pursuit, but also it was a way to kill time and avoid drooling on myself if I nodded off at the gate. Some of the shops were a bit more upscale than I imagined, and it surprised me I hadn't noticed them earlier. A few stood out, and I paused at one of them to inspect a set of lined leather gloves and matching cashmere scarf. Both were obscenely expensive and I frowned at a predictable airport markup philosophy that preys on thoughtless assholes who forget to buy something for loved ones until the last minute. I was glad Vienne wasn't there to see me because she believes (accurately or otherwise) my frugal nature is only a confirmation that I have no soul and fretting about the price tag would have won me severe and lengthy ridicule.

After detailed questioning by a girl behind the counter to establish correct size for the gloves, I surrendered and paid the money. It felt strange and yet satisfying to buy a gift, but I worried Aline would think it presumptuous until the sales girls assured me the thought would be appreciated. Was the charming show just a skillful sales ploy? Probably, but the risk of failure was worth taking if only to see Aline smile. I found a vacant spot along the wall and closed my eyes until the Air Canada gate agent called passengers to prepare for boarding—the signal another aerial plod was about to begin.

WALES SHARES A common, informal border with England, but getting there by airplane from North America is a fatiguing process that finally ended when the taxi eased down my driveway on a bright morning under clearing skies. An overnight dusting of snow made for a lovely scene suited to a Currier & Ives catalogue, and I stood in the cold air for a moment simply to enjoy the quiet. When I closed the door, my phone buzzed from a pocket and I answered with a wide grin.

"Good morning, Aline; your timing is perfect."

"Welcome home, Evan," she replied softly. "How was your trip?"

"Tiring, but it was good to see my sister. How about you—did you have a nice holiday?"

"It was lovely," she replied. "I spent some of the time with Margaret and her family."

She went silent suddenly and the pause seemed excessive until she finally spoke again.

"I'm glad you're back home and safe."

It sounded strange, the reference to safety, but I put it down to what may have been an ordinary aversion to flying.

"It's good to *be* back," I said, nodding. "The flights took forever but at least I made it without going insane, so…"

I cringed immediately, silent and furious with myself for so thoughtless a comment. I wanted to apologize and tell her I hadn't said it for any reason other than decrying the stress of airline travel, but she didn't seem to notice. After another second, she said, "You must be very tired."

"I'm fine," I replied. "I fly a lot and it's easy to sleep on airplanes without any trouble."

It was surprising she called at the precise moment I arrived but I didn't think more of it. I heard her throat clear and it was obvious she held the phone away from her face by the muted sound.

"Are you going into town or staying home for a while?" she asked.

"Oh, I'm done moving for now, believe me; there's nothing like coming home after a long trip, so I'll probably hang out and…"

"I missed you," she said, nearly at a whisper.

In another time and place her words might reasonably have seemed abrupt and unexpected, considering we'd only known each other a few months, but it wasn't any of those things and I answered her without a thought.

"I missed you, too. I thought about calling from the airport last night while I waited for my flight."

"Why didn't you?"

"It was late—almost one o'clock in the morning back here. I was sitting at the gate and…"

"I wouldn't have minded, Evan."

At once, a shiver ran through me, immediate and delightful. Had another door opened, I wondered?

"You were probably sleeping," I offered.

"I can go back to sleep, can't I? It's nice whenever you call."

I stood in my kitchen the way people do when their attention is so focused little else matters. I hadn't asked for them, but Aline's words poured into me like a tonic and I basked in the moment.

"It's nice to hear your voice again, too. I guess it's why I wanted to call you from Montreal, but…"

In that second, before I could finish my thought, another image flooded into my brain like a tidal wave—unstoppable and unexpected. She stood motionless in the woods as clear as the moment I first saw her on that hillside in the flowing, sheer material of her cloak. I saw her eyes, shining out from a gathering mist and fixed upon me like cool, blue lasers—unwavering and steady. She was silent but I felt as if she called out to me from that place, and the sensation was overwhelming. There were no words I could form and no sound I could make, transfixed and held in time like an obedient statue, waiting for an unknown command or order. Only her face, framed by the gentle curls of her hair, remained in my thoughts, and the paralysis gripped me until she broke through the strange, trance-like pause.

"If you're not doing anything later, I'm off to Wrexham to run a few errands…"

I heard her but still I couldn't speak, and the images persisted in my mind.

"Evan?"

"Oh, uh…yes, I'm here—sorry."

"I was just wondering if you'd like to come along to Wrexham?"

"Of course," I said at once. "Just tell me when to be ready."

"I'll be 'round at one o'clock?"

"One o'clock," I answered automatically.

She disconnected and I sat for a while until the image faded. In a sudden and inexplicable moment, I could smell the faint odor of her pine incense again. There was no reason, yet it wafted through my kitchen distinct and unmistakable. The strange occurrence of another "vision" disappeared, but I didn't take the time to consider what it meant. I finished unpacking and waited until Aline's Land Rover wandered down the driveway.

8
WHILE WE'RE BUSY BARING SOULS…

AS we sped along the highway east, Aline seemed happy to see me, and I was certainly delighted to see her, but there was something more. She smiled for no apparent reason and I saw it from the corner of my eye. A random thought or humorous memory, perhaps? It didn't matter and we spent time on the things people chat about as they catch up—life's ordinary processes and the obligations between friends who haven't seen each other in a while.

She told me about Margaret's twin nephews and their excitement to find the Star Wars toys on Christmas morning Aline had concealed in her truck until the boys were finally asleep the night before. It seemed so normal and I smiled at the thought of her wrapping gifts on the floor of her living room. In her description I heard the voice of contentment and satisfaction as anyone would in the warmth of the season. I listened and heard stability, too. I won't allow the intrusion of vanity to suggest it was anything to do with me, but the thought teased from a distance just the same.

After discussions with a shipping agency, plus a few turns through a handful of clothing stores as a reconnaissance mission to check out the competition, we lunched at a Wrexham pub called the Nags Head. I watched her and the change was obvious: distance between us *had* lessened since our first meeting in the trees and recognizing it lifted me. Now, she seemed more at ease as though a requisite condition had been met and the aloof, mysterious persona was dismantled and put away for another time.

It was nothing out of the ordinary because people often remain at arm's length until they get to know each other as a matter of course. Those invisible, protective barriers are there for a reason, and only fools or drunks ignore them in the first moments. The loud ones—overly friendly and gushing because they need acceptance more than the rest of us—are the tedious exceptions. It takes time to move through the days and weeks when we decide if another is acceptable, and we shifted quietly into a friendship far beyond the social limits of mere neighbors.

I remembered my first day and Jeremy's careful description of Damon's neighbor, suggesting her treatment for a mental condition shouldn't color my impressions of her as he walked the thin line between reasonable caution and undue worry. They accepted her, he said, and she was at least comfortable with them, but I know Jeremy saw in me a stranger and one who needed to understand. Aline's relationship with Damon was, at least in Jeremy's mind, sometimes strained, and he worried I was in danger of making matters worse. After all, they knew nothing of me beyond that connection, and Aline's distant nature was widely regarded as an unfortunate by-product of her time in Scotland.

As the days passed, my encounters with Aline proved nothing like the tense, confrontational picture I first formed in my mind; whatever malady that kept her in an institution for months was likely gone, and she seemed hesitant only for the same reasons a shy person waits and watches until satisfied no hidden threats are waiting.

I shook my head at the thought of her stay in a psychiatric ward. Was Aline's recovery completed on a predictable schedule, or was she simply not so ill after all? Perhaps she reached the invisible limits of what she could tolerate and the circuits inside her mind closed as a measure of self-protection in what is so often called a breakdown. Plenty of people find themselves at such a juncture and for reasons that don't necessarily include a loss of their sanity. On a cold, sunny afternoon she didn't look like a girl fighting unseen demons, and I smiled at the thought when we climbed back into her truck and aimed it toward home.

When we arrived, Aline wondered if I would like to come inside for a while. I nodded, knowing it likely meant yet another cup of tea and stretches of silence on the couch in her living room, but the practice was becoming our routine. As it is for so many others who meet and form a growing friendship, we walked beside each other, waiting but unwilling to interrupt the natural process. I noticed a new LED television hanging from a wall although she seemed to never watch it. I stood to inspect and admire the machine, imagining an enhanced experience on Super Bowl Sunday, just as Aline's phone chirped where she had left it on a lamp table.

I remember the moment because it was the first time anyone called her while I was there. Probably Margaret, I figured, calling from Colwyn Bay to discuss shop business, but when Aline smiled broadly and said, "Thank you so much; I have your address and I'm leaving now," it was clear the caller was somebody else. When she disconnected Aline told me she needed to leave, and I moved quickly to put my cup in her sink.

"I'll get going, but give me a buzz if you want to hang out later?"

She smiled again and said, "If it's all right, I'd like to stop in on my way home?"

"I'll be there when you get back," I replied, turning for the door.

I pause here because the officials stopped us at this point during our interrogations. Oh, they called them "conversations," but they were always the ones asking questions and we were the ones with answers. At Burke's direction, a thin woman with an unpronounceable last name they called "Mo" had been given control of the process, and she wanted to go into detail I didn't think was important. She insisted, which meant the delay would be made worse if we didn't cooperate, so I played along. I called her "Miss Persimmon" but not for anything to do with the Mary Poppins character and mostly out of spite because I wanted her to know I didn't subscribe to the implied authority she held. It annoyed her, of course, but there wasn't much she could do about it.

There were others like her, too—psychologists they thoughtfully rebranded as "behavioral analysts"—and she wandered around the interview room's bland government-issue table like a film director handing out instructions and commentary while an assistant dutifully typed notes into a laptop. Mo was curious about the process by which my relationship with Aline crossed over from acquaintance to something more.

"Were there any particular signs?" she asked. "Indicators that made clear your preference for each other's company had grown into the early stages of an emotional commitment?"

Still defiant and unwilling to entertain their demands without a fight, I simply answered, "No."

Mo wasn't amused, but her questions were at least understandable and nothing I hadn't asked myself long before. I remembered that time and the confusing moments when images and "visions" appeared suddenly and for no reason, but I had no intention of pouring those memories out for her to inspect.

ALINE WALKED ME to the door and watched again in the cold air as I made my way down her meadow where the tree line guided me around our hill. The snow was gathered in patches where sunlight couldn't reach, but as I went, the quiet of the forest wrapped around me like an old, familiar blanket and was no longer a place of mystery or worry. When I hung my coat on an ornate wooden lattice screwed into the kitchen wall, my laptop showed an unread e-mail from Vienne.

Her message detailed the last sign offs with a finance firm she'd hired to transport most of the contents from Damon's safe deposit boxes into a vault somewhere outside London. The gold and silver, plus a few additional pieces of jewelry no one seemed to have mentioned earlier, would be assessed and sold outright or, for those pieces with historic value, auctioned off to the highest bidder. Bundles of hard currency in local banks were transferred into modest-yield savings accounts, simply to avoid the killing application of British tax laws. Vienne's plan made sense and I replied to that effect, but the note only reminded me of my conversation with Birgit Nyström and an unresolved mystery still waiting somewhere in the future. I closed the computer and searched for my keys, determined to do the week's grocery shopping while I had nothing better to do.

I went through the shops, chatting with clerks and owners the way most people do in small towns, enjoying acceptance among those who once referred to me only as "Damon Morgan's very quiet brother." How was it, they chided, a good Welsh boy couldn't speak the language? Was there no one in all of America willing to instruct me? It was good-natured teasing, but I did look up some tutorials and grammar basics online when I returned home. Even butchered, an honest attempt at sorting out the confusing jumble of consonants and duplicate letters that makes Welsh a challenge would be noticed with an approving nod.

Dusk was settling and I went to switch on my front porch lights so that Aline would know I was home just as her truck swung around to a stop. I went outside to wait as she parked and stepped lightly through the slush to my door.

"Come in, come in," I said, motioning with one hand in the fashion of a traffic cop. I took her coat and asked how it went, though I had no idea where she went or why. It seemed like a good question, and she held up an index finger to signal for me to wait.

"I have something for you," she said, pulling from her handbag a small cardstock box.

It was wrapped with a narrow purple ribbon made of a cloth material, not the cheap plastic stuff, and I looked at her with a smile.

"What's this?"

The ribbon's bow fell away and I pulled the lid carefully to reveal a simple coin-shaped medallion made of pewter roughly the size of a nickel attached to a delicate curb chain necklace. I lifted it free from its velvet bed with a smile at the notion Aline had thought to buy me a gift.

"It's beautiful—thank you! This is really very thoughtful, Aline."

It was unpolished and on its face was a raised image of an ordinary oak leaf. She stood beside me and said, "There's a man near Denbigh who makes metal castings from wooden patterns. I carved the original from oak and left it with him while you were in Canada."

I placed it around my neck and let it dangle in the fashion of a St. Christopher medal for a moment, thumbing its texture and unable to stop smiling. I understood the importance of the moment, but Aline decided to finish the explanation anyway.

"You were away at Christmas but I wanted to give you something. I'm sorry it took so long."

"Wait a minute; you made the original blank yourself?"

"An old oak became diseased two years ago and a branch fell behind my house in a windstorm. My father taught me how to carve when I was young, so I kept some of it because the growth ring pattern was beautiful."

"But you carved it with your own hand and that alone makes it unique and special to me."

"Do you like it?" she asked quickly.

"Yes—I like it very much," I answered. "It's going to stay where it is from now on."

It was my turn. I grinned and told her not to move as I hurried to my bedroom to fetch the gloves and scarf. My wrapping efforts were sub-par but an obvious (and excessive) application of stick-on bows made her laugh. I know the gloves were nice, and the scarf would keep her warm, but it was clear the age-old truth of intent and thoughtfulness counted more to Aline than the gift itself, and she did nothing to hide a wide smile as she tried them on.

"They're lovely, Evan; thank you very much."

Her voice was soft and measured and she reached for my palm instinctively to squeeze it, uncaring if it seemed forced or overt. There was no signal—no menu for appropriate responses from the book of relationships—but we knew it was time. It was a gentle, soft kiss, but I could feel my heart begin to pound inside my chest. That moment is still burned into my memories as if its meaning soared above all others. Aline's smile faded and she placed her hand against my cheek before a second more purposeful kiss that seemed to go on for minutes. When we stood away at last, I looked again at the little medallion.

"The oak leaf…a Celtic symbol of life."

"It joins us," she whispered.

Aline positioned herself on a stool in my kitchen where she usually sat whenever she came to visit. She gathered her knees close and crossed her feet to capture them in place as I stood beside her.

"You told me it would be interesting as we got to know each other, remember? I was surprised because you seemed to know I was staying in Wales permanently, even before *I* did."

"Yes, I remember."

She nodded again, but her expression changed—pensive and almost sad. I saw it clearly as she looked at me and spoke.

"You worried about this," she whispered again.

I wondered what she meant, but there was no clue in her eyes.

"Worried?" I said.

"You were concerned about how we would get on."

"I just didn't want to show up out of the blue and…"

"May I ask you something?"

"Of course."

"Does it bother you now, knowing I was in hospital? We aren't just acquaintances anymore, Evan."

It was a matter of time, and I always knew we would return to the question at some point, but it seemed so sudden and abrupt. I wished at once she hadn't asked but there was no way out—no clever, easy escape.

"I thought about it when I first heard, I guess, but it doesn't matter."

"Why not?"

"Well, as you said, we've become more than just friends, and you never gave me a reason to *be* bothered."

She walked toward the windows.

"You don't know why I was in that place."

"No," I answered slowly, "but I'm not sure it makes any difference. Should I worry about something that happened a long time ago and long before we met?"

"Others do," she replied, looking away quickly.

"I'm not them."

Aline turned and looked again through the window toward the trees.

"Some will tell you to keep your distance; they'll warn you I'm trouble to be avoided."

"Who will—the people in town? I got the impression from Jeremy they're cheering for you; they like to see you're healed and doing well, Aline."

She looked over her shoulder and said, "Not them. But there will be others—people you haven't met."

"I don't understand; have I done something wrong?"

She turned and shook her head quickly.

"No, not at all! I just don't want you to think of me that way—as if I'd gone mad and had to be cured of something that went wrong inside my brain."

I watched her closely for an indicator to guide me when people who've endured emotional shock are forced to confront those most painful things. Instead, she spoke in a direct manner and not with the voice of a recovering patient holding fast to a lifeline connecting her with sanity suddenly threatened. Her tone made it clear the experience in Scotland had left unfinished business, and I guessed the ordeal was forced upon her against her will.

In my thoughts I saw them: pale inmates in striped pajamas and shabby bathrobes, curled in the fetal position on a metal-framed bed painted the institutional shade of white to match the walls of an isolation ward. I could see reddened eyes peering out from a tangle of matted, unkempt hair in desperation at the clank of locks and a rattle from key rings that make such places sound fittingly equivalent to prisons. Was it that way for her? Did an emergency room doctor see the signs of mental distress and call for special help? I know the images were contrived and only what my imagination conjured up from the memories of movies or television shows, but it bothered me. I hoped Aline wouldn't notice, but she sat again and smiled sadly.

"You're worried right now; I can see it in your eyes. We've grown closer but you're wary of becoming attached to a crazy girl."

"That's not it," I replied evenly. Had my expression told her something she waited to see? "I like our friendship just the way it is, and I wouldn't be much of a friend if I thought only of myself."

She stood and walked toward the door where her boots and jacket waited. Did she not believe me, I wondered?

"I like our friendship, too, Evan; I like it very much. But one day you'll understand why I was there. They will tell you to turn away; that you're a fool if you let yourself be drawn in."

"The doctors?"

"No; they were only trying to help me, but there are others. It's inevitable, but I want you to know I understand if you prefer our relationship remains casual—to keep it as it is. I don't want you to feel obligated or moved by pity because I don't need any."

"I'm not afraid, Aline, if that's what you're saying."

"Are you sure?" she replied at once. "I can smell the fear inside you. I know you want to fight back against your instincts with logic and intelligent reasoning, but the fear is still there."

Her words came at me like machine gun fire—staggering and without pause. I listened to her but in those brief seconds, when our minds judge and compare what we hear against what we know, I felt suddenly lifted by a strange, steadfast purpose.

"You're wrong," I declared. "I know how I feel better than anyone, and you're dead wrong if you think I'm looking for a convenient excuse or a way to get out of this gracefully."

She moved closer, but her brow had furrowed.

"Don't say these things out of bravado, Evan; it's easy to pretend when you need to believe."

Was it Aline's way of closing the book before the first chapter's conclusion? I'd seen the trick enough times to recognize it and I threw it back as fast as I could.

"If you'd rather be left alone, I will, but only if you want it that way and not because I'm worried about your time in Scotland."

She reached for my hand and we stood before each other in silence. A gate opened and through it I saw the first glimpses of those things I know today but couldn't have contemplated then. Aline moved us both past the existing boundaries of our growing relationship and into the next, but she stopped it to offer me an escape—a way out—even if I couldn't understand what it would mean. I think of that moment sometimes, but I have no regret for where it led and my part in it. We held onto each other for a while in the silence, and I felt the strange sensation of knowing my life was changing. There was no hesitation or reason for concern; it simply was and I had no interest in going any other direction.

When she hugged me a last time and turned for the door, Aline made me promise not to be late for our breakfast date the next morning, reminding me she was eager to try her hand at a new recipe for eggs Benedict. The understanding between us had been formed in rough shapes, like the oak leaf medallion she'd made for me, but the days and months ahead would become a lathe to shape and refine its contours into what she already knew it would become. I felt better about things, alone in the quiet of my kitchen, when she drove up to the road. Tame though it may have been, our first physical encounter was a signal and one of the few I *did* manage to interpret successfully.

I looked at the television for a while, but it was more a distraction while I pretended the past hours had been nothing out of the ordinary. After a while I caught myself nodding off when a blaring commercial about margarine woke me with its loud, irritating beat. I crawled into bed still thumbing the little oak leaf and thinking mostly of her. Sleep found me quickly but barely an hour passed when it began.

DREAMS ARE FUNNY things. They can be goofy, amusing romps in a made-up world where anything is possible and limited only by the boundaries of our imagination. Sometimes, a dream is so disjointed and surreal it becomes a bizarre, inexplicable slide show of disturbing horrors we would rather not recount, grateful "it was just a dream" when we wake. When this one began, I could hear the sound of voices echo in the darkness until they faded to a uniform whisper.

The unmistakable aroma of charred wood and freshly wetted earth surrounded me, but there were no visual cues—no reference points—until finally I watched from a featureless, empty room as a shape moved toward me from the shadows and into the light. I couldn't see a face but I knew it was Aline in that odd moment when the transmitter of memory sends instructions we accept without question. The voices of others faded in and out, though I couldn't see them, and her hair had been pulled up into a high knot on her head like an upside-down shock of wheat. I could smell her, too, and the unique odor of her skin was unmistakable.

She spoke at last but I couldn't make out the words as she moved closer. She wore a strange gossamer material around her shoulders so sheer and thin that her naked body glistened beneath it in the dim light, and upon it was a swirl of tattoos, like elaborate commas, in groups of three. I think of them today and the image created was cryptic—primitive—as though applied at random and not by a skilled artist.

"Wake up boy; wake now and take your share!" she said with a distant, lurid giggle, and it was clear what she meant when her hands moved along my body, trailing scented oil from a thin glass tube. Her hands guided mine and I felt no hesitation or reason to withdraw as the encounter slipped deeper into the primal, instinct-driven frenzy of animals. A montage of images and sensations held me like a vise, and I watched it as if suspended from above or looking on during an out-of-body experience. No dream is so powerful and as real as any living moment, but today, of course, I know more than I did then.

The sequence was profoundly erotic—raw and graphic in the extreme—yet I was a willing participant; I *wanted* to do those things. I felt cheated when it ended abruptly and it was difficult to shake away the powerful visions as I hovered between consciousness and a place where there were few behavioral limits and no restraints. Throughout the compelling moments I could hear, taste, and smell, and I remember hoping in the midst of it all no one would intrude and discover us. This was not from modesty, and only because I didn't want the dream to end, but when it did I felt cold where my perspiring head soaked the pillow.

At last, I sat on the edge of my bed while the final images were replaced slowly by consciousness. I could feel the rapid pulse at my temples and shallow, measured breaths like a runner forced to hide with terror that his panting gasps will give him away. It took a few moments—I can't remember how long—until I tasted the distinctive flavor of blood. I went quickly to my bathroom and squinted against the harsh light but there was no injury—no pain. I looked and felt about in tentative probes with the tip of my tongue, expecting a wound where I had bitten a lip or my cheek, perhaps, but there was nothing. I swirled warm water again, spitting out the pink solution into the sink, and as I splashed and dried my face, the reflection stared back with dark, dilated eyes like a stranger struggling in a haze of confusion.

I resented waking from the dream before it could reach a conclusion, though few dreams ever do, and I nearly sulked from being denied the climactic ending such dreams suggest. The feeling stayed with me for many minutes despite nagging echoes of shame pecking at me from the fringes of my conscience as a reminder good people of character don't do such things.

When I returned to my bed the sheets and blanket had been pulled from where I tucked them neatly, and my pillow showed three blood spots: one on the left and two others on the right. Had I swung my head back and forth, dribbling out the stains with each motion? It was quiet and I worked slowly, gathering the sheets to swap out for fresh linen, and a deep breath seemed to settle things at last.

I switched off the light and lay quietly in the aqua glow of my bedside clock with memories of the raw sequence fresh in my thoughts. I hoped with an absurd desperation Aline would never find out the depravity made by my dream state and the animal behavior my imagination assigned to us both. She never would, I decided, but mostly I was grateful being relieved of the need to explain why I dwelled on graphic details without the slightest regret. As I settled, a faint smell of wet soil drifted through and I sat up, awake and alert.

Maybe it's understandable, but I worried my subconscious had somehow assumed authority to revive the dream and invite the puerile images waiting inside. Of course, that was wishful thinking; instead, I simply missed the clues and signals offered by impossible realism no dream can match. There wasn't a rational explanation for me to grasp and hold tightly, even if some sell it as a rare window into the human psyche. To me, interpreting dreams is emotional snake oil and another reminder of the darker corners of my nature I'd rather not reveal.

9

ANOTHER STEP, ANOTHER GLIMPSE

IN the morning I woke slowly, and it was difficult just pulling myself out of bed. Could a dream, regardless of its content, create so debilitating an aftereffect? I thought about Aline that morning with silent gratitude there would be no need to explain myself and the obscene moments in a dream that reflected my own depraved imagination. I felt dirty and dishonest, but that is the inevitable burden after suffering creepy dreams and images of things we would never do in our "awake" lives.

WHEN DUSK CAME to end the afternoon, Aline called suddenly and I stared at my phone for a moment before answering. To my great relief, she simply wanted to know if I had dinner plans, and when I reported none she suggested a "date" at her favorite place in Liverpool. There was no particular reason, she insisted, and mostly because she hadn't been on a "dress up" dinner date in a while. I agreed quickly, of course, and when I pulled into her drive near seven o'clock, the tension I created for myself seemed to fall away like water draining from a bathtub.

We chatted about ordinary things on the hour ride up to Merseyside and none of it seemed odd or forced. Instead, Aline showed only anticipation for an evening out and it went that way for a long time—two people on the same path, if for very different reasons, adjusting and finding those places where one fits neatly with the other. We settled into it and found a sort of equilibrium that seemed natural, learning more about each other in small but continuing increments.

We sipped wine in the restaurant bar while waiting for our table, and through it all Aline's history remained elusive and she spoke mostly of her childhood in details that became fewer and less defined when topics shifted to her adult life. I wondered where and when the difficulties for her began and by what event; was it something specific, or a slow burn to an unfortunate conclusion in Scotland? I knew better than to ask and I wasn't concerned enough to worry about it anyway.

WEEKS PASSED, THE customary pace was established, and with it, an informal schedule by which we each knew how to go over the hill—she to my house, or I to hers. In town, we had become an "item" and a few knowing smiles from shopkeepers seemed to apply a final, approving gloss to it all. Aline, they said, was changed. Now, she wore a smile for no reason and stopped to chat about things that would never have concerned her before. In my private moments ideas of something more flirted with me from a distance, but I ignored them with a determination not to screw it up with unwanted expectations. It stayed that way until a message chimed its arrival in my phone late in the night to pull me from my sleep.

Uncaring for the time difference between us, Vienne forwarded an amusing meme about Buffalo Sabres fans' historic dislike of rival Toronto and I laughed out loud as the back and forth process consumed thirty minutes. Trying to sleep again would be a wasted effort and it occurred to me in a comical moment I had no books with which to become bored in the late hour. I stood and pulled on my robe, looking again at the clock that showed another twenty minutes until midnight. In that second, I thought of the Air Canada gate in Montreal and a call to Aline I didn't place. Was she still awake, I wondered? Could I soothe myself with the sound of her voice without seeming a needy, selfish pest? Once more I flirted with the idea, but unwilling to reverse what was built in those first careful moments. Instead, I decided to follow a hidden, more private course.

In the darkness, with no others around who might notice, I would be secure and alone. No one needed to know anyway, and without hope of a return to sleep, I dressed quickly and slipped out through my back door on an angle toward the woods. It seemed childish but I stepped slowly around occasional patches of snow in the cold air.

A penlight that once dangled from my key fob lit the way with its artificial blue glow, and it seemed fitting as the moon above bathed the forest in similar tones. Past the hillside and along the dry creek bed I wandered until I reached the bottom edge of Aline's field. I simply wanted to see her house, even from that distance and look for a lit room to reveal she might yet be awake.

As I cleared the trees and angled left in sodden grass she was there, waiting motionless in the moonlight. It startled me and I stopped to aim my light at her for a moment before replacing it in my pocket—the night's strange glow was more than enough, and she walked slowly toward me. As it was on our first encounter months before, Aline appeared out of nowhere and at precisely the right moment. When she stopped in front of me, all of it seemed expected and inevitable.

"Couldn't sleep?" I asked.

"No," she replied.

"Me neither. I was going to call you but I chickened out and decided to take a walk instead. You saw my flashlight?"

She moved closer.

"I knew where you were."

Her words were soft and spoken with ease, but I didn't hear the hidden meaning. Instead, I reached for her if only by instinct and we held each other for a moment. She was dressed in her robe with heavy boots and a winter jacket that made for a mildly amusing picture, but before I could comment she pulled me close and kissed me. I wish I could say I understood, like a film star in a romantic movie perhaps, but all I could do was stand in that moment and give in to the powerful sensation. She took my hand and turned for her house without a word. I walked beside her in silence while we crossed the lawn, aiming for her back porch. I could smell fragrant shampoo when she laid her head on my shoulder for a second or two until we went quickly through her door. She turned, only for a moment, but her expression changed. I've seen it many times since, but the first remains prominent in my memories because it was so unexpected—almost feral.

Aline turned quickly and walked backward to her front room, pulling me by my outstretched arms until she stopped and moved a low table away to leave a wide throw rug in front of her fireplace clear and uncluttered. It sounds strange to say it now, but it was the sort of thing we might do before a wrestling match and not the slow, romantic ballet sex becomes when its first moment arrives.

In the orange light of her hearth, watching as she pulled the robe from her shoulders, I saw ornate, swirling tattoos, just as they appeared in my powerful dream. They were not uniform and mostly in the distinctive shapes of ancient, Celtic art—random triads and elaborate knots—but none connected deliberately to another. I couldn't understand how those same designs across her body could be nearly identical to the scenes of my shocking dream days before, yet it was a stunning replay and I let myself live within it once more.

She watched me as she went, but still I couldn't speak. Her movement was not a burlesque-inspired strip for the purpose of building anticipation; instead, her thigh-length nightgown and panties were simply in the way and she nearly tore them from her body.

I stood before her, motionless like a repentant waiting for judgment, until a flurry of movement left my own clothes in a heap near my feet, and I waited until her fingertips found me.

Aline moved like a serpent writhing and molding its shape to fit the world around it. I felt breathless—captive to the moment—as time became static and irrelevant. She said nothing and I couldn't speak. We moved together, first with a deliberate, almost violent cadence but later rising and inexorable like water below the decks of a sinking ship.

I couldn't recognize it at first, but the air changed around us, moving from the breath of a stone oven in this moment to a crackling, electric swirl in the next. Her face changed, too, swapping a gentle smile beneath lovely eyes for a sneering and twisted expression of purpose and determined power. Her teeth clenched as she pulled my face to her with a hiss and a handful of my hair to direct me wherever she wanted.

She commanded me to taste her and breathe in her scent, but I heard a faint warble of laughter in that same moment and it was the first time I understood how captive I had become. It didn't matter the demand or perversion, I waited eagerly for anything she ordered me to do. I don't remember when we moved at last to her bed but the clutching and groping became desperate and even violent. She bit my lip and I saw my blood on hers as she grinned and said in a deep, guttural growl, "You're mine! Love me proper now."

The shuddering explosions followed again and again as if made without limit and I worried my pounding heart would burst out of my chest or the ringing inside my ears might leave me deaf. They didn't, and all I could see was her glistening, naked body moving in the twilight as she twisted me into position so that we could begin again. The sound of wet skin on skin in a steady cadence was loud and alone in the silence until I heard whispered words coming at me as she held my head with a firm grasp. I wasn't sure if it was my imagination until I saw her eyes close as she bucked back and forth above me and the strange whispers became a chanting song. The words were foreign, but I didn't care or worry for anything beyond the moment and each breathtaking convulsion. Her sudden, strange language offered no clue and I wondered in a brief moment if she was pouring out another product of her old difficulties—speaking "in tongues" by another name.

There was no line of demarcation; no discernable starting point. I didn't know if each forceful thrust was my doing or hers, but the physical pleasure was, in the last moments, a compulsion bending me to its will. Desire and primal lust overran any sense of romantic connection between us and still I couldn't stop myself from obeying any command. Her thighs closed tightly against my ears in this moment but turned into pounding spurs like a jockey compelling a horse in the next. Everything was slippery and hot to the touch and I could think of nothing else.

When she pushed me onto my back and moved slowly into a tight straddling position, her hair fell forward like a golden tent around my head and all I could see were her narrowed eyes and the sound of breathing through flared nostrils with each movement. Again, the images swirled through in my mind and I could smell an unexpected odor, like wet moss clinging to the branches of an old tree. I had no time to consider its meaning but I remember it clearly today.

Through it all, what should have been tiny gasps and polite moans of two joined by the power of love became something else: gravelly shouts and warbling screams anyone else might regard as the voice of pain. I never once thought to stop or slow and she gave no hint of a reason I should. No experience in my life could match the fury and desperation holding me to her like a vise until finally it began to slow. I can't say how long it continued until we finally gave in to exhaustion, but the trees outside stood motionless in the early dawn light.

We were breathless, pouring sweat, and still she watched me in the final seconds as her expression eased and the lovely, gentle face returned. Calling our first night earsplitting sex is the easy, boastful description today, but it was much more than that and months would pass until I understood the difference—and an explanation why.

Mo will be disappointed when she discovers I didn't go further in the details of my first time in bed with Aline for their narrative. It isn't for the sake of modesty but because Aline asked me not to. Mo will see the brief, generalized description and convince herself my hesitation is made from a defiant need to protect and secure a private place where no one else should be allowed to go—a place reserved only for us. She wants to believe it was undeniable attraction and the emerging power of love that brought us together that cold night, but Burke knows better. We all understand it was much more than a romantic interlude, but Mo will shake her head and insist it was that unseen force which makes one devoted to another for a lifetime. She's right about some of it, of course, but she will refuse to allow the rest of the story to shatter a charming illusion. Miss Persimmon is a scientist but she's also a hopeless romantic; I've never been able to figure out how she reconciles the divide between fundamentally competing interests but that's who and what she is.

WHEN I WOKE in late morning, the snow was dissolving in a steady, cold drizzle. Aline shifted herself closer and pulled me close.

"Let's stay here a while," she whispered and it was obvious she wanted to revisit the passionate moments from the night before. "I'll start breakfast later."

When it resumed, the moments were unlike before—gentle and with an ease the way most people imagine lovemaking should be. The moments were abbreviated, but noticeably absent were the powerful thoughts and fierce, passionate images that took me over and released what anyone else might call animal nature. I said nothing and Aline's manner was once more the way it had been a day before. I felt dehydrated and as I drained two full glasses of water, she laid her head softly against my shoulders. Whatever spell carried us to another, surreal place only hours earlier, it was gone and the calm returned.

My moonlight walk hadn't been made for those reasons or the base instincts of sexual desire; I went over the hill simply to satisfy a private need and to look the way parents do when their children are fast asleep. I had no expectation or deluded idea of knocking on Aline's door, but when she met me unannounced in her field, explaining myself became needless. Had she woken and felt a parallel compulsion of her own, I wondered, unable to sleep and driven by the same desire in an impossible moment of shared thoughts? It didn't matter and I was relieved when we continued afterward without the awkward "talk" to define boundaries, make excuses, or to ensure no repeats because the encounter was only "in the moment."

We spent most of that day together watching television and planning my next trip up to her shop. I wondered if our late-night rendezvous would come up and when it did, Aline seemed to regard the previous evening's raw exhibition only in tones of affection and not tied to lurid details or wondering when we intended to do it again. Once complete, our first intimate moment—no matter its intense push against the borders of acceptable behavior—brought us finally through to a calm and understanding place that needed no analysis or qualifying argument. It simply was and we were free to follow our new path together without slobbering declarations of love or pornographic overtures aimed at this pleasure or that.

There was no effort made to establish rules or make pledges of devotion others find necessary in exclusive relationships because they weren't required. Aline was in no hurry and neither was I, so we picked up where we left off the day before and simply enjoyed breakfast together. She asked me to rinse some blueberries and I gave in to a silly impulse to shoot her with a spray from the faucet. She squealed a little, but a battle for control of the sprayer was on and she didn't let up until the front of my shirt was soaked. It sounds childish today, but I enjoyed our rough-housing and loud laughter that ended with a hug and a truce.

With order restored, I watched her again. It was interesting, although a bit dull to describe now, but seeing her at domestic tasks like any other girl without the mystery and unknown worries I'd assigned to her only months before was somehow expected and soothing. She prepared the eggs as I would; she tucked a dishrag in her waist and hurried from the stove to the refrigerator, and it occurred to me in a sudden and enjoyable moment whatever landed her in a mental ward was no longer in control; Aline Lloyd had taken her life back.

AFTER A WHILE, the unanswered questions about Damon's finances came up again in a phone conversation with Vienne. She had decided it was a problem for a future day and since most of the contents from his safe deposit boxes had been secured locally, or at a bank in London, there was no special hurry to investigate further. I was prepared to take it up again, but I admit relief from that duty was very welcome. We agreed a more involved, direct approach to managing our newly acquired business interests was needless as the property rights and ownership holdings Damon had secured were largely self-regulating. We were always given the option of attending financial meetings each quarter, but neither of us felt a pressing need to go, particularly with Liam Donnelley's banking friends to keep an eye (however expensive it turned out to be) on such matters.

We spoke in abstract terms about the changes our sudden wealth had brought, but it seemed Vienne was enjoying the money more than I. She bought a suitably expensive high-rise condo in Montreal's fashionable Ville-Marie neighborhood and, in a parking garage nearby, one of the severe battlecruisers Mercedes-Benz offers in its seemingly endless line of sedans. Not for the image, she insisted, but because it was "that damn nice" to drive. She wondered if I intended to splurge a bit as well but my defense of the used Nissan X-Trail I'd bought in November—one of the cars American soccer moms drive these days in order to avoid looking like soccer moms—only made her laugh. "You can afford a new car, Evan," she said. "Live a little!"

I promised to upgrade before summer, but I think she knew it was mostly big talk with no intention of backing it up unless and until somebody forced me.

She asked how it was going with "the mysterious neighbor girl" and I hoped the question had been asked only in passing. After I first told her, my description was colored by the things I thought I knew. In those earliest days I avoided a suggestion that Damon had bolted from the place in part because of difficulties with Aline. When I explained things had changed dramatically, and a growing relationship had become something more, Vienne went suddenly silent.

"Wait a minute," she said. "Are we still talking about that same girl from before—the crazy one who did time in a looney bin?"

She couldn't know but it was irritating to hear the words.

"Yes," I replied, "but it turns out she's nothing like that. I had it wrong and she's not crazy at all."

"Then why was she institutionalized?" Vienne asked bluntly.

"I don't know the specifics, but I think she went through a bad time and needed to reset. People shut down sometimes, Vienne. Everyone has a breaking point and just because Aline reached hers doesn't mean she's crazy!"

I heard my own words—clumsy and loud—like a desperate explanation from a lovestruck teenager to others who don't understand, or worse, don't *want* to. I knew of her past only those things Aline allowed me to see; I couldn't describe the details because she wouldn't reveal them and I assumed it was best that she hadn't.

In the silence as I waited for Vienne to speak, I felt a dull ache rising again and with it the nagging questions I wouldn't press Aline to answer. Had I done so out of considered deference to her position, or was it only my selfish unwillingness to disturb a friendship that moved to a much deeper affection? But worse still, was there still a lingering bigotry about mental illness I needed to destroy so that I would become worthy?

"Okay, okay!" Vienne replied. "I shouldn't have said it like that. I didn't realize you've become close but it's not like you offered me clues or updates in the last three months!"

Again, the air went dead. Of all people in the world I would rather not offend, my sister is at the top of that list. I felt horrible, fumbling for something to say.

"I know, Vienne, and…look, I'm sorry for being an asshole about it and not telling you earlier."

"It's okay," she muttered, and I heard the softened voice she always uses to let me off the hook. "Anyway, how did you get from where you were to where you are now? Did you just show up one day and knock at her door, or what?"

"No," I answered, "and it's a good thing I didn't. Damon tried that when he was here and it didn't end well."

"Wait; are you saying he hit on the neighbor girl while Isolda was waiting for him down in Spain?"

"No, nothing like that," I said quickly. "Aline said he was a bit too loud. Not a jerk, or anything, but just all over the place."

"Well," Vienne added, "that does describe Damon when he was on some new adventure."

"I know, so I kept myself at a distance and let her get used to things in her own time. After a few days, I went for a walk out in the back part of my property and she was there. She knew I was Damon's brother before I told her but we just talked for a while in the woods and she seemed very nice…quiet as hell, but nice."

"Okay," Vienne continued, "fast-forward to now; are you just friends with her, or has it gone beyond that?"

"A little beyond. Okay, a *lot* beyond."

"Evan, are you sleeping with her?"

"Jesus, Vienne, is this an interrogation?"

"Okay, so you are—at least I know the landscape. When did you get so cozy with this girl?"

"After I got back from Montreal."

"What's her story; is she from there?"

"Not originally but she's been here for a few years. She came down from Scotland right after…"

I stopped for only a moment, but Vienne understood.

"After they let her go?"

"Yeah. She was born and raised in Cardiff but she owns a little dress shop in a resort town up on the coast not too far down the highway from Anglesey."

"Is this strictly casual or should I consider it exclusive?"

"I'm not sure."

"Take a guess!" she insisted.

"I suppose you could say it's exclusive but I can't speak for Aline."

"It's been a while since you had a girlfriend, Evan; are you okay with this?"

Vienne's question was understandable, but it was the first time anyone had used the dreaded "G" word. I felt like a middle school kid, blushing and fidgety when a sibling pulls out a private detail for all to see at the dinner table while parents are watching over the rims of their glasses to measure the response.

"When I first got here, I saw her a few times but always at a distance. I didn't know if that was because of Damon or if she was just cautious. After I got to know her better, she seemed like a different person than the one Jeremy Collingwood described."

"How was she different?"

"I thought she was going to be a wacked-out hermit, twitchy and weird because of her earlier problems. I was expecting an eccentric zone-brain teetering on the edge of insanity, but she's not like that at all."

"She acts normal, like anyone else?"

"I don't think it's an act; she *is* normal, at least now."

"Don't screw around with this," Vienne cautioned. "If you don't know enough about all the stuff that happened to her from before, it's hard to know for sure she's normal."

"She hasn't said or done anything that would make me worry, so I figured she got herself squared away and past all that. They wouldn't have released her if she couldn't manage on her own, right?"

"I suppose so, but I'd give it some time before I made a final assessment."

"What do you mean?"

"I mean playing with her in bed is one thing; some kind of deep, emotional commitment is another matter."

My thoughts screamed "too late" but I ignored it.

"I'm taking it day by day and that's all; nobody's making wedding plans, okay?"

"All right, but I want to meet this girl and look her over for myself."

"I'm fine, Vienne; you don't have to do the big sister inspection."

"Yes, I do. Are you going to bring her over at some point or do I have to come to you?"

"I haven't really thought about it, to be honest."

"Well, think about it now. Actually, we're in a down cycle at work so it could be a good time for me to catch a plane. And anyway, I want to see this rural estate of yours."

"It's just a little farmhouse, Vienne."

"I want to see it anyway."

After we hung up, I sat for a while to consider our conversation and maybe just to reflect. I couldn't tell her the reason there had been no plan for dragging Aline to North America because I didn't have one. It wasn't for any hesitance or need to delay until we spent more time together in order to satisfy the unspoken requirement for a number of months to pass before such things are appropriate. We want our people to understand we've taken the necessary steps to assure them we're not merely enamored; we need them to know the new person is more than an acquaintance. For both of us, now alone in the world after Damon's death, it was something different—something more—and I had to make sure of my own intent before selling it to Vienne. I looked around my house in anticipation of the cleaning marathon coming at me like a tidal wave, but more than that, I had to sort out the time and manner in which I would have to tell Aline and hope it wouldn't arrive as news she didn't want to hear.

10
A STRANGE EVENT IN FLANDERS

TEMPERATURES began their slow climb in spring, and the relentless, delightful tides of green swept through the valley to welcome the new season. We spent more time in the trees walking and chatting in a silent explosion of life renewed. Jeremy told me about Aline's love of the forest, and I remembered the conversation wondering if she hid an alter ego—a passionate environmental activist who talks to her plants and washes them with a spray bottle filled with distilled water, but she was none of those things.

She went to another place among the giant oaks and stands of birch, a private zone where she changed a little, welcoming and comfortable there in ways I couldn't fully understand. It wasn't fashion, cultural identity, or a political imperative. Instead, her comfort among the trees came from something deeper and without regard for image and a perceived need to change the world.

When we sat on the trunk of a fallen tree, or cross-legged on the carpet of leaves forever covering the forest floor, she smiled at me and asked if I had done those things as a kid. I nodded and told her of a special place in a pine grove not far from our childhood home that seemed to belong only to Damon, Vienne and me. We went there to pretend we were explorers looking for treasure in a faraway land where dragons and wizards lurked in the shadows. A creek wandering through a deep depression with steep walls of sandstone made a good setting for entertaining those fantasies, and I wondered if Vienne would think of the place when we took her for walks in the valley. Aline listened, but she seemed to drift in and out, wandering back through her own memories and childhood adventures, perhaps.

BARELY A WEEK before Vienne's arrival from Montreal I completed the furious cleaning exercises, determined she wouldn't find me slovenly and undisciplined in my new life as a country gentleman. Aline watched and smiled from my couch, and I envied her calm, disaffected manner considering the circumstances. I told her everything there was to know about Vienne, including the certainty she would come under fierce scrutiny as the new lady friend of a little brother, yet it didn't seem to bother her.

When she called as they began boarding for her flight in Montreal, Vienne wondered if I intended to bring Aline to meet her at the airport in Liverpool, since her chosen air route from Montreal went through Dublin instead of London. I didn't know because I hadn't asked but there was little doubt Aline would quickly agree. Girls from our school days held uniform dread at the prospect of running head-on into my very protective big sister, but not Aline. I had been down that path once or twice, enough to feel the nerves begin to fray when we crossed over the Mersey at Runcorn, angling west toward Lennon Airport.

Vienne smiled and waved as she moved through a group of travelers after clearing Customs, but she bypassed me and went immediately to Aline. They embraced warmly for a moment, exchanging the expected niceties, but it seemed honest and genuine. Vienne raised her eyebrows and tilted her head at me to signal her approval as we made our way along the concourse. My first moments with Aline had been nowhere near as cordial, but I was grateful for the unspoken détente and decided (wisely) to keep my mouth shut.

Vienne stayed for a week and we marched her through the routine, showing her the sights in southeast Denbighshire: the abbey and Dinas Brân castle (what's left of it), the Plas Newydd house because Aline insisted, and again in Liverpool to inspect the array of shrines made to the memory of the Beatles so Vienne could place another check mark next to a completed bucket list item. I introduced her to Jeremy before running her through the local shops, and it was interesting when I felt suddenly like a local.

We watched rugby replays because Aline assured Vienne it was necessary. I tried my best as we went through an online tutorial for the sole purpose of learning to sing "Land of My Fathers" properly. Aline insisted so we wouldn't be lost come the day we would be expected to belt it out like a native, so we obliged. She showed us a video online and even I blinked back a tear or two as seventy-five thousand Welsh voices in Cardiff's Millennium Stadium thundered their anthem as one before the national team went on to beat rival England.

Some of our time was spent walking in the woods and through the gap where my property points quietly toward Aline's field, but a day trip to Colwyn Bay was Aline's chance to spoil Vienne and she didn't waste it. Both found a comfortable common ground—a summit, perhaps—where each could enjoy the company of the other without concern for me. I'm still unsure how that happened and whether it was allowed to develop of its own accord, but they became friends in that week. When I asked Aline if she 'helped' Vienne's perceptions of friendship, a returned glare and a very firm "no" answered the question.

I think of those days sometimes and how we crossed over from mildly suspicious new neighbors to a local item and finally to holding hands and strolling without a care in the same place where Aline had startled me as she stood motionless in the leaves. We spoke of Damon and his time there, but mostly we listened to amusing anecdotes Aline recalled after an evening's discussions matured and wine bottles stood empty on the kitchen counter. It was unexpected and Aline delivered with a skillful comedic timing I never knew she had, but it seemed a stark contrast to the quiet girl staring at me through the trees and I sent a quiet "thank you" up to the heavens for a small favor.

On the morning of Vienne's last day in the valley, Aline gave her a woven leather bracelet made of thin straps interlaced in groups of three, and stitched within were seven large beads made of polished amber she bought from a shop over in Chester. I couldn't know then the significance of seven beads, but it seemed important only that the bracelet had been made by her own hand just as my oak leaf medallion had been.

Vienne understood the moment's meaning and she was prepared. While we waited, she went to retrieve something from her suitcase—something for Aline, she said. Vienne returned with two thin, oblong pieces of wood barely eight inches in length and four in width. The halves were joined by a tiny brass piano hinge on one long edge and fastened with a single delicate latch no bigger than a fingernail on the opposite side so that the object opened like a book. The wood was stained and finished in hand-rubbed Tung oil and Vienne handed it carefully to Aline as she opened one half to reveal a length of intricate lace, faded and yellow, on a bed of black satin.

Aline placed it on my coffee table and knelt to inspect it like a patron in a museum. Vienne spoke quietly and with a voice I've rarely heard from her—soft and almost reverent—as she explained the lace was made by our great-great-grandmother, Catrin Rees. She did the lacework for an evening gown given to the daughter of a friend, Vienne said, and that girl was wearing it aboard RMS Titanic the night it slid beneath those icy Atlantic waves. She was still wearing it when the Carpathia's crew pulled her from a lifeboat the next day, and she insisted the lace had been a good luck charm. The girl returned some of it to Catrin and told her it would bring *her* good fortune, too. For generations, pieces were handed down (and usually forgotten), but Vienne found it among our mother's things after our parents were killed. A small length of it seemed a fitting gift for Aline, and I was astonished Vienne would be willing to part with any of it.

I watched Aline as she held the intricate material in her palm, and her brow furrowed suddenly the way it does when we struggle to fight back against gathering tears, but it was too late and one coursed its way down her cheek. I looked at her in silence as Vienne reached for her and they held each other a moment until Aline smiled and laughed a little before thanking Vienne for her thoughtfulness.

We put Vienne on her return flight late in the afternoon during a misting rain, and the ride home to Lllangollen was passed mostly in silence. Aline looped her hand around my forearm and the quiet shift from one place in our lives to the next was complete. There was no special requirement or expectation, but knowing Vienne and Aline were at least temperamentally aligned became a signal—an anchor, perhaps. Beyond the unusual circumstances that brought me to the valley, small and unnoticed indicators began to blur and the clues became more difficult to find. It stayed that way until summer when the tourist season arrived, and with it, Inspector Andre Renard.

When I drafted our narrative for Burke, I understood Renard's involvement would be of extreme importance because he was the one who lit the fuse. Their determined interest was clear but mostly because of the inspector's friendship with Gregory Hurd (who, it turns out, was more than Burke's political sponsor inside Whitehall). I don't blame them, but Renard's association with a high-level bureaucrat in the British government made problems both for them and for us because few politicians are good at keeping secrets and fewer still at keeping their word. We went through the notes carefully so as not to miss meaningful context, but there were no startling revelations or the memory jogs they hoped would shine light on those first days when Renard came up from Liège.

As I began the recollection task it was only that: laying out the events as they occurred. I remembered and noted a precise timeline from the moment he arrived and the rapid burn that brought us to where we are today; by any useful measure, it was the moment everything changed.

After a while those days became more difficult for me to describe, and I suppose that is true only because I can't do anything to Renard for the hate and discontent he put us through. I know it's not an admirable thing to say, but privately, I still regret passing on the opportunity to get in at least one decent punch.

Burke was running things again when we got to this point in the debriefing sessions because Hurd's people needed all the information they could get in the event of a diplomatic "episode" with the Brussels government.

"Describe those first interactions dispassionately," he said. "Tell us in academic terms, if you can, and try to bear in mind why Renard was there."

Dispassionately? That got a laugh, mostly from Halliwell and the security boys, but even Miss Persimmon snickered a bit. I couldn't tell them what happened on Renard's first day in Llangollen because we didn't find out he was there until later when he asked around in town.

THE SUMMER SEASON was underway and more than a few cars with continental license plates passed by my house with cameras out the window. Tour groups filter through from time to time and the occasional lost soul pulls into my driveway to ask directions. They don't seem to make it as far as Aline's farm because my property is positioned on a more traveled road, but even she gets one or two when the air warms and a full press of people on holiday begins. In town, faces come and go the way they do in all popular tourist destinations and Renard's appeared in the second week of June.

He went under an assumed name; we know that from his conversations with people at the Texaco station. Late information from Burke himself confirmed that Renard popped up days earlier in Colwyn Bay, predictably beginning his search with available public records and the relentless efficiency of the internet when you know how to use it. He called himself "Jean-Paul Jacquet," ostensibly looking for a couple who had been helpful when his nephew was there earlier in the spring. His story sounded plausible enough: college kid on a bike tour through Denbighshire stranded when a wobbly, miscalculated turn landed him in the ditch with some road rash and a damaged pedal. A nice couple—one of whom was an American—gave the boy a lift, and since he was in the area on holiday, he told them, a grateful uncle wanted to stop in and express his thanks. It was clear who he meant so they mentioned us by name. It's perfectly understandable, and I don't fault the gas station guys, but it was the confirmation Renard needed.

All the while we knew nothing of a student in distress because there hadn't been one. It was a risky move in a small town where everyone knows everyone, but Renard's play worked well enough when two ladies I won't name innocently pointed him our way. Armed with an address, it didn't take long for the theatre to begin.

AFTER A MORNING spent attacking the growth overrunning my backyard, I dialed Aline's number to see if her dinner plans would call for a night out in Liverpool or something more local. It rang for a long time and I was sure she was in the shower until she answered at last. It was the tone of her voice—suddenly low and cautious—that told me something was wrong, and when I asked her she simply said, "I need you." There was no explanation or reason given, but when I hurried to her door she was waiting with an expression I'd never seen before.

She wasn't shaken or wearing the face of worry. Instead I saw only steely determination before she began, not anger, precisely, but more a look that telegraphed her irritated state. A man had been there to see her only moments earlier—a Belgian policeman—called Andre Renard.

"What did he want?" I asked.

"He thinks I did something horrible," she replied.

Aline pointed me toward her kitchen and waited until I was settled at her table. Thirteen years earlier, she began, a group of Dutch students she'd met in college invited her to join them for a cultural exchange event at the university in Leiden. Because it wrapped early, she took a pleasant side trip to the coast for a visit with a friend in Brugge. The acquaintance, another econ major called Marion Van Den Broeck, worked a finance analyst job and Aline went over so the two could spend a few days catching up.

I listened closely because it was the first time she included details about her adult life before Denbighshire, but the story turned suddenly when Aline said Marion was out of town on business and she decided to stay a while to look around. She explained there was an idea of possibly relocating there, as Marion had been lobbying her boss to find Aline a position. It seemed innocuous enough and made a reconnaissance mission to look at apartments routine and understandable. On her second day an unexpected moment turned an ordinary visit into a nightmare.

As she made her way along the sidewalk near a canal, Aline said, a screech of tires pulled her attention to an intersection where a delivery truck had slammed into a small car. At once, the fuel tank's rupture sent gasoline into the street as a crowd gathered. Two men rushed to pull the occupants—an unconscious woman and her infant child—free from the wreckage before a potential fire could overwhelm them. Seconds later, Aline said, flames ignited and engulfed the little sedan just as firetrucks arrived.

Her words were measured and precise, but when I asked what any of it had to do with her or the Belgian cop who came to see her, she said Renard was speaking about the unexpected death of a man only a day later, and he believed she was somehow connected. It was confusing so I waved my hand and said, "Hold on a minute; who's the second guy?"

"A man called Claude Dumont," Aline answered. "He was there when the lorry ran through a traffic light and crashed."

"He got hit, too?"

"No, no, but he was there, amongst the crowd."

Aline walked to the window and spoke with her back to me. I took it for lingering memories of a desperate and harrowing experience, waiting for bystanders to save the trapped mother and child, but it was much more.

"After the fire brigade arrived there was nothing more to see, so I walked to my hotel. The second man must have followed because he called out to me."

"What did he want with you?"

"He was shouting at me and I began to hurry, but he caught me in the middle of the street, insisting I explain."

"Explain *what*?"

"He kept at me, demanding that I talk to him. The hotel people must've noticed and they came out to help. The man tried again, begging me to speak with him until they led me inside."

Her voice changed again and was nothing like the tone you would expect in the description of so odd and threatening a moment. Instead of emotion, I heard the muted patterns of a commentator on the sidelines of a tennis match.

"The next morning, he was there. I turned back but he rushed past and blocked my way, insisting that I talk with him. I was frightened because the hotel people hadn't seen. I tried to run around him but he shouted and lunged at me."

The image formed in my mind as Aline continued her description.

"I thought he would miss but his hand caught the collar of my shirt. It tore away the buttons and his nails scratched my neck. I tried to hit his arm—to force him so he would let go—but then he fell."

At first, I didn't understand what she meant. Had he tripped on the curb in an awkward, embarrassing moment? When she explained the man collapsed onto the sidewalk, I saw in her expression something new, a look that made me frown in reflex, even if I couldn't understand its meaning in that brief moment. Her eyes moved left and downward while she spoke, as if suspecting somebody moving close from behind. She appeared free of empathy and I have only seen that look one time since. I remember swallowing hard and sitting perfectly still as she went on.

"The hotel people were around me by then and there was a lot of commotion until somebody gasped and stood away from where he was lying on the sidewalk. There was blood from his nose and ears…some from his mouth as well."

Aline looked at me and I presumed she wanted to gauge my reaction, but in my thoughts, I could see images of her confrontation with astonishing detail. I heard his voice and the clatter around him as they called for an ambulance. Through it all, the fragrance of perfume—delicate and unmistakable as if recently applied—was suddenly stronger than it had been and I felt sharp pain near my collarbone.

"Anyway," she continued with a bored tone as if she had run out of interesting things to say, "the paramedics tended to him but he was dead. The police were there and the hotel manager explained."

She went silent for a moment and I asked softly what happened next.

"After they were finished, an employee told us the ambulance driver believed the man might have died from a massive stroke. I haven't thought about that day in a very long time."

"But this cop obviously *has*," I said at last.

"He told me Claude Dumont, the man who died, was his friend."

"That was a long time ago, Aline; why would he ask about it now? And anyway, how did he know where to find you?"

She reached for a card on the counter and handed it to me. On it was Renard's name and his position as a former detective in the Liège police department.

"What did you tell him?"

"I told him the same thing I told the police in Brugge," she replied sadly, "but he thinks I'm lying."

"He said that?" I demanded.

"No, but it was very clear in his voice. He told me it 'wasn't finished' and then he drove away."

I stayed with her, presuming wrongly she needed time to come back from a place in her memory and a tragic, unexplained incident years before. When she finished, I decided to leave it alone, and for a few days things returned to normal. I resumed my fight with the shrubbery, and a search for new work gloves (mine had been worn through at the palm) sent me into town to buy a fresh pair. As I walked from Watkin & Williams to where my car was parked, he was waiting.

"Evan Morgan?"

The accent was obvious and I knew at once Renard didn't give up so easily.

"Yeah, that's me," I replied.

"May I speak with you a moment?"

"Sure," I answered, but my agitation was growing and I know he could see it easily.

"I am Andre Renard, and…"

"I know who you are, Inspector, but I don't think there's anything I can do for you."

He paused when my answer made it obvious any pretense otherwise would be a wasted effort.

"Then you know why I am here."

"I know enough."

"Do you? I don't wish to seem impudent, but I don't believe that's true."

I could feel my face flush when the moment arrived—that certain point where customary, polite deference is blown away by rising anger.

"I know you're here about some guy who died after assaulting Aline thirteen years ago, but apparently, her answers weren't good enough."

He smiled the way people do when they hear ignorance and a demand for patience they'd rather not extend. It was unlikely Aline would have neglected to tell me about their encounter, but Renard was sure the story had been told in carefully segmented half-truths.

"Miss Lloyd is understandably hesitant to discuss the event, but there's more to this than you know."

I looked at him with the intent of putting him in his place. I wanted to make clear his intrusion was neither wanted nor would it be tolerated, but I thought better of it and tried to beg off.

"I'm sorry, Inspector, but I wasn't there. Aline has already told you what happened; if you'll excuse me…"

When I reached for the car door, Renard blocked me.

"Why don't we just talk for a moment, eh?"

I looked again and said, "I don't have time right now, so if you wouldn't mind…"

"I *do* mind, Mr. Morgan," he said softly. "I think you would be well-advised to listen."

"Or what?" I demanded. "Look around, Inspector—this isn't Belgium and you're out of your jurisdiction. Take your hand off my car or I'll do it for you."

He smiled again and stood away. I thought it was finished, but as I hurried to fasten my seatbelt he leaned close and said, "This won't go away only because Aline Lloyd wants to pretend!"

I turned the ignition and slammed the car into drive, but as I looked for traffic he called out from the sidewalk.

"Have you seen things, Mr. Morgan? Visions, like dreams from nowhere?"

I ignored him and did an abrupt U-turn in the narrow street, speeding away as he shouted my name again. The ride home was made in nervous agitation as his words echoed in my mind. I *had* seen things, of course, but I was too angry to give Renard a reason for hope. As I turned into my driveway the thoughts were running rampant. How could he know about the sudden unexplained images? The "visions" Renard meant *were* strange, but I hadn't revealed them to anyone.

I sat in my garage as memories showed me again those moments when daydreams become silent movies—stark and realistic beyond all reason. Dreams are never so vivid, leaving us lost in a netherworld where reality blurs and sensory input has no limit, but worse still, Renard seemed to know as if I'd described them in painstaking detail. Had he experienced the phenomenon too? I thought at once of Aline and with a disturbing sensation that went far beyond suggestion. Was there something she hadn't bothered to tell me?

She was in Colwyn Bay for three days, but when I told her about Renard's sudden appearance in town she didn't seem overly concerned and I wondered why she didn't react with anger at the news. A policeman knocking on the door might rattle most people, but most people are not Aline. When she returned from the coast the following Friday there was no sign of Renard. On Saturday, my hopes were dashed when I heard a car door in the driveway as I finished clearing my breakfast things, already late for a customary tea date with Jeremy.

I knew it wasn't Aline, and when I glanced out the front window, Renard stood beside his car, surveying my house. He carried a thick manila envelope under an arm, but the rage swelled up at once, boiling over as I burst from the house on a straight line to meet him.

"You're pushing your luck now, Inspector," I declared firmly, but he simply held out the envelope.

"I've included the transcriptions into English so you will understand, Mr. Morgan. My mobile number is on the card; call when you're ready to talk."

He returned to his car and aimed it toward my gate as I stood in silence eyeing the envelope. I pulled its contents and it was clear Renard was deliberate and thorough, separating photocopied documents into distinct groups according to a timeline. Some of the annotations were in French, but I could understand well enough to know most of them were copies of his original source material.

PART OF ME demanded the papers' return to their envelope unread, if only to demonstrate my indifference to the inspector's annoying persistence. The other parts of my nature—those which guided my professional career as an objective analyst—demanded at the minimum a simple review. The latter won out and I walked with them to my kitchen.

It was unclear why Renard was so determined to connect Aline with the death of his friend, but soon a picture began to emerge. He'd jotted contemporaneous notes for the purpose of explaining, but he did so likely knowing his attempts at speaking with Aline would get him nowhere. The words were a chronology—a menu, of sorts—designed to distill a clutter of police reports and medical examination results into plain language.

As I guessed it would, the story began with the unfortunate death of Claude Dumont, a jewelry store owner who moved his shop from Liège over to Brugge in 1991 so that he could be closer to a relocated son. The text didn't say so directly, but it became clear the two were lifelong friends, and I read carefully when the chronology described a frantic call to Renard. Transcribed text showed the detective jotting notes at a furious pace as Dumont told of a traffic accident involving a large truck and a young mother with her infant child trapped inside their car. The words were hastily written as Renard listened to his friend's desperate and impassioned tale. Accompanying documentation from the local cops showed much of what Aline already told me, but there was more.

A truck had indeed crashed into the young woman's car, but the fuel ignited almost immediately. In the rising heat and flames there was no chance for bystanders to reach the driver where she sat unconscious inside with her baby. I remembered Aline's account and she had said specifically the gasoline didn't begin to burn until *after* the car's occupants had been rescued. I frowned at the inconsistency but Dumont's description of the event continued.

The old man made his way across the street toward a gathering crowd, the notes read, but he stopped when the wind came up suddenly. A powerful, frightening gust from above blasted downward onto the stricken Renault, sending a cloud of smoke, loose dirt and dust roiling into the sky like an upside-down mushroom cloud. There was nothing else, he said: no sweeping breeze along that narrow street on an otherwise calm and clear afternoon. For a full minute, Dumont continued, the wind screamed straight down onto the car as if pushed by a jet engine, forcing the flames away to create an opening for two brave men who rushed to pull the mother and child free. Once they were safely removed, the powerful wind subsided as quickly as it appeared and when it did, the flames grew again until the little hatchback was completely engulfed.

There were supporting accounts for police made by witnesses gathered at the scene, each describing the solitary column of impossibly strong wind, but Dumont saw something else—something he couldn't explain. Nearby, he reported, a girl in her early twenties stood alone and away from the crowd between Dumont and the wreckage. Her hand was slightly raised, he said, and her eyes were closed. It struck Dumont as a strange sight in the midst of a desperate attempt to rescue the driver and child, but he was compelled to watch her. After they pulled the woman and baby from her car, the girl lowered her hand and turned to go just as the gust died out and the flames resumed as if with a vengeance.

I read Renard's comments in the margins of his notes and Dumont's reason for calling made me stop and reread to make sure there was no mistake. The two had been friends for nearly thirty years; it made sense Dumont would alert Renard immediately, but the words sent a shiver up my spine and Renard underlined the translated sentence twice to affirm its importance:

Witnessed a miracle? Not a joke or having me on—he believes.

I continued to read as if pulled by an unseen force demanding more. The notes resumed and Renard's commentary was at least as valuable when Dumont described his first attempt to make contact with the mysterious girl after following her to a local hotel. He begged her to speak with him, to make him understand how she could accomplish such a thing. The girl refused, he said, but it was clear Dumont believed she was an instrument in divine hands, perhaps not knowing herself what happened. Still, he tried to convince her to tell him what she knew and how it felt. Dumont described a sudden, inexplicable parade of thoughts and images as though his mind had been taken over "by a demon" and made to see things that weren't there, frightening images filled with violence and a terrifying sensation of dread. When he recovered, she was gone.

I stood and paced around my table where the pile of papers seemed to mock me as I searched for a reason to stop reading. None of it should have made sense and yet *all* of it did. An eerie sensation filtered through my body and I knew better than to think Renard was chasing phantoms. The condensed police reports included still images from security cameras at a hotel the following day, and in them Claude Dumont embroiled in a heated argument with a guest. I looked closely but supporting statements made by witnesses were needless; it was her. The report and accompanying video showed an obvious assault made by Dumont against a hotel guest only seconds before he collapsed, and a police report identified the girl as Aline M. Lloyd—a citizen of the United Kingdom.

I continued to read in numb silence, troubled by the details Aline hadn't included when she told me of Renard's visit. There had been no mention or reference to Claude Dumont's dramatic declaration he'd seen a modern-day miracle and assigned its existence to Aline. The next pages described the results from a medical examiner and an autopsy performed at the request of the police. I read it all but their words shocked me back to reality.

At the height of his shouting match with Aline, Dumont fell to the sidewalk like a marionette suddenly cut from its strings, and what the examiner found made it clear he suffered significant paralysis and was likely dead in minutes. The cause of death was determined and reported as multiple, massive aneurysms throughout Dumont's brain: a fatal series of hemorrhages unlike anything they'd seen. Dozens of blood vessels suddenly exploded with so devastating an effect the coroner's report noted the term "catastrophic" couldn't fully describe the extent of the old man's injuries.

There were interviews with bystanders at the accident scene the day before but also guests and staff at the hotel where Aline stayed; most of the accounts went along parallel lines with minor variations. Outwardly, and with no reason or suspicion to give them pause, the authorities theorized Dumont's advanced age and hidden weaknesses inside his brain's crucial arteries may have taken him literally to the breaking point. Unsure of a cause, and without a reason to suspect wrongdoing, the cops told Aline she was free to go and she did so the next day.

Renard's annotations told of his doubts, however, and an emerging mystery. The phone conversation with Dumont seemed odd in the extreme, but his death less than twenty-four hours later raised flags for an experienced detective and Renard was determined to find answers. Absent an identifiable crime, the police in Brugge had no case and the matter had to be dropped; there would be no more interviews with the British girl and it was best, Renard's bosses told him, to leave things as they were. I looked at the side notes and it was clear he couldn't accept what the local authorities regarded as obvious: Claude Dumont may have died suddenly, but the tragic event was the product of natural causes.

As I thumbed through the pages I felt an odd compulsion to skip ahead to the second bundle Renard had secured beneath a blank cover page. Again, the inspector's commentary made a sort of briefing to set the stage, but the second group of documents were transcriptions from police interviews regarding an odd episode in Glasgow and nothing to do with Dumont's bizarre, unexplained death. The timeline shifted, too: forward six years and hundreds of miles from Brugge. I continued, driven by a need to know and the notion Renard's presence in town carried with it darker intent. Whatever brought him all the way from Belgium would surely be found in those pages.

Renard's path began to show, and it was clear he made up his mind Claude Dumont's death, although listed officially as aneurysms, collided with what he knew of his friend and the disturbing late-night conversation that passed between them. The inspector wouldn't (or couldn't) let it go and he became obsessed with finding and speaking with Aline. The Brugge police records showed her in residence at a flat in Croydon, but his attempts to reach her by phone ran aground when a manager reported no person by that name lived there.

Renard took matters a step further, calling a former colleague working at Interpol in Lyon. Without a case there was no justification for an official inquiry, but his friend agreed to keep an eye out in the agency's database if Aline's name ever popped up. Renard believed in the power of electronic record-keeping and he knew even a simple traffic violation might expose her location. The idea was wishful thinking, at best, but a clever cop will spread his net wide on the mere chance it might snag a clue. In the summer of 2006, the Interpol man was alerted by his database's automated search function and from it a reference to a person of interest in an unresolved assault case. The record showed Aline Marie Lloyd was injured during an altercation and interviewed by Scottish police in connection to life-threatening injuries suffered by two men at a Glasgow bus stop. I remembered Jeremy's description of Aline's difficulties in the Scottish city.

With those words, and his memory of Claude Dumont's description of visions during his confrontation with Aline, Renard saw enough to know his search had likely found another connection. More notes showed interest in a then-unnamed female in her twenties who, it said, had likely been the victim of a robbery attempt. I resumed flipping the pages one by one, shaking my head as another scenario played itself out in more police reports and witness accounts.

Officers responded to a call from a distraught woman reporting two men seriously injured at a bus stop. She described them as "pushy lads" who'd cornered a lone girl with clear intent to steal her handbag. The girl resisted, and as the caller was dialing police, one of the men struck her in the face. The witness began to shout for help to anyone within earshot when one of the men fell suddenly to the sidewalk and the second was on his knees, grasping at his throat. The female, a young woman with blonde hair, turned abruptly and walked away as if, the witness said, "she was only late for a meeting." The bystander moved slowly closer until she had a decent line of sight to the bus stop. Finding both men were in desperate trouble, she waited until paramedics arrived a few moments later.

It was strange, the witness told police, that a girl in her position wouldn't be in tears and shaking after such an ordeal. Instead, the victim simply hurried down the street as though nothing had happened. There was a struggle and one severe punch that left her bloodied, but the men who attacked her went down in pain and the girl only glanced at them for a moment the way she might at a lost wallet or a set of keys in the gutter.

Ambulance drivers arrived to find one of the men unconscious but otherwise unharmed. The second man, their report continued, displayed symptoms that included eyes swollen completely shut and an obvious constricted airway, suggesting at once he was possibly in the grip of anaphylactic shock. They were transported at once to West Glasgow Hospital, but the cops turned their attention to the missing girl and apparent victim of a mugging-gone-wrong, intent on speaking with her before she disappeared into the night.

It didn't take long for the search to bear fruit when an alert hotel clerk reported a guest moving quickly through his lobby with a "smashed face" and blood down the front of her shirt. When police arrived and knocked at a second-floor room, a woman answered toweling wet hair and fresh from a shower with a split lip and swollen nose but oddly calm and unconcerned. As I knew it would, the report showed her as Aline M. Lloyd, visiting Glasgow from Cardiff for a job interview at Royal Bank of Scotland. Renard knew it, too.

I read on, moving quickly to hospital reports about the would-be muggers filled out by attending physicians who described unusual injuries hospital staff couldn't explain. One collapsed unconscious and could not be wakened. Though he suffered no outward injuries, the man was clinging to life with dangerously low blood pressure and an unstable pulse. The other fared no better but his injuries seemed to defy logic. His face was severely swollen and a tracheotomy procedure in the ambulance was needed to relieve a windpipe constricted so badly, little or no oxygen was flowing into his lungs.

Suddenly, the reports said, and for no apparent reason, the first man woke slowly. He was disoriented and confused, leaving police officers to wait it out until he regained consciousness. The second attacker's symptoms eased only minutes later and swelling that threatened his life where he lay near the bus stop was nearly gone. Emergency staff had no explanation for the abrupt reversal, but bloodwork and toxicology results showed nothing out of the ordinary beyond cotinine, alcohol, and trace residue of amphetamine. In each subject, the hospital records noted, there were no unusual, foreign compounds or a history of allergies, leaving doctors unable to establish cause and identify appropriate treatments. Both men simply lost their symptoms and were resting comfortably.

I continued and saw the prognoses for both men were encouraging, at least from *their* perspective, but attention shifted once more to the lone girl who would surely have become a victim but for the sudden and inexplicable injuries to her attackers. The police made Aline sit in a patrol car for a while as their colleagues took statements from witnesses. They were in agreement, yet no one could reconcile the outcome; the men had indeed meant to isolate and rob her. Once stable and out of danger, hospital staff cleared them both for interviews by the Glasgow police, but the result was unexpected as both freely admitted their intent to rob Aline. The second man asked if anyone knew they had been taken to West Glasgow's emergency room and when a cop asked why, the man worried she might "find them and finish the job."

I read his words in disbelief but the mugger-turned-victim had no problem confessing so long as they kept the "mad bitch" away. He said she "looked at them in a queer manner and mumbled." There were horrible images forming in his mind—images he couldn't describe—and then the pain. The man likened his experience to being strangled by invisible hands, and his companion said it felt as if he'd been "knocked out by a mean bastard with a bloody great pipe."

Investigating officers scoured the bus stop for clues and, of course, found nothing. There was no physical evidence or weapons and Aline's disheveled appearance and bloodied face only confirmed eyewitness accounts. There was no plausible way a slight girl could have meted out such terrible injury, they said, which pointed logically to the actions of another—a vigilante or very dangerous Good Samaritan, perhaps—yet none of the witnesses reported a fourth actor. A mystery had been dropped in the lap of Glasgow P.D. and the answer, they said, would likely be found from a conversation with Aline Lloyd.

The document flow went suddenly (and inexplicably) blank, but I felt my heart sink when a final entry recorded a week after the attempted assault showed an abrupt transfer authorization moving Aline to a psychiatric facility outside the city, the kind of place that cares for people unable to care for themselves and does so under lock and key. At last, and in the midst of Renard's determined hunt for answers, I understood: though she never allowed me in close enough to speak of it, her admittance to a mental ward was laid bare in the reference to a "sectioning" order.

I read the reports again as if the words might have changed somehow or that my understanding was incomplete. The notes suggested her stay for "observation, evaluation, and treatment" would, by its very definition, involve weeks or even months, and I shuddered under the weight of my own imagination and how it must've been for her in that dark, frightening bus stop, cornered by thugs who meant her harm.

It seems unlikely today, but in that moment, I thought only of Aline. I cared nothing for two criminals who wanted to hurt her—they deserved the horrible result—but more than that, I didn't consider Renard's persistent belief Aline was somehow connected to Claude Dumont's death in Belgium. It meant nothing to me that a skilled and seasoned police veteran's nose smelled something off; I didn't care what he thought or why. I simply wanted to see her and let her know I understood.

Still, the commentary and sidenotes from Renard remained and within them his unwavering belief there was more to Aline's story. Something was wrong, he wrote in a desperate scribble, and it was now a mystery that needed to be explained. I looked at his card but it wasn't with the sensation of noble self-reproach Miss Persimmon wanted to hear. Mo still thinks the better half of my conscience drove me to call, that I overcame my romantic attachment to Aline by the sheer force of goodness and proper human behavior. Instead, I wanted only to see how far the man was willing to go and what it would mean. I had to gauge him and find for myself if his pile of papers was supposed to take him across the finish line and bring relief to a grieving friend or if he meant to force Aline into a corner and make her spill out the full story so that action could be taken. It wasn't clear what that might be, but I thumbed a message into the phone and waited until he arrived twenty minutes later.

11
YOU'RE NOT READY

WHEN I met him in the driveway, Renard leaned against the side of his car with folded arms as if annoyed and waiting for me.

"Have you examined the documents, Mr. Morgan?" he asked.

"I read them, but I don't find anything that tells me where you're going with this."

"I am not certain," he replied.

"That's helpful."

Renard heard the sarcasm clearly but he wouldn't take the bait.

"When it happened years ago, I wanted only to learn what my friend was trying to understand: how so unnatural an event could be possible, but…"

"But?"

"He died, Mr. Morgan. I knew Claude since we were children and he never once showed signs of mental distress. They dismissed it as though he had gone mad and his insanity caused the blood vessels in his brain to burst. He couldn't find the answer from Miss Lloyd, but he shouldn't have to pay for curiosity with his life."

"He shouldn't have grabbed at her, either," I answered at once, "but he *did*. Was assault and battery supposed to convince her to talk to him, Inspector?"

"Of course not, but things happen—accidents! Claude was not a violent man; he would never have harmed her."

"He damn near tore her shirt off!"

"You're losing sight of the larger issue, Mr. Morgan."

"Am I? Enlighten me, please!"

Renard walked slowly from his car but his eyes were aimed at the hill behind my house.

"Your girlfriend played a direct part in two unrelated incidents over six years; the first resulted in sudden and unexplained death and the second could have as well. Each time, each incident, she was there."

"Yes," I replied, "and each time, there was no crime committed and no charges against Aline were brought, nor *could* they be. You say I'm forgetting the big picture, but I think you're just pissing around with a mystery you can't solve, trying to find and lay blame for the death of your friend."

"Then what of the two men in Scotland, eh?" he said quickly and with a louder tone to show determined purpose.

"I don't give a shit about them," I replied evenly. "And I don't give a shit about you."

Renard looked at me and it was easy to see his temper was being tested. Suddenly under stress and long-held frustration, his accent was growing thicker but he held his bearing.

"And the visions?" he demanded. "Claude spoke of seeing things in his mind; *frightening* things. In Scotland the men who attacked her begged police to keep her away; both of them report sudden, horrible thoughts, like watching at the cinema."

"That doesn't prove a damn thing," I replied, dismissing his direction at once, but it felt wrong and I knew it. Before I could withdraw, he went to the bone.

"And you? Have you seen these strange things in *your* mind since you became involved with Aline Lloyd?"

I wanted to know how it was Renard knew my name, let alone my relationship with Aline, but his voice was growing louder and years of chasing Aline pulled him past a point at which decorum still mattered. In his mind, she was a detached and uncaring figure standing in front of Claude Dumont the moment he died. Worse still, her name surfaced again under strange and inexplicable circumstances that resulted in severe injury, only as a prelude to certain death were it not for the skilled and timely intervention of Scottish emergency crews. For Renard, the connection ceased to be mere coincidence long ago; despite a glaring lack of evidence that might explain or bring him a measure of peace, the old detective was unwilling to let it go.

I couldn't speak. For moments that seemed like hours, I couldn't tell him what I knew perfectly well was true. I *had* seen sudden and unexpected thoughts so real and vivid calling them "visions" was at least as accurate as anything I could manage. I swallowed hard and it made me angry to think Renard knew he'd found the flaw in my armor—that my hesitance would somehow stamp his assertions with a mark of validity and force me into a corner.

"What do you want, Inspector?" I asked at last. "Aline hasn't committed a crime and your badge doesn't work here anyway. What do you hope to gain by all of this?"

He only blinked at me and I thought I saw the edge of his chin quiver slightly with the rage that was building, but I went on quickly.

"I'm sorry your friend's brain exploded, and I can understand how that must feel for you, but it wasn't her fault!"

"How do *you* know, eh?" he shouted suddenly. "Just because you are fucking her?"

"Careful, Inspector," I replied slowly, but he went on without pause.

"Claude believed she was moved by the hand of God—the bringer of a miracle! But godly servants don't kill innocent people, Mr. Morgan; they don't perform wonderful, selfless acts this day and then murder on the next!"

I felt my own restraint failing and I went toward him in response.

"But Aline *does*? You think she's some kind of hell-sent demon, bent on destroying the world?"

"No, I think she is something much worse than that," he replied evenly. "I think she is a murderer who has been clever for a long time. I think she will murder again, and that is something *you* should consider, Monsieur."

"Are things that dull down in Liège, Inspector? Too bored with retired life and looking for a reason to be relevant again?"

On his face, there was only the expression of astonishment and disbelief. He shook his head and smiled, telling me without words he saw only an ignorant fool, desperate to protect a love interest—a failed defense in the face of truth.

"I know who you were," he said with a voice that was low and quiet. "In America, you looked after air accidents; you were also an investigator. Can't you hear the stupidity in your own words? Don't *you* wonder why these unexplained events all point to her?"

I felt a churn in the pit of my stomach as Renard's logic blasted its way through every wall of scornful disbelief I'd built around me to protect against my own suspicions and doubt. The documentation was thorough and the case he could make was disturbing. If moved at all by the inspector's accusatory tone, I decided, there would be nothing done until I could reach her and ask Aline's side of so strange and unlikely a tale. I owed far more consideration to her than Renard.

After a moment, I found my way back from the edge and a place that threatened to land me in jail for beating an old man to a pulp. I looked away and said, "I need to think about this for a while."

"To what purpose, Mr. Morgan?" he protested. "You can see everything is there!"

"Everything?" I snorted. "I see an angry man trying to find a reason for his friend's death."

Renard looked away. The moment remained intense and I watched him closely, not at all sure he wouldn't pull out a gun or try something stupid, but he only stared at me.

"Has she told you why they kept her in that hospital?" he asked.

"What difference does it make?"

He showed me a suddenly satisfied smile and said, "You don't know, do you?"

"No, and I don't give a damn."

He put his hands in his pockets for the purpose of demonstrating he had no intention of attacking me, perhaps, but determined that I would hear him clearly.

"Keep reading the papers, Mr. Morgan. The doctors and psychiatrists in Glasgow, she told them everything went black. Miss Lloyd insisted she couldn't remember but the police reminded her what happened to those two men. Injuries so severe and unexplained but she remembered nothing? They diagnosed her with a mental disorder, Mr. Morgan, and they kept her locked up for treatment."

Renard moved closer.

"But Scottish detectives don't agree. No, they hear a convenient excuse, maybe; a clever lie hiding inside her mind where the police can't go!"

Renard's voice was climbing and it was clear he didn't give a damn what I thought about it.

"Is this criminal insanity?" he continued. "Who will ever know because she walks free after only a few months and nothing more is done!"

The question was never asked but I heard Aline's voice from my thoughts warn me that someday the answer would be revealed. She had said they would tell me to keep away; that I was a fool to trust her. I presumed she had only meant to test our relationship and lay out those pieces of a puzzle made by her past, knowing the stigma of mental illness hung over her like a cloud. Was it only to prepare me? Had she done so to provide an escape before we went too far and the emotional bonds had been made fast? I couldn't know but Renard's words still stabbed at me. A breakdown is one thing but traumatic amnesia as a false and contrived excuse for avoiding arrest and imprisonment is another.

I fought back silently against the dreadful possibility she had been something much worse than I imagined, and I needed time to think things through.

"I'll read through the notes again," I said at last, "but no promises; I can't make her talk to you, Inspector."

"I leave for Belgium this evening, but you can reach me by mobile phone," Renard replied. "It would be better talking to me before Welsh authorities are the next ones to her door." He leveled his eyes at me and said, "It would be better for *you*, too."

Again, Renard's implied threat slipped through and I'm sure it was no accident. I moved toward him quickly.

"You think I'm going to roll on Aline because your private sleuthing adventure didn't pan out? She's more important to me than you or any other assholes you bring into it but be my guest; call them now, if you like. Let's see what the local cops think of your pet theory, shall we?"

"Maybe they will take a different view when I give them copies of my documentation, Mr. Morgan. I wonder if you will be so arrogant then, hmm?"

"Time for you to leave, Inspector—the show is over."

Renard smirked and I can still hear his voice today.

"Oh, the show is just beginning, my friend. Tell that bitch her time has run out!"

As Renard turned onto the road toward town, I stood alone on the tiny, smooth stones of my driveway with trembling hands and a sticky-dry mouth. A breeze came up and it felt good where it brushed past my temples to cool them as I struggled to make sense of all he said. My head swirled with images made by the words in his paperwork and justifications I offered myself no longer mattered. When I turned slowly toward my door, she was already moving to meet me. Again, Aline appeared out of nowhere and it was clear she had listened to my heated exchange with Renard.

"You heard?"

"Yes," she replied softly. "I called, but when you didn't answer I walked over. There were loud voices and I stopped beside your house when I heard his."

"How much did you get?"

"All of it."

When we settled on the couch Aline's face was one of near indifference, at first, but she must have seen the torment in mine. I gave her the pile of Renard's documents and sat quietly while she thumbed through them without a word. She took her time, reading and nodding silently like a schoolteacher grading essays, but there was no doubt it all made sense to her. At last, she set them aside and looked at me.

"I'm sorry you were dragged into this."

"He thinks you're some kind of lunatic serial killer."

"Of course he does."

"This is serious, Aline. He can't explain how but he's sure of it; Renard believes you killed Claude Dumont deliberately and attacked those assholes in Glasgow. Everyone involved over in Belgium said the same thing: that Dumont died of natural causes. The Scottish cops couldn't figure out what happened at that bus stop but they've left the case open until they do."

"That's not what's bothering you, is it?" she asked.

She knew it wasn't but still she felt compelled to ask. Was it simply to test me and what I thought I knew? I didn't want to bring it up, but since she went straight to the problem of amnesia and convenient blackouts, I moved close and continued.

"They held you in that place after diagnosing you with selective amnesia caused by a traumatic event, but Renard isn't buying it. He thinks you lied to them just to avoid arrest, and he's threatening to show this stuff to the police if you don't talk to him."

"Yes, I know."

It was so quiet and I teetered as if perched on the tip of a needle, unsure of anything but wishing only that she would tell me it was all wrong and Renard contrived his incredible tale. She took my hands in hers.

"I need to ask you something," she said softly. "It doesn't matter how you respond but I can't explain any of this unless I know you will tell me the truth. Can you promise me that?"

"Promise," I answered.

She waited for a moment and I thought she was only collecting her thoughts. I know now the pause was for my benefit instead of hers but only to allow me time to consider and decide.

"I know this might seem a bit abrupt, and I wish we had more time to let things sort out on their own, but…"

"Go ahead."

"Do you think we belong together, Evan; is it what you want?"

The question was sudden and out of place. I *had* thought about it since our first encounter in the snowy field beside her house, and there was no point in avoiding it any longer. I don't deny it made me feel strange to speak the words, but the answer had always been there, waiting for its moment to be freed.

"Yeah—I do."

"Do you trust me? If you don't, or Renard's papers have made you afraid, it's all right and I'll understand."

"I trust you, Aline, just tell me what the hell is going on here."

She smiled and touched my cheek very gently.

"You mean the world to me; I need to know you know that. I've never felt a love like this, and I won't again, so I'm giving you the chance to walk away before it goes any further."

"My escape hatch again?" I asked.

"It's so painful when I say that but I could never do anything to hurt you, and when you understand, it will lead you to a decision; you will have to make up your mind because what you discover will change things between us forever; it can't be any other way."

We had been there before, walking on the fringes of a notion I mistakenly believed was only a part in the ridiculous drama we make for ourselves when we've met another. Confronting our desires and hopes becomes a sort of prod, I suppose, and one that is used to make things clear or wash away frivolity and carelessness in those first moments when simple attraction has shifted quietly into a deeper, more meaningful affection. We offer a way out but only because we hope it won't be taken; we need to know the other *wants* to stay. Aline's words reprised those earlier thoughts, and once more I was presented with the opportunity—a last chance—to stay clean and leave her behind before the mysterious conditions that brought Renard to the valley could cause me harm. Of course, I had no intention of leaving and it stung a bit that she would feel obliged to make the offer.

"I'm not going anywhere," I said at last. "Whatever this is, we'll deal with it together."

They stopped us here, of course, but I found it odd that Halliwell, and not Miss Persimmon, wondered carefully if my choice to stay with Aline was made from conviction, or if it was just bravado and an unwillingness to let go for no other reason than stubborn selfishness. The question was certainly understandable but it surprised me to hear it from him. Mo wondered too, but she only watched when I laughed and affirmed my commitment was honest. Halliwell knew the others held the obvious, subsequent question but I intercepted it and told them the choice had been made without Aline's influence. They seemed to accept the decision was mine alone, but only after a long deliberation we weren't privy to.

Berezan, meanwhile, needed more. He is a maneuvering, unprincipled weasel in my book but in fairness, he's also a highly intelligent man who pays attention and he held up a hand as a signal to Halliwell. It's still unclear to me if his involvement was authorized solely on Burke and Halliwell's authority, or if Gregory Hurd's people invited him as an easy way to placate their American allies. I guess it didn't matter and he paused, tapping his trademark pencil like a drumstick on the desk with a screwed-up frown and narrowed eyes. Right on schedule, he wondered why I hadn't thought to turn the tables on Renard and demand to know how he had scrounged up privileged and personal documentation, especially as a retired cop without access to the customary channels.

It was somewhat of an embarrassment but I'd never considered the idea in those tense, combative moments with the inspector, and I told them so. Surprisingly, Berezan closed the thought himself by reminding everyone Renard would not have been eager to answer anyway, and with that, we moved on. Mo smiled at him and I still wonder if the gesture was Berezan's idea of an olive branch.

Aline paused and I know it was the torment of reaching her own portal and the finality waiting on the other side in those last, tense seconds. As I would cross over, she explained, so would she. The moment became electric—profound. She always knew the outcome long before it arrived, but there was no way of getting me there without showing those things I would need to know so that mystery and disbelief could be transformed into understanding.

"Do you believe him?" she asked.

"I'm not sure *what* to believe," I replied, but her question seemed like a test with no correct answer.

"What if he *was* right?" she continued softly. "What would you think of me if Renard's accusations turned out to be true?"

"Are they?" I asked with expectant, raised eyes in the way we do when we're sure the answer will be "no."

She didn't draw back in stunned shock and disappointment that I would even consider such a thing. It was surprising but she simply nodded.

"Yes, they are."

I'm sure there is a clinical description somewhere in a textbook that explains in medical terms what we call a "sinking feeling"; that sudden, unavoidable punch in the stomach catapulting us from the comfort of what we thought we knew into a minefield of things we didn't *want* to know. In that breathless moment, I felt like a man left to die marooned in misery and shock with no hope of rescue. I expected her to tell me Renard was just a "loose cannon with a grudge." I thought she would tell me his tale was absurd and without merit, made in desperation because nothing could bring his friend back from the grave and no one else seemed to care.

I couldn't speak, wandering in a lonely daze where once-intoxicating notions of our future life together were being torn apart and scattered on a powerful wind. It couldn't be, I said at last; there was no way she could do such things because *no one can*. People don't make others descend into a coma or collapse with near-fatal reaction to allergies they don't have. Normal people certainly have no power to create hemorrhages or direct and focus the wind. She listened in silence and when I ran out of words she knelt on the floor in front of me.

"A few people *can* do those things, Evan. I can do them."

Without warning the thoughts poured in and I couldn't stop them. I am unable even now to describe the sensation of loss and desperate sadness swarming over me like a suffocating blanket when Renard's words echoed through my mind. The doctors found symptoms of traumatic, selective amnesia, but the therapy and treatments they gave her were misplaced and ineffective because she hid a deeper and more serious condition behind the wall of a convenient "blackout." I wasn't angry in those seconds, and mostly I felt a growing sadness for Aline and what she endured. It seems obvious now, but I was not moved by a simple process of feeling sorry for myself. I hoped she wouldn't notice it in my face and understand. Instead, she pulled it into the open—raw and stark—as if she could hear my thoughts.

"I know what it suggests; you hear a lost mind but that's not what this is," she said softly. "It never was."

Aline's bearing was astonishingly calm and her expression was the picture of knowing patience. There was no desperation in her voice or an impassioned need to explain what couldn't be understood. In that quiet moment she simply waited for the bomb to complete its detonation before the cleanup could begin. I couldn't see it then, but Aline always knew the time would arrive and when it did, she was prepared.

"Dumont died because I pushed inside his brain; I didn't intend to go that far, but it happened. Those men in Glasgow *would* be dead but the paramedics kept them alive until I was far enough away that they could recover. Renard sorted it out because Dumont saw what happened in Brugge; he knew I was responsible for something no one could explain."

"The fire."

She nodded with a sad smile.

"I couldn't let that woman and her child burn alive because I didn't *have* to; I had the way to stop it and I did."

"Are you telling me the sudden wind was…"

"I made it happen so the people standing nearby would have a chance to save them."

I shook my head and looked at my feet.

"I want to believe you, I really do, but listen to what you're saying, Aline. Nobody can summon up a giant blast of air and aim it at a car on fire!"

"Are you sure?" she asked softly.

I stared at her, blank and dumbfounded, but she just smiled and continued.

"Dumont saw it. I thought no one would notice, but he saw it and he knew."

"You're saying this is the reason he followed you?"

"In his experience, what he saw was impossible. The only explanation that made sense was divine intervention; in his eyes, it truly *was* a miracle."

"But this wind…"

"It wasn't God, Evan; it was just me."

I felt lost. There was no chance the event she described was made by her hand and only a crazy person would ever think it could. I simply followed Aline to that dark place where her illness blurred the line between fantasy and reality. The doctors in Scotland were unable to break through the lapse in her memory and no one can blame them; by any competent psychiatric analysis, her trauma blotted out the entire experience. They tried, and I'm sure they believed the treatments would help her return, but something much worse hid inside Aline's mind and it never found a way out. I hated to think it in that moment, but I knew they should never have let her go.

I wanted to ask them; I needed guidance from mental health professionals because I had no idea how to respond. It no longer mattered that I was in love with Aline, and the torment from knowing we wouldn't live and grow old together made clear it was simply a matter of time before they found and returned her to that place, or another just like it. I had to tread lightly so that my own inexperience and blundering stupidity wouldn't make things worse. I wanted to run—to get away from her—but the thought made me feel ashamed and disgusted. How, I wondered, could a true friend even think of abandoning her when she needed me most? Still she waited and watched. It must've been difficult as she sat out the seconds, knowing what could only have been the storm of helplessness and indecision closing in on my thoughts. At last, I held up my hand to signal I heard, even if it was just a tactic to delay until I thought of something better.

"The next day," I continued, "when Dumont cornered you at the hotel, I saw the stills from surveillance videos and it's clear he assaulted you, but then he went down and…"

She looked away for a moment.

"I was just a scared kid, Evan; he hurt me and I overreacted. It was too much, and I'm sorry for what it did to him, but that was long ago and before I learned to control what I can do."

"They found dozens of ruptured blood vessels in his brain, Aline. His injuries were horrible—*fatal*—but you never laid a hand on him."

"I didn't have to," she said sadly.

"So how does this work, exactly? You just *made* those blood vessels hemorrhage?"

The question was childish and asked with clumsy, patronizing condescension. I wanted to see how she would react—to establish her borders. I thought I was clever enough to help her build a trap and let her fall into it on her own so that logic and common sense might find a way through. I believed in my ability to force reason into a cave where reason never goes. Maybe I could become a light to guide her out. I watched and waited for the signs of confusion, hoping to throw a lifeline for her to grab, but she wasn't drowning and the effort was wasted.

"You could say that, yes."

With her answer the numbing sensation of finality slammed shut a doorway out. There was no chance Aline had induced blood vessels in Dumont's brain to burst, yet there was also no hesitation in her voice. She wasn't testing me to gauge my reaction as Claude Dumont had done more than fifteen years before; Aline *believed*. I accepted the unexplained blast of air was more likely an opportune gust of wind and nothing as dramatic as witness accounts by people who didn't have a better answer. Pushed by a sudden, emotionally charged moment and extraordinary circumstances, one person's "good, stiff gust" could so easily become another's biblical "breath of God."

Far less thrilling or dramatic, Dumont's untimely death was surely a product of his own fragile physiology. The structure of his brain was taken beyond a breaking point perhaps, but with the same result regardless of Aline's presence, and nothing could change that unfortunate truth. Renard's suspicions didn't explain anything but they weren't unsubstantiated after all. Still, I hated him for it. It was difficult to accept but it would be more accurate to say I hated him for dredging up what surely meant the problems that had landed Aline in a mental hospital would do so again; I understood at last there was much more at work than only his desire for closure and a misplaced application of justice.

I wondered about the muggers at a darkened bus stop in Glasgow, too. The police wisely left the investigation "open" despite committing Aline to the care of a psychiatric facility, but that fact did nothing to describe how a 115-pound girl could possibly overcome two hardened street thugs, both intent on stealing her purse. Would she say the second event was the product of her hand as well? There was no point in asking because I knew it couldn't be, and my remaining thoughts went to the despair that would follow when they came to take her away.

My spine tingled the way it does when reality breaks through in the end. Trapped in a corner made of logic and the crush of despair, I understood at last all I hoped for would soon evaporate. She reached for me but I could only think of myself and I just wanted her to go. It was the first time I'd seen the face of insanity at close range, but worse still, from the very person I was least prepared to accept in so horrible a state.

I wanted to offer an excuse—something benign and far from the moment—so she wouldn't see and understand I had to get distance between us. I wish I could say it was only for the understandable purpose of gathering my thoughts or thinking through everything Inspector Renard claimed in the pages of his folio to avoid prejudgment, but that wasn't true. Instead, I felt revulsion and then a numb feeling of loss. Secrets again—always unwanted and usually delivered with a measure of regret or sadness when the truth is revealed. Aline was no longer a picture of warmth and the place where I felt most comfortable; she had been transformed into a different person and was far worse in reality than I ever imagined, remembering those who bought my little farm years before, only to sell it and run away a few months later. I saw the faces in my imagination, drawn up into worried frowns and desperate expressions, forced to abandon their property and escape a lunatic on the far side of their shared hill. In those terrible first seconds of despair, I thought of Damon.

I hoped Aline would sense the uneasiness until I looked at her and it was clear she had, nodding with a faint smile and closed eyes. I've given up being embarrassed by my thoughts from a time when I didn't (or *couldn't*) understand, and that moment was such an occasion. She stood and placed her hand softly against my cheek.

"You're not ready," she whispered, turning slowly for the path and a return through the forest to her house.

12
CALM BEFORE THE STORM

I felt sullen and alone pacing slowly in my kitchen as a strange analogue to the grieving process began. I know perfectly well how self-absorbed and dramatic it sounds today, but it took a while before the shock went quietly from disbelief to a place where we go to accept what cannot be avoided and begin to plan how best to deal with the aftermath.

Few of us can prepare for so profound and sudden a change, but I was determined to stiffen my back and face it head-on. No amount of handwringing or worry could make things better, and until they came for her we would spend our remaining time no differently than we had before. Whatever course loomed in an unseen future, I refused to withdraw and leave her to follow it alone.

The cold truth behind a sudden, horrible revelation seemed overwhelming and I worked hard to avoid wallowing in a pool of self-pity, oblivious to what Aline's condition would mean for her. I mention it now because Burke and Halliwell stopped the conversation again and not from a fear of what Aline might think or do. Instead, they paused with surprising and deliberate sympathy knowing a moment in time so far from ordinary simply made continuing without regard for the emotional wreckage it would cause unacceptable.

Mo waited in polite, considerate silence, and even Berezan understood, solemn-faced and quiet in deference to an impossible pit of despair I couldn't escape. After a while, and reassured the narrative could resume, they wondered why Aline had waited—why she went home to allow time so that I could adjust to what I thought I knew instead of putting it right, then and there. She only smiled at them and said simply, "There was plenty of time for that, and Evan just needed to be alone for a while."

Burke nodded and smiled, too, and his small gesture changed the way I felt about him afterward. He knew what Aline's words meant from hindsight, but he approved because her answer was correct.

STANDING ALONE IN my kitchen, I looked without purpose at anything in my line of sight, somehow hoping the best course of action might appear out of nowhere if only I would look hard enough. I didn't notice the sun was setting behind distant hills to the west until I stood at a window with unexpected determination to shake off my funk; there were things to do and preparations to make. Renard's words echoed in my thoughts as I opened my computer and began a search through the internet to learn all I could on the subject of acute mental conditions and the most likely regimen of treatment to prepare for the moment when they came to take Aline away. Her likelihood of escaping a return to an isolation ward seemed remote, but I read the articles closely for no better reason than to prepare for the inevitable separation it would mean.

Would she accept and go along without a struggle, I wondered? Worse still, how would the authorities even know to search for her? The answer, I reasoned, would lie with Renard and the conclusion of his tireless investigation; *he* would tell them and the sad ending would begin. I won't pretend I didn't consider alternatives—intercepting the detective with an impassioned plea to simply leave her alone, for example. In my desperation all kinds of thoughts paraded through, even if most of them were absurd, but I held them just the same.

Could Jeremy intercede on the chance Renard's impossible tale might yet be discredited and made worthless? What could I say that would be truthful without making things worse? Any testimony from me might only add fuel to the fire and accelerate the very nightmare for Aline I wanted so badly to avoid.

She had claimed no memory of the Glasgow incident despite a bloodied face and policemen at her hotel room door. Perhaps momentary amnesia as a shield raised by her traumatized mind against further damage was possible, but Renard never believed, and it seemed odd to the police investigators, too. There had to be another answer: a condition or illness consistent with their decision to admit her to an isolation ward. I returned to Renard's notes, with references to the first interviews conducted shortly after Aline's arrival at an inpatient facility, but something seemed off. I noticed a questionnaire apparently crucial to the process was missing, but sidenotes photocopied and stapled to administrative documents made it clear they considered something much worse than amnesia. I looked twice to be sure at secondary analysis fixed on the possibility of "bizarre delusional disorder" and a cautionary note directed at attending staff to watch for associated symptoms.

I pored over each paper carefully, but it was obvious Renard had been denied much of what the psychiatrists saw and did to treat Aline. It made sense, understanding the intensely private nature of medical record keeping, but little of what remained helped explain the treatment schedule and how it turned out. When the paper trail stopped suddenly with an authorization to shift from inpatient care to a transitional facility in Stornoway—a halfway house—there was nothing more to see. The records were incomplete and I could only estimate how many of them must have been withheld or redacted. I wondered (as Berezan did during our interviews) how Renard got his hands on *any* of them.

WHEN ALINE CALLED as I was turning off the lights on my way to bed, I felt the adrenaline jolt and reddening face, wishing she hadn't bothered. After the day's events, I simply wanted to be left alone. For the first time since we'd met, I had no desire to speak with her. My phone buzzed repeatedly as the voicemails mounted until it was clear she wouldn't take "no" for an answer, and it seemed I was making things worse by refusing to pick up. At last I gave in and selected her number, but she didn't pick up. I tried again, but the unique sound of her Rover pulled me to the window to wait for her headlights to appear and wander through my gate.

I opened the door and stood aside, bracing for what looked to be round one of our first real fight, but she only smiled and took my hands in hers.

"I know this has made you worry," she began, "but don't; everything will be fine."

We sat for a while in silence and I know she waited for me to speak, but when I did the tone must have been severe because I watched the gentle smile disappear, replaced by a face of one who's been injured.

"Do you understand where this is going?" I asked sharply. "Renard doesn't believe for a minute your memories from that night are gone; he thinks you've been lying all this time and he's determined to expose it—to expose *you*."

"Yes," she replied softly. "I know."

"He's not going to stop until somebody arrests you or sends you back to that hospital, Aline."

She looked on with an expression I will never forget because it placed before me two options to consider and one was just as plausible as the other. In her eyes I saw at once the disturbing evidence of a mind corrupted beyond redemption, but with it, the unavoidable possibility of something else and not a product of delusion or insanity. I couldn't see it clearly then, but she tossed her own rope for *me* to grab and hold tight: a fleeting image suggesting perhaps the old Belgian cop was right and an army of experienced doctors had gotten it wrong.

"Renard will lose interest, Evan," she said at last.

"He's been building his case for fifteen years!" I replied with a voice much louder than I intended. "There's no way he's letting go of it now, especially when he has copies ready to hand over when he gets in front of the North Wales Police."

"He will lose interest," she repeated. "They always do."

"Who are 'they'?" I asked with a frown.

"It doesn't matter right now," she answered, "but trust me. Renard has no case to make and when the police tell him as much he'll go back to Liège and forget about it."

"There's no telling *what* the police will do," I protested. "Renard's a retired cop and that has to carry weight with other cops."

"Maybe it does but I can't tell them any more today than I already have. Allegiances between policemen can't change that; Renard will run out of things to say and when he does, his fantasy will die out."

I listened to her words, troubled not by their meaning but instead an absolute certainty and disinterest in a growing problem that might well land her back in a psychiatric hospital. Did the nature of her condition force Aline to ignore or dismiss tangible facts in the present merely because they are connected to an episode in her past she cannot recall? I felt myself floundering, unable to make her see and understand the profound risk and likelihood her liberty would be taken from her once more. She saw it and placed a hand gently against my face.

"You mustn't let this bother you, Evan. Inspector Renard is the one who has run out of time, and I'm telling you as plainly as I can: he won't be able to make a case because there isn't one—there never will be. They may listen politely, but in the end, he will go back to Belgium empty-handed and there will be an end to it."

I had nothing more to say. Aline's mind must surely have shifted to another world where the consequences of Renard's threat didn't exist and, in her mind, brought no reason to worry. I felt my anxiety begin to ease suddenly, although I couldn't understand why. Whatever the result when Renard made his play, I was in no position to compel Aline toward anything and least of all a magical return from the dark recesses of her illness. As night fell over our valley my only choice became obvious: I would stay close and ride out the days until the authorities arrived with a new sectioning order and a return to Glasgow or (at worst) a warrant for her arrest.

THE FOLLOWING DAY passed quietly, and the day after and the day after that were no different. In slow increments, our lives returned to normal and I began to lose the nagging, daily expectation they would show up at any moment. For weeks it went on like that, with sudden bouts of worry and constant glances at the gate whenever she visited, watchful for a van to make its way down my driveway filled with burly attendants carrying straitjackets and loaded syringes to ensure Aline's eventless return to the wards. It's the dramatic (and badly misrepresented) notions we get from movies or the television that does it, I suppose, leaving dire images of brutal insane asylums and lost, screaming souls behind heavy doors that will never open for them again. I knew better, of course, but the mysterious world hiding behind the walls of inpatient facilities seems to invite and amplify those scenes because few of us have been inside one to see and know for sure.

THE FULL CRUSH of summer arrived with caravans of tourists in its wake and still there was nothing from Renard. The police didn't roar in and take Aline away in shackles, nor did the padded van bound for Glasgow, yet all of it seemed little more than a cruel delay in a conspiracy to make me miserable. Each morning I heard the old expression in my mind "if it seems too good to be true, it probably is," but the effort (and a prickly sensation of worry) was wasted. It took a while but I came to a juncture and another decision point demanding an answer. Perhaps it was my nature and personality, or even my training as an investigator, but either way I had to know.

On a bright Saturday afternoon in late July when Aline was up in Colwyn Bay, I gave in to the urge at last. I won't pretend it didn't make me feel guilty for going behind her back, but I found Renard's card in a drawer where I'd stuffed the documents to keep them out of sight. I accepted the risk of stirring up trouble, but without confirmation one way or another, the threat of his return would hover above us like a black cloud and I had reached the point at which I'd simply had enough.

My first attempt failed because I mangled the phone number input, but a second try found its mark. When Renard answered, I thought he was just awake from a nap because he mumbled and it seemed he didn't recognize my name.

"Inspector," I repeated slowly, "this is Evan Morgan."

My pulse quickened in the long pause that followed until he seemed to come alive at last.

"What do you want?" he demanded in a gravelly voice.

"I was about to ask you the same thing," I replied. "It's been a few months since…"

"Don't ever call me again, do you understand?" he demanded. "*Never!*"

There was silence and I stared at my phone as if it could explain but mostly to make sure the call had dropped. I touched the number once more, and it only rang once before Renard picked up.

"Leave me alone, bastard!" he thundered. "Goddamn you, it's finished!"

I blinked with astonishment in that moment, taken off guard by Renard's sudden, profane outburst. I wanted to believe his words were delivered with anger and resentment because he had discovered at last no one cared enough to bother with Aline. I was sure he'd lashed out in rage after learning the Welsh police had no intention of pursuing a Belgian cold case with so scant a collection of evidence and most of it circumstantial at best. His rant might easily have been one built on fury and his own failures, but that's not what it was. Instead, Renard's strained voice sounded more a siren of desperation and fear.

I sat on the arm of my couch for a while, trying to sort out the abrupt, unlikely conclusion of more than a decade of work and Renard's obsessive hunt to find justice for Claude Dumont. What had the police told him, I wondered? The scenario played out in my imagination and I nodded involuntarily at what must've been his last hopes being dashed. Renard likely *did* approach detectives in Denbighshire to show them his papers, but the locals turned him away for lack of evidence, motive, or cause. Did they see an old cop past his prime and grasping at a chance to win a decade-long search? Maybe a call to counterparts in Liège's police department with a request to stand Renard down and aim him again toward the reality of a pensioner's sunset days had resulted in a rebuke and warning to leave things alone and move on. Either way, Aline was right; there was no longer interest and Andre Renard would fade into the distance.

She stopped by on her way home from the coast and I decided to tell her of my strange call to Belgium. She smiled politely as I described Renard's bizarre outburst and it seemed her thoughts were elsewhere. Others hearing a similar story might've perked up simply for the novelty of a loud and vulgar speech, but Aline only asked if I preferred chicken or fish for dinner. As she always knew it would, life in our valley returned to normal.

TOWARD THE END of the month we spent a long weekend in Cardiff so Aline could show me her childhood home and stomping grounds at the university. It's a vibrant city and I saw a lot more on that trip than I did my last time there, but it was the nice, slow drive down from Llangollen I enjoyed most. We made needless stops simply to walk a bit and look around in clean country air that was fragrant and nothing like D.C. It took a while to reach that point but I remember nodding in quiet satisfaction that my choice to stay on had been correct, and suddenly northern Virginia seemed a million miles away.

On a quiet Sunday morning her phone buzzed while we lounged with nothing better to do, and when she saw the number, Aline motioned me quickly toward her. I felt a jolt of uneasiness until she said very loudly, "Yes, I can hear you!" She looked at me with a broad smile as her parents made their periodic check-in call, this time from Senegal on the coast of Africa where they paused for minor repairs on an adventure to visit friends in Dakar. They intended to follow the shoreline all the way to Cape Town, but problems with the boat's electrical system compelled them to save that journey for another time.

I listened to Aline shouting and laughing with her dad or exchanging updates about cousins with her mother, and it was the first time she ever spoke to them when I was around. There's no good reason why I found it so extraordinary but I did; for all her mysteries and the caution of others when I first arrived, here was a daughter chatting with her parents no different than any girl would do. Perhaps it was simply watching her being an ordinary person in an ordinary moment, but I felt better when she nodded and pointed suddenly at me.

"No, Mother," she said, "I don't think he came all the way from America just to meet me."

She smiled and winked in the middle of the teasing joke but it was clear they had spoken earlier. There were approximations and guesses as to return dates and potential locations, but without being told, I was already committed to meeting the parents. When at last they disconnected, Aline raised her eyebrows high and said through a gentle, slightly nervous laugh, "I think they want to meet you before the end of summer."

"Aren't I lucky!" I replied with enough sarcasm to let her know I would've preferred an alert after she told them of our involvement. "Okay, where and when?"

"Maybe Mallorca, but I think my dad would rather not commit to a hard date. They'll be sailing back before winter, so I expect it will be sometime in late September or October."

"I hope they don't hate me."

"So do I," she replied to close out the duel with a chide of her own.

BECAUSE IT'S IMPORTANT, she insisted, Aline booked us on a leisurely ferry ride across the Channel to Le Havre. The famous port city was not her goal and I didn't realize why we made the effort until she maneuvered a rented car along the rue de Nesmond in Bayeux, aiming me toward the magnificent Musée de la Tapisserie. It took a while to navigate along glassed enclosures where the historic tapestry described in 230 continuous feet of embroidered images events that culminated in the legendary medieval Battle of Hastings. I couldn't understand its importance to her but in time, she said, it would be different. I shrugged in my ignorance, unable to see what she really meant.

I recall them with fondness but our road trips brought other sensations, too, and not all of them so pleasing. In the wake of our debacle with Andre Renard, I caught myself fighting a subtle feeling of anxiety each time we passed a police car, wondering if they might've changed their minds after all. Aline didn't notice, and I said nothing, but the nagging worry was always there. I decided on our way home the lingering doubts and concerns were more trouble than they were worth and, determined to close the circle, I dialed Jeremy's number while Aline was busy buying gas at a Shell station in Shrewsbury.

Jeremy's neighbor is a North Wales Police officer and, I reasoned, if anyone could help determine how far Renard had gone, he would be the likely choice. At the time, we knew nothing of Renard's cover story as the uncle of a college kid come to grief on a bike tour. It didn't matter because I left names out of it and asked only if an older Belgian gentleman came to see the police in the spring. Jeremy passed the question to his pal and he called back half an hour later to report the cops hadn't heard from any Belgians that season except for a bus carrying a tour group on holiday from Antwerp involved in a minor fender bender on their ride over to Holyhead.

I felt the tension ease and despite Renard's big talk and loud threats, there was no longer any doubt his best efforts to drag Aline off to jail had gone for nothing. When I maneuvered the car into my tiny garage, intent on beating Aline to the bathroom, a weight lifted and the laughter returned.

I noticed she was more often on the phone with Vienne and their growing friendship produced a slightly wicked tone of collusion and shared intent to mold me into a better person. Aline sided with Vienne in the long-running argument over my frugal habits, now characterized as "Evan the cheapskate." The mild insult was tolerable, but it carried with it a renewed demand that I find a better car. I balked, of course, but despite my reminder that her military surplus Land Rover was no spring chicken, Aline deflected the contradiction with one of her "I dare you to argue with me" expressions.

When the leaves began to turn once more, the anniversary of my arrival to the valley came up and Aline seemed more charmed by it than I. Still, the season was changing and she was becoming restless to finalize plans for a vacation week with Vienne and her outrageous friends in Montreal.

It seemed strange and unlikely Aline would openly court such an adventure, taking careful steps to remain at a distance just a year before, but when I told Jeremy of the idea he smiled and nodded approval as if reminding me he'd been right all along. Vienne went to work planning out every second of our week and Aline did nothing to stop her, so I was obliged to lay out suitable clothes for the trip and arrange flights. I admit the tedium of another transatlantic airline adventure was no longer enough to dampen my spirits at a chance to see my big sister again, and with it came the quiet satisfaction of bringing Aline out for our first "big-time" road trip.

When we boarded our plane, she explained it had been many years since she last flew. I splurged considerably and bought business class tickets, but she seemed to take the relative opulence and pampered treatment in stride. It was my first time on an airliner not jammed with the masses back in "steerage," but I think the distinction mattered more to me than it did to her.

THE EXPLOSION OF autumn colors was nearly gone when we started a cloudless descent into Montreal in late afternoon, and I frowned, knowing Aline would miss October leaves and the yearly renewal of nature's loveliest works of art in a place where it is always spectacular. Vienne waited for us to clear Customs, but it seemed a bit insulting that again, she was more excited to see Aline than her own brother.

I begged her not to drag us through a gauntlet of fashion industry sycophants and hangers-on but she ignored me and I resented it until, in a skillful move, Vienne bought me off with luxury box tickets to watch our beloved Sabres play the Canadiens at Centre Bell Arena. For the occasion I bought and wore a Gilbert Perreault number 11 throwback jersey with defiant pride, determined to show the "Habs faithful" a Buffalo man was in their house. The experience was satisfying—the Sabres won 3-2 in overtime—but also entertaining as my sister explained to Aline why NHL players are allowed to beat the shit out of each other and not go to jail for assault.

We went on an all-day trip up to a little town in the Laurentians where Vienne's friend and her husband run a general store, but the visit was mostly an excuse to get out of the city for a while. We waited through a shower turning to snow with quietly powerful cider and a huge plate of poutine that tastes a lot better than it looks. In both directions the ride was an understandable exercise in catching up, but I listened as they did most of the talking and I wondered if Aline considered the events of summer and Andre Renard's mistaken belief he could rattle her.

Of course, we couldn't tell Vienne any of it and a deliberate silence brought the first pangs of guilt and discomfort that gnawed at me watching as she celebrated the couple Aline and I had become. I soothed myself with the belief a time might arrive when all of it could be revealed to her; a moment when circumstance would allow me to unburden myself. I wanted to tell Vienne the full story but mostly because I needed the little voices inside my injured conscience to stop whispering "liar" from that hidden place where our character is kept and measured.

ON THE FOURTH day in Montreal, Vienne went into the office for a couple of hours to sort out a logistics snag threatening a recruiting event, leaving Aline and me to relax on our own. It was considerably cooler when we stood at a broad window in Vienne's apartment high above the streets, looking south with mugs of coffee as a slow parade of cargo ships eased their way along the river. Time had passed since Aline startled the hell out of me in the woods separating our farms, but at last the invisible boundaries between us were finally dissolved.

It was suddenly quiet and I asked her about her relatives, wondering if they were distant from her. Aline nodded and told me an aunt, her mother's sister Laine, lived in Newcastle with her second husband. The cousins, Audra and Glyn, both lived outside the UK; Glyn teaches music to high school students in Halifax and Audra lives in Windhoek, Namibia, where her husband took on the family's construction business. Aline's grandparents were gone when the last one—her maternal grandfather—died in 2000 but other aunts, uncles, and cousins lost regular contact over the years, and I heard in her voice an adult life lived mostly alone.

As our Canadian week ended with another boarding process, the most notable change was the progression of Aline's deeper kinship with Vienne. It was somehow surprising to me, the closeness and ease with which each adjusted to the other. Romantic attachment has its limits and the void Aline endured by distance from her relatives became a target Vienne seemed more than willing to attack without being asked. I watched with quiet satisfaction, knowing they would likely remain close regardless of my relationship with Aline.

When we finished unpacking and collapsed in my front room to inspect collected mail and catch up on local news from the television, it felt as if a necessary trial had been won and time to do nothing but recover from our journey was well-earned.

13
"WHEN THE LEVEE BREAKS"

MY phone buzzed from the kitchen and I was sure it would be Vienne calling to make sure our airliner hadn't plunged into the ocean. Instead, Jeremy's name appeared and when I answered, his voice was low to ensure no one overheard.

"Evan," he began, "are you home yet?"

"We just got back an hour ago. Why?"

"Have you been contacted by anyone else today? From here, I mean."

"No one but you just now; what's going on?"

He paused again and I could hear his door close as he repositioned the phone against his shoulder.

"My mate Danny called this morning and said some people were asking about Aline."

I sat forward at once as the gnawing fear returned like a silent battering ram.

"What people?"

"Government people, Evan—three of them with credentials tied to Special Branch—and they wanted to know about a België detective who was here in the spring. I assume this has something to do with your earlier question?"

I felt the color drain from my face as the image seeped in and Aline saw it.

"Who is it?" she whispered.

I mouthed Jeremy's name silently, but she only smiled a little and nodded.

"It's a long story," I offered. "Why do they want to talk to Aline?" I asked.

"No idea," Jeremy answered, "but they came 'round here wondering if I knew where you might be; Danny said they asked for my contact info straight away."

"What did you tell them?"

"I told them you were away in Canada visiting relatives. The head boy—a quiet little bloke called Marsden—smiled politely and suggested my mouth ought to remain shut about their visit to avoid injuring sensitive diplomatic interests, or some such rubbish."

"Anything else?"

"I told them I'm already bound by legal professional privilege but I don't think they were impressed. Evan, if you're in difficulties, you need to tell me!"

"It's not as bad as it sounds," I lied. "If they come back, let me know and I'll deal with it." I felt the uneasiness building, but when I looked at Aline, she seemed disinterested. Jeremy's words were a shock and my mind began to race with the possibilities of an aggravated army of bureaucrats trying to avoid an international incident. What seemed an issue dead and buried when Renard went home to Liège was somehow resurrected. No one could know about the Brugge incident unless Andre told them, making it a near certainty the faceless Marsden would return.

"Don't let this go too far," Jeremy whispered. "If you need help, bloody-well say so, all right?"

"It's covered," I answered, "but I'll keep you in the loop."

She waited until I tossed the phone aside.

"What did he say?"

I explained as best I could without sounding paranoid, but she stood and walked slowly to the window.

"It was always a matter of time," she said, turning toward me with a sad smile. "Renard must've spoken with somebody before he ever came to see me."

"Which means," I continued, "Andre's been clever; he planted seeds in case he couldn't get it done on his own, but something's wrong."

"What's wrong?" Aline asked without looking.

"How the hell did a retired Belgian detective get in front of high-level British officials, and worse still, what kind of bullshit story did he give them?"

"He was only hedging his bet, Evan," Aline replied with a strange, distant voice.

The terse phone call replayed in my mind and Renard's demand to be left alone suddenly made less sense than before. "It's finished!" he'd insisted, yet Jeremy's news told a different tale and one now driven by powerful intelligence agents from Her Majesty's famed Special Branch.

Uneasiness in the pit of my stomach became a tempest, but Aline stood suddenly alert and an urgency was plain in her expression. Today, I know it was inevitable, but I watched in that moment as her eyes darted left and right until she nodded twice.

"There's no other way," she said firmly as she pulled her hair back and secured it into a ponytail with an elastic tie.

"I can't explain this in words; I wanted to ease through the process and allow the answers to find you naturally, but that is no longer possible. Are you ready to see?"

"I don't understand what you mean," I replied as the torment returned like fingernails scratching along an old blackboard at the prospect of facing the true measure of her illness, alive again and holding her tightly in its grip. She leaned close and reached for my forehead like a mother concerned for a fever in a young child.

"How do you feel?"

The question seemed out of place—disconnected to so serious a moment.

"A little anxious and confused, I guess, but other than that..."

"No, I meant to ask how you feel *physically*."

"I feel fine."

"Are you sure?"

"Yeah, I'm sure," I answered with an unconvincing smile as she knelt and sat slowly on her heels.

"And now?" she asked as her eyes narrowed.

It happened with the suddenness of a switch thrown by an unseen hand when throbbing pain swirled through the sides of my head—pulsing and electric. It felt as though my brain was connected with a high-pressure air hose, inflating it beyond the space of my skull, and I cried out involuntarily. There were no other thoughts beyond the shock and abrupt agony—the kind of stunning and immediate pain that consumes every thought.

My sight blurred so badly, only light and faint shapes appeared before me. I heard the raspy moan escaping through my nostrils because my teeth were clenched tightly, but as suddenly as it gripped me, the pain was gone and only the familiar ringing in my ears remained. When my vision began to clear, Aline wrapped my trembling body securely in her arms. I don't remember moving but I was on the floor, and she held on tightly with her head pressed against mine.

"I'm so sorry, my love," she said softly, "but you would never believe any other way."

I felt paralyzed as Aline brushed back the hair from my forehead, beaded now with perspiration, and she waited. After some minutes, I don't know how long, she leaned close.

"Can you taste anything?" she asked, but all I could do was shake my head.

With the same suddenness, my tongue reported the unmistakable, acrid flavor of a penny, somehow dissolved and pooling inside my mouth.

"Do you taste copper?"

This time I nodded and said "yes, I can taste it" but the words were slurred and clumsy. She helped me onto the couch gently, but when we settled the foul taste was gone. In my ears the persistent ringing was gone, too, and she told me to sit still while the last of the effects faded.

The air was quiet and a breeze wafted through an open front door I hadn't touched. When she pointed to it, I turned to look. Without a sound it moved slowly closed. I stared in disbelief but Aline saw it quickly.

"Don't be afraid—it's all right."

She pulled me slowly to her and guided my head against her shoulder. It was subtle and yet powerful—her touch drained off the tension like a sponge. I went without a thought, obedient and compliant like a child in her arms. My terror from moments before was taken away as if waking from a nightmare, soothing and meant to reassure I was safe again. When I felt myself returning to normal, I looked at her.

"How?" was all I could say.

She went quickly to the bathroom and returned with a wet washcloth, dabbing the sweat from my head and neck.

"People called it magic when I was first young but it's not that at all. Some of us were given a very special ability, and it takes time to even recognize it, but this is just the power of nature, Evan. When we came of age we learned to use it, adding something from before each time we began to mature."

"I...I don't understand," I said feebly. "*Nature?* What the hell is this?"

I wanted somebody to rush in and expose the trick. I needed to see a laughing crowd behind the curtain and know I'd been fooled by a clever illusion; that it was all made-up and everything I knew would be restored. I would laugh with them, if only for the relief that I'd been conned and there really *is* no such thing as magic, but no one appeared to stop the show and tell me it had been a carefully arranged, elaborate prank. Instead, Aline kept me close and stroked my wetted temples.

"Shhh," she whispered. "None of this makes sense right now, I know, but there was no other way to show you so that you would see and understand. After a while, it will be easier as you adjust. Only a handful outside our numbers have ever seen and experienced it like this, Evan; give yourself some time."

I sat forward with my face in my hands like a repentant partygoer recovering from an epic bender. There was no more pain but the unbelievable had turned in seconds to a harsh reality no one can prepare us to accept. Telekinesis and mind control? The inexplicable realm of the supernatural had all been a comic sideshow to me and never part of the normal world where we say "magic" in offhand ways to describe something wonderful. It isn't real, and yet there I was in the aftermath of its grip, struggling to complete a singular, impossible transition.

"This isn't happening," I mumbled. "There has to be an explanation."

Aline leaned her head to one side and positioned it directly in front of mine. "You still don't see?"

"I don't know how you did this, but it's not real, Aline—it can't be. There's something else going on here and just because I haven't figured it out yet doesn't mean I won't!"

The pain was real and I wondered how I would hold on and function when the last of my doubts came down in a heap. I knew it was no skillful illusion and yet I fought with every bit of my strength to deny.

I was comfortable in my ignorance, safe inside a presumption created when those pieces of a known puzzle made in the image of mental illness waited patiently as my only rational explanation. Only those who can't find a better answer hide behind mysticism and supernatural wonders because they have little choice. I was better than that and my belief systems were always subordinate to the reliable scientific method. Sometimes boring, and often the bringer of disappointment for some who need more, demonstrable truth was the single most important vehicle that delivered us from stone-tipped spears to excursions across the powdery surface of the moon.

I wish I could say only disbelief plagued me in the moment but that wasn't true. Slight though it may have been, just the possibility it was real pressed hard against the walls we build to hold back those deepest, most terrifying sensations of vulnerability. When Aline began, a tiny fissure was opened and fear came through in waves.

"This can't be happening," I repeated, but it was only for my own comfort.

She nodded silently and lifted my chin to kiss me very gently.

"What do you need so that you'll see and understand?" she asked softly. "We don't do these things for show, Evan, but if you want more…"

"The fireplace," I said suddenly. "When I went to your house the first time, it was empty and then it was alive. Was that part of this?"

Instead of answering, Aline turned and pointed to my own hearth where it lay void of logs. After a moment or two, tongues of beautiful blue flame appeared, growing straight up from the empty iron grate. I watched in dumbfounded silence as they swirled and danced and I could hear its muffled rumble. For a full minute, the fire intensified as I reached toward it to feel heat radiating outward, and in those final seconds there was nowhere left to hide.

She held my hand as the fire subsided into a flicker for a few seconds and then it was gone. Aline waited while I went through the last, maddening process of acceptance, and the weight of a revelation few have endured made of me a new and different man. I know she wanted only to protect me from my own doubts, and in an absurd gesture I somehow needed to make, I stood and stumbled awkwardly to my kitchen. In a drawer I found and retrieved a digital deep-fry thermometer, racing back to the fireplace with the last shreds of uncertainty pushing me onward like desperate voices in a distant past demanding to be heard. I remembered seeing the instrument in a drawer and the image it made in my mind of Damon's amateur cooking dreams and the odd dishes he tried to prepare. On that day, it would register something much greater.

I knelt and placed the probe against the wrought iron grate, and when I read the LCD display it showed 154 degrees. I couldn't speak and all I managed to do was stare. At last, the trial and emotional gauntlet I ran was complete; there was no longer any reasonable doubt, and I felt suddenly heavy where I sat in silence. She pulled me upright and steered me back to my couch.

I could hear her words but they came at me in echoes, louder this moment but muted in the next. She cradled my head softly in her palms and told me not to be afraid. She said she could never do anything to hurt me, but all I had was the thin lifeline of faith and a need to believe her. My hand tightened its grip on hers and I held onto it like a buoy in dark, pitching seas suddenly within reach.

She leaned close to my ear and whispered, "You will always be safe with me...*always*."

I'd like to tell you the transition was long and tortuous, that I fought courageously against the attack on my common sense, but there was no use. In ten minutes I went from the firm ground where most of us live—comfortable with our place in the physical universe—to a minefield of uncertainty. After a while, it occurred to me my reaction was exactly as Aline knew it would be, but more than that, it was selfish and stupid when I realized *she* had been living with a secret all her life. The evidence we hold onto for explanations is always hiding beneath the surface and when we discover it, moments of fear or indecision are washed away and we smile in gratitude. The doctors in Scotland looked and listened and a hundred years of psychiatric research told them to find and treat a known disorder. It was precisely what anyone else in their position would do, but the stark reality glared at me like a flare in the night: they saw only what she had placed carefully before them.

Aline's diminished mental state was never more than a disguise—a useful tool to deceive and redirect others. There was no emotional condition or malady corrupting her mind and her deliberate illusion became an insurance policy guaranteeing no one would be any the wiser. Like successive hammer blows, the realization I could never have envisioned pounded against the door of reason and I understood at last.

Claude Dumont watched the power of Aline's hand but he too saw what he wanted (or needed) to see: God's will only meters away and by it, salvation for an innocent and her child. Two men at a Glasgow bus stop felt her power in their turn but for different reasons and to terrible effect. Years later, Andre Renard's best efforts followed his instincts and a path that pointed toward an insane killer. I know he thought a triumphant end to the journey was within reach but his sudden silence, and a struggle against untold fears, could only mean he also found himself a target within range. In a stunning conclusion, the inspector's passionate search for truth and justice halted inexplicably and almost overnight.

I looked at her and even then, she waited patiently as those final moments passed.

"How long have you been able to do these things?" I whispered.

"A very long time," she replied, but I was too consumed in the moment to understand what that really meant. She would complete the thought later, but for the moment, it was enough.

"Then he was on the right path," I said with a sad smile. "Renard wasn't chasing phantoms after all."

"Yes," she answered, "but he will never understand how or why."

I was too tired and reeling from her stunning revelation to consider what that meant.

"Enough now," she said. "I want you to lie down and rest. When you wake, all this will make more sense, I promise."

I DON'T REMEMBER much beyond a distant sound I knew was Aline tidying up in my kitchen until I woke in the dark. It was disorienting, and I struggled to clear my head, but she was beside me and propped on an elbow.

"It's still early," she whispered. "Go back to sleep."

"What time is it?" I asked automatically, but my phone showed 6:36.

I slept through the night but I could see she was watching me carefully when I returned from the bathroom and dressed slowly. It was silent as we sat for a while and I wondered how long it would go before one of us spoke. There are few occasions when change comes to us more profoundly and without the possibility of a return to where we began. I stood beside her at the window, watching sunlight fight its way through the oaks in the solitude of our valley.

She asked me if I wanted to end it and walk away—if I was moved only by an assumed obligation to stay on—but I shook my head. I couldn't tolerate the idea of being anywhere else, and when I told her so she seemed surprised. It wouldn't be of any particular importance otherwise, but seeing her wait out my answer like the rest of us brings a strange sense of satisfaction and calm because today I know what it meant. Aline stayed deliberately outside my mind when she asked, leaving it for me to decide on my own.

SHE WENT HOME to answer messages and make sure a sale at the shop was underway as planned. When she returned midmorning, I waited in the kitchen as quietly as I could. A secret exposed (and truth of her power) shook me in ways I still can't fully describe, but the result went far beyond my living room. Far away from our valley, in a place no one can access, a new problem festered in the files of a hidden government agency made suddenly aware of Renard's failed play. Worse still, there was no way of knowing how much they knew and what they intended to do about it.

I thought I understood stress and the burden of dealing with fear, but those first hours in the swirl of a life changed forever left me drained simply knowing at last what we always regarded as the absurd was real, tangible, and perhaps dangerous. "They used to call it magic," she had said, but that was little more than a name applied by people with no way to understand, driven by superstition in a time long before science could arrive and save the day. It didn't matter as I paced in nervous anticipation until suddenly, the connections were made and I thought of Renard's sudden, unexplained reversal when Aline returned.

"Feeling better?" she asked in a whisper.

"I don't know what to feel," I replied.

Before the debacle made by Renard's accusations, she had become my reason and purpose; just a girl making her way out from understandable difficulties but dear to me and the face of my future where people love and live like any other. Now, she was something much more and the destroyer of common sense. I held on in desperation as the memories of sudden pain from the day before swirled around me like hornets daring me to disbelieve again.

"What did you do to Renard?"

The air seemed alive and crackling with energy, a strange effect like static electricity.

"I didn't hurt him, Evan," she replied softly. "I simply gave him a glimpse of his future and what it would bring if he didn't forget this nonsense and go home to Belgium."

"You went to see him before he left Wales?"

"Of course."

I looked into her eyes but they showed nothing new. I thought there would be an expression of malevolence but she was unchanged.

"When he answered the phone," I continued, "it was clear and I could hear it in his voice; he was terrified, Aline."

"I should hope so," she replied, and it was frightening to watch her move, so calm and unconcerned.

"Was it the same thing you did to me?"

"No," she answered, "it was nothing like that. I just gave him a glimpse. It doesn't matter, Evan; Renard understands now and he won't be a problem for us anymore."

"He showed them copies of those documents," I said sadly. "Not the cops here, but he must've given those papers to somebody high up in the British government. They asked him why he came here and it's just a matter of time before they figure it out."

"They can ask all they like but I'm sure it's the last thing Andre Renard will want to talk about for the rest of his life."

It required little imagination for me to know what that meant and the horrors Renard must've seen when the images began to pour in and with them, the truth of what she could do. I guessed correctly Aline left no doubt as to her purpose and the thought gave me a chill when I realized there was no longer a fear of being found out. Instead, she *wanted* him to know and understand it was she who took him to a dark, horrifying place. With no hope of convincing others of so outrageous a tale, Renard was alone and exposed. The inevitable comparisons followed when I considered that truth.

A simple, harmless peek inside to convince her own boyfriend—the one she loves—sent me to my knees in agony. A more aggressive demonstration of her power to a man she dislikes could only have been a nightmare so real and terrifying his stability was torn from him and scattered into the night when the demons of Aline's thoughts raced in to torment Renard in ways he could never have imagined. I didn't mention it then but the irony was obvious: Claude Dumont looked at her and saw an angel acting as an extension of God's hand; Renard looked and saw through a window into Hell.

Three more days passed but still there was no visit from the police. They made no connection to us because none existed; Renard hadn't spoken with Jeremy's neighbor and the extent of police involvement was confined to an exercise in cooperation with shadowy figures carrying heavy credentials. Inspector Renard was no longer part of the problem, perhaps, but officials with authority of the Crown to back them up most certainly *were*.

It's amusing today, but when I told them of that moment during one of our breaks in the conversation, Burke and Halliwell watched and listened in reverent silence because they'd seen the result; they too had been taken to the edge when Aline's defenses brought terrible and final consequences to those who push her. It's not a nice thing to say, but it was fun watching them squirm, knowing how loudly a powerful, high-level bureaucrat like Gregory Hurd once scoffed at the notion and threatened the others with "pejorative reassignment" when he was briefed for the first time. They all listened but without the dismissive, self-assurance they once held. For them, the "power of nature" had been made all too clear.

In a surprising demonstration of his intuitive skills, Burke wondered if I experienced fear of her that day or if it had been instead a rising sensation of extended power available for me to use. Had I suddenly realized, he asked, she might become an instrument in my hands and one that could be aimed at anyone I wished? He seemed genuinely surprised when I shook my head. I saw a degree of callous disappointment in Burke's expression, but Mo just smiled, reassured once more the best qualities of my character still held and guided me.

14
TURNING POINT

IT felt a bit like walking each moment across a thin sheet of ice covering a deep, freezing lake, and Aline waited with a patience I couldn't appreciate until the questions rolled through my thoughts often enough that answers were needed. I wanted to avoid the topic and look toward the future, but the details in Renard's stack of papers remained unexplained and with them, the missing pieces of her life now blended into my own. At last, I gave in and asked her if she would tell me about the truth inside a Belgian policeman's misperceptions. She always knew the time would come and with it, an obligation to bring me closer. Another soft breeze through the valley welcomed a quiet Sunday and we set off on one of our customary walks in the trees.

Dumont's unfortunate experience was the obvious starting point, but Renard's notes on the night his friend called with a frantic declaration of a miracle witnessed were accurate. She described the moment Dumont lunged at her and the involuntary reaction that brought so terrible a result when blood vessels in his brain were quickly (and inexplicably) shredded. It was sobering to hear, but she never claimed his death was an accident. Instead, she *meant* to harm him. It was too much, and she regretted reacting so violently, only because she hadn't yet developed the control of a power her age and experience would bring later. Measured and appropriate response was not yet a skill well-polished, she said, but Dumont's death became a lesson to her on the importance of knowing her own limits. It sounds cold and indifferent today, but I remember wondering if her matter-of-fact description was another peek through the veil and within, a look at the darker corners of her nature.

I listened to the words, but they became drowned out in the moment I thought of Damon's odd behavior, suddenly demanding tangible assets as payment for his services, moving abruptly away from established and traditional electronic transfers into an ordinary bank. Like a siren blaring out its warning, the obvious conclusion blasted through and I felt a tug of uncertainty and anxious worry once more. There couldn't be any doubt; Aline's influence was written on the face of Damon's sudden and unexplained requirement that left his clients surprised and confused. His "changes regarding a woman" *were* Aline and not Isolda Marquez. I had to understand, but I felt uneasy asking her. I know it sounds strange and absurd, but in that moment, the tiny barbs of caution brushed against me as though walking through a patch of nettles, and for the first time I felt the persistent, gnawing effect of fear.

She told me I would always be safe with her. I wanted to believe that but only because I needed to know *she* believed. Suddenly, her assurances were cast into doubt. It was inevitable the question would come up at some point, so I held my breath and hoped for the best.

"Did you help Damon with his finances?" I asked.

She turned to me where we sat on my favorite dead tree trunk, covered in moss and carrying the silent history of an ancient place that became important to me as it had been to Aline.

"I didn't give him money, if that's what you're asking," she replied warily. "Why?"

"Not money," I said quickly, "he had plenty of that. I just meant advice; you were trained in finance and economics but Damon was anything *but*."

I expected her to nod and explain, but she waited a moment with an odd expression. In a smooth and effortless movement, Aline swung a foot over the log to straddle it like a horse, and she leaned toward me with an obvious frown.

"Are you all right?" she asked.

I said nothing but Aline stood quickly, and I felt my cheeks redden when she turned her back. I didn't know what to say, but she spun to face me at last and her expression was unlike any I'd seen since we first met on that cold October day. She shook her head as she paced slowly past me, and I couldn't decide if she carried anger or the sting of betrayal. Either way, our first moment of conflict had arrived.

"Did you think I wouldn't notice?"

"What are you talking about?" I demanded.

She stopped and said, "You're afraid of me."

It wasn't confusion or mystery; instead, she exposed me like cockroaches in a kitchen scurrying for cover when the lights go on. There was no way to explain in that moment because I didn't understand enough to make a decent point. It was unnerving to realize she could sense my uneasiness, and with that ability she had become something different—unnatural. They say animals can detect fear, and it shouldn't have been surprising, but there were no images flooding in—no intense vision as a clue I could recognize. She simply reacted to those markers only she could see and understand.

"I'm *not* afraid, Aline," I answered loudly, "but only an idiot would look at a fight he can't win and try to act tough!"

"Do you believe them, Evan? When you look at me, do you see a mad woman—a *murderer*?"

"No!" I said at once. "It's not like that at all, damn it!"

"Then why?" she asked, moving toward me. "After all this, do you honestly think I could ever hurt you?"

I had nothing that would explain and no words I could offer to justify the involuntary reaction. I understood why Dumont had died and the rare occasions when we are forced to fight. She couldn't know he never planned to harm her and her heavy-handed reaction was at least understandable, but the details in Renard's mountain of papers suggested more in records from the Glasgow Police Department. She waited and watched as I fumbled through my own thoughts, unsure if they would remain my own if I ever angered her and how swiftly I could be made to pay for them.

"I *don't* know!" I thundered, trying to navigate an impossible argument. "I guess it's human instinct, but how can you expect me to accept all this—what you can do—without feeling at least a little wary of it? You can make me see, think, or feel anything you like and there's no defense! With a thought, you could destroy my brain, just like you did to Dumont, and I am powerless to stop it."

Aline walked right up to me and I had to fight the urge to stand away—to keep her at a distance, as if *that* would make a difference.

"I could also draw a knife across your throat as you sleep, couldn't I? I could smash your skull with a hammer and you would be just as dead!"

"People go to prison for doing those things," I replied defiantly. "No one can be arrested for killing people by *thinking* them to death!"

"Oh, you poor, stupid bastard!" she said with a sad smile. "It doesn't take much effort to kill somebody, Evan, and it certainly doesn't require my abilities. It just takes the will and desire. I don't have either of those things because I am in love with you and I need you with me as you *are*!"

"Is there anything else you haven't told me?" I asked at last. "What other secrets are you keeping?"

"There is more but I'll explain that to you in time."

"Explain it now!" I demanded.

"Not yet, Evan, it's…"

"Then *when*? What's a good time on your calendar?"

"You're still not ready!" she shouted. Aline's voice echoed through the trees and in an odd, secondary moment I remember being startled by the volume and how loud she could yell. She closed her eyes and waited to calm herself. I waited, too, until her smile returned as she continued.

"It's not time yet. I will explain the rest of it at the proper moment. Evan, you have to trust me; I've been through this once or twice and I know what I'm doing."

I wanted to believe—to understand. I needed to know and not worry, but the truth behind her words held a lethal ability no one else has and it could be turned on me if Aline ever changed her mind. The process took a while to root but finally the connections were made, and I felt bold enough to seek out confirmation, if only to satisfy my own troubled mind.

"Back in the spring when Renard was here," I said softly. "Before you showed me…"

"Yes?"

"You asked me to tell you the truth before you could continue; you said it wouldn't matter how I answered, so long as I was honest about it."

"I remember."

"If I ask something, will *you* do the same? Will you promise me your answer will be only the truth?"

"Of course!" she answered.

"Those images I saw—the visions I've had ever since I came up here…that was you, working inside my thoughts?"

"Yes."

I knew the answer before I asked the question, but it brought at least a small amount of relief because she didn't hesitate, not for a moment. There were other questions and I couldn't stop myself from asking them.

"If you can run around in my head, then you know how I feel; you have to know I'm in love with you, too."

"Yes, I know," she replied softly, "and it's given me more joy than you can imagine."

"Is it just my own emotions, made for the same reasons we fall in love with anyone, or do I love you because you *made* me? Is this what it seems, or an invisible spell I can't fight?"

"I'm not a witch, Evan!" she said quickly. "We can't cast stupid *spells*!"

"Just answer the question."

She smiled and cradled my face in her palms as I waited out the seconds.

"It's only you," she whispered. "None of this would be worth anything if it wasn't."

"But you could do that if you wanted to?"

"I don't really know," she replied with a strange, distant voice. "I've never tried."

I felt the doubts ease but not in the sudden, manufactured way you might expect if my relief was made by her hand alone and simply to continue an illusion. It's not an everyday thing, and we so often take for granted those small details, but trust is always won and never given. In that silent, magical moment, I felt closer to Aline than I had ever been.

"I need to know one more thing."

She leaned her head to one side and said, "What thing?"

"Did you intend to kill those men in Glasgow?"

She looked straight at me and nodded.

"Others were near, and I knew they would call the police, so I ran away before it was finished."

"What if no one else had been there?" I asked.

"They would both be dead," she replied flatly.

She sat beside me again and a wash of affection for her swept through me. I can't explain why in that particular moment, but the sensation was powerful, and I know she could feel my thoughts in hers when she turned and held me. The stark admission without remorse would have made others recoil in disgust but it had no such effect on me, and I walked without worry along a thin, invisible line separating good from evil. What she described was, in any meaningful way, attempted murder, yet I felt no revulsion.

"Death penalty for purse snatching?"

She smiled and shook her head.

"Robbery was not the only thing they had in mind for me, Evan."

Like a bow drawn over the strings of an out-of-tune violin, a screeching sound tore through my thoughts at what she clearly meant.

"What did they say to give you that impression?"

"It's not what they said," she answered. "Their thoughts were plain and obvious."

"You went inside?"

"It didn't take much effort. I've heard it before when others were threatened, but in those moments long ago, there was nothing I could do. This time it was meant for me and so I stopped it."

Perhaps she learned from her mistake when she went too far with Claude Dumont as a young girl, but the lesson wasn't lost on me and I wondered about the lingering effect on her attackers in Glasgow and how close to death she had taken *them*. They would remember that night, she said, the rest of their days and without doubt who had done those horrible things. Were the images she made them see as bad as their injuries, I asked, or was it the other way around? Aline stood to continue our walk but she turned to me and said, "They received what they deserved."

I don't know if the months she had sacrificed in a psychiatric ward were worth the effort, but it seemed as though she accepted it in the natural course: a necessary step in a long process and one taken only to protect herself. If the doctors looked and saw a treatable disorder, she argued, they would waste no time entertaining the thoughts that plagued Andre Renard, suggesting an evil serial killer looking only for more victims. I understood the same logic applied to two muggers lying in wait at a darkened bus stop.

"You didn't belong in that place," I said at last. "You weren't crazy at all—you never were."

"No," Aline replied, "but sometimes it's better to let people see what they want to see and avoid explaining things that can't be explained."

I remember considering the distance I had gone in so little time, and when she spoke with casual indifference about the manipulation of others as a defense mechanism it seemed suddenly understandable—almost normal. I asked again what she meant when she told me I "wasn't ready," but that description would wait patiently for another time when the full truth finally emerged.

15
BE CAREFUL WHAT YOU WISH FOR

FOR weeks we waited and watched, but there were no visits from the police and no further contact with Andre Renard. Though she offered an escape on two occasions, I didn't need to be saved and each day put more distance between us and the moment she showed me what she was. It would take some time before I would be allowed to see *who* she was, but I was at least smart enough to go at a slower pace and take things as they came.

As the days wore on, I found myself wondering about the nature of her strange power as curiosity and fascination with the impossible finally overran the shock and confusion of knowing it even exists. I learned not to refer casually to any of it as "magic" and invite the immediate nuclear response, and the skill became more valuable when details began to emerge slowly. I asked her if she could make people see and think things not necessarily for the purpose of warning or punishing them. When she demanded to know what I meant by it, I stupidly pointed to our own relationship and the way we interact.

"I'm not saying you need to," I began, "but if you wanted, could you slip inside my mind and shape the thoughts to steer me in a particular direction?"

She eyed me warily for a moment but I think she already knew where I was going.

"Which direction are you talking about, exactly?"

It seemed harmless enough, and with that first powerful, lurid dream in mind, I went in with a hopeful smile and the innocence that once kept me happy in my ignorance.

"Well, romantic things, I guess. If you were *in the mood*, for example, could you invade my mind and make me desire you so powerfully nothing else would matter?"

"I shouldn't have to!" she replied at once and I knew I was sailing blind into dangerous waters. "And anyway," she said, pouting, "I don't remember *you* putting up much of a fight whenever the urge arrives."

She was right, of course, but I wanted to experience something she could do that wasn't painful or horrifying—an experiment, I suppose, but one that wouldn't put me on the floor in agony.

"Yes," I persisted, "and that's all true, but I just wondered what it would feel like if you decided to pull the strings for something other than making me regret pissing you off; a better sort of demonstration, maybe?"

"It's not a silly carnival ride, Evan!"

I held up a hand in silent capitulation; if she found my questions ridiculous and immature, I understood at least enough to know leaving it alone was my best course. She looked at me for a while and I thought she was preparing for another round. Finally, she sat beside me and said, "Very well—if you absolutely have to know…"

It took a few moments but when it began the sensation was beyond my expectations. There was no sudden increase in temperature, the way the movies seem to suggest when an intimate moment approaches, but instead it was an odd wash of movement through my neck and back like nerve endings suddenly awakened. Not unpleasant or uncomfortable but enough to remind me they were there. She later told me the tingling sensations are only a mechanism to seize and hold my attention so that nothing else can interfere.

I've thought about that moment and how best to describe it to those who have never experienced such a thing, and the only way I know as an analogue might be a veil made from thin, delicate material draped over you. It lets you see movement, but only just, and it serves to insulate you from animal instincts until the moment they are released. When the veil is removed, a sudden shock of realization is powerful and singular in its purpose. The feeling wasn't so much a physical sensation but rather an unstoppable wash of pure emotion. Those twinges of desire and arousal, she said, are only extensions of a need that lives in the mind;

the goal is not immediate sexual gratification but instead an unshakable devotion and obedience to the desires of another.

I sat in silence as it came on like a wave, cresting in this moment but ebbing in the next, serving only to tease and enhance the experience. I looked at her and though she appeared no different I was consumed by an absolute and irresistible command to touch her. She moved closer but her expression remained unchanged. Aline watched closely and the power of her gaze was almost tactile and I felt her looking through me.

At last, the raw images appeared to run rampant through my mind like faded negatives being scattered on the wind, vivid enough but fleeting and incomplete. I recognized them from our earliest encounters, but the effect was powerful. She reached for my hand, guiding it to the buttons on her shirt and we began without a word. I did what she commanded only by the force of her will—precisely how and where—without regard for anything beyond obeying and satisfying her desires. I imagined it would be similar to living inside a dream but it wasn't like that at all; I was fully aware and awake, yet every movement seemed to be made as a reaction to her orders and I could think of nothing else.

It went on for a while and she later told me, "You wanted to see and feel what it's like, so I gave you the full treatment." I don't remember all of it because the pace quickened, and her dull expression changed into a powerfully erotic gaze, holding me in its grip with each movement. I did anything she wished me to do, and I went willingly to a darker place not unlike the images from that first dreamlike state in the moments before we met in a snowy field behind her house. The experience became much more than sexual release, and I felt like an instrument in her hands until we lay naked on her living room floor.

When the sensation eased I could feel myself return to where we started—once more in the quiet moments when reality assumes control. She said nothing until after we showered and dressed, but I suppose nothing needed to *be* said; I wanted to see and experience what it meant to be a willing servant to her wishes and she showed me. Today, what I experienced could be regarded more accurately as a symbol of her *restraint*. It sounds strange to portray it that way, but her demonstration was made for the purpose of showing me a benign example of her abilities and that lesson was made clear. Aline waited a while but then she took my hand in hers.

"I can make you do those things, Evan; I can hold your thoughts and compel you to want me more than anything in life, but was it ever necessary? You were interested long before I came to you in your thoughts that night."

I smiled, but her words brought another truth: I was no longer burdened by the understandable hesitance that tormented me when I came to realize what she could do with a mere thought. The incredible and unlikely power she can wield was part of us and no longer an object of fear or reproach. It didn't matter that few, if any, knew it exists or the care we would be obliged to observe to keep the secret hidden; I had gone to another place and so long as Aline was there, I knew I would never go back. Of course, the still-hidden truth she *hadn't* revealed couldn't touch me in that quiet moment, but it was always there.

It brought a quiet sense of relief, the process of becoming a different person, but the remaining, ordinary parts of our lives hadn't changed and knowing it became an anchor. I had learned not to fear her, too, and the distinction made things easier when we found ourselves in the rare moments of disagreement. It seemed as though I enjoyed a special and absolute exemption from what she could do. "Just because I can," she said, "doesn't mean I will." Aside from her extraordinary abilities, we were just another couple with all the usual joys, disputes and resolutions all couples find when they become committed to each other. Today, I am more grateful than ever.

I WENT UP to the shop on a blustery day in August to help Aline unpack new inventory and deal with the boxes while they racked their new items. On the way, as I always knew it would, the question of who and how much to tell returned. Obviously, that meant Vienne and the continued prospect of lying to her I hated to consider.

We talked about it over dinner and Aline seemed strangely calm. Instead of dire warnings and a demand for utter silence, she told me her circumstances made things different from what they had been before and with those changes, a door opened. I asked her if she really meant what it seemed; if there would come a time when my sister could be told and taken through a similar process so that she would understand, but Aline would only say it depended on the need and an inescapable scenario demanding Vienne's inclusion into our bizarre and unbelievable secret.

There were no precise conditions or events that would require such a thing, Aline said, but it was something we would think about. The idea became more immediate when Aline suggested another visit to Montreal once the holiday season died out in January.

"I know you want to tell Vienne about all this," she began, but I cut her words short.

"I'm not big on lying to my sister, Aline, but I understand why she can't know."

"Not right now," she replied with an odd and unexpected smile, "but one day, you may *have* to tell her."

"I don't understand what that means."

It was one of the many moments when my ignorance, and a process not complete, created for Aline another test of her patience, and she looked at me for a moment while she considered her response.

"This is all new to you," she began, "and I know perfectly well how strange and unbelievable it must seem. But you must trust me, Evan; I have been here before and I know what could happen if these things were revealed."

"Like it was when you brought the hammer down on Renard?"

"No," she replied at once. "It was enough to frighten him off, but that's all; he doesn't know what this is and he never will."

"I'm standing right in the middle of it and *I* don't even know what this is!"

"At the proper time," she said softly, "you will."

"I watched a fire burning without logs, and when I called Renard there wasn't much left of him; you simply aimed a thought or two and he ended up a quivering blob of shit on the floor! Is there anything more you could say to top *this*?"

"Yes," she said with a smile. "A lot more."

There is a difference between deliberate silence and the inability to speak, and that distinction was never clearer to me than it was in that moment. Despite all that had happened in the months before—indescribable effects of a supernatural power I had to experience for myself to know was no illusion—there *was* more. I thought I had done well adjusting to a tidal wave of stunning revelations that, if published to the world, would change everything we thought we knew about the paranormal and shake more than a few of society's cultural foundations into rubble. Was there anyone else who stood alone in such a place, forced by the evidence of personal experience, and struggling to reconcile the irreconcilable? Aline rails at the use of the term but in my singular corner of reality the only word that crept into every analysis I could make in my private moments was "magic."

She said "I'm not a witch" because the image points to a contemplation of good and evil as a function of religious conflict—God's power battling Satan and his servants who follow the occult code, for example. Faith has nothing to do with it, she insisted, lecturing me that magic and witches were convenient excuses for terrible acts to protect the soul. Sometimes, she said after a long pause, a chance to lash out at the devil by burning one of his minions at the stake was the only course. How beautifully ironic, I thought, knowing she could do those things many would associate with covens and malevolent practitioners of the dark arts, yet she was dismissive of the idea as reality. Still, I held a question in need of an answer if only to rationalize events that were, at their core, irrational. It was a question I would rather have avoided but such a chance was long gone and it hit me in a single, powerful blast:

What do you do when you discover magic *is* real?

I bathed in a strange sensation of belonging, at least as far as I can be allowed to borrow the term, since I was not a target for the horrors she could inflict. It felt a bit like being a civilian on a battlefield; neither a belligerent for this side or the other. I stood beside Aline, accepting my assumed role as companion to a sorceress and grateful for the distinction; if others tested her or threatened to expose what she could do, it was *they* who would pay the price. I suppose it brought a certain calm in knowing the bad people who walk in cities and prey upon the ordinary or weak would find something else if they looked and saw vulnerability. The two rough boys in Glasgow found that truth the hard way, but Aline made it more than clear there would be no frivolous use of it and only as the last of possible resorts. No carnival ride indeed.

They paused as I described that quiet conversation, and in one of her occasional moments of thoughtfulness, Mo signaled for a question. Because it was late in the night and we were getting tired, I said in a snotty, combative tone, "Hit the brakes, everybody; Miss Persimmon missed something!" She ignored the insult quite surprisingly and pulled a chair to sit directly between us. It was abrupt and unexpected because the suits always stayed on the other side of the table, and she waited a moment, looking at me while she formed her questions. "I know you won't...or can't," she began, "but in that time—after she first showed you—did you ever consider running?" I laughed a little and asked her if it would have made any difference.

Mo nodded with an unusually understanding expression and said, "Others might've tried, but I wanted to know why you did not."

The message was poorly concealed and I knew she meant Aline's influence. Were my thoughts invaded and controlled so completely, she wondered, that any chance of breaking free was an unreachable goal? She wasn't asking to test my resolve or tempt me with the possibility; Mo was simply fascinated by my choices and from them the clearest declaration of love and no possibility of betrayal. I think she changed a little that night and I lost some of my disdain for her in the process. There were moments when Mo saw more than Burke, Halliwell, or even Berezan ever could, and a single, almost imperceptible nod told me she understood.

16
BURKE FINDS HIS WAY TO COLWYN BAY

THE sky surrendered to heavy overcast and a lonely drizzle when Aline decided to sign the paperwork for a new custodial service Margaret wanted to try out. We drove up in the afternoon to sunbreaks along the coast sending beautiful rays of gold and yellow in cheerful swaths across the highway. For once, I had the presence of mind to pull my phone from a pocket and click photos out the window with the intent of sending them to Vienne, and in that brief second or two, I felt different somehow: content and at peace with the world for the first time in a long time. Aline just smiled and I know she could feel it by remote inside my thoughts, but I didn't care in the slightest. When we parked and scurried against the gathering wind a new surprise waited—another change moment.

No one noticed them until I turned from inspecting new sweaters on one of the shop's floor display tables as a pale, balding man in his mid-forties stood with hands stuffed inside his pockets at the checkout counter. Another walked slowly along the racks, pretending to look at Helly Hansen foul weather jackets and a third figure stood quietly behind and to the first man's left. Aline appeared from the back office, and she looked at me immediately.

"Good afternoon, Miss Lloyd," the older one said as he offered his card. "My name is William Marsden. May we have a moment of your time?"

One of them stepped lightly between us with an extended palm. It was abrupt and awkward but he smiled and said, "You're the American lad!" I tried to move around him but he grabbed and shook my hand vigorously, if only to distract and short-circuit any move I might make toward Marsden. Aline just smiled and motioned them toward the office. At once, Marsden paused and gestured toward one he called Kevin.

"We don't need to trouble Mr. Morgan with all this; could you look after him for a moment?"

It was clear what that meant, but my racing heart and heightened senses were more powerful than his false consideration.

"It's no trouble at all," I said with as even a tone as I could manage, and Aline finished the thought.

"I would rather he stayed."

Marsden returned the automatic smile bureaucrats practice because they're taught and believe the appearance of civility in an otherwise contentious or distasteful setting is an important behavioral distinction separating them from the unwashed masses.

"Ah. Well, Mr. Morgan is certainly welcome to join and observe!"

The poorly hidden note was meant to imply I had no authority or particular standing in the matter, and I followed them to the shop's office where Marsden and one of his men waited until Aline closed the door.

"Now then," he began, but she cut him off immediately.

"If you want to discuss Andre Renard's visit, please have the courtesy of beginning it without a lie, Mr. Burke."

I expected him to fumble for a response, or to show at least an understandable degree of confusion, but his expression changed as though somebody had pushed an unseen button when the suddenly needless pretense dissolved. I watched closely but he was neither angry nor even embarrassed. Instead, he showed only relief and I didn't know enough to realize why.

"We would arrive here at some point, I suppose," he said with a smile.

Aline just looked at him, and I noticed her eyes never blinked.

"Alan Burke," he said at last. "I won't waste your time with department names or mysterious, hidden offices for which I am responsible because you've never heard of them."

"I've heard of Special Branch," I said at once, but Burke only smiled.

"A necessary fiction to ensure the cooperation of your local constabulary. We are representatives of Her Majesty's government and that is really all I'm at liberty to reveal. May we proceed?"

I wondered how much time and contrived cat-and-mouse had been averted when Aline tore away Burke's "William Marsden" façade from the start, forcing the process ahead without a goofy charade. Burke seemed just as happy about it, and he held out a palm until the other man filled it with a small notepad. Burke thumbed through it for a moment until Aline nodded, and then it was his turn.

"Inspector Renard had a very interesting tale to tell," he continued, "very interesting indeed."

"I'm sure he did," Aline replied, "but I wonder how *you* came by it, Mr. Burke?"

"Oh, we are provided with lots of interesting things, Miss Lloyd, but I'm not certain its origin can make any meaningful difference here."

"Hurd," she said suddenly, "and he told…a military officer called Halliwell."

Burke's face went blank. He stared at her for a moment and there was only a slight pause until the clawing, screeching sensation of fear swept through my mind again when I realized she was inside *his*—and transmitting it to me in a shared thought so real it felt like my own. It was the first time Aline had let me see and feel the thoughts of another through her—an unnatural and frightening eavesdrop that brought a shiver up my spine. She looked at me and I nodded very slightly to signal I understood, but Burke seemed like a man suddenly unable to speak his own language. It went on like that for a few moments, and I know Aline sat quietly so he would know who and what he was dealing with. At last, the sensation eased and I could no longer feel his thoughts.

It must be said Burke is hardly the image of an imposing physical presence, but his intellect is powerful and it shone when he recovered so quickly. Others would likely have cut and run, hoping to plan another way, but not Burke. Instead, he placed his hands once more into his pockets and that "cold oatmeal" smile of his returned.

"We didn't believe his story, by the way," Burke said with a new, more familiar tone. "But now it would seem Detective Inspector Renard's fantastical narrative wasn't so absurd after all, was it?"

"I didn't ask him to start all this, Mr. Burke," Aline said. "Those things in Brugge happened but Renard misunderstood."

"What was it he misunderstood, if I may ask?"

"All of it," she replied simply. "He is convinced I murdered his friend for no reason."

"Indeed he does, but it was a rather odd indictment, considering he now refuses to speak of it entirely," Burke said with an obvious, questioning frown.

"What are you talking about?" I asked, and to my surprise, he sat on Margaret's desk to answer the way people do when they're about to take you into their confidence. Tedious though I now know Burke can sometimes be, the man is a cool runner.

"Oh, we learned of his condition afterward, but by then, poor old Andre… well, he didn't have much to say, did he?"

"I don't understand," I said, but it was clear Aline's prediction Renard would lose interest was correct, and it became one of the red flags people like Burke see better than others.

"No one spends more than a decade collecting information to lay blame for murder, only to reverse his position almost overnight. Inspector Renard suddenly wanted nothing more to do with this so that his life could return to normal. Well…normal in the relative sense, of course."

"And Dumont?" I asked.

"We thought at first Renard might've been telling tales, but the scans showed significant distress throughout Monsieur Dumont's cerebral cortex and *nobody* can pretend something like that."

"So?"

"So, Mr. Morgan, a discreet phone call to his old mates here, some of our own monitoring software there, and we saw enough to understand there was something unusual flitting about inside Andre's head, if you'll pardon the expression. We went over to Belgium but he refused to talk. He told us to sod off and leave him alone, in fact, and…"

"And that's when *you* saw his files?"

"To be precise, certain functionaries in government had them already, but yes, we were given copies and that's when the numbers began to add up all wrong."

Aline knew he meant Hurd. Through it all, she sat quietly listening, but it was clear she regarded the exercise as a waste of time.

"What numbers, Mr. Burke?" she asked.

"To begin with," he replied, "there is the question of Claude Dumont's injuries. We were given the MRI results and our pathologists agreed at once: there is no medical explanation for a human brain to have suffered what they referred to in the notes as a radical and abnormal proliferation of subarachnoid hemorrhages."

"I'm not a doctor," she said, and Burke waited for her to finish a sentence she had no intention of continuing. I thought he might take the bait but he went right on without a pause.

"It's not a question of the diagnosis, Miss Lloyd; we are speaking of *cause*, not effect."

"Dumont was very agitated when he attacked me," she replied simply. "Perhaps his brain was stressed beyond its limits."

Still Burke wasn't fazed.

"We watched the video segments, Miss Lloyd. Dumont went a bit too far in his zeal to speak with you, but that was hardly a life-threatening attack."

"It was to me," she answered in a precise and even tone.

Burke blinked a few times, but it was clear he was getting nowhere, and Aline hadn't shown the slightest sign of weakness. He turned away for a moment but his smile was gone.

"We can return to the injuries another time, but I should tell you our lads were very keen to hear your account of the sudden downblast of air Dumont described; so powerful and focused, he said, it seemed like…what did he say, 'an invisible rocket engine'?"

"Perhaps a weather anomaly," she replied. "There's nothing so extraordinary about a sudden wind, is there?"

Burke waited to see if Aline would show signs of anxiety—the nervous reaction of one running out of answers—but she stared at him with an expression free of emotion.

"It is possible the description was overstated from Dumont's excited condition," he said, "but there was also your unfortunate encounter at a Glasgow bus stop; we saw the reports of that misadventure as well."

"Those men weren't looking for answers," she answered coolly. "I have the photos of my face they took at hospital, if you've not seen them."

"We saw, and one can hardly blame you for defending yourself, but there was and remains no rational explanation for the condition in which you left them, is there? The emergency staff at West Glasgow saw something none of them could diagnose."

"I can't help what they saw."

"But then you told investigating authorities of a blackout; a sudden dance with amnesia brought about by an understandably traumatic event."

"Yes?" she replied coolly, and I found myself looking at the exchange as I would a tense chess match with something on the line much deeper than pride or notoriety. I watched Burke and his knowing grin made it clear he understood Aline wasn't going to budge. I know it didn't surprise him and he went on as though reciting from a lawyer's notes.

"In each case—Brugge and the bus stop—you were in close proximity, but there's still more. I don't pretend to hold any sorrow for the two in Glasgow," he said with feigned seriousness, "but even *you* must admit their astonishing recovery and utter lack of identifiable cause defies all logic."

"If you say so," she said with a subtle shrug, but Burke was on a roll.

"I can also tell you the emergency physician's notes declared with absolute certainty their very painful brush with death would have become permanent had they not been discovered and treated so quickly."

Aline said nothing, and through the moments of awkward silence, Burke waited until it was obvious she couldn't be pushed.

"And now, after pouring out an amazing story better suited to a suspense film, Andre Renard comes to Denbighshire, only to spin about quite abruptly and refuse to discuss the matter further. The collection of documents filled with dots he took such deliberate care connecting is suddenly the last thing on Earth he's willing to talk about. So, Miss Lloyd," he continued, "there you have it, and one can easily see our dilemma, hmm?"

"I don't see a dilemma at all," she replied.

"No?" Burke answered. "Well then, let's add up what we *do* know, shall we?"

Burke grabbed his index finger and looked at the ceiling for a moment before he began. I thought it a bit dramatic and amateurish, but I have since learned there is nothing amateur about Alan Burke.

"An old man in Belgium has a bit of a contretemps with a Welsh girl on holiday called Aline Marie Lloyd, but he drops very suddenly dead when no less than thirty-seven blood vessels in his brain burst simultaneously and for no apparent reason."

She didn't move and her expression remained unchanged as Burke went on.

"Six years later, a pair of mildly insane lads with too much drink and too few brain cells assault the very same Aline Lloyd at a bus stop in Scotland, only to find themselves at death's door with injuries Glasgow's best doctors cannot explain. The chances…well, it's got to be more than any of the oddsmakers at the derby would take, doesn't it?"

I know Aline didn't need help, but the words poured out before I could stop them.

"We've been through this before, Mr. Burke, and nothing changes: Aline hasn't committed a crime and there's nothing you can charge her with, so…"

"I do apologize, Mr. Morgan," he interrupted quickly, "but you've mistaken our purpose. We are not policemen, you see, so any idea of arrest is not our goal."

"Then why *are* you here?" I demanded. "Renard tried to muscle her and he was wrong. Now, you and your men are doing the same thing but you have no case! Just leave her alone and go home; there's nothing more to see."

The room was silent and still she showed no emotion or even interest. It was beautiful, in a horrible-sounding way, but watching her in that moment made me appreciate the nature of one who controls so much yet resists deploying it. If armed with her abilities, plagued by my own fears and short temper, I might've given Burke and his bodyguards a tiny glimpse, but she simply waited. He waited, too, but soon the calm returned and with it, his final pitch.

"Renard wanted somebody to explain why a lifelong friend died. That was all he needed, but when he looked closer—with the help of a contact at Interpol, I might add—he found something much deeper, didn't he?"

Aline raised her eyebrows in the way we do to signal little or no interest, but Burke didn't miss a beat.

"What did you say to him, Miss Lloyd; what did you see when you were prying about inside *his* thoughts? He moved away recently to the south of France, we're told, but nothing can remove the terror he takes with him."

I looked at her when it became clear Burke knew enough to zero in on her powerful abilities.

"I'm not sure there's anything more I can do, Mr. Burke," she said evenly.

"Yes, I see," Burke said with that idiotic, upside-down smile he wears while thinking in silence, "and that is a pity, isn't it? We rather hoped you could shed some light on two unique and separate events you were directly involved with, one of which resulted in a fatality."

He glanced at her one last time, motioning for the others to follow, but he paused for a moment and said in a low, even voice, "It's no good, you know. All this evasive pretense is little more than delaying the inevitable."

"The inevitable?" I asked quickly.

"Our operation looks into the things that are widely held to be impossible, Mr. Morgan. As you can surely imagine the importance of dialogue cannot be overstated. We would rather keep this as only a conversation, so I do hope Aline will reconsider."

"Maybe I missed something, but did that line about dialogue just turn into a threat, Mr. Burke?" I replied.

His smile evaporated quickly, and I wondered if I found the limit of his patience.

"The work must be done, Mr. Morgan, by collegial discussion if possible, but our responsibility to the people of the United Kingdom may require a more purposeful approach."

"Ah," I said with a nod, "I thought so."

Aline was silent as Burke strolled slowly from the office, stopping near the counter to fasten the snaps on his coat where Margaret waited with a customer.

"You have my card," he said, nodding and smiling. "If you'd like to think about it and ring us later, we shall keep a line open for you, hmm?"

We watched them go, and I think Aline's relief was confined to the unlikelihood Margaret or the floor girls heard any of it. She returned to the office to grab a sales brochure from the new cleaning firm, and then she asked if I'd like to walk along the waterfront and take some air. We turned right and then right again, but she stopped in the cool afternoon breeze coming in off the ocean and smiled at me. I remember shaking my head in wonder at how coolly she waited after so harrowing an experience, but the only frayed nerves were clearly mine.

"That little bastard Renard," I said, snarling involuntarily. "He sent copies to this guy Hurd, whoever *he* is, long before he came up here."

"Yes," Aline replied, "and they obviously had a word with Mr. Burke."

"Who *are* these assholes?" I asked. "MI5 or something?"

"I don't think so," she answered. "I could feel Burke's thoughts and he was honest about one thing—they're not policemen. His associates may have been at one point, but I think they were military because the little one standing with Burke reacted very powerfully when I mentioned Halliwell."

"You heard *his* thoughts, too?"

"They were impossible to miss."

I smiled and looked away for a moment as the concept gelled in my mind, and a clue emerged I wouldn't have considered before. If the cops in Llangollen had been kept deliberately at a distance, then Burke's hidden agency was not worried about spies or terrorists.

"Have you heard of the other two—Hurd and Halliwell?" I asked.

"Not until I could hear their names in Burke's thoughts," she answered. "We can search government websites tonight, but I would be very surprised to see either of them appear."

"How does this connect to Renard?" I wondered.

"We're missing something," Aline replied. "Burke's thoughts weren't clear enough to reveal more than Halliwell's position as a soldier."

"Is Hurd military, too?"

She shook her head and said, "I couldn't hear anything beyond his name."

Renard's pile of documents had clearly won the attention of somebody with considerable authority, and once more Aline was under scrutiny. We stood at a tenuous place where the past wormed its way into the present with questions she was unwilling to answer, at least for unknown officials who live in secret worlds. The tenacious old detective took a head-on approach when he went to Aline's farm, and regardless of what he knew (or *thought* he knew), Renard was still grossly overmatched. Burke, on the other hand, enjoyed the full weight of the government and frightening him off was unlikely in the extreme.

ALINE REFUSED TO reconsider, and Burke seemed to disappear as quickly as he and his men arrived. I called Jeremy to ask his police officer friend, but all *he* had was the sudden meeting at their station with people from Special

Branch and nothing more. It was a reasonable conclusion Burke returned to London for a while, but we both knew that condition was temporary.

On a hunch I decided to dig a little and see if there was help available in other places. Aline was away in Chester for the day helping Margaret get her sister settled into a new flat, so I opened my old contacts notebook.

The scrawled names and numbers represented colleagues from my first days at the NTSB, but others were friends of friends I had run across on occasion, and one of them—a retired SEAL named Andy Leach—spent time as a military liaison between the Navy and a handful of NATO military units. He was attached for a brief time to a Special Air Service group carrying out pre-op raids in the hours before the first Gulf War; if anyone could make inquiries to identify a member of Britain's celebrated commando unit at the least, and possibly Hurd as well, he would be my choice.

When he answered, I learned Andy was in Gainesville teaching NROTC students at the University of Florida. We went through the usual catch-up process, exchanging stories about those with whom we had shared experiences, but the conversation worked its way around to the reason for my call and Andy's hushed question about the nature of my search. "Is this in the open," he asked, "or down in the weeds?" When I said it was best kept between us, the news didn't faze him and he simply replied, "No problem, Evan; I just needed to know how to work it."

"I'm trying to get an identification on three guys," I began. "Two are Brits—possibly inside Special Branch—and a retired Belgian police inspector."

"Names?"

"Hurd; maybe connected to MI5, plus another called Halliwell. No first names, but we believe Halliwell is a soldier. The detective's name is Andre Renard."

"Wait," Andy said at once. "Are you talking about *Stuart* Halliwell?"

"No idea," I replied. "All we have is the last name."

"I don't know if he's the same guy you're looking for," he continued, "but we had a liaison officer named Stuart Halliwell with my unit during Gulf One—an SAS guy. It was an exchange deal; I went with his squad for a while and he came with us after that. I lost track of him when we rotated back to San Diego, but last I heard he was living in Munich, coordinating covert stuff between SAS and the German Police's elite GSG 9 anti-terrorism guys about ten years ago."

"Could be him," I said as Andy continued.

"I still have a few eyes and ears inside the Pentagon and one at State; I'll see if they have anything on this guy Hurd and the Belgian. Give me a few minutes and I'll call you back; some of these folks are a little hard to track down."

I didn't tell him where I was and he wouldn't want to know anyway. When he called back an hour later, I reached for a pen and pad to keep notes.

"Okay," he began, "my contact at State has a Gregory Hurd on the roster of Brits she deals with sometimes," Andy began. "Officially he's listed as 'special advisor to the Director General for Roads,' but that turned out to be a ghost entry."

"What do you mean?" I asked.

"When she looked him up in a general personnel registry, there's no such position and his name doesn't appear anywhere in that department's directory."

"Is there any way to cross-reference against other British government agencies?" I asked.

"I didn't have to," he replied. "My contact asked around to some of her guys while I checked with mine at the Pentagon, and Hurd's name showed on some internal documentation with an address in Westminster."

"Does that give us anything useful?"

"Gregory Hurd is Whitehall, Evan; he's way the hell up a hidden food chain connected to their version of the Defense Department. No one knows exactly where, but it's obvious he's a heavy hitter who doesn't have shit to do with the roads."

I was jotting down Andy's words furiously as the blurred picture began to clear.

"This is good stuff, and I'm on the right track, but how about Andre Renard—anything on him?"

"Nope," he replied. "My contact at State had nothing, and one of her archive guys at the Pentagon asked around, but the only thing *he* had that was even close is a civilian contractor working for Dassault Systèmes at a Belgian Air Force base named Valerie Renard—a woman in her thirties. Sorry, Evan, but that's all I could find."

"It's a lot more than I had an hour ago," I replied. "And thanks, Andy; this answers a lot of questions."

We promised to keep in touch, knowing it was little more than polite obligation, but I had learned a few things about the utility of access to a network of professionals, and I was determined that if Andy ever called me one day, I would do whatever it took to reciprocate.

WHEN ALINE RETURNED from her trip to Chester, I told her the details of my conversation with Andy Leach.

"There are people from my past I wanted to speak with—ex-military, most of them—to see if they could help me find out about Hurd and Halliwell but also Renard to show us how he got inside the British government."

"And?"

"My friend knew a Stuart Halliwell from way back; said he was SAS, too. I don't know for sure if that Halliwell is the same individual in Burke's mind, but the coincidence was too obvious to ignore."

"And Hurd?"

"That's where it gets weird," I replied. "Government org charts show a Gregory Hurd as some sort of advisor to the UK's Transportation Department, or whatever it's really called, but that's an elaborate cover story; Hurd is deep inside the British Defense apparatus."

"A bureaucrat," she said.

"Yes, but they couldn't find anything on Renard or his connection to Hurd. If you didn't get anything from Burke's thoughts, I don't know what else we can do."

Aline sat back and looked up to the ceiling. I thought she was only pondering the question but her expression changed and showed what I can only describe as resignation. I saw it and asked if she was all right.

"I can't promise anything," she said with an obvious note of caution, "but there may be a way."

"Okay, so how do we do that?" I asked, not realizing what it meant to her, and she hesitated as though the answer lived in a place she wanted to avoid.

"You remember why I went to Belgium when I was younger?"

"A road trip to see about a job, right?"

"Partially, yes, but I went there to visit a friend called Marion Van Den Broeck. We were at university together, but she took a job at a firm in Brugge and we kept in touch…well, until the incident with Claude Dumont."

"Did something change?"

"Yes, but it wasn't Marion's fault. I couldn't go back there, and she thought it was something *she* did, but…"

"But you couldn't explain any of it and for a lot of reasons."

"Exactly. We lost contact for a long time but reconnected a few years ago when she got engaged. It's better now, and she's come up to visit a couple of times, but whenever she invited me down to Brugge I always found an excuse not to go."

"And now?"

"Marion and her husband moved to Brussels last year. I've been meaning to go see her, but then you arrived suddenly so I've had…other things to do."

"You should plan a road trip—there's nothing in Brussels to bother you, right?"

"No, but the reason I bring it up is because Marion works for the Belgian government now; she's a manager in their Treasury Department."

"Should that mean something?" I asked. "Sorry, but I don't get how that moves us any closer."

Aline sat forward and looked straight at me.

"She has access to a lot of confidential information, Evan."

"I'm sure she does, but…"

"Multiple systems connect one department with another, at least at her level, and that includes law enforcement personnel. There has to be something inside one of them that can tell us about Andre Renard."

The picture became clear in the expression she wore, obliging Aline to burden a friend with tasks that could be construed as unethical at best and even criminal if taken too far.

"She doesn't know anything about the Claude Dumont incident, does she?"

"No."

"I'm guessing the same thing holds true on your abilities—about what you can do?"

"You're the only one who knows about that, Evan."

"Well, me and Renard—maybe Burke, too," I replied with a grin. "I think he got enough of a peek at that mind reading thing you pulled at your shop."

"I suppose so," she replied, but her tone had changed and she spoke at a near whisper.

"I'm sorry, Aline," I offered immediately. "I shouldn't have put it like that."

She smiled and took my hand.

"It's all right," she said. "I should be able to approach Marion without going into much detail."

"What happens if she asks the wrong sorts of questions?"

"Let's take this one step at a time," she answered.

"When did you plan on contacting her?"

"Right now."

Aline dialed and when Marion answered, they spent twenty minutes catching up and finding again one of the places where friends go to firm up their bonds and reassure each other time's passage hasn't changed things between them. It was interesting to hear and the honest, genuine voice of one so different from any other was surprising. I don't know why I thought of it in that way, but the secrets hiding inside *make* Aline different, even if no one else can know.

At last, the moment of opportunity was revealed when Marion told Aline about her position at the Belgian Treasury and with it a clear understanding of her authority. Aline waited through the descriptions of what Marion did, talking shop the way kindred professionals do, and primarily to avoid the perception she had called only to enlist Marion's help. I suppose that was true, but reconnecting with a friend made Aline's ultimate goal something that could wait a while.

At last she mentioned a frustrated search for a Belgian national, and when Marion offered to help find Renard, Aline nodded at me silently to signal the process was beginning. The first-pass inspection revealed more than one Andre Renard, but armed with enough information to provide differentiators, Marion said she would probably have something within a day or two, and they hung up after promises to meet up in Brussels.

We knew a rundown on Renard might solve the riddle and reveal a pathway through to Gregory Hurd, but the essential information still eluded us from my conversations with Andy Leach. There was no longer any doubt as to Burke's influence and power, but with Halliwell's addition, the intelligence angle had taken a darker, more menacing turn: Special Branch or otherwise, an ex-SAS commando's involvement made it clear the British government had given Burke a significant level of discretionary authority and with it an ability to move unfettered.

Did Burke's horsepower extend to lethal force, I wondered? The pains they took to keep his organization carefully hidden in the shadows suggested something more than traditional surveillance duties of groups responsible for national security and intelligence gathering. Unless Burke showed again, we were left with little more than supposition.

AFTER TWO EVENTLESS days, Marion called while we were on the road home from a shopping excursion to Wrexham. Aline pulled over so we could change positions and give her the freedom to listen and take notes without distraction, but the call didn't last long. When she disconnected and looked at me, I was sure we were out of luck, but she smiled and said, "Andre's story wasn't hard for Marion to find." I asked her what that meant, and she began a narrative that brought at least some satisfaction and understanding.

Renard himself was unremarkable, and even his connection to Hurd turned out to be ordinary and free of the intrigues I'd expected to hear. Instead of a shared experience in a distant, unpublished past colored by sneaky bilateral operations no one ever hears about, Hurd and Renard had become relatives by marriage. Marion was thorough and followed the clues in a simple notice taken from a Liège newspaper nearly eight years earlier of the impending wedding joining a British diplomat and a local girl. The groom, Keith Hurd, was Gregory's youngest son and a junior actuary in the British Embassy's vast array of trade missions. His soon-to-be bride—a graduate student named Camille Jenneau—also happened to be Andre Renard's niece. I thought about that for a moment as the picture emerged.

Over time, Renard and Hurd clearly developed a friendship, and from it an avenue opened few enjoy. Somewhere along the process, Renard must have been given enough of a glimpse into Hurd's world that brought the comfort of knowing a senior operative within the British Defence Ministry had his back in the event anything went wrong. It wasn't the kind of relationship one would likely need, given their respective positions and nationalities, but Renard knew enough to reach across the English Channel before his ill-fated trip to Denbighshire on the chance he would need additional, political firepower. It seemed a bit excessive to me, but there was an understandable wisdom to it, and we wondered what Renard knew about Hurd that *couldn't* be found in Marion's database investigations.

"There has to be more to it than that," I declared. "Renard's a cop—why would he feel the need to bolster his position by calling Hurd?"

Aline didn't know, and we were left to speculate about something deeper, but at least we understood how they came within one another's sphere of influence. We found ourselves closer to the end story than we had been, but it only invited more questions about Burke. A lone detective trying to find meaning in his friend's unexplained death was a solvable problem because he had mounted a search completely on his own initiative. It didn't matter that Renard's former position as a cop wasn't enough to finish the job when matched against Aline's power. Burke, on the other hand, was differently placed. We would wait but the inevitable conclusion was obvious to Aline, even if I couldn't see it, and with that truth another step in a long, strange process began.

17
TEGWEN MERCH NYFAIN

NOVEMBER arrived and the leaves were nearly gone as we walked among the trees on our customary morning stroll. I pointed to them and wondered what she thought of our life together that grew from origins in that very place. Aline turned and held my hands in hers.

"I knew you would stay, but after Renard's involvement I wasn't at all sure how it would turn out."

"And now?"

"We are exactly where we're supposed to be, Evan," she said. "Where we will always be."

It was a simple reply made without hesitation, and her words seemed to wash over me like a warm tide. It felt wonderful to hear them, for all the reasons it should, but there was more than romantic attachment and I can only describe that moment as the feeling when fears and doubts are suddenly beyond your thoughts. She didn't mean a path through the woods where we went each day but rather our place beside each other where only we could go.

We went into town and strolled along the river walk, free of tourists and clatter of the summer season, and by any measure I was no longer a strange foreigner. Glances toward the Berwyn Mountains seemed as familiar as those from my childhood in Batavia where Vienne and I ran and played. I mention this only to remind myself how quickly things change and the transition from calm and quiet contentment that's so often fragile and temporary.

As it had been in the days after Andre Renard went home to Belgium, there was no sign of Burke or his people. Well, I should say no sign we could *detect*. Aline's powerful "thought radar" hadn't gone off suddenly, and it became clear a waiting game was being played out. We knew he'd be back eventually, but I was grateful for the break and a chance to live without fear or suspicion for a change.

I wanted Aline to show me new and exciting examples of what she could do but not by the painful method she released in my living room. I decided to leave it alone for fear it would seem a frivolous ploy for cheap entertainment—which it absolutely was—but also because she scared the hell out of me and I wanted nothing to do with a repeat at that level. Still, there was more to learn and her words echoed in my thoughts as I considered all that had happened and what it would mean. We watched the needles of sunlight pry their way through thick clouds at dusk, but the need to move out of a haze made by simple ignorance pushed me finally to speak.

"How did you talk your way out of that hospital?" I asked. "It doesn't matter to me, and I know that sounds terrible, but you didn't black out for a second at that bus stop, did you?"

"Is that what you believe?" she asked suddenly. "That I'm an insane murderer who kills for sport?"

I heard the echoes of betrayal in her voice, but that was not what I meant, and it felt strange to explain what I thought had become obvious.

"No, I don't believe that, but there's more to this than you're telling me, and you said so yourself."

"Did I?" she replied with a noticeable tone of defiance.

"Yes, you did," I answered. "You said I wasn't ready but knowing what you can do makes me wonder when I *will* be ready."

I was prying without regard to consequence, but what she had already demonstrated brought us to a new and coldly different place.

"I can't imagine anything more weird and unlikely but there must be *something*, so what is it, Aline?"

She looked away, and it was obvious we waited at the end of one mystery as another was about to begin. Time, and our shared experiences, tested me, but I hadn't wavered or turned away, and it was a bit insulting to think she couldn't bring herself to open that final door and show me *who* she was. I watched her in those last seconds, tormented by worry and doubt, never suspecting what waited on the other side. I wasn't afraid but I had to know the final, most guarded secret she held. I know she'd hoped it wouldn't come up again, but when it did she was ready: at last, it was time.

Aline stared at me for a moment before steering me toward her house. When she turned to me again I saw the lovely, comforting face I'd come to adore and in her eyes no trace of malice or ill will.

"My time in hospital, and the things I had to do to protect myself, are not what I meant when I told you there is something more."

"But I thought…"

She held up a hand to shift the discussion where she always knew it would land.

"When I showed you that first time," she began, "it was necessary so you would understand the things that brought Renard up here. It was the only way because no one believes that sort of thing without seeing and experiencing it."

"I hear that," I replied with a smile.

"I didn't want this for you, Evan," she said softly. "I'd hoped we could live a normal life; to love each other and grow old together. Renard put things in motion we cannot avoid any longer because Burke isn't going to leave it alone the way the inspector did."

The narrative was needless because I'd lived through the details she described. Still, I knew enough to keep my mouth shut as she continued.

"I showed you those images and made you feel pain because there was not enough time to explain and let you adjust easily. Now, everything is going to change again, and I need you to see and understand what I could never tell you before."

"I'm not afraid, Aline," I said bravely, but she just smiled and placed her palm gently against my cheek.

"I know, but this is different, and what you know about me in this moment and the things I can do will seem insignificant an hour from now."

"It can't be *that* bad," I said with a smirk to show her I could take it like a man.

"I know you worried about my sanity, but it's nothing to do with this. You will fight against something impossible for you to accept—something that cannot be—until it becomes plain and inescapable. When that moment arrives, there will be fear and confusion but *you* will become a different person, too."

I felt a chill when she asked me if I was truly ready because there would be no way back, no chance to unlearn what she was about to reveal. I told her the question was a formality; I had no intention of turning away, but Aline already knew.

"Do you have to pee?" she asked abruptly, and the question seemed absurd and out of place.

"Well, no, not right now…"

"This will take a while, Evan. I can't have any distractions, so if you need to go, now is the time."

"I don't have to pee!" I said with a laugh, but she could hear my nerves fraying in that odd, uncomfortable place between the things we know and those we are about to discover.

"Come on, then," she said as she took my hand. "I want you to come to bed with me."

"Wait; right *now*?" I said, but she laughed and pinched my side.

"Not in that way! But it is important for you to be relaxed completely; no clothes to distract you and just our skin touching so you will feel at ease the way you did when you were a baby."

I nodded and we walked hand in hand to her bedroom, undressing in the fading light. Aline climbed slowly onto her bed and knelt where she propped her pillows against the headboard, motioning for me to lie on my back. She slid her legs down each side of my body, pulling me toward her until the back of my head rested against her breasts. She brushed back my hair for a moment, cradling my head in her hands, and I could feel the tension and worry begin to ease as though drawn away by an invisible force. It occurred to me Aline's power was at work once more, but it didn't matter, and I had no reason to complain. I reached for her hand because I couldn't see her face behind me.

"If Renard hadn't come up here to start all this, would you still be showing me this today?"

"No," she replied flatly. "It's a horrible thing to say, but I never intended to tell you about *any* of this."

"*Ever?*" I asked.

"What I am," she said in a near whisper, "is so far from your reality, it would be wrong to burden you with the knowledge unless I had no other option. You struggled when I showed you my abilities, but this…it will be much harder still for you to accept."

"You make it sound as if you're some kind of alien. I hope you don't grow two more heads or sprout dragon wings."

She leaned forward and placed a soft, gentle kiss on my forehead.

"When we first met in the wood, I wondered about your family and how long it's been since they left Wales."

"Yes."

"You asked me if I was a student of history; do you remember my answer?"

"You said, 'I *am* history,' which I thought was a little weird, but…"

"It was a mistake to say it that way, but I didn't think we would ever speak of it again."

"And now?"

"Now that everything has changed," she continued, "what I couldn't tell you then is something I *must* show you tonight. I lied to you about what happened in Brugge, but I will never do that again; you need to see what this is…who I am."

I took in a deep breath and nodded when she paused for a moment to offer a last chance for me to remain innocent.

"When you see…when you *understand*, there's no way back to where you are in this moment, Evan. You can never forget or pretend not to know, and if you don't want this after all, then say so right now."

"I'm not leaving and I'm not afraid," I replied firmly. "Show me, so we can get past it and move on."

"Then it's time," she said at last. "The images will seem strange and foreign, but in time you will understand them. This is just the beginning, a first of many journeys. Be patient and all of it will make sense in time."

"Will it hurt?" I asked innocently. "The way it did when you first showed me?"

"Not at all," she answered quickly. "Relax now; it will be a bit like a vivid dream, but we'll be able to speak to each other. You can ask questions as we go because I will see what *you* see. Are you ready?"

"I'm ready."

AFTER ALINE SHOWED me a relatively tame example of her abilities, I was sure there was nothing left in life that might leave me in awe, but the presumption was made too soon. Another mystery—another secret—waited to be discovered. I told her I was ready (and I believed it), but behind me Aline came at last to her own decision point and another fork in life's road that required action.

I take deliberate care to remember these things because I spent too long seeing it from only my own, limited perspective. It was selfish and inconsiderate, perhaps, but without real understanding I had little choice. As I struggled just to accept her incredible powers of the mind, *she* fought a hidden battle against an inevitable day when her true identity would be pulled from its hiding place and laid at my feet. Aline knew the risk, but our future together compelled her to what she once refused to reveal. It was getting dark outside but she turned on no lights or lit even one of her many candles. It was "better this way," she insisted, and I went along at her direction without a word.

It began with a physical sensation I still can't fully describe: a strange feeling, like cool fluid flowing through my veins, spreading out from my head and down through my torso to my extremities as the first images began to emerge. I thought perhaps my imagination was anticipating—filling in the blanks—but it wasn't that at all. She didn't tell me before we started, and I shouldn't have been surprised by it, but there were so much more than visual cues. She said I would *feel* things—that I could smell and taste them, too. I waited, watching as my understanding of life changed, and when the objects around me began to clear in my vision, it was crisp and different from the vague images of an ordinary dream.

I saw people across a broad patch of bare dirt, but they were dressed in odd costumes and their words were distant—unintelligible. The smell of smoke met me at once and with it the crackling sound of a carefully kept fire. I saw houses left and right, but they were little more than large huts and circular in their construction with heavily thatched roofs at a severe pitch to form a distinctive, conical shape, like a giant Hershey's Kiss, perhaps. Between them, people moved through, yet they didn't notice me. It seemed like a clip from a documentary or dramatic history series describing a place long ago in a time I couldn't recognize by any outward signs.

I felt a cool breeze moving past me and above, the sun was blotted out by heavy overcast that seemed to hug gentle, barren hills nearby. It took a moment or two before I heard an odd echo, as though from a recording being run backward, until at last I recognized Aline's voice calling out.

"Evan, can you hear me?"

"Yes," I mumbled stupidly.

"What do you see?" she asked, but still her voice was distant.

"A village, I think—huts and people moving around a compound," I answered. "What is this place?"

"Watch a while," she said, "I'll explain when we finish."

The images faded and re-emerged, but each time it was different. I saw a woman's face appear more than once and her importance was somehow obvious, even if it remained strange and undefined. I saw a group gathered in a glen near an ancient, gnarled tree, watching as an elderly man with a snow-white beard reached upward to the sky. As he spoke, the others replied in what seemed a bizarre conversation with no one.

"Can you see the old man, Evan?"

"I see him."

"He is very important, so watch carefully; he will speak to us soon."

More images passed through like slides in a presentation, but I could feel physical sensations as minute and precise as the uneven ground beneath my feet, cloth against my skin or the sound of rain as more images showed a different place, and I knew without being told time had passed. In an open area bordered by thin plates of slate half-buried vertically in the soil, the old man, wrapped in a heavy, beige-colored robe with folds gathered around his neck, leaned against a smooth wooden staff as he spoke. Beside me three others not more than fifteen years of age sat in a close group to listen.

His language was unlike any I had ever heard, and it lilted like a song filled with odd phonemes from an alien place I couldn't know. He appeared again in a new image but speaking only to me with a solemn expression meant to hold my attention. Gray, flowing hair framed the creased, leathery skin of his face and within, eyes like Aline's, blue and shining like the sky on a summer day. Though his words were strange gibberish, I felt a sudden, inexplicable feeling of gratitude for where I was and the reason he spoke. I was held in the embrace of an unexpected sensation of reverence as I listened, and it didn't matter that I understood none of it. Soon after, the images began to dissipate, and I remember mumbling out loud in complaint because I simply wanted to see more. When the darkness closed in, Aline's voice called out to me a last time.

"Open your eyes now," she said. I could hear and feel her breath against the back of my neck. I blinked a few times as the strange, trance-like haze lifted.

"How do you feel?" she asked at a whisper. It seemed she knew before I could respond, but fatigue dragged me down like gravity turned up a notch; my body was heavy, and it was difficult to hold my head straight.

"What the hell *was* that?"

"Rest a moment," she said. "It will take time to clear."

Aline pulled me gently to her and eased my cheek against her shoulder until my vision sharpened once more. The experience was fresh in my mind, and the questions mounted to make my confusion all the worse until she spoke again.

"I know how it must seem to you right now, but this is no different than before: you wouldn't be able to understand unless you saw and experienced it for yourself."

"I have no idea *what* I just saw," I replied. "I hope you're going to explain because I'm about as confused as I can be right now."

She took my hands in hers the way she always does when another bizarre surprise is about to be revealed.

"I brought you there so we could start at the beginning," she began. "I know it seemed strange and unrecognizable to you, but what you saw were moments from my past. I will show you many more of them later, but for the moment, it was important for you to see from the earliest days."

I stared at her as the uneasiness returned.

"I don't understand what you're saying; that looked like walking around inside a scene from a weird movie, not the memories from a little kid in Cardiff!"

Aline smiled and said, "When we sat in your living room that day, would you have believed if I only *told* you the things I can do?"

"Well, no, but…"

"As it was then, it was important for you to see and feel before I explain."

It was clear her next words would take me down a similar path, and I felt my stomach churn when I nodded and asked her to continue.

"I was first born in a small village on the southeastern coast of what is now called Anglesey. I'll take you there, but our village was near to where Pentraeth stands today."

"Wait a second," I interrupted. "I thought you were born in Cardiff."

"I *was* born in Cardiff, but not the first time."

"The *first* time?"

"This person—the one you know as Aline Lloyd—was born in 1980 at University Hospital in Heath, north side of Cardiff."

I could feel my brow furrow as confusion and the suddenness of fear and worry wrapped me like cold tendrils.

"But you just said you were born Pentraeth!"

"Yes, I was."

I shook my head quickly, trying to keep track of the confusing and contradictory words.

"This is starting to sound like some half-ass version of Who's on First!"

She smiled and nodded because, as usual, she was waiting for me to catch up—to walk a solitary path of discovery and reach her where she waited patiently.

"I can't tell you something like this in easy to understand stages, Evan, so here goes: the images you saw were from the early days in the life of a young girl called Tegwen merch Nyfain. It means Tegwen, daughter of Nyfain."

"The woman looking at me was Nyfain?"

"That's right. I don't know exactly when or even the time of year because we didn't keep track of birthdays on anything like modern calendars. By today's calculation of time and era, the closest I can put it is sometime around 460 AD."

"Those were her memories?"

"They're very much like memories," she replied quickly, "but not the way we think of them now. It's difficult to explain, but those images are places in time; you can call them memories, but that's not what they are."

"Then what *are* they?" I asked, fighting back against the confusion.

"They're rather like living snapshots, I suppose, waiting inside to be found and experienced whenever we like through a sort of portal, or doorway. We can't go back in time physically, but I *can* take you to some of those moments, and you can see and experience for yourself a distant past and places now gone from history."

"How can you see memories...*moments*...from a kid who lived fifteen hundred years ago? How do you know her name?"

"I know because those moments were mine, Evan; I am Tegwen."

I could hear my heart begin to pound and the ringing started low in my ears, growing to a high-pitched screech, just as it had on my first day sitting with Jeremy. Aline was inside again and I could feel the uneasiness begin to ebb. She was moving to calm the storm gathering in my imagination, where yet again, the impossible was held up before me as an inescapable truth I couldn't avoid. When the ringing stopped, I looked at her.

"This is ridiculous; are you telling me you're...*reincarnated?*"

Though I didn't understand, Aline had been preparing for that moment since the earliest days of our relationship, and she answered immediately.

"Not in the way most people use the term today, but yes—I have lived other lives and my first was a girl called Tegwen."

"How can you know when this happened?"

"The old ones who visited our village spoke of a time long before when foreign soldiers came and conquered our people. They endured, and the soldiers went away, but many hundreds of seasons had passed, and I now understand they meant the withdrawal of Roman legions from Britain."

I could feel the blood drain from my face where I sat in the darkness. I couldn't move, and Aline's words brought a single, spirit-crushing realization: the girl I loved was delusional at best and perhaps a criminally insane murderer at the very worst. Seeing and feeling what she claimed was a moment in the past as though I lived through it myself was a powerful experience, but not enough to pull me across the dividing line between us.

"Reincarnation is just a perception of life people use to make themselves feel better about death, Aline. Heaven, Paradise, Nirvana...it's all the same. You have the power to make me see or think anything you like, but what you're saying is just not possible."

She took in a deep breath, and I could see her smiling in the dim light.

"If this wasn't real, why would I bother to show you? What would be the point?"

"You tell me!"

"Think about it, Evan. What could I possibly gain by dragging you through such a thing? None of it matters for Renard's purpose *or* Burke's, so why would I go through the bother? You don't believe, and it only confirms your suspicions about madness and the reasons they kept me in that hospital. In my place, would *you* perpetrate a lie and the turmoil it will bring?"

The seconds ticked by as I considered, but there was no easy answer. Clever people can make logical arguments and still be stark raving mad, I reminded myself, but none of them can walk into my conscious mind and make me see, think, or feel. I needed to buy time, even at the risk of obvious condescension.

"Okay, let's say it's all real and you're not jerking my chain; how many times *have* you lived?"

"Six," she replied firmly. "This life is my seventh."

"And you say you were born in the middle of the fifth century…"

She smiled sadly and said softly, "I knew you would resist this. It's not something most people could grasp, but you must see and understand what *was* before I can show you what *is*."

"After all that stuff in my living room, I was ready to believe *anything*, but this is just…"

"Crazy?" she said quickly.

"It's not something you hear every day, is it? And anyway, I thought each life that ended was supposed to blend immediately into the next; you'd live a hell of a lot more lives than only seven in fifteen hundred years."

She leaned forward on her hands like a teenager at a slumber party, neither overexcited nor shying away from a description she waited a year to make.

"When I was first born, we *did* believe the soul passed seamlessly through from one life into another, but it turned out to be something quite different. I can't explain how or why it happens because there was no one who ever explained it to me—it simply *was*. When it happens, and we recognize the moment, we accept it."

"Are there more of these *moments* from that first life?" I asked. "Beyond what you showed me just now?"

She nodded and said, "Many more, and I'll take you there when we have time. If it makes you feel any better, I had no idea what they were when I first experienced them. As I grew older, I learned what they really are and how to move through them. It's hard to describe in words, but over time, I knew without understanding why. Does that make sense?"

"Not really."

"It will become easier as we go because there are qualities that allow you to simply know things without being told—you won't have to ask."

We moved closer; the process continued, and I felt myself shifting to another place. It wasn't fear holding me, and I didn't need rescue, but other thoughts pulled at my sleeve.

"Who were those people?"

She paused for a moment so that her reply could be made without adding to my confusion—careful and precise.

"The old man you saw speaking to me alone was called Cadwal; he was a very wise, very learned man—a bard."

"I didn't understand a word he said."

"Today's historians and linguists would call it an ancient Brythonic dialect—a dead language, obviously. We didn't speak Welsh or English the way we do now, at least not yet."

"What was he saying?"

"It was a warning," she said. "I was different than the other children in my village, and he knew it."

"Different because of your special abilities?"

"The old ways were dying out, and he wanted to make me understand those things I could do would become dangerous in the eyes of others one day."

"The arrival of Christians."

"Not specifically, but they were a part of it. The Romans were gone more than a century before I was born; by then, Christianity was spreading everywhere—it wasn't new or strange to us."

"But the old man had a problem with it."

"He was one of the last who kept strictly to the old ways, but that wasn't what worried him. Instead, he knew there were very few like me and what I could do would make people afraid. He simply knew where it would end, and he demanded that I keep that knowledge to myself—to never reveal it."

"Afraid and violent," I said with a sad smile. "That sounds a lot like Claude Dumont."

"Yes, and now you can understand why he was compelled with such desperation. For him, the things I did that day in Brugge could only be described as either a miracle and the work of God or some sort of Satanic spell," she said with a sad expression. "He saw the impossible and it frightened him."

"And the old man," I continued. "He worried the Christians might see you as a threat?"

She smiled and shook her head, knowing at once I didn't understand.

"Many of our people *were* Christians by that point, Evan—there was no conflict."

"But Cadwal wasn't buying it?"

"He listened when the holy men came through our village from time to time, but I don't remember him resenting it or fighting against them. The images are incomplete, but it wasn't the old ways he was worried about or the acceptance of Christianity; all of it was inevitable and I think he knew."

"What bothered him?"

"My abilities had nothing to do with faith or religion. He was very wise and making me promise to never tell or show anyone was a practical matter, not a theological contradiction."

I pictured again in my mind the old man and the solemn expression he wore as he spoke to her. I couldn't understand his words, but his sincerity was obvious.

"Who was he," I asked after a pause. "An elder?"

"Cadwal didn't live in our village, but he came to us quite often. I never knew where he was born, and it's likely he had no longer kept a home at all, moving from village to village in a routine circle to teach some of us. My generation was among the last who were trained in the old ways."

"When you say 'old ways,' you mean he was like a Druid priest, or something?"

"That is exactly what he was," she answered, "but it was a normal part of life and not the way they characterize in the modern era; he didn't pop up one day and say, 'Right! I'm a powerful, mystical Druid, so everyone pay attention.' The Romans drove Druids to near extinction long before I was born, but the traditions were still practiced during my lifetime…Tegwen's life."

"But the term is accurate and what historians would call him today?"

"It's who we were. Cadwal was an influential and revered person—a seer and interpreter of auguries—but mostly, he was a teacher and judge who was called upon to hear and settle disputes. Those duties were always ours."

"He must've been a powerful man."

"Cadwal didn't carry a title or some kind of badge, but he held considerable authority, and it was never questioned even when the Christian holy men came to the village. He told me to keep our traditions—and my abilities—inside and hold them for another time."

"What time did he have in mind?" I asked, suddenly riveted to Aline's description.

"He believed the old ways would be embraced again one day; he didn't trust the Christian God would be forever powerful as the holy men did."

"But he understood your special abilities?"

"Not the way you mean; I didn't develop telekinetic, *physical* abilities because I was too young. As I moved from childhood, Cadwal knew I could hear thoughts however, and it was the reason I was chosen to learn from him. We to visit neighboring villages and I assisted as he heard complaints or disputes."

"A roaming magistrate?"

"In a sense. People would offer their arguments and he would consider them. I could hear the thoughts of others and when he discovered that, I was brought along to listen. When a difficult dispute became one that could go either way, I told him if I heard truth or a lie in a person's thoughts and he would give his judgment accordingly."

"You were inside *their* heads, too?"

"I could hear it well enough."

As I sat in the darkness a scene paraded through my thoughts and with it, images that gave form to her description. I knew only bits and pieces about our ancient ancestry and nearly nothing about life in post-Roman Britain. The mysterious Druids held considerable power and influence over their people for centuries as Celtic tribes spread west and north across Europe. There was clearly a deep connection to the land and elements, but Druidic traditions were much more than a charming environmental activist's dream; there was a practical application of their learning that observed the physical world and obeyed natural law. Understanding those things, and the seasons that rose and fell each year, meant the difference between thriving or dying from starvation.

I imagined her in that place and time, sitting at the elbow of a grand Druid who was a judge, a healer or diviner to summon the favor of nature's gods. But Aline—*Tegwen*—was special and a powerful resource to root out the truth and hand down equitable solutions to disputes. Like hidden eyes above a poker table, any Druidic judge armed with her abilities would get it right every time and the distinction could only have made her a favorite student. I smiled at the likelihood Aline's power wasn't regarded as an abnormality but instead an understandable quality for those revered men and women who guided the course of a civilization for a thousand years.

"Did you become a priestess, or whatever they called it?"

"I learned from Cadwal because he took me on as a student and it was a huge honor to be asked. I remember my parents were very proud of me but also they were sad because it obliged me to a life often far from our village."

"Couldn't they say 'no' when Cadwal selected you?"

Aline smiled and shook her head slowly.

"Nobody said 'no' to a man like Cadwal, Evan; they accepted it and that was that. I studied and learned from him, traveling great distances to meet with others who kept the old ways or to see after disputes in neighboring villages."

"How long were you with Cadwal?"

"He was very old when I first knew him but he prepared me to carry on. I was in my early twenties when he died, but I continued with what I knew until my own authority nearly equaled his. I can't say with certainty *how* long, but my hair had gone gray and many years passed until the moments stopped. Maybe sixty or even seventy years."

"And there's no way to know exactly when you…when *Tegwen* died because they didn't keep records back then."

"We had no written language at all and because of it nothing to show what became of me. The Christians brought Latin as the old ways died out and our people shifted from oral, pagan traditions, but that was never part of my life."

Just the thought held me like an invisible hand as I came to understand what it meant. If what she said was true, how strange and confounding it must be to think of yourself as another person who lived fifteen centuries before.

Could there be any other condition as surreal, I wondered? But the dreamlike state was more than a description in mere words; I saw and experienced it for myself, just as she said I would, and the effect was stunning. Who among us can discuss such things without fear of being heard and labeled a crank or outright lunatic? How could she manage in the twenty-first century, I thought silently, knowing what she had been so long ago? But as I allowed the thoughts to drift through, the inevitable question slammed into me, and I looked at her where she knelt on the bed.

"That was a very long time ago, Aline."

"Yes, it was."

"But you said it was your *first* life—that you've lived six more times since?"

"Yes, that's right," she answered simply.

"And you remember them, too?"

"I remember five, not including my life today."

"And the other?"

"My second life," she said sadly. "I have few moments or images from it and I know only that I lived."

"Hold on a second," I said as the confusion wormed its way back inside my thoughts. "If you can't remember, or there aren't any more of these moments and images, how do you know you lived at all?"

She took in a deep breath as she waited to speak, and I felt instant regret at having asked. Was there something more she couldn't tell me, I wondered?

"I can see enough in the moments to know."

"Okay, if it took you fifteen centuries to live seven lives…"

"With each life, I was born when I was born. It was random and I don't know how or why."

My head was swimming, just trying to process all she told me as a concept, let alone the unworkable math it presented, but she heard it in my thoughts and moved close.

"I'm very sorry if this collides with your comfortable belief systems, Evan, but I can't change any of it and I wouldn't if I could!"

The frustration and building anger were clear in her voice.

"Look at it from my perspective!" I said in desperation. "After the episode in my living room, and all the shit you can do with just a thought, how do I know what I saw in that moment wasn't a projection you sent to me from your own imagination?"

"It's not the same thing!" she protested. "I wasn't sending images to you; I let you inside so you could see them through me."

"I want to understand, Aline, but you have to admit how impossible it sounds! Never mind what I think, how do *you* know it's real? All these things that seem like memories or moments, whatever the hell you call them, might be something else—something made up in…"

"Made up inside a lost, insane mind?" she said curtly, finishing my sentence with her own words.

"That's not what I was going to say!"

"Yes, it is, and you should know better than to think I wouldn't hear it in your thoughts."

I felt myself go red, grateful she couldn't see it in the dark, but an argument was building. Again, I had blundered out my doubts and fears, but before I could qualify them, or even apologize, Aline was moving.

"Get dressed," she said with a noticeably impatient tone, and I thought for a sudden, surprising moment she was going to throw me out.

"Where are we going?"

"I can't go on while you're held back by your doubts. We may as well get it done and over with now so you won't continue to look at me as if I was a fucking looney!"

"What does 'get it over with' mean?" I asked at once, but she either didn't hear the fear in my voice, or she didn't care.

"Come along downstairs," she answered. "I'll show you so we can finish this once and for all."

A flood of apprehension swept through me with swirling images of my own death. I tried to mask it as I pulled on my socks, but she felt it and spun around quickly.

"For God's sake, Evan!" she shouted. "Do you ever stop to consider how it feels to *me* when you have those stupid thoughts?"

"I'm terribly sorry, Aline," I said much too loudly, "but 'finish it once and for all' sounds like a bad deal!"

"Oh, come on," she said, turning for the stairs in frustration. I followed without a word, wishing she wouldn't rummage around in my brain so often, and when we stopped in her dining room, she nodded toward an antique sideboard and it was clear she wanted it moved.

"What are we doing?" I asked.

"Just give it a bit of a shove," she replied.

I braced my knee against one side and it glided surprisingly well across the plank floor on hidden rollers I'd never noticed before.

"More," she said, and I pushed again until it revealed a framed wooden panel set flush into the wall.

"What's this?" I asked as she handed me a cordless drill aiming at eight screws holding the panel in place. When I finished, it tilted outward, and she lifted it free to reveal a hidden space and within a few cardboard boxes and small, plastic tubs stacked one on top of the other. She knelt to pull one of the tubs out and onto her dining table. With her hands on its lid, Aline looked at me for a moment.

"I'm going to show you what you need to see."

"What do you think I need to see?" I demanded.

"Proof," she replied quickly. "Your precious, goddamn evidence, all right?"

For the first time I heard impatience becoming a "last straw" in her tone, but I knew she was right: a life lived scoffing at the things we call "impossible" kept me on the fringes of belief because everyone knows better—you are born, you live out your life and then you die. Only those who *have* died can know with certainty what, if anything, happens after.

I wanted to believe because I felt and knew all too well the extent of Aline's power; there was nothing else to explain the shock and pain that day. But this was different, and the idea of dancing from one life into another across fifteen centuries was more than I could accept. Despite the perceived images from a child's mind in a distant, ancient past where I had wandered in breathtaking realism, no one can be who Aline claimed she was and nothing I could do would release me from my doubts. She knew it and a moment that should never have happened was finally upon us.

She laid several papers on the table and pointed to one: a summary document written on Cardiff University letterhead from the office of Dr. Monica

Williams. Beneath it, printed e-mails and letters between Professor Williams and Aline that looked like questionnaires or tabulated surveys. She stood and led me to her garage where a small wooden crate made of half-inch boards within a 4x4 frame was nestled in a corner and surrounded by garden tools, a bicycle and her lawn mower.

"That's it," she said softly, but her voice was cautious and only just above a whisper, the way kids speak taking shortcuts through a creepy cemetery with imaginations running high.

Beneath a blue tarp, an object roughly twice the dimensions of a bowling pin lay in a cradle made of diagonal blocks of wood. I knelt to get a better look and found it was made of incredibly thick glass—two inches at the least—and open at one end in a wide, yawning space big enough to accept my hand with ease. It seemed to be a gigantic, amber Mason jar, and Aline reached for a circular piece of tin the size of a big saucer. It was slightly corroded but otherwise wearing only surface tarnish that matched the diameter of the opening. She handed it to me, explaining it had been set into beeswax as a seal and then wrapped in thick cloth soaked in a sticky resin for good measure. All of it had been removed during cleaning after the contents were emptied out, she continued, leaving only the big jar and its metal lid.

"What am I looking at?"

"It is a time capsule," she answered.

"It looks like an overgrown medicine bottle. Who buried it?"

"A family in Aberystwyth put inside ordinary things from their life so others would find it one day and understand who they were; it was sealed up and buried under a field one hundred and twenty-two years ago."

"Interesting," I replied, "but what does it have to do with your big secret?"

"It has everything to do with it," she said evenly. "I wasn't certain this would ever become necessary but it has. It's time for you to see, and when you do, you'll understand."

"*You* dug this up?" I asked.

"Come with me."

When we sat again at her table, I looked at printed e-mails and process documents. Professor Williams, Aline said, had made a name for herself at Oxford teaching historical anthropology. Her work at Cardiff expanded into applied archaeology, and Aline asked for her help finding the capsule's precise location. I thought of Damon with a sad smile, knowing he would certainly have been in his element had Aline approached him. I read further to find a fee amount was settled, and Williams noted the search and excavation would be an invaluable teaching opportunity. Not long after, a project for undergrad students was organized. I felt lost in a swirl of confusion.

"Okay, I'll bite; how did they know where it was buried?"

"They didn't," she answered.

"*Somebody* had to know," I countered, "or it wouldn't be sitting out in your garage right now."

Aline went to the counter to boot her laptop.

"Before we met, you were in the business of examining evidence and drawing conclusions," she began. "Now, I'm going to show you what no one else ever could, and when you understand what it means there will be no more doubt or worry—you'll have the proof you need to know I'm not insane and the moments you experienced tonight are real."

"You don't have to prove anything," I said, but she waved me away.

"Yes, I do. It's understandable, and this is the only way. Keep reading."

The communications with Monica Williams resumed three months later when Aline sent a note declaring the capsule's general location was known, and it was time to place it precisely in order to begin the process of bringing it up. Professor Williams was excited at the news, and she replied a few weeks afterward that all the preparations for excavating it were complete. I wondered why she didn't ask how Aline had found the capsule, but the professor ended the note by expressing her joy knowing their work would reunite a family from the past with their descendants in the present. When I asked her what it meant, Aline deflected the question and pointed to a conversation with the owner of a field south of Aberystwyth kept as a pasture for grazing sheep.

In the northwest corner of the plot near a medieval church where the Ystwyth River flows, the capsule waited under four or five feet of dirt. She asked for and received the landowner's permission to mount a search so long as the activity "didn't frighten" his sheep. Professor Williams and her team arrived a week later to set up their awnings and tables as the dig site took shape.

Aline motioned me beside her and selected from her computer videos made by the students to chronicle their project and use as a teaching aid. I looked as they began with a wheeled ground-penetrating radar unit following an invisible path laid out on a grid inside one of their laptops. The machine looked like an anemic, engineless lawn mower, but it didn't take long before a strong return fixed the spot twenty yards from where the road makes an abrupt turn to form a sharp right angle.

Since no other meaningful targets were revealed, it was obvious they had found the capsule where Aline predicted it would be, and the unearthing process began with stakes in the ground to establish a perimeter. Layer by layer, the grass was shaved away and soil removed in a precise, deliberate order until the first scrape of an ordinary garden trowel clacked along the capsule's glass body. In their video I saw Aline waiting at the edge of the excavation, looking on as the surrounding soil was shoveled aside, but her reaction seemed muted and far less than the students' grins of satisfaction as they isolated the big jar and dug around until it rested on a narrow pedestal of dirt.

Lots of measurements followed more photographs to indicate depth and relative position as part of their instructional video until finally it was lifted gently up. They placed it carefully on a makeshift bed constructed of crosshatched boards while a fiberglass transportation case was prepared. When it was ready, they laid the capsule into foam padding to secure and protect it on the journey back to Cardiff for cleaning and the all-important opening to reveal its contents.

I read on and watched more footage as the capsule, now in Professor Williams' lab, was rinsed of dirt. They even brought in champagne for the event and toasted a successful recovery when student technicians began the slow and precise task of unwrapping a ribbon of hardened cloth from the capsule's amber-tinted glass.

One of the students noted immediately a raised inscription on the jar's bottom as the manufacturer's mark, showing the molten glass had been blown into and around a two-piece metal die by "*R.F. Hamilton & Co.*" and beneath the name was "*1891.*" Behind the students, Aline stood with folded arms, and when she wiped away tears, no one noticed. I *did*, however, and the meaning of so simple a gesture is far greater today than it was when those students gathered around to watch.

A wrap of cloth roughly two inches wide and infused with resin formed a layer of protection around the vessel's uppermost third, Williams said, to add an extra measure of seal integrity. The students unraveled the wrap inch by inch until a mildly tarnished tin cap emerged where it was set deep into a trough of pale, stiffened beeswax. Individual strips of resin cloth were laid over the metal cap in crossed layers, and then the wrap became a last, thorough step. The resin had hardened and aged over time, but it was intact and unbroken.

After removing the wrap carefully and in pieces, Williams and her team used small probes and dental spades to work the metal cap free of its wax bed, and with an odd sucking sound, the capsule opened to the air for the first time in over a century. Aline only watched, and I could see the process was not as compelling to her as it was for Williams and her team until the first item—a gray paper envelope—was carefully withdrawn and placed onto a long table. Aline moved closer when they held up a photograph, and its clarity brought smiles and approving nods as they looked at history before them.

Aline skipped ahead in the video presentation because, she said, the items inside the capsule were packaged and given to her after Williams and her team made detailed studies of condition and durability against the passage of time. A secondary inspection was conducted to analyze materials used to create the container and its elaborate system of watertight seals. She pointed to one of the folios, and in it was the full set of documents and verifying attestations as to age and authenticity, but also results of soil analysis confirming the surrounding dirt was uniform and undisturbed.

I did my best to focus my attention, but Aline offered no clues and I sat it out until she stopped the video and turned to me.

"I have the items in a secure lockbox," she said, "but you need to finish reading Doctor Williams' letter."

With a shrug I leaned forward and resumed the professor's narrative where she laid out the details of their agreement and Aline's stated goals. After removing the artifacts, her team followed a precise and carefully prescribed regimen aimed at isolating otherwise innocuous bits and pieces. I didn't understand why until the text noted transport of certain samples to a colleague at Oxford who specializes in forensic examinations conducted for British law enforcement agencies. It made me uneasy, at first, but the intent became clear when the results detailed a painstaking effort made to answer Aline's questions.

Dr. Williams' colleague had used microscopy techniques to map the exact placement of cloth in order to identify a distinct pattern he called a "fingerprint" in the resin so that any irregularities or deviations created by movement of the cloth afterward would show immediately. When none were revealed, analysis resumed with a focus on chemical composition of the resin. I wondered why they went to such lengths, but the notes showed an interesting detail and one I would never have considered: there were four layers of cloth wrap and tests conducted on them discovered the effects of exposure to moisture and oxygen, typically resulting in a breakdown of the once-sticky resin, diminished the deeper they went. It meant the outer layers, exposed to the soil, fared worse than the inner wrap where it hugged the capsule's glass directly.

At last, fiber analysis confirmed what they already knew—the wrap had gone untouched since the day it was applied in 1891. Professor Williams compiled the forensic findings into a summary to answer Aline's most pressing request, declaring "a near zero probability of compound perturbation across ten disparate samples of resin and wax." In simple terms, it meant the glass capsule had stayed exactly where it was buried a century before, but more importantly, it hadn't been opened.

I figured the effort (and considerable expense) Aline had gone to was simply an exercise in confirming historical authenticity against the day she would look to sell it off to a museum or collector, but her true purpose was something altogether different.

"Okay, you know it's the genuine article," I said at last, "but what was the point of it all?"

"That," Aline replied, "is the last, most important part."

18
SKIPPING STONES

ALINE grabbed a folding step stool from its place beside her refrigerator and walked slowly to a coat closet near the front door. I've put my own there more times than I could count, and I thought we were off on another leg in her wandering scavenger hunt. Instead, she opened and positioned the stool inside the closet, reaching up toward an unseen space above the door's casing.

I leaned in and saw a small panel on hinges that gave access to something within, and it became clear a modest safe was the lockbox she mentioned earlier and she pulled from it an ordinary manila envelope. It was another piece from a strange puzzle but it was also, she said, the most crucial of them all.

"As it was on that day when I first showed you," she began, "this will seem ridiculous and impossible, but you have to see and understand or none of it will matter."

I remembered the foul taste of copper.

"Thanks, but I'll pass on more of the invisible mind-beatings."

"That's not what I meant."

I felt a sudden rush of cold, and it made me hunch my shoulders in reflex. Aline's thoughts carried collateral effect as she pulled me through another moment—another brush with her abilities—to remind me of the hidden power and how easily it can be delivered.

"I knew what was inside the capsule before it was dug up," she began.

"How?" I asked. "Did you find a list somewhere?"

"No list or location notes were ever made," she replied. "It would spoil the surprise."

"That you *know* of," I replied gently. "Somebody could have found it and memorized the words before burning it and no one would be able to dispute a claim."

For a brief, glorious moment, I was sure my logic and reason had won out, but Aline just smiled.

"I know you mean me, Evan," she said. "If I found a list somewhere with the intent of playing a stupid joke by claiming such a thing, what would be the point of waiting until now to reveal it?"

Her response was cryptic and loaded, but before I could go further, Aline pulled a small cardboard box from her safe and handed it down to me. Inside, she said, were the pieces of a family's life collected and placed into the capsule on a bright summer day in 1891. When she opened the box, a musty odor drifted out and Aline waited for a moment in silence. I watched her and she seemed to drift away to a place where no one could follow.

In those final seconds, the storm of emotion sweeping through her could only have been intense and I could see her tears.

"We can leave it for another time," I offered, but she straightened herself and brushed the wetness from her face.

"No," she said softly, "we have to finish it; this is for you. Open the box, Evan."

Inside I found a delicate lady's hairbrush made of pewter and inlaid with an intricate design in mother-of-pearl. Behind it was a small metal container, and its faded red label announced "Peek Freans Famous Biscuits." I reached again and pulled out an antique photograph of four people—parents and two young children—sitting close together for a formal portrait. I couldn't see in detail, but their faces were stern and serious. Aline motioned for me to flip it over, and there was a brief handwritten annotation made with a quill or old-fashioned fountain pen:

Mr. H. Pryce and family, Aberystwyth, 14th June 1891

Aline reached for another envelope, but this one was smaller and likely made for sending formal invitations to guests at a wedding. I looked inside and found a single tooth—a small molar—clearly taken from a younger jaw. I looked at Aline, but there was one more object to go in the box, and a tiny cedar case with a beautiful cameo made of ivory opened easily to reveal matching opal cuff links.

She selected one and brought it to her lips as her eyes closed. There was no explanation, but little was needed: an otherwise ordinary item from any Victorian-era haberdashery meant something to her, and I waited through the moment in silence. We returned to her kitchen, and she placed each of the five objects carefully onto her table. It was obvious they were taken from the capsule, but still she wasn't finished.

At last she handed me the manila envelope. I looked inside and found a single unopened letter addressed from Aline to herself and posted from Colwyn Bay. When I looked up with a frown of confusion she said, "There are three additional copies, and my solicitor has one of them at her office in Rhyl; the other two are kept in safety deposit boxes outside the country."

"This is what you couldn't tell me before?" I asked, almost afraid to hear the answer.

"This is the final step," she replied, handing me a paring knife for a letter opener.

One sheet of expensive bond unfolded to reveal a standard red seal of a notary public registered in Denbighshire, and at the top was a column of words I recognized immediately.

> List of items prior to excavation. Pryce family time capsule buried off Morfa Bychan road near Abersytwyth on 14 June 1891. Recorded here, 5 March 2010—Aline M. Lloyd.
>
> - biscuits (1 tin)
> - gentleman's opal cuff links (2)
> - girl's tooth (1)
> - family photograph (Huw, Paulette, Rhian & Thomas Pryce) hairbrush (1)

"You made your own list?" I asked with a shrug.

"Yes," she answered, but her voice was low and almost a whisper.

"Why mail it to yourself; is it *that* important?"

"Look again at the date, Evan."

The notary's signature date was also "5 March 2010" but it meant nothing. She handed me Professor Williams' assessment letter next, pointing with her little finger at its date: "21 September 2011." Once more I looked at the list of items and again at the date before the obvious screamed through in my thoughts at last. The letter was much more than an itemized list of the capsule's contents; it was her proof—her insurance policy—and I sat immediately in the grip of a cold reality I could no longer ignore. My doubts still lived, but they teetered on the edge of a reality I never thought possible. My resolve was weakening under the weight of the capsule's contents and the truth Aline knew what waited inside before Dr. Williams' team set up shop in a sheep pasture.

The capsule had been examined by professionals across several disciplines for the express purpose of confirming or denying a simple premise that no hands had touched the heavy glass container in over a century. Her list, handwritten and witnessed by her lawyer, was made eighteen months *before* the capsule was pulled up and into the light. No one could possibly have known what waited inside unless they had an original list…or they had witnessed its burial in that remote Welsh field.

"It will take time, Evan, but you will see it; I promise."

"All this," I mumbled. "I don't understand…"

"Yes, you do," she replied softly. "You simply haven't adjusted to it yet. I could help you see and understand right now, but it would be wrong; you would never be sure my influence wasn't at work to deceive you."

"What does this mean?"

"It's not a trick; you can see with your own eyes and this is exactly as it seems. You can search the Earth for the rest of your life, and you will never find the list you suspected because we didn't make one—my mother wouldn't have it."

She reached for the old photo and handed it to me, circling with her finger one of the children—a girl standing at her mother's side—where the photographer had posed them in a time when cameras were gigantic and made of wood and brass. I could barely speak as a tempest of confusion swirled in my thoughts until I choked out the words.

"This little girl…"

"Her name was Rhian Pryce," Aline replied.

I looked again, but there was no point in fighting against a truth looking out at me across a century from cool, shining eyes.

"She was…she's *you*?"

"I went there almost ten years ago," she began. "The moments were easy to find and live again, but it took a lot of driving back and forth until I matched my memory to what's there now and sorted out the spot. It wasn't a pasture then, and the trees were different, but I wanted to see how much the place had changed since I was Rhian. I expected a block of flats, or maybe some houses…"

"Was there a landmark, or something from before you remembered?"

"The shape of the hills beyond, but mostly it was the distance to a sharp bend in the road and I could see beyond it to the river in my memories. They dug the hole quite close to the road because my father and Uncle got tired of carrying it. I worked it backward, walking that field until the distance looked right."

I pictured her pacing in this direction or that, dodging sheep shit and looking off toward the Ystwyth River with a hand above her brow. She told me it took more than one trip until the images from her moments as Rhian had become stark and vivid in *Aline's* memory and the distances finally matched. A few years later, she made her list, and a year or so after that, a call to Monica Williams in Cardiff.

"You knew it was there, but why dig it up at all?" I asked. "Why go to all the bother and expense?"

"I wanted to see it again," she answered. "I never felt that way before, but I just wanted to touch it and know it's real. But after Glasgow, I worried another incident might one day force me to prove who and what I am."

"What would force you?"

"To prevent being sent back there ever again."

I felt numb, and I knew she could feel it through my thoughts as the last of my doubts flickered and died.

"After you rest," she replied gently, "I will take you to other moments, just as we did when I let you see some from my first life, but these are new and happened since we met."

"Why show me?"

"Because you are in them. You will hear your own words as you spoke them to me and you will know they are real. After, I will show you the moments when we made and sealed up the capsule. You will watch through Rhian's eyes—*my* eyes— as workmen buried it in that field and there will be no more doubts."

Since that first day, when she tore through my mind with such terrible effect so I would see for myself and let go the stubborn belief no one could do those things, I had held fast. I refused in defiant confidence there is no such thing as a soul moving through time in the lives of others, but all the forces of logic that make us rational and sure in our convictions were disappearing. I thought it should be a moment of despair and lonely abandonment, but it wasn't either of those things. What couldn't be had become something that could be nothing else, and I smiled as the pestering needles of disbelief were withdrawn.

"You're tired," Aline whispered. "Let's go to bed now. In the morning, I'll explain it more."

She was right, and the fatigue pulled at me in an endless wave, so I gave her a sad smile and followed as she gathered up the capsule's contents and turned off the lights. It was the night my life's changes became permanent, but also the moment I found a new path where I would walk only with her.

A YEAR AFTER it began, a strange journey no one else can know pulled me stumbling at last to the final, unavoidable conclusion. I wish I could say I fought a good and honorable fight so as not to be fooled, but in truth, I simply ran out of excuses. It wasn't enough she could start fires with her mind or poke around inside my deepest, most guarded thoughts; instead, I surrendered to the sobering truth Aline walked the earth 1,500 years before I was born, and she did so as another person—a separate life.

There are no instruction manuals or self-help videos to shield against the collision between those things we regard as unquestionable truths and others we know are absurd impossibilities. When the moment arrived, and all rational answers were gone, I stood and walked to her kitchen window watching as a polite Welsh rain made tiny ripples across the surface of a stone birdbath in the middle of her backyard. I wasn't dumbstruck or lost for words, and there was no more tension or rising fear. Instead, I just felt spent and naked at the doorway of a life I had never thought possible. One more time, the ultimate expression of secrets held me as if by the scruff of my neck. Of course, the battle was already fought and lost. With only the two of us, alone and in silence, I had no more arguments.

In the quiet, as she waited for me to speak, I questioned my own sanity for the first time. I reconsidered the lingering possibility of an elaborate hoax, but I knew better. If indeed I felt compelled to examine stability, it was mostly to reassure myself it hadn't gone *that* horribly wrong. Insane people, they say, never wonder if they're crazy, but Aline heard my thoughts and I could hear hers before she spoke.

"You're not crazy," she whispered.

I smiled with closed eyes, and she stood close to steady me as I crossed over from what *was* to a place where she waited quietly for me to follow—where she always waited. No longer burdened by a need to challenge and expose a charade that didn't exist, I was lifted by a strange and liberating breeze because I knew the stunning revelation in her garage wasn't a sinister mechanism operating to harm me.

The days ahead would be cluttered with questions spurred by mere curiosity, and I wondered if she would grow tired of explaining it. How could I hope to catch up and truly understand when her experience crossed a millennium and more while mine plodded along in only decades? She knew what I faced, and it surprises me still she went patiently beside me with an understanding I could never match. There was so much to learn, and suddenly I wanted to hear it all, even as the life I once led fell away. Aline's giant bottle was opened to the light after more than a hundred years and finally, on an otherwise dull, rainy day, I was ready to take my first step into *her* world.

Aline made breakfast as I sat quietly behind her counter nursing a cup of coffee until I noticed the capsule's contents on her countertop where she'd placed them the night before. I took the family photo to her table and sat with it for a while, wondering what it must be like for *her* to look at the face of a child in another distant life and see herself. When she glanced at me from her stove, I held up the photo.

"Tell me about them."

"Huw Pryce," she said. "He was a bank manager where we lived in Aberystwyth and my father in Rhian's life—my sixth life."

"The cuff links," I said involuntarily.

"They were his contribution to the capsule."

"Your mother doesn't look very thrilled to be there."

Aline smiled and shook her head as the memory rushed through.

"Thomas—my brother—was squirming and fidgety because the shirt collar irritated the back of his neck. My mother took him behind a screen in the photographer's studio to get his attention, and when they returned, we sat for the portrait."

"That day in Professor Williams' laboratory was the first time you saw this picture since it went inside the capsule?"

"I would never have believed a photo could be so important to me, but…"

"Who decided to do this in the first place?" I asked.

"My uncle Edward saw one being buried at a park near Rouen while he was visiting in France, and when he told us about it my mother thought it would be great fun to create one of our own."

"This was your mom's idea?"

"When the weather was horrid, my father read Jules Verne novels to us in the parlor; my mother loved the idea of going to the moon or living under the sea."

I looked at the solemn faces in Aline's photograph and then at her, but she intercepted the thought immediately.

"My parents were not stodgy and prim, Evan. I know it looks that way in the photo, but we were a loud and loving family. They decided to make a time capsule and my father started planning."

"Was there a particular reason for making it out of glass?" I asked.

Aline laughed a little and said, "Oh yes, there was a reason. My father and Uncle Edward went 'round and 'round about the very thing, arguing and making diagrams on the dinner table…it was quite lively."

"Who won?"

"My mother beat them both. They were arguing about this metal or that and how long it could last before it rusted away. They hit on brass as a possibility, but then she told them glass doesn't rust and it keeps the water out, which ended the argument, and that's what we did."

"It looks custom-made," I said, and Aline nodded.

"My father knew a man in Yorkshire who owned a glassworks. I was a bit of a tomboy then, and he took me with him so I could see how they made the pieces for a mold and watch as the melted glass was forced in and around it. It was the first time I'd been that far from home; I felt so grown-up…"

I listened with a smile because her voice came alive as she described a very special time, but there was something more. I realized after a while she spoke of her parents only in the formal "mother" or "father"—there was no shift to an informal "mom" or "dad." The detail might seem insignificant in any other context, and I wondered if *she* realized it as I reached for the tin.

"I can understand a photograph for a time capsule but…*cookies*?"

"After the photo, we each chose something important to us, and believe me, the biscuits were *very* important to my little brother."

"And the brush?"

"My mother received it as a wedding gift from my great aunt. I remember she wanted to send something else, but when my father chose the cuff links, she decided to sacrifice her favorite brush."

The photograph was next, and I held it for a moment.

"How old were you in this shot?"

"I celebrated my eleventh birthday in March, only a few months before."

"The tooth was yours."

"Yes," she said with a smile. "I had an abscess, and the dentist pulled it without telling my mother. It was very painful and he pulled it immediately. She was furious with him for not asking first, but then she kept the tooth and held it up as a warning to choose dentists carefully. I think she just didn't like him and the excuse was convenient. She laughed and hugged me for my sense of humor when I chose it for my contribution."

Aline's mood lightened, and her description of a family moment could just as easily have happened twenty years before. I listened with a new ear, knowing my place was special and privileged, hearing a nineteenth century girl speaking across time through Aline. She told me about her life in Aberystwyth with a promise to show me places from her childhood so I could see and experience them, too.

After a while, and the time she always knew it would take for me to adjust, I felt better. There was no crescendo to a dramatic cymbal crash when I understood at last and the immovable, stubborn parts of my nature that once called out for an end of it had been stilled. She watched me, and I felt the delicate fingers of her thoughts moving through my own, but she was inside only to smooth the edges and steady me in the final mile of an unbelievable journey. I was suddenly delighted with myself for finally learning to recognize the sensation unprompted, and she nodded with pride.

"I understand how difficult this was to accept. If our roles were reversed, I would be just as suspicious, but you have crossed over and now you're with me on *this* side."

"I wasn't trying to be a pain in the ass, Aline…"

"You don't have to feel badly, Evan; I have wondered about it more times than you."

"All along," I said. "You knew where that thing was, and yet you waited so long to open it up to look inside?"

"When Monica's students pulled it up," she replied, "it was confirmation, not a discovery. I didn't want to touch the letter to myself at all, but then you arrived and everything changed."

She looked away for a moment, and I knew the first explanations she could never make before were about to begin.

"How does this work?" I asked. "What happened so you would know who you were before?"

"In every life," she began, "I reached a point where suddenly nothing made sense and it took time to remember *what* I am."

"Your powers?" I asked.

"No, not that," she replied. "Awareness always emerged earlier, always when I was moving from adolescence into adulthood, but the moments and what you call 'memories' surface at a slower pace, and it takes a while to recognize and remember them."

"That has to be a shitty, confusing time," I added.

"Some were worse than others until I learned to find and see those moments in each new life. A few times, the thoughts made me worry that Satan was controlling me, or that maybe I had gone mad. After a while, it became clear, and each time—each life—I remembered."

"Why now?" I asked. "You said I was never supposed to see or learn about any of this."

Aline moved close and slid her feet under my legs because, she says, the pressure feels good. Her face wore a thoughtful, almost sad expression.

"Have you kept a secret all your life, something you never revealed to anyone, not even once?"

"I'd have to think about it," I replied, but the question flustered me and my answer seemed inadequate.

"Think about it now," she said. "I've kept this secret for a thousand and a half years because Cadwal was right: the time for our ways has passed and it will never return."

Aline's voice became distant and strange, the way an actress might adjust to direction for an ethnic or foreign accent. It was disturbing, and I hoped she wouldn't hear the concern filter out from my thoughts, so I shifted topics just a little to distract her.

"After you…well, after you die…you're reborn into a new family line?"

"Each life was unique and not connected to another physically or genetically, but I was always a part of them. My firstborn spirit, soul, or essence—whichever you prefer—remained through them all."

I listened closely because Aline's nature was being revealed and laid bare for me to see; with one word—*firstborn*—the last veil in a mystery fell away, and the moment seemed removed and eerie when I looked and saw two in the face of one. It happens that way sometimes; we clomp along in happy ignorance until, like a white-hot bolt of lightning, understanding waits in front of us with an upheld hand we can no longer avoid. In those seconds, it felt like that, and I smiled with a slow shake of my head as the final pieces fell into place.

"Seven lives. Every time, it was always you; always *Tegwen*. The lives you lived since were never just one person."

"Yes. I am Aline in this life, but I have always been Tegwen."

Her answer was immediate, direct, and the destroyer of my perceptions of existence built on the faith of accepted truth. Of course, that belief had been torn away, and I felt like a lone man in the middle of a featureless plane with no horizon. Aline—and every life that went before—was a shared identity.

"Rhian wasn't reborn as Aline Lloyd," I said at last, "*Tegwen* was."

She nodded, but we were moving to another place where her manner seemed to shift a little, and the uneasiness crept back in despite my best efforts to ignore it. As usual, she heard.

"Evan, this is not a split personality disorder; there is no 'Sybil' in here."

I shook my head in wonder and said, "I can't imagine how this must feel for *you*."

"It's funny you put it that way because this is perfectly normal for me, and it always has been," she answered. "I can't imagine what it would be like any other way."

"How can you be two people at the same time?"

"That's not how to think of it," she said. "I wouldn't be who I am as Aline Lloyd without Tegwen; it's rather like echoes or instinct guiding me. I know where it comes from, and *why*, but it has never been a superior-to-subordinate experience."

"Aline is not under Tegwen's control?" I asked.

"Not in the way you mean. It's more accurate to say Aline's consciousness is *assisted* by Tegwen, not directed by it."

It hadn't occurred to me earlier, but one question became suddenly obvious, and I moved closer to Aline.

"These lives," I began, "always lived here…in Wales."

She nodded the way people do when they think you need support, even if you do not.

"Does anything from your past explain?" I wondered. "Maybe from Tegwen's life or part of your time as a Druid to tell you it would always begin here?"

Aline smiled for a moment, and it seemed my question surprised her. Of course, it hadn't and she knelt on the floor, leaning to draw her hand across the ancient planks very slowly.

"Our gods made it that way, I suppose," she replied in a hushed voice. "I've been many places and other countries, but it's never right until I return to this land."

It was the first time our talks went to her pagan origins and she pulled it into the light deliberately and without regard for how I might react.

"Did Cadwal tell you about this when you were young?" I asked. "Did he explain the lives yet to be lived…being born again and again?"

"Only in broad terms," she answered. "I knew it would happen, but he described rebirths as something much like skipping a smooth stone across a quiet pond; it bounces from spot to spot until it finally slows and sinks. It was a simple way to tell me about the importance of my original life—*the stone*—meeting and joining with other lives until I finally die."

"Until Tegwen dies."

"Yes."

I listened and learned as she went, privy to a window into the past no one else has been given, but other questions seeped through and I posed them carefully. I imagined her in that life, making her way through the fifth century, learning, growing and how it was in an age (and culture) mostly erased from history.

"Were Druids allowed to marry?"

Aline grinned at me and what she knew was another query made with caution against a reply I wouldn't want to hear.

"Of course," she answered.

"Did you?"

Her expression changed again, and I remember watching with a blended sense of curiosity and dread.

"There was another; a member of our class I met when we journeyed across from the island and down the coast to a gathering where Harlech stands today. He was called Fáelán and we formed a friendship during that time. There was an idea of marriage, but it never happened."

"Why not?"

"He died," she answered simply. I said nothing because the memories could only have been painful, but she finished the thought.

"Cadwal took me to an important conclave and from it, we were given several requests for hearings at two villages near present-day Llanidloes. It took many weeks before we returned, but during that time Fáelán became gravely ill."

"I suppose that happened with some regularity back then?"

"By comparison, I suppose it did," she answered. "A ruptured appendix or punctured lung from broken ribs was always fatal."

"What happened to Fáelán?"

"They said it was a plague, but smallpox is more likely. The village where he lived built a pyre, and so I could never visit a gravesite to ask our gods for favors in his name."

"Favors?"

"When one of our own died, especially before his or her time, words were offered to the gods of wind, sun, and rain to honor the dead by extending kindness to those left behind—abundant crops, for example, or an end of raids by foreigners."

"You meant to marry this man?"

"No formal announcement or arrangements were made but it was understood, yes."

With her solemn answer, the implications became clear: Tegwen followed a course on her own, and one life was changed by the death of another. It was difficult for me to contemplate the reality and a man long dead who won her heart many centuries before, but that truth was unavoidable, and I made up my mind to take it for what it was and avoid peevish jealousies that could never affect me. It made me wonder if she understood my emotional dilemma, but Aline didn't mention it and I was at least wise enough to leave it buried with the ashes of the past.

19
THE SECOND, AND ENYDD

"TELL me about the others; I'm ready to learn now, and anyway, it can't get any stranger than *this*, right?"

She reached for my hand and said, "When I was first born, what I am was no longer common and that was the reason Cadwal made me promise to never reveal what I could do. Today, it's much worse."

"Why was it becoming less common?" I asked. "A product of the Roman experience?"

"As the old ways died out, there were fewer and fewer of us. I don't understand why, and maybe it was accelerated evolution, but the Romans killed so many, it's reasonable to connect them to it."

"But something else changed?"

"For my duties and responsibility to Cadwal, hearing the thoughts of others was useful because we were trusted to render fair judgment. But he knew those abilities were bound at some point to be noticed in a changing world, and it would expose us to dangerous risks."

I listened and heard the conclusion before she reached it.

"Claude Dumont's reaction is a good example."

"Yes, and that is why I have never spoken of it since. My other lives are similar; can you imagine what anyone else would say if I told them I was born fifteen hundred years ago?"

I passed through a final gate separating the life I'd lived from the days and years still ahead: a one-way threshold it was pointless to resist. The moment was not as dramatic as I would expect, and I remember smiling sadly as I considered my own reaction. In those first moments of a revelation like no other, I told her digging up a giant glass bottle didn't prove anything; I needed to show her my intellect prevented me from giving myself over to a fantastical illusion that defied the laws of physics without a fight, but the effort would certainly have been wasted. Somehow, in ways I can't justify or even describe, the last of my doubts faded. There is no way for me to quantify such things—to apply scientific analysis and find a truth no one else can see. Instead, in a beautiful parallel to those times in Aline's former lives, I simply knew.

"You showed me a glimpse of Tegwen's life," I began, "but what about Rhian and the lives you lived in between; can you show me?"

"First, I want to tell you about them and who I was so the images will make sense when you see and experience those moments."

"Where the hell do you start with something like this?" I asked. "It's not exactly a slide show from summer camp."

Aline held up a reassuring hand and it was clear she anticipated the question.

"After Renard came here," she replied, "this was inevitable, so I thought about it and how best to take you through."

It didn't matter to me which life she chose, but I understood the importance of her first existence as Tegwen and the common bridge connecting it to all her lives. Lives, *plural*. It still sounds strange to me but it really *is* the only way to describe her accurately. It was time to move things forward, but those first minutes were colored by the unnerving reality Aline was no longer a singular entity—a unique personality. Tegwen was with her, and always had been, but my perceptions were forced into a new framework and reality we're not trained by life's experiences to accept easily. When she began, I looked and listened as a man forever altered.

ALINE BROUGHT GLASSES of wine and settled on her couch to start my lessons about a girl I would never see but who also sat right beside me in her newest life. Without a written language, she said, history that was passed down by word of mouth over centuries provided few meaningful clues as to when Tegwen was born. Elder Druids she'd met on her journeys with Cadwal spoke of a time before and measured, in their words, by the passage of "three generations since the invaders disappeared from the land."

I asked her what it meant and she jotted notes on a pad from her kitchen, laying out timelines I could recognize. Presuming three generations spans nearly a century, she explained, it's an easy enough task to work the math forward.

"I didn't know any of this before my life as Rhian," she began, "but I sat with history professors while I was at university in Cardiff, and they showed me what I didn't know about the times corresponding to my earlier lives. For them, it was just my curiosity about western civilization, but it helped me understand my own, hidden history and fill in the blanks."

"When you lived the first time, your people didn't keep written records," I complained. Aline just smiled patiently and said, "No, but the Romans *did* and some of theirs have been useful to this purpose."

"In what way?"

"We knew Roman legions were recalled from Britain late in the fourth century, which means I was born sometime late in the fifth century, anywhere between 460 and 480. And just to be clear, my 'people' were *your* people, too, Evan; we are both descended from the same distinct culture."

"So noted," I replied with my best apologetic smile.

She pulled out an old milk crate filled with texts and history books describing Britain and Wales during the Middle Ages but also an internet "favorites" folder on her laptop with at least fifty saved websites dedicated to the various eras in which she had lived. It didn't make any difference to her story, but she reacted badly when I referred to Tegwen's time as the "*Dark* Ages," regarding it innocently as a common historic reference.

"Because it came along before the Renaissance," she said with a scowl, "doesn't mean those times were dark!"

I listened she reminded me Tegwen "didn't have to endure the Saxons and Normans, Vikings, or goddamned Henry the Eighth." I nodded in silence, deciding to never open *that* wound again, but the mysterious world of the Druids became more interesting to me than it had been.

Little of them is known today because of the maddening absence of a written Celtic language. There is slight evidence by way of artifacts and remnants of their settlements, leaving mostly the transcribed accounts of others to describe (in miniscule detail) who and what they were. Worse still, those commentaries were made primarily by Romans (or Greek scholars on their behalf) and could hardly be regarded as objective or fair, considering such open hostility the Empire held for Druids over 500 years.

Julius Caesar's commentaries on Druidic influence, made from his experience fighting the Gauls in modern-day France, Belgium, and northern Italy, seemed to me little more than offhand, surface-level notes and certainly not a thorough academic white paper telling us things about the Druids other historical analyses cannot. The texts in Aline's collection included observations from the odd Roman soldier or attending commentator keeping track of the Roman Empire's western-most domain, but it was clear they had no use for Druids and all of them said so. Pliny spoke of "monstrous rites," and the revulsion he reported from human sacrifice (including cannibalism as a part of the ritual sacrifice process) suggests an obvious, deliberate bias against the Druids, and I wondered if any of it made a difference to Aline. The Roman experience with Druids in Gaul, she reminded me, was not hers and happened long before she was born.

A class of people within the Celtic tribes, mystery-shrouded Druids were priestly keepers of knowledge and a connection to the physical world around them; teachers, judges and powerful seers were the link between natural and supernatural. The questions piled up and I could barely contain myself.

"You know how much people today *don't* know about the Druids, right?" I asked.

"Oh yes," she replied simply.

"Doesn't it bother you?"

"No," she answered. "Should it?"

"It would be impossible for me to know what *you* know and not be tempted to straighten out their misperceptions!"

"It wouldn't if you were me."

Her answer stopped me cold. She showed none of the frustration I expected, and I wondered if she was just that patient or if there was another force operating to make the question irrelevant. Of course, presenting herself as the only living person who can tell the world precisely what it was to be a Druid priestess in post-Roman Wales meant exposing herself to a nightmare of intense scrutiny and plenty of vehement disbelief the rest of her life, and I was silently proud of myself for not taking it further.

"And Druids today?" I asked, hoping to steer the conversation away from an uncomfortable reality she could never allow into the light.

"There aren't any," she answered blandly. "At least none that I know of."

"There must be *some*," I countered. "They gather at Stonehenge every year and commune with the oaks during one solstice or another, right?"

"They're not Druids, Evan," she replied, and her expression changed to one of caution. "Stonehenge had nothing to do with us; it was built at least a thousand years before Celtic people came out from continental Europe, probably by Neolithic Britons who lived there three or four millennia ago. I didn't even know there *was* a Stonehenge until my fifth life when I learned of it from my tutor."

"If they're not Druids, who *are* they?"

"People who feel a deep connection to nature, I suppose," she said with a new distant tone. "They practice what they believe to be the traditions we kept, or what they would *like* to believe, and most of them have Celtic ancestries."

An image from a documentary came quickly into my thoughts, showing white-robed people carrying stylized gold sickles across a field, clearly somewhere on Salisbury Plain, making their way to the ancient and mysterious monument.

"I always thought of them as flakes and dirt-worshipers who think it's cool to call themselves 'Druids.'"

"They're not all flakes, Evan; they simply hold onto a modern interpretation of Druidic traditions no differently than Christians or Muslims hold onto theirs. I suppose some are charmed by the trappings of what they perceive as Druid life, but for many, it represents wonder and respect for the earth."

"What is the 'modern interpretation,'" I continued. "Are they missing something?"

"A few have worked to revive our traditions but mostly in the last century and from beliefs they either created or interpreted to a deliberate purpose," she answered. "People today who call themselves 'Druids' are not, but their chosen lifestyle celebrates nature's power, just as we did. They cause no harm and you can't say that about *all* religious or spiritual pursuits."

Aline's characterization was honest and made without the prejudices and personal dislikes from my own limited perspective. I admit many *are* drawn to modern Druid culture by the inspirational qualities of their Celtic heritage and a powerful sense of ancestral place. (I suppose I am, too.) Either way, it was surprising she, of all people, rose to their defense until I came to understand the difference because Aline judges with a better, more generous spirit than I. Neither magical nor harmful, she sees people who look toward a time in a distant past from the uncertain chaos of the present, reaching for meaning among the same trees and grassy hills *she* loves so much. Today, I admire her for it even more.

She stood at the window beside me for a while, and I wondered if her mind wanders as any other person's might or if it takes her instead to the places where she lived long before, always there and waiting for her return. There would be time, she said, to show me more images and moments from a remote, post-Roman village in the late 400s, but I anticipated a description of the next.

"And the second life?" I asked with suddenly growing interest.

"I wish I could tell you," she replied, but her answer seemed distant, disaffected, and nothing like the breeze of nostalgic joy she'd brought with the description of Tegwen's existence.

"What's stopping you?"

"My second life is not the same," she answered. "I have no idea when or where it was, and I can't even tell you what I was called because I never knew."

"Then how do you know it was your second life?"

"I can see moments, and they appear between Tegwen and my third life, but they're distant and vague as it would be in a very short dream," she said. "There are faces but little else; those images were likely my mother and father when I was very young and then the moments end abruptly."

There was no doubt what she meant and the sad conclusion was obvious.

"You died in early childhood."

Aline nodded the confirmation, but she did so with an odd expression of detachment I couldn't decide was either reflective contemplation or simple lack of interest. The time could have been any point between Tegwen's life and the eleventh century—almost six hundred years—but there was nothing to indicate *where*. Her young life, as it was for most children during the Middle Ages, was fragile and always at risk of disease, starvation, or genetic malady, and because of that truth its early end was hardly surprising; Aline only knew she was born.

I asked her if she regarded her second existence differently than the others, simply because it was so brief, but she looked away and said, "It wasn't the only time that happened."

The moment seemed longer than it was, and I expected her to elaborate. Instead, Aline turned to me and pointed to a photocopy of a textbook page with notes scrawled in the margins. I looked and saw a name underlined and bracketed to indicate its importance.

"Enydd merch Uuin?"

"My third life," she answered. "I spent hours living again in the moments because there are no records to tell me where and when. I went there, searching for clues or an indicator from discussions between my mother and father but also neighbors who spoke with travelers passing through."

"What did you learn?"

"I was born in or near Aberffraw and I know at least that much hearing my father tell another where we were from. I think we were traveling because the place looked strange and different; it was clearly not our home."

"Could you deduce the timeline from those moments?"

"Yes, but only because of a power struggle in the southern kingdom of Gwent and news that arrived in our village telling of a Danish king called Canute who invaded. The history texts today show this happened around 1030."

"How old were you?"

"I was probably nine or ten because the images are quite vivid, which they would not have been if I was much younger."

"Which means you were born around 1020."

"I can see moments near the end of my life and another war that changed Gwent when Gruffydd ap Llywelyn took control in 1055. I didn't survive to old age and died probably in my thirties, which aligns with these historic dates."

A new life—another person. Aline began her third existence at a time when the kingdoms of Wales (and all of Britain) were often violent, ever-changing, and unsettled places. She sat patiently while I scanned through her documentation, most of it culled from library books or internet sources, and it was clear her homework was thorough. She told me about life and how it was lived, but the reality she described was sobering to the ears of a twenty-first century man.

"It was always hard going then," she said, "and the moments I can see are the first since Tegwen's life that bring physical sensations."

"Physical?" I asked. "In what way?"

"In Enydd's time we were usually cold and always hungry. A lot of dreadful odors—everything smelled of smoke and shit…unwashed bodies. We scratched constantly at lice, and my mother pulled a fine-tooth comb through my hair to remove the nits. I remember the snapping sound when she crushed them between her fingernails…it wasn't very pleasant."

"I can't understand how anyone lived that way," I said with a slow shake of my head. "What kept you all from going mad?"

"That's just the way life was lived then; we had nothing to compare it against and so we didn't really notice. When I tell you about it now, a thousand years has passed and many things we consider normal today weren't possible in the eleventh century."

"What did your family do?"

"My father was a sawyer," she continued. "I liked to watch them cut logs into boards and beams. There was a trench dug out of the ground—a cousin down inside and my father up on the log. They pushed and pulled a big saw up and down. In summer it usually attracted hornets, though…the sap."

"Food must've been a challenge in those days," I offered.

"My father and mother tended what crops they could grow in a sort of garden behind our little house, but much of what they earned went to the local Lord and the Church anyway."

"What did you eat on an average day?" I asked.

"Bread and vegetables, mostly," she answered. "Meat was rarely on our table, and chickens were eaten only when they stopped laying eggs."

"It sounds to me as if your family and neighbors were…I don't know, serfs?"

"Most common folk *were*," she replied. "Unless you were noble-born, you worked the fields and used whatever skills you had to feed your family; that's all there was."

More than once my mind wandered to Damon and what he would make of it had Aline taken *him* on equivalent trips through the magic of her mental time machine. As an archaeologist, my brother might well have offered her every penny he owned in exchange for personal views of those moments and a chance to see what no one alive has ever experienced.

"How did it end up for Enydd...for *you*, I mean?"

"I can't be certain, but I believe I died from complications during childbirth," she replied softly. "I was married off to a young man in town called Cynwrig. I didn't like him, but he stood to inherit a tannery from his father and that meant stability."

"It was arranged?" I asked.

"My father simply wanted me to have a roof over my head and food to eat; Cynwrig had both but he needed a wife. The match was agreed and I had to accept it."

"You don't often visit that time in your thoughts, do you?" I asked.

"Not very," she replied. "He wasn't cruel, and he never mistreated me, but Cynwrig worked hides all day and the vile smells were always there, a persistent odor of death. He was acceptable as a husband but certainly not preferable. I did my duty without complaint and we had two children: a boy called Gwion and a girl, Angharad."

Aline's voice softened suddenly, and I saw her head tilt gently to one side the way people do when a memory takes them to another, more solemn place. I wondered if it was the lingering power of maternal instinct and helplessness knowing her children were long dead and gone, but her silence was made by something more. I sat beside her and watched for a moment until she seemed to recover and finish the story of Enydd's life.

"I became pregnant again and Cynwrig was worried because we would have another mouth to feed. He softened on the idea after a while, but there was a conscription and they took him to fight in the king's army against soldiers from Mercia far away to the east...I never saw him again."

I knew most rulers in that time didn't maintain a standing army unless their kingdom was under attack, or alternatively, when they wanted to attack somebody *else's* kingdom.

"They said he died in service to the King."

"You were left alone?" I asked.

"I was left without a husband; Cynwrig's younger brother, Hywel, would inherit the tannery, but I wasn't thrown out. There were lots of war widows in those times and I carried on with it until…"

Her expression changed again and I think she just needed to move beyond the memory.

"When it was time, my mother-in-law and my own sister were with me, and I remember they were terribly worried and there was a lot of pain. I know it was the day our third child was born but the moments stop so suddenly."

"Are you sure?" I asked gently. "Your description sounds as if…"

"I didn't survive," she replied at nearly a whisper. "I have few memories of my child, and only those made when they held him up for me to see. There was so much blood…"

While Aline moved through time in her thoughts, I felt badly for her but there was nothing to say. After a while she smiled when the memory of her final breath as Enydd merch Uuin slipped away. I found myself stuck at an uncomfortable place, looking on without the slightest idea how it must feel for her to relive that time and endure its cost a thousand years gone.

"No public records in villages back then?" I asked.

"The Church kept most but we were illiterate and wouldn't know what to do with them anyway."

I understood what that problem meant in tangible terms.

"It's impossible to know what became of your kids."

"I've wondered," she said. "But no; there isn't a chance to research an ordinary family in a poor village so long ago."

"Then it's possible you have descendants from that life, or your others, running around out there today?"

"Yes," she answered, but there was no hint of excitement at the prospect, and I knew enough to know it was time to leave it alone and change the subject.

"Obviously you couldn't in your second life, but when you lived as Enydd, did your abilities surface?"

Aline seemed to brighten up when I asked the question, relieved perhaps of continuing a painful narrative.

"They did but it wasn't in the way you mean."

"How so?"

"I could hear thoughts of others, as I had in Tegwen's life, but I couldn't manipulate the physical world around me the way I can today."

"Did Cynwrig know?"

"Absolutely not," she replied at once. "In my early life as Enydd, I didn't know if it was the voice of a demon or an angel speaking to me from Heaven. It was frightening, at first, but as I grew older it became easier to accept when I began to see the moments from Tegwen's life and understand again."

"If you were frightened at the prospect of the devil inside your mind, why didn't you say something to your husband, or maybe the priests?"

"I remember considering it," she said, "but Cadwal's warning was always there and it frightened me enough to keep quiet."

"You mean it scared *Tegwen* enough."

"Yes, but remember, Evan, the wrong person could just as easily regard me as an agent of Satan. In that time and place, faith and superstition were often the same thing; telling *anyone* I could read minds could have gotten me killed."

The image of Enydd beneath an executioner's axe or chained to a stake and burned alive made me shudder. I looked at her and waited as she closed her eyes. For a moment, I thought Aline was finishing a last stroll through a life that went dark a thousand years before, but when she reached for me it was only fatigue. I pointed her toward the stairs and followed quietly; there would be time enough to return and wander through events of the past. She wanted to watch television for a while, but another thought crept in and I waited for a decent opening to bring up the sore subject.

"Okay," I said at last. "I can't argue with this, any of this, but the endgame is still coming, and Burke isn't going away."

"No, he's not," she replied softly.

There was little doubt she read and felt the swirl of competing emotions inside my mind, but I needed to talk it out with her just the same.

"He's got a lot of firepower behind him, Aline."

"Those people live in the shadows, Evan," she replied. "They can't discuss what they do outside their world because they know pulling it into the light would make questions they can't answer."

"What are you saying?"

"Burke has no interest in Renard's plan to have me arrested."

"Does that matter?"

"Of course! He may be a smarmy bastard, but Burke has been down this path before, and his desire for knowledge outweighs anything the government might do to interfere."

Aline's words suggested something deeper, and the imaginary, "yowling cat" sounds went off inside my head when I thought it through to its obvious conclusion.

"What do you mean 'down this path'?"

She looked with a strange, momentary distance in her eyes, perhaps taken by her thoughts to another place.

"I could hear it when Burke was just leaving the shop," she said. "There were signals…clear and easy to find. This is not the first time he's encountered people with abilities like mine."

"He didn't seem overly skeptical, I'll give you that; as if it was expected."

The Colwyn Bay scene played out in my memories and the meaning became clear: Burke's conspicuous calm hid something more.

"He wants to talk," she said. "It's clear he knows at least some of the things I can do, but he needs to understand *how*."

"He's afraid of losing containment," I added. "No one beyond his sphere is supposed to know, and Renard's little road trip to Wales has forced Burke's hand."

Aline turned suddenly to me and said, "I know you won't, but it's all right if you want to leave for a while."

My shoulders sagged and the expression I wore only confirmed what Aline already knew: I wasn't going anywhere.

"I'm sorry, Evan, it's just that…"

"I don't need to escape, Aline."

She smiled to let me know the question was only a formality.

"We'll have to call him sooner or later," I added.

"Yes," she replied softly, "and it may not end well."

A WEEK WENT by and inventory duties at the shop kept Aline in Colwyn Bay until late afternoon most days, but I sat at the counter in her kitchen while she emptied steaming linguini from her colander into a shallow bowl.

"Can I ask you something?"

"Of course," she answered.

"The others…your earlier lives."

"Yes?"

"Why are some of the moments easier to find than others?"

She leaned against a wall for a moment and her eyes narrowed as she considered the best way to describe the things I needed to know. There would be time to show me all of it, she said, but the process is lengthy. I knew there was more but teasing it out of her had become an interesting investigation aimed at a past no one else could see. Aline sat beside me and took in a deep breath, pausing a last second or two before she began.

"In this life," she said, "with all the power of technology and history at my fingertips, it's been much easier to study and research the time from my memories—those moments."

"Libraries, the internet…" I echoed.

"Yes, but even still, there is so much that cannot be described with precision. I've had to piece together the things history knows and try to weed out the things it doesn't."

"Isn't it frustrating to know when they're wrong and not be able to tell them?"

"When I was younger, perhaps, but would it make any difference?" she asked warily.

"It might to a history PhD trying to get tenure!" I said, snorting.

She laughed at the notion to remind me of Cadwal's words and a promise she made. There was a reason he insisted on her silence, she said, and his wisdom had proved correct too many times for her to ignore. I think of that promise now and it holds me as firmly as Aline; I have accepted the responsibility of her secrets as my own whether I like it or not.

20
ONE AMONG MANY

WHEN I met Aline on our shared hillside, our first moment of change passed by unnoticed because I simply didn't know then what I know now. Andre Renard's ill-fated visit created another, and Aline's willingness to expose who and what she was became the next. On a cool day of mist and drizzle, the next steps in a long and indescribable journey were about to begin.

Aline told me about Enydd's life, and I listened with a different ear because of its direct connection to her, but also for the unique view of history her description allowed. During quiet moments in bed or on her couch, she found and guided my thoughts beyond the here and now, and I went along with her like a tourist admitted through the gates of ancient, forbidden places. In an odd moment, I felt a wash of gratitude for the gift of my place as the only one to see backward in time along so vivid and personal a path, privileged to watch and listen for myself as if I too had walked there.

We stayed away from the brief time of her second life and I suppose it's just as well; aside from the uncomfortable reality it brought to Aline, there was nothing for me to experience or understand about a mother's death. Enydd's life, however, was another matter, and I smiled in spite of the wretched conditions she endured because it poured out a thousand more questions to every answer. I imagined again how it might be for an audience of historians, scholars, and archaeologists—people like Damon—listening in dumbfounded awe to Aline's every word and the priceless opportunity to find and hold onto truth and real understanding of a distant past.

In the morning, she mixed up some cocoa and when she poured it into cups beneath a trail of steam, we settled for my next "lesson." I asked her who she was in the fourth of her seven lives, but her expression became solemn and she looked at the floor. She pulled from her archive box more papers and printed pages from who knows how many historical reference documents and websites. At the beginning of the notes on an ordinary spiral-bound pad, I saw a name that seemed more modern Welsh to me than any given to an Iron Age girl, and Aline spoke as I read.

"Marged Caffyn," she began. "Born in winter 1338 near Caernarfon."

After plowing through European history to refresh my understanding of the Middle Ages (mostly because Aline made me), obscure dates I'd learned in school made a lot more sense in that process than they ever did when I was young.

"Right at the beginning of the Hundred Years' War," I declared proudly, and just to show her I *did* pay attention, my report continued. "Long after William showed up at Hastings, which means pretty much everyone was speaking French by then?"

"Not quite," she replied blandly, "particularly among the common folk, but you have the correct timeline."

Aline's tone left no doubt she wasn't in a playful mood. I retreated and asked for the story, but it was the ending that made for her suddenly somber mood. Marged was the middle of three children by a blacksmith who spent most of his time forging weapons for the king's foot soldiers and lesser knights—a single-purpose production line for iron spear tips, simple daggers, and arrowheads by the hundred. Her description of daily existence in the 1300s didn't sound meaningfully different to me from those she made of Enydd's life three hundred years before, and the stark similarity reminded me in today's age of rapid and incessant technological progress how *little* things changed once upon a time.

Anticipating a fast-forward to another marriage and the drudgeries of village life in the shadow of a Norman castle, I wondered if "Caffyn" was her maiden name or that of her eventual husband. Aline looked at me with sad eyes and said, "I didn't make it that far."

She pointed to a single line on a page from her notes and in it, a date: "*11 March 1350.*" She showed me more photocopies of public notice documents in an ongoing process of memorializing each day's casualties in Monmouth.

Sometime in the late eighteenth century, she reported, an academic exercise was completed for the purpose of creating duplicate records, translated from Latin into English, to the benefit of scholars without access to archived originals. The information a scrivener recreated faithfully showed the March 11 date and names of people in the southern Welsh city who succumbed. A notation still in Latin near the top of the page cited "*Pestis*" as the cause for each of the twenty-two deaths registered only the day before, and on the list was a simple line that explained Aline's mood. It was brief, concise, and sent a shiver up my spine:

"*Marged Caffyn, 12 years. Died this day 'neath Monnow Gate.*"

Nothing needed to be said. A relentless and efficient killer, the Black Death swept across Europe from its apparent origins in southern Russia, taking at least 25 million people—a third of the population of Europe—in less than a decade. One of the victims when the plague finally reached southeastern Wales was a young girl called Marged.

I waited until Aline nodded for us to continue, but it seemed weird and wrong to dwell on so horrible an end to her fourth life. Perhaps it was Marged's tender age, or the unspeakable agony she endured until the end found and delivered her to darkness, but I hoped Aline would leave it and return to finish the history later. Instead, she sat and tried to smile, so I knelt beside her and asked if she was sure.

"Marged's life was brief, but it was also mine and you need to understand."

"I can see what happened but how did she begin?"

"I was born in Caernarfon where my father worked as a blacksmith. My grandfather—also a smith—was badly injured in a fall and he died a few days later. They sent word for my father to assume ownership of the family's shop, but it meant leaving everything behind and moving to Monmouth."

"That's a big step," I noted and Aline agreed.

"People weren't mobile like they are today."

I thought about that time and the logistics involved, knowing a move of everything you own 150 miles away was no simple hop in the fourteenth century.

"Fill up the ox cart and put one foot in front of the other?"

"The journey to Monmouth is one of the most vivid times I can see from that life. It took forever. We were near starvation and out of money by the time we arrived, and I hated my father for making us go."

She waited a while and when she went on, I could sense the growing tension because she filtered it through to my thoughts so I would feel and understand how her life went from ordinary and relatively comfortable (for a medieval family) to a long and taxing plod the length of the country. I saw images and the somber mood of her parents, bickering back and forth throughout to make it obvious her mother wasn't overjoyed at the prospect, either. Shabby, remote way-houses smelled vile and were often hives of greasy, unwashed locals who aimed leering stares at Marged and she knew, even at her age, what it meant.

Their journey was lengthy but once arrived, she said, the welcome extended by the wife of her father's cousin was cold and forced. Marged never knew why their own relatives held such resentment, but it was likely made from disappointment when Marged's father assumed property the cousin wanted for himself. Regardless, new arrangements only made worse her feeling of isolation and loneliness until the cousin's family moved away, but their settled life didn't last long. A neighbor told them of reports spreading quickly through town that a merchant's son returning from Weymouth on a small cargo vessel had fallen gravely ill, and his sickness was obvious: the plague had come with him and its horrors would soon change everything.

Aline stopped a while, walking slowly between her kitchen and front room as the images passed through her mind. I couldn't see or feel them, and when I asked, she told me there was no reason I should; the pain and fear of a little girl when the first telltale sores appeared was not something she would allow beyond Tegwen's memories.

They knew what it meant, she said, and her grandmother's worry the pestilence was God's fierce punishment for their lack of piety made little sense (or difference) to a child who hadn't been alive long enough to understand the idea of sin. All too soon, calls from the street to "bring the dead" were shouted out with demands from their priest for help digging huge pits into which the day's victims would be dumped and covered over with a thin layer of dirt. Every evening, the ghastly task was repeated.

Accounts recorded all across Europe were grim and mostly uniform regardless of kingdom or citizenship: The Black Death cut down rich and poor alike, and it moved with astonishing speed. Whole villages fell in weeks and the body count soared so badly, many of the corpses were burned atop pyramids of tree branches in a desperate attempt to cleanse the land. Those with any kind of wealth fled the towns (and what few cities there were), hoping to find refuge in the countryside, but there was little chance of escaping the invisible horror.

I asked Aline if she remembered the pain, but she would only say the "moments" stopped so abruptly it was likely she died within a day or two after the first symptoms appeared. Sufferers may well have been submerged in a semi-lucid state as the fever took them over, and because of it, I reasoned, Marged was likely unconscious when it ended for her. I still find it interesting Aline's reaction to that particular life was so strong, and it made me wonder if there were other moments and the ravages of the Black Death she wouldn't show, shielding me perhaps from its terrible effect.

On the following morning I noticed the plastic tub and cardboard boxes littering her dining room table were returned to their hole in the wall, but she didn't ask me to push the heavy sideboard to hide it from view; there were two more lives for me to learn about and understand.

WE WENT ON a Saturday road trip up to Liverpool as a deliberate (and welcome) diversion from the somber mood left behind by the details of Marged Caffyn's short, unpleasant life. The purpose, Aline told me, was an earlier promise she'd made to Vienne that I would be forced to consider a new car, and since she favored the brand, Hatfields Land Rover near the banks of the Mersey was our destination.

It was a wonderful outing and a convenient excuse for Aline to get in some "big city" Liverpool shopping, a perfect choice for venturing out and away from the history lessons for a while. Poking around the dealership's display floor didn't do much to improve my notorious and stubborn ideas of thrift. I'd had no intention of committing to such a thing when we left her house, but the decent trade-in value they offered for my used Nissan, and Aline's relentless goading, resulted in bank transfers and signatures for an ice-blue Range Rover Sport model before I could change my mind. When I asked Aline why she didn't take her own advice and look at one for herself, she just smiled and said, "Maybe in the summer."

"They have a bunch to choose from," I countered. "Why not let them fix you up with one of the big ones?"

"Next time," she said with a grin. "I want two doors and a lot more horsepower."

It was nice to hear a giggle and her return from the solemn moments seeing and remembering her life as Marged and the sadness of knowing how and why she died so young. Aline didn't need my pity, and I didn't offer, but I wondered if the remaining of her seven lives would take her to another past she'd rather avoid. It wasn't the right time to ask, so we spent the afternoon figuring out how to work all the features in my expensive new car until her phone buzzed with an incoming call. When I asked who it was, the number originated in London and we knew at once: Burke waited on the other end of the line.

21
A ROAD TRIP TO SOMERSET

ALINE put the phone in speaker mode and the drama resumed.

"Miss Lloyd," he began, "I wonder if you've given some thought to our earlier inquiries?"

"We've been busy, Mr. Burke," she answered, and her tone was anything but friendly. It didn't deter him and he moved the conversation along quickly.

"No doubt, but I rather hoped you might find a few moments for us," he continued. "Time has passed, you see, and our masters…well, they're becoming twitchy, worrying you may decide to slip away in the dark of night."

"They are mistaken," she replied defiantly. "I have no intention of running from you or anyone else."

"Then perhaps we could meet and continue our discussion?"

She looked at me, and I shrugged with indifference; there was no point in expecting Burke would let it go, and my fight-or-flight instinct was trending decidedly toward fight.

"I don't want to see you in my shop again," she said curtly, "but I suppose another spot would do for your purposes. What did you have in mind?"

"We do have a cooperative arrangement with one or two military installations, and a secure space at Norton Manor in Somerset has been put at our disposal for this sort of thing."

"Go on."

"It's a Royal Marines camp very near Taunton."

She looked at me once more and I shook my head to signal my doubts, but I knew she could hear them anyway.

"No," she answered simply.

Watching her dismiss a man with Burke's power and influence was particularly satisfying and maybe more amusing that I should admit. His sudden awkward pause made it clear she had caught him off guard, and I expected a disjointed, fumbled reply. Instead, the ever-cool and unflappable Burke held course.

"May I ask why not?"

"Really, Mr. Burke," she said with a sneer, "do you expect us to go into a military camp and watch stupidly as they lock the gate behind us?"

"You misunderstand," he replied. "We have no interest in detaining you."

I imagined he was speaking through another of his automatic, disingenuous smiles. I hoped Aline would tell him to piss off, but she closed her eyes and said, "Very well, Mr. Burke; what do you propose?"

"I'll make arrangements and meet you at the gate, shall we say, this time tomorrow?"

"And then?"

"There are relatively comfortable quarters that will be made available where we can sit together and have a private conversation."

"What is the purpose of this visit?"

"We are simply interested in learning and understanding, Miss Lloyd—there will be *only* conversation, and you are always free to go any time you wish."

Burke was thinking ahead, but I didn't see it in those tense moments.

"No promises," she answered bluntly.

It didn't faze him, and Burke said, "Mr. Morgan, I presume you will be joining as well?"

I found it needless to make a point of showing me he wasn't concerned or worried about my involvement, but it was no surprise. A last glance from Aline and she said, "Perhaps tomorrow, Mr. Burke."

Before he could answer, she disconnected and sat on a bar stool in her kitchen waiting for me to say something, but there was no need. Wherever Burke was going with his persistent interest, she wasn't willing to encourage it by a cordial (and committed) agreement. I knew she was ready to go, but it was still fun to watch her make him squirm.

ON SUNDAY MORNING we finished breakfast and pointed the car south toward Cardiff. Aline hadn't been to Somerset in a while and I never had. She wasn't interested in idle chitchat, so I paid attention to the road and kept quiet; if Aline felt my rising anxiety (which was a given in my experience), she made no mention of it. By the time we followed the M4 across the Bristol Channel by way of a new bridge at Severn Beach, the churn in my stomach was a distraction and still she seemed unmoved by it all. An hour later we eased slowly along a gentle country highway until the fence line of Norton Manor Camp appeared on our left, wearing a predictable crown of razor wire as it funneled us downhill past an old artillery piece and a simple blue sign announcing "40 Commando, Royal Marines."

Burke was waiting at a guard house, and we sat quietly as the credential inspection began, and when it concluded, a very stout corporal motioned us briskly toward a shiny black Jaguar sedan for a quick ride along the narrow streets of the camp until it stopped in front of an ordinary building. Somebody opened the doors for us, and we followed inside to what appeared to be a small classroom where mission briefings might be held, and within, four others leaned against tables behind false smiles we knew not to trust. After the door closed with a solid "clunk," Burke began.

"The demure accommodations were arranged last minute, so I do hope you'll bear with us?"

I watched Aline watching Burke, and for a terrifying moment the anger seeped through from her thoughts, threatening to derail a discussion yet to begin.

"We're here," she began. "Let's get on with it."

Burke nodded with a smile and it was obvious he'd expected her short reply as he extended a hand at the two who came with him to Colwyn Bay.

"You may remember Kevin and William from our first visit to your shop, but also with us today is Colonel Halliwell and to his right, Mr. Gregory Hurd representing the interests of Downing Street."

I smiled and nodded.

"Stuart Halliwell?"

"Yes, that's right," he replied with a confused glance at Burke.

"Andy Leach says hello; wanted me to tell you he still owes you a beer."

Halliwell grinned immediately and the tension surrounding us seemed to disappear. Dropping Andy's name brought a sudden legitimacy I could never have won on my own, and the silent, ironclad bond joining "Spec Ops" people became a bridge between worlds. Burke nodded with a smile, knowing I had made a few calls since that first day at Aline's shop, but I didn't care.

I wanted to smile and nod now that the mysterious Hurd/Halliwell duo was finally known, but Aline was not as forgiving, and she walked straight at Hurd. When he stiffened suddenly and leaned back in reflex, it was clear she was already inside and probing.

"If he wanted to speak with me," she said, and only to Burke, "why wait until now?"

Hurd's disaffected expression changed at once, and I saw in his eyes a worry turning quickly to fear.

"I'm quite certain our colleagues are grateful you've chosen to join us," Burke interjected hopefully as he moved forward, but Aline wasn't finished, and Hurd winced just as the ever-present Kevin stepped quickly between them to shield his chief. It took only a moment—a second in time—before the silent soldier's eyes closed tightly (just as Hurd's had), and I reached for her.

"Let's hear them out," I offered.

When she released him at last, Kevin stood away and the sudden, confusing effect of Aline's thoughts sawing through unhindered left him shaken. There is a clear distinction between those moments when she's merely "listening" and the jolting sensation when a target feels the dull ache of purposeful intrusion. As it was for me, Kevin had no idea she'd wandered through his mind on that cold, blustery day at her shop, but this was something else when the needling, invisible probes slipped through and the pain took him.

"Aline," I whispered softly, guiding her away so that Burke's bodyguard (and Hurd) could recover.

I didn't feel what she gave them but it could only have been unpleasant. A message was sent and they understood at last how effortless it really is for her. Burke's smarm was gone, too, and yet he did nothing to interfere; was it his way of convincing Hurd? Aline suspected the haughty politician wasn't fully on board with Burke's mandate, and his dismissive posture did nothing to disprove her theory. We waited another minute or two until Burke motioned for us to sit. Aline shook her head "no" but he pulled a chair for her anyway and said, "Please?"

When things had settled Hurd kept a respectful distance. In a contradiction to Burke's slightly bald and slouching presence, the powerful politician looked more a manufactured talking head on the television. Gleaming titanium cuff links peeked out conspicuously from the sleeves of an expensive tailored suit covering a frame that was fit and lean from jogging or squash matches beneath a precise, drawn-back hairstyle you can't get at an ordinary barber shop. Tanned skin betrayed a vacation home in places where the sun always shines (somewhere on the Mediterranean, I guessed), but none of it mattered to Aline; government power broker or otherwise, Hurd was noticeably rattled, and Burke continued without hesitation.

"The purpose of this meeting, Miss Lloyd, is merely to establish a dialogue in anticipation of further talks. As I mentioned before, we have seen Inspector Renard's documentation but also a lengthy, interesting collection of records from Scottish police and more than a few doctors."

"We've been through this before, Mr. Burke," I said quickly.

"Indeed, but you must see by now our interest has become…well, *enhanced* shall we say?"

"Enhanced?"

"Our own staff has reviewed internally, and their assessment of Miss Lloyd's condition was bound to be somewhat different from those at hospital, wouldn't you agree?"

"How is it different?" I said with a deliberate sneer. "She was attacked! What would *you* do in her place?"

"The physicians in Glasgow had no idea what sorts of things Aline can do, whereas our laboratory chaps *do*; I would say that is a significant difference."

Instead of blurting it out directly, Burke laid hard truth on the table by a mere detail so that no more time would be wasted pretending they were no closer to it than the cops in Glasgow or psychiatrists who looked and saw an emotional malady to be isolated and treated.

"We understand their conclusions," he continued, "and they can hardly be blamed for diagnosing the condition because she simply gave them precisely what they expected to find. In their position, one would be hard-pressed to conclude otherwise."

"But you know better," Aline said abruptly and with a deliberate, unnerving smile.

"I hoped you might help us with that," Burke replied. "We know enough to press on but not to the specific degree necessary."

"Am I to be your latest experiment?" Aline asked. "A cooperative rat to be run through one of your mazes or to drool whenever you ring the bell?"

Before Burke could answer, Hurd regained enough composure to take control.

"Alan is acting on my direction, Miss Lloyd."

It was the first time we heard him speak, and I think he believed pushing his weight around earlier rather than later might pay dividends when Aline realized how important he was.

It didn't work.

She let him move closer in the mistaken belief our discussion was now his to lead until a single glance stopped him cold. Hurd's head was turned a little, and he regarded her like a carnival sideshow spectator expecting her to say "boo" at any moment. I knew he worried she might open that invisible valve and release the dull pain again but worse than what she'd aimed at poor Kevin. Aline faced him squarely as she spoke.

"Are you in charge here, Mr. Hurd?"

"I am the senior authority, yes," he replied with as much confidence as he could muster, but the perspiration was gathering at his temples and his face wore the sheen of a man walking quickly on a hot day.

I was sure he was going to get a second dose, but Aline turned suddenly and her eyes fell instead on Halliwell. The air became charged as she reached out with those first thin fingers of thought—exploring and probing—until the landscape of his mind was opened for her to inspect. A momentary pause and then it resumed, but this time the familiar tone came alive in *my* ears and with it, an abrupt and disturbing realization she wasn't concerned with collateral effect. At once, Halliwell's jaw tightened and his mouth formed a screwed-up frown the way people do when anger and frustration take them to their limit. He fought it bravely until she increased the pressure and pain to remind him there was no place to hide.

Like a timid person flinching from the sound of a loud and unexpected bang, Halliwell's eyes flickered and his shoulders hunched when tiny unseen knives stabbed from within. He moaned out loud in reflex, and I think it made things worse for Hurd watching in frozen silence until Burke stepped forward with an outstretched hand.

"We don't need this, Aline; you have our attention most certainly!"

She looked at him, and I wondered if the power inside would shift his way, but instead she exhaled a deep breath and it was clear her entire body tensed as her invasion of Halliwell's brain gained momentum. When she was finished, the colonel tried hard to mask the terrible effect, but it seemed juvenile and stupid. I smirked with a slow shake of my head; I know Hurd noticed but it was unlikely Halliwell had any clue how mild and easy his moment of discovery had been when compared with the rough boys at a Glasgow bus stop.

Aline maneuvered suddenly between Hurd and Halliwell, leaning against the table like a loafer on a stoop waiting for something interesting to happen. The move was so brazen—fearless and deliberate—I knew it had to be disturbing for them until she looked finally at Hurd.

"You didn't believe Mr. Burke's description," she said softly, but she turned again, only inches from Halliwell. "You needed to see and feel—to know that it's real after all."

She waited another moment, likely to maximize the effect, and then she returned to take my hand in hers. It was chilling to see the metamorphosis of her personality into something else, and as she looked deep into Halliwell's eyes, Aline finished the point.

"Now you do."

Hurd had been mostly irrelevant to the moment, and it took me a second or two before realizing Halliwell was her primary target all along. I wondered what she knew that hadn't been said; what secrets glowed like a scorpion under a black light, suddenly exposed to her and torn from the colonel's mind?

Burke stood out the moment to let Hurd and Halliwell recover, but Aline's power, and a demonstration she wanted so desperately to avoid, left no doubt in their minds. Hurd's casual, disaffected pose when we arrived was gone as he struggled to gather himself. With Halliwell and the reliable Kevin in tow, he aimed a glare at Burke on his way to the door.

"I'll expect a briefing and situation report on this by end of day," he said (deliberately avoiding eye contact with Aline, I noticed), and then he was gone.

We heard car doors slam outside and a revved engine that signaled a hurried man in need of distance between the world he knew and another frightening place where the impossible kicked down the door to his life of surety and tradition along the corridors of Whitehall. In an odd sort of way, I almost felt sorry for him, having been there myself, pulled into a harsh light where nothing escapes Aline's attention.

Burke held up a hand at a profoundly nervous William to assure him the show was ended and that he wouldn't be next.

"May we continue?" Burke asked.

"Please do," Aline said, smiling.

With calm and order returned, Burke positioned himself on the other side of a table from us and clasped his hands together in what seemed a show that neither he nor William would appear the slightest bit threatening.

"Since you possess such extraordinary skills," he began, "I'm sure you can see enough in my thoughts to know we operate for the purpose of investigation of subjects who are similar to you in many ways."

"I know what you are, Mr. Burke," Aline replied evenly.

"Then you also know our desire to understand your unique nature is supported by a larger authority and not merely by way of scientific interest."

"Hurd?" I asked.

Burke nodded and inspected his nails while he decided how best to tell us of his group and what they do.

"Only a handful know anything at all about our organization," he continued, "and fewer still have any idea people like Aline even exist. There is no point in advertising because the common person wouldn't know what to do with the information if we presented it to them prime time on BBC; it is simply a reality they cannot see."

"Which," I noted with clear sarcasm, "keeps you safely in the shadows and free from inspection by British taxpayers or the accountability they might demand."

"I suppose that's true, Mr. Morgan, but in the end, their safety is the reason and goal; we don't look into these cases as though we have nothing better to do."

Burke spoke to me but his eyes never left Aline. There was a tone of resentment in his voice, and it came from a thin suggestion in my words his nearly invisible department was somehow immoral or wrongheaded. In truth, Burke walked between two opposing interests, holding the impossibility of the supernatural in one hand while carrying the weight of his position and a responsibility to the people of the United Kingdom in the other. I had enough sympathy for his tight spot to recognize why they chose him for the job and at least a measure of respect that he maintained it without disaster. If sufficiently provoked, people like Aline could unravel the threads holding modern society in place, and Burke's task is learning how and why they exist but also to keep them willingly in a box where they can do no harm. The Glasgow bus stop incident threatened that tenuous equilibrium, and it was Burke's obligation to ensure it went no further.

"What is it you want her to do, Alan?" I asked at last.

"We want her to teach us," he answered, "and that is all. Our facility is configured for studies of this nature, and we merely wish to have an honest conversation."

"*Honest?*" I snorted. "I find it difficult to believe a nice chat will satisfy your curiosity. What's the real game?"

"Our understanding of telekinesis and thought projection is growing, but investigations have been conducted on the fly and rarely in a controlled environment properly equipped and staffed. Gregory's sponsorship and funding has changed that, but he expects results, you see."

I wasn't sure if Burke's explanation was good news or bad. On the one hand, it meant there was enough serious attention given to studying weird paranormal events so that hard-to-justify taxpayer money was spent to equip and staff his group. On the other, there was a nagging possibility bureaucratic interference would expect of him a tangible product and one not necessarily to the favor of those being studied, including Aline. I thought about it for a moment and in my mind a picture emerged: a politician like Hurd fancies himself a man of action—a results getter—who faces a never-ending requirement to qualify his position. For us, he is something altogether different, and a government official is the secondary image that can't be overlooked or underestimated.

"What kind of process did you have in mind?" I asked.

"Our section's facility," he continued, "is tenant to a Royal Air Force installation and functions as a base of operations. Resident laboratory, research, and administrative staff conduct affairs apart from the military. We are obliged to suffer the noise of jets flitting about, but it is private and quite secure."

"Go on."

"Temporary quarters will be provided, as this will likely require a week or two of your time," Burke said, "but the process itself is merely a series of discussions or 'interviews,' if you like."

"What is the purpose of a medical annex?" Aline asked abruptly.

Burke smiled at what he knew was another of Aline's forays inside his thoughts and an involuntary image of the group's headquarters she could see clearly, but something Burke hadn't bothered to mention.

"There are physiological aspects," he answered, "which made it necessary to install a thoroughly equipped infirmary and biosciences lab. We hoped you might agree to provide minor blood and tissue samples, in addition to specialized tests such as MRI and CAT scanning, but also experimental routines to establish parameters and take the full measure of the more…*direct* of your abilities."

"You were right," I said as I turned to Aline. "A lab rat experience."

"Do not be alarmed," Burke said quickly. "Other than the occasional pinprick of a needle, it's mostly a series of physical examinations and a simple test regimen to study Aline's distinctive talents."

"In Scotland," she replied, "I endured more medical tests than anyone I know, and it didn't reveal anything to *their* expensive machines; why do you believe it would be any different with yours?"

Burke's automatic smile returned.

"Perhaps the tests you speak of weren't looking for the proper indicators."

"Or maybe," I interjected quickly, "there's nothing *to* see and you're jerking her around because you can't find an answer, or a tidy math equation, to explain it for assholes like Hurd."

"You may be quite right, Mr. Morgan," Burke said, "but we are left with an obligation to try, aren't we?"

Our perception of Burke's determined, unrelenting persistence was confirmed and it became clear Aline had to decide one way or another. If she agreed, and Burke's words weren't hollow, it would mean time spent inside another secluded military base where questions would be asked and tests administered. If, on the other hand, she said "no" it was unlikely to end the process, and just as

Burke had done ten minutes before, I wanted to push the border and see how *he* would react.

"What happens if she opts out of your intrusive little sweepstakes, Mr. Burke? Maybe we just wish you a pleasant day and walk out right now."

I didn't want to speak for Aline, but I wasn't certain she *would* and the pivotal question needed to be asked. I suppose she already knew what I was going to say because I thought about how I would word it, and the conversation with myself would surely have been wide open to her thoughts, but she only smiled and raised her eyebrows as if to say, "Well?" when the ball was returned to Burke's court.

"As I said before," he answered coolly, "you are always free to go any time you wish but doing so will only invite more scrutiny from Mr. Hurd and his associates, none of whom as interested in your welfare as we."

I felt the hair go up on the back of my neck, and I'm sure the anger made my face run red.

"Is that another threat, Alan?" I demanded.

"Not at all; I simply want you to understand this engagement has now progressed to a point at which a civil and mutually beneficial solution can be reached without further intrusions. If you choose to delay, our superiors are likely to take a different, less cooperative course."

"It sounds like a threat to me," Aline said, but Burke assured us otherwise.

I watched him in the silence of that room, and it was clear he'd arrived at a break point: a place where false cordiality was no longer required and plain English became the best way out.

"Mr. Hurd is a man who wants to be somebody," he said. "Family connections may have influenced his acceptance into a very powerful fraternity, but it is a temporary condition; Gregory has eyes on a much larger chair."

"His politics don't mean a damn to me," I replied.

"Regardless, the problem remains, and he expects a return on his investment. A lot of money is spent maintaining our quiet enterprise, but there are limits to what the government will accept, and Gregory's word alone keeps the funding in place; if he doesn't get what he thinks he needs in a timely fashion, he *will* react."

"Which means the cash is shut off and you're out of business."

"It means, Mr. Morgan, Aline's privacy will become compromised and that is something we would all prefer to avoid."

Burke's description was deliberate, and the endgame was clear: cooperate or those beyond his control would demand action. It occurred to me his goal to keep Hurd and the Whitehall crowd at a distance was as much for his own professional benefit as it was for our safety. When Aline motioned for me to stand down, I understood her position was shifting and likely because she could feel Burke's sincerity and a genuine desire to prevent an escalation.

"I want to consider it with Evan a while longer," she said. "I'm inclined to go along with this but I won't be pushed or prodded, do you understand? If and when I decide to agree, it will happen on *our* schedule and not Mr. Hurd's."

Burke's expression changed again, and it returned to one of relief.

"I understand," he said simply. "I do hope it won't be too long, but you have my number and we look forward to meeting with you again."

Always anticipating, William had called for their car and we went back to the gate in silence. I'm sure Burke knew Aline was still searching and listening, but you wouldn't know it to look at him. Instead, he just shook hands with us, smiled, and said, "Until next time?"

THE RIDE HOME began in silence, but after our first stop for a break and some fuel for the car, Aline smiled at me from her seat.

"Burke is getting nervous," she began.

"He's afraid you're going to bail on him?" I asked, but that wasn't it.

"The people above are pushing him."

"Hurd?"

"Yes, but there is another—a high-level Minister who has deep reservations about paying for a project like this."

"It has to be a dicey proposition," I added, "for a Minister to okay the money knowing exposure would quickly end his career."

"*Her* career," she replied. "Burke was telling the truth about one thing, at least: Hurd's goal is purely political, and he had no real interest in the outcome… until today."

I knew what she meant.

"You scared the shit out of him back there; it's no wonder he left in a tailspin. How many of these bastards even know about Burke's team; can you tell from their thoughts?"

"Not many," she answered, "but Burke has put himself on the line, and it will go badly for him if I don't agree and tell them what they want to know."

"Why now? Did the fiasco in Scotland leak out or put them in the spotlight with the heavies in London?"

Aline turned in her seat and pulled her ankles up beneath her the way she does when we're about to go off on another lengthy and wandering discussion.

"I could hear it in their thoughts but mostly from Burke. They've had others in this position—people with extraordinary abilities—and all of them went along with it quietly; no one before me has resisted."

"But you *have*, and now they're getting jumpy that others beyond their tight little circle will find out. Maybe the press or some kind of stupid whistle-blower nightmare they can't keep under wraps?"

"Yes, but I don't think Burke sees it that way; he really is interested in understanding, whereas Hurd is only looking after himself."

"None of these assholes suspect your other lives, do they?" I asked warily. I would have been surprised if they had, but Aline just smiled and said, "No, and they never will."

It was bound to arrive, but Aline's decision pointed to an uncertain future and I wondered if she already knew.

"You're going to cooperate with Burke, aren't you?"

Aline looked at me with a sudden scowl and said, "If you want to stay home, you can."

She misunderstood my question. I assured her I would go wherever it leads, and I could see her watching me from the corner of my eye. Unable to conceal anything from her when she's determined to pry into my brain meant no amount of lying skills would ever be enough, and my thoughts would be forever open to her. It was insulting she worried I wouldn't stick it out, but worse, the sudden and suspicious turn in her mood left me alone and isolated. It brought a disturbing thought, but one I had to consider: could we reach a day so badly at odds that *I* might become an enemy in her eyes? I hoped she would sense and hear only agitation which, under the circumstances, would be easy to explain away, but again she found something more.

"I wish you wouldn't do that," she said in a pout.

"Do what?" I asked quickly, but the pretense of ignorance just sounded stupid.

"You know what I mean," she replied. "Worrying that I might hurt you—that you would even *consider* it."

"How *should* I react, Aline? You can hear my thoughts—any secret I try to hide—but you couldn't hear and know I wasn't looking for a way to weasel out of this?"

She turned away in silence, but another possibility surfaced I hadn't considered. Perhaps she *can't* hear my every thought after all; maybe it's situational and requires focus or concentration. Was her own emotional turmoil clouding that ability? I decided to test the theory. With the cruise control fixed and our car humming along, I looked off into the distance and thought the words "I love you, Aline" quickly in my mind. She didn't say anything for a while, but when I realized she was watching, I turned to find her smiling again.

"I love you, too, Evan."

22
IN THIS LAND...

FOR the rest of the week we went about our normal routine, and I kept away from the subject of Burke's invitation as Aline considered options. I decided the best way to support her was staying out of it unless she asked for help. When she didn't it seemed as good a time as any to learn again through the images and "moments" from a life lived long ago.

"Tell me about your fifth time through."

"Jane Mower," she replied with a surprising grin. "Born the 20th of February 1701 in Llanelli, not far to the west from Swansea. My father and another man were coachbuilders; they made carriages for wealthy customers in the city."

"Almost four hundred years since Marged," I noted. "A lot of things must've changed in that amount of time."

"A lot of things changed *every* time," she said.

After her first birth in the fifth century, Aline's lives seemed mostly uncomfortable or brief, and I hesitated to ask further against the possibility Jane Mower had been only the next in a series, but Aline brightened considerably.

"It was an ordinary life," she began. "My father's business was fairly successful, and I was brought up in what today you might call an upper middle-class home. We weren't terribly well-off, but we were never poor, either."

"How long did you live?"

I was almost afraid to ask, but Aline returned to the big plastic tub and more folders filled with photocopied documents.

"Into my seventies," she replied with a smile. "It was a better life compared with Marged or Enydd."

I grinned and asked her what made Jane's life special.

"It was the first time I used my abilities deliberately…well, since I was first born."

"*Which* abilities?" I asked, knowing they were considerable and potentially dangerous.

"Until I was older and settled, it was mostly listening to thoughts," she answered. "Anything more would've been an enormous risk, but as it was in my first life, I could hear them."

"Passive only," I replied, "but I'm guessing that didn't last long?"

"As the abilities emerged—when I remembered and understood who I once was—I began to explore and experiment."

"Jane met Tegwen."

Aline glared and her irritation hit me with a sudden, uncomfortable pressure inside my ears.

"I was *always* there," she said at a near growl. "Jane didn't need to be introduced to me!"

The sound of her voice changed and the moment went from merely awkward to frightening. I knew I had gone too far (again), but she looked down immediately with a palm to her forehead. After a moment, I could see she was angry with herself for losing her temper.

"Always there," I echoed. "I felt it, and all of a sudden you're very touchy about something you once told me was an equal arrangement—half and half."

"I shouldn't have said it like that," she said.

"But you did," I replied quickly, "and while I can't hear *your* thoughts, it's pretty clear when you said 'I was always there,' you meant Tegwen."

"I'm sorry, Evan, but you made it sound as if I was lurking around inside, waiting to take control of her!"

"Of *her*," I said, just to emphasize the point.

"Of *me*! Damn it, Evan, you know what I mean!"

The moment had descended into a needlessly heated argument, and yet I couldn't shake the unsettling truth of her words and a nagging, persistent effect it left on our relationship. I watched her struggle with an impossible dilemma, fighting hard against the duality and unique nature of being two people inside one body. After minutes in silence, I decided to move slowly; there were no easy explanations—how could there be? Instead, I returned to her description of Jane Mower's life, suddenly fascinating because of her unguarded comments about something more than merely listening to the thoughts of others.

"You're not living Aline's seventh life," I said as softly as I could, "this is *Tegwen's*."

"Yes," she answered, but her eyes showed equal parts resignation and defiance. It didn't matter that I understood at last. Instead, Aline wanted it made clear she didn't give a damn what I thought about it and nothing would change who and what she is. I decided to pull back and shift topics, if only as a measure of self-protection.

"Tell me about Jane," I said at last. "How far beyond just listening to them did you go?"

Aline waited another moment or two, and I could see she was grateful for an end to the tension and harsh tone.

"When I married, it was during the phase of life when I usually discovered who and what I am," she began. "It was always that way and it took time to adjust."

"But once you did…"

"It helped my husband in his business dealings."

"What did he do?"

"He was a manager in a trading house and was often given the task of entertaining men with whom his masters did business; I arranged afternoon teas or evening dinner parties and the idea was getting closer to those with considerable influence and power."

"This should be an interesting story," I said, grinning.

She nodded quickly, and it felt good to know our confrontation only moments before was finished. Despite her assurances she would never harm me, I noticed an increase in our combative exchanges and my own stubborn will pushing its way through. Aline hated our fights (and still does), but I was determined to show her rational concerns for my own safety were not equivalent to timid fear.

She opened a text book about life in the 1700s, waiting as I studied an article describing daily routines for people of her social station.

"I played the part and showed a happy hostess," she continued. "After enough champagne and gushing attention, their thoughts were easy to hear. I listened and told my husband what they were thinking, and it gave him a considerable advantage when they negotiated terms or struck bargains later on."

"Your husband knew about your abilities?"

"Not as you do," she said. "I was always careful to characterize them as merely hunches, but when they proved correct enough times, he began to trust."

"What about Cadwal's warning?" I asked. "Didn't you remember it?"

"Of course!" she replied. "But that was different, and I never revealed the truth behind it. In my first life, such things weren't strange or frightening so it wasn't a risk, and Cadwal saw no reason to worry. When I helped my husband, he never suspected it could be something more, and I wasn't about to tell him."

"He just put it down to female intuition and left it at that?"

"It was a simpler time, Evan; no one thought to suspect something more, at least not in our sphere."

"What was your husband's name?"

"Edwin Clarke. We met in 1719 through mutual friends when I was visiting my mother's family in Portsmouth. His uncle was a manager for the East India Company, and when a position opened, Edwin was sent from London to learn and gain experience."

"Your parents were shopping you out for a husband?"

"We didn't go there for just that purpose," she replied, "but my mother was always looking by that time in my life; it was the way things were when a young woman with social standing came of age."

"Did you like him?"

"I wasn't bowled over in love, but I certainly didn't protest, either. Edwin was a handsome, rather dashing man, and I loved listening to tales from all the places he'd visited. He was fourteen years my senior, but my mother saw a good match and we were married that same year."

"How long before you decided to give him special help in his business dealings?"

"Five or six years," she replied. "It took time for Edwin to rise in importance enough to warrant those meetings I could attend."

"Eavesdropping garden parties?"

"I didn't have to work very hard to hear them, Evan."

"When did you take it further?" I asked.

She returned a sort of smirk, and it was easy to see she carried the satisfaction of applying her own hand to the affairs of her husband's work in an era when few women could.

"Much later. There was a man who came to our house for tea," she said. "He represented a group of ship owners and even members of the Lords who supported the Prime Minister in a fight over import taxation."

"How long ago?" I asked.

"1730s," she replied.

"I didn't know England had prime ministers back then."

"Mr. Walpole; he was the first. Authority was starting to shift from absolute power of the Crown to Parliament and a two-party system of government."

"But this guy who came to tea was a pain in the ass?"

"He favored excise taxation on imports, but Edwin's firm opposed it. He was a powerful man with influence, and I decided to…*encourage* him just a little."

"*How* little?"

"When he spoke, I sent him sensations of discomfort, you could say, especially when he argued for the tax."

"Are we speaking of intense pain, like you gave me?"

"Not pain," she replied, "but very unsettling feelings of dread and doubt. Through the entire afternoon I watched and listened, applying pressure until he declared an illness and asked us to excuse him."

"He left the party early?"

"Yes, and he withdrew his support for the Prime Minister's excise scheme only days later. He came to our house once or twice after, but I left him alone."

"Did it make a difference to Edwin's business?"

"I can't say with certainty, but that man had a lot of power, and when he turned away from the PM, others did as well. I think it just helped them stand against the tax."

"As a woman in that time, it must've been awfully nice to know you had the power to steer things better than the boys could hope for?"

"It was," she said, grinning. "When I first tried, and it worked, I helped Edwin whenever the opportunity presented itself. It probably sounds arrogant now, but my efforts helped his career in ways no one else could."

"Did you ever lay down the law on one of Edwin's opponents?" I asked. "Let them know what they were dealing with the way you did with Andre Renard?"

"No," she replied, "nothing like that. I never felt compelled to it, but also, I was afraid of going too far; I remembered Cadwal's warning."

Aline's mood was light again, and she described Jane's life differently than she had of her earlier lives and the hard times she'd endured. When I asked her if there were moments or memories more prominent than others, she laughed and said, "It was the first time since Tegwen's life I never went to sleep hungry."

She described life in Jane Mower's era: knee-length breeches and waistcoats, three-pointed hats and cloaks. Her dresses were elegant, she said, but heavy and forever in the way. Stays and corsets were uncomfortable, but the echoes of Tegwen's voice was always there to remind her it could be a lot worse. On her wedding tour, she could barely contain herself at the prospect of visiting France and Italy. I hadn't considered it, but Aline announced with noticeable pride the weeks-long event was also the first time she'd ever traveled overseas. The society splendor of Paris gave way to the ancient majesty of Florence and Naples until his work responsibilities forced Edwin's return to Portsmouth.

They took up residence in North End on Kingston Road and remained there for ten years. During this time, Aline said, her first child—a boy they named Gerald—was born on a warm August day in 1722. Another son, Elias, arrived two years later.

Aline's detail and the clarity of those moments were astonishing, and she took me there so I could see for myself while it poured down rain outside. It was a mild time, politically at least, and the Empire that would grow in strength and influence until it spanned the planet was guiding the course of western civilization. Edwin struck out on his own with two partners and they bought their first ship, a cargo packet making regular stops between England and the bustling French seaports at Brest and Le Havre.

Their position in society was at the upper echelon, but she spoke with regret that too much of the work raising Gerald and Elias fell to a governess while she kept a close eye on Edwin's affairs, always ready to twist the silent, unseen thumbscrew should a deal became threatened. As Edwin's business expanded, he opened his own trading house on the western reaches of London. Jane was hesitant to move away permanently, but their proximity to the city was both exciting and convenient, so they settled near Wimbledon Village. She showed me old photos of their house taken almost a century later, and it would've been considered a mansion in any era.

Their sons grew to manhood, and Gerald decided on a career at sea, awarded a commission in the Royal Navy during the autumn of 1740. Jane wiped tears as they watched him board a coach bound for Plymouth and his position as a junior officer aboard a newly built ship of the line. He wanted to become a navigator, and Aline reported proudly the vessel carried 80 cannons, but she went suddenly silent and I could guess the reason why.

She told me a man came to see Edwin at his offices a year later with the terrible news their eldest son had been killed in action against the Spanish fleet somewhere in the Caribbean Sea. They told of a fierce battle and Gerald's steadfast bravery, but a musket ball took his life where he stood on the quarterdeck of his burning ship, struggling to maneuver in tight quarters. I imagined the scene, and even if it was a contrived story to make grieving parents feel better, neither wanted to know and they preferred instead to hold the memory of their son's life as one of nobility.

"And Elias?" I asked.

"He read law at Cambridge and took a position in the Foreign Office," she said with a smile. "He became a diplomat, advising our ambassador in Vienna to the court of Empress Maria Theresa until 1752 when he took a posting in Lisbon at the court of Joseph the First."

Her voice trailed off suddenly.

"Elias was badly burned in Lisbon during a terrible earthquake in the autumn of 1755. He recovered and came home, but never married. My son's face and upper body were slightly disfigured by the fire and because of it, unsuitable to further diplomatic work. Elias retired from service and worked in Edwin's firm until his death in 1786."

I waited quietly, and Aline said nothing for a while. Lost in her thoughts, I saw her brow furrow suddenly as she endured old memories and Gerald's untimely end. There's no effective way to describe it, but I felt myself shifting again and the way I thought of her previous lives. Before, it felt like hearing the history of distant people I could never know, sitting out the hours while she let the wash of memories ease past. But in that moment, I suffered with her because Jane was no longer a name. Instead, she lived again in Aline's voice and it didn't matter that Tegwen was the hidden force allowing me to see and feel for myself. Finally, she stood and told the last chapter of Jane Mower's life.

The years passed quietly, and Jane spent a lot of her time entertaining guests and acquaintances alone as Edwin's importance to Britain's expansion grew. His ever-increasing wealth and influence were nice, she said, but it took a toll on his health. A preference for excessive doses of rich food and drink didn't help, and a summer they spent with cousins in Grimsby (and a healthier lifestyle) proved temporary. Aline spoke nearly at a whisper as she told me a man came to her door on a windy day in 1770 with the news Edwin had died in his office and likely, she said, from a heart attack. A year later, Jane sold their grand house and went to live with a cousin in Poole. Elias stayed behind in London, eventually selling off the family's interest before calling it a day and removing himself to a small home in the Cotswolds.

She recalled Jane's move to Poole with a clear detachment I found strange, and it was then when I realized the story of her own life diminished in Aline's eyes the further it went. I'm sure that was Tegwen's preferences and the only remaining voice, but the sadness I expected her to display wasn't there. She showed me church records and a simple paragraph in Jane's obituary. There were prominent references to "Edwin Clarke" throughout the notice, and it was obvious her death was worth noting only because she had been married to a prominent and successful man.

I asked as softly as I could if she knew where Jane's body was laid to rest. She nodded and told me of a small cemetery near their church, and when I asked if she ever went there in her lives since, she said she had, but only once. She looked and told me there wouldn't be a second time. When I wondered if there was a reason to avoid it, she said, "I had no choice; they buried me beside the church but I didn't belong there…in England."

"Where *did* you belong?"

"Here," she answered simply, "in this land where I began."

Finally, I understood. From her first existence in a Druidic village on Anglesey, all the way through to her seventh life as a modern woman making her way in the twenty-first century, Aline's identity—*Tegwen's* life force—began within the borders of Wales, and I felt suddenly stupid for not seeing it earlier. "Our gods made it that way," she once said. It was never random in Aline's mind that her beginnings in an ancient and mystical time of Celts and post-Roman Britons demanded a geographic constant for reasons beyond even *her* understanding. I decided not to ask about it again, and the answer may never be revealed, but it still brings strange feelings today.

VIENNE CALLED THE following evening, and Aline paced around her house as they went through their customary catching-up exercise. Plans for a vacation "somewhere warm" resumed, and a resort hotel on a beach in Malta surged into the lead over other potential Mediterranean destinations. She became loud and lively speaking with my sister and, for a while at least, the interference of Andre Renard and the cascade of stressful events in the weeks and months since were kept at bay.

Aline jotted notes hastily on a pad in her kitchen as reminders to check into available flights or arrangements for rental cars and what level of opulence each of them required from a hotel to make the trip worth taking. There was no point in offering perspective because my authority was always subordinate to theirs, but it didn't stop Aline from asking what I thought about the preferred hotel. It wouldn't make any difference, of course, but it was nice she made the effort anyway.

While she and Vienne finished up their call, I pawed through the plastic tub's trove of documents, just to pass the time but also to learn a little more about the lives she'd lived spanning fifteen centuries. After a while, she noticed and sat beside me.

"In all those lives," I asked quietly, "were you able to do the things you can do today, even if you didn't use them?"

"It took a long time for me to even understand each time I entered a new life. I was aware only of my ability to hear inside—I never manipulated the physical world and it's not even clear I *could*."

"But later?"

"The thoughts and feelings of others were obvious to Enydd; it wasn't disturbing but I never considered acting on them."

"Cadwal's influence?"

"He was so deliberate and serious…I suppose his caution carried over."

We sat in silence, and I know she waited for me to adjust. Listening to a description I once regarded as an exercise with a history professor had changed because I understood it was real; there was no contrived fantasy by a crazy girl with a rampant imagination. I listened as she spoke of her lives in present terms despite the truth they happened centuries before. She watched me for a while, but another clue surfaced and my questions resumed.

"I don't know much about Druids…well, *nobody* does except you, I guess, but Cadwal didn't magically hand over these abilities, did he?"

"It wasn't something we spent much time talking about."

The only conclusion I could reach seems obvious today, but she waited patiently until I found my way through.

"Your powers didn't emerge after becoming a Druid priestess," I said at last. "Cadwal accepted and trained you *because* of them."

"I knew my ability to hear thoughts was the reason he decided to begin my training, but it never occurred to me to wonder how or why I had them; I simply did, and it wasn't questioned."

Aline looked at me with the pride of a mother as if I had learned to read a clock or tie my shoes. It felt a bit like acing a big college exam to qualify for the next as a condition for graduating. I didn't realize until that moment the progression of Aline's lives was a parallel to my discovery of them as each layer was peeled back for me to see and understand in careful and deliberate increments.

23
LIFE AND DEATH AT SUNRISE

IN the hours after our tense and uncomfortable trip to Somerset, a nagging sensation of dread began to ease when Burke understood Aline was closer to a summit. The potential for in-depth study that could, under the right circumstances, vault his section's hidden efforts miles ahead of where it lingered in little more than informed suspicion was finally within his grasp.

The usual tasks kept Aline in Colwyn Bay for a few days, and I stayed behind to deal with a maddening leak from her downstairs bathroom faucet. I didn't mind being an unpaid, amateur plumber because those mundane parts of life we take for granted were signals that things had returned to normal. When she came home on an otherwise dull Saturday morning, we lazed around and did precisely nothing simply because we could. Deep in the night we slept like kittens and didn't see the clock beside her bed click over to 5:44 when she sat up sharply and whacked my shoulder; I couldn't know it then, but the last and final act was already underway.

They came in over the hill north of her farm at dawn, moving silently and swiftly as only trained specialists can, and I would never have realized but for Aline's unique (and peculiar) abilities. I asked her what was wrong, but she held out her hand to silence me. It's the sort of reaction from people who hear an unexplained thump or knock in the distance, but after a second or two, she was moving.

"Get dressed," she said calmly. "We have to go."

"Where are we going?" I asked in a bewildered mumble, but she was nearly at the bedroom door when she shouted for me to hurry.

I followed downstairs as quickly as I could, pulling on a shirt as I went, but she stopped and aimed me toward her back door. I fumbled with my shoes, and I remember wondering how she'd dressed so quickly. Again, I asked her what she had heard, but she slipped quickly across her lawn in the pale light on a brick walkway leading to the lower field and beyond it my old path home. It was clear she meant to make for the dry creek bed at the low point in our shared hill, but the way was blocked when the first two men slipped into the open. At once, I understood: Burke's people had sent a covert team to burst in and take Aline by force. As we watched, one of them crept slowly forward with a stubby machine gun aimed straight at us.

"Get on the ground," he shouted firmly. "Now!"

I began to raise my hands in reflex when Aline turned slowly and looked past me toward her house where four more figures in black tactical uniforms and ski masks went laterally across her grass to flank us. My heart was pounding and again, the first soldier shouted at us to lie face down, but Aline did nothing.

"We'd better do as he says," I whispered, but she was unmoved, and it was stunning to see her calm in a place where many people would wet themselves.

"Not yet," she replied, nudging me ever closer to the trees.

"Lay down, *now!*" the soldier shouted again, "or we *will* force you!"

With each command they inched closer until Aline's invisible border was breached, and she pushed me away in a single, sudden movement that brought the commandos' guns up in an instant. I wanted to say something—to talk them down from a tense and needless moment—but there were no words I could form, and I watched with a strange, detached fascination when it began.

Aline's eyes narrowed and she tilted her head slightly backward in an odd sort of frown when the first soldier cried out. He straightened quickly and his back arched, but it was his scream of pain that seemed to stop time. Another moved quickly forward, unsure if he should keep his aim fixed on Aline or tend to his stricken comrade, but she made no distinction and he felt the first waves send him to his knees. Instinctively, the hooded trooper raised his hands to each ear as though trying to protect himself from a piercing noise, but the motion made clear both men were in desperate trouble.

From behind us, more shouts as the second group moved up quickly. They separated into pairs, and Aline pivoted to aim her gaze at the closest two. They stopped and stood up straight, letting their guns dangle from shoulder straps as though gripped by an unseen paralysis. Their knees were bent slightly and heads bowed so that each man's chin rested against his chest. Through it all, I couldn't move or speak, and even today I wonder if it was simply the inability to react from fear and the suddenness of it all, or if it was Aline's influence holding me safely at a distance.

I remember most of what followed, but I think that is only true because I've had time to replay it in my mind and watch the memories and a flurry of movement so startling and swift, I couldn't keep up. The second soldier in front us had fought through the pain and he aimed his gun as he moved quickly up the hill, shouting for us to get down or he would open fire. I don't know if it was worry for my own life or for Aline's, but I tried again to speak without success.

She didn't move as the remaining pair behind us went left and into the open field to form a chevron-shaped cross fire zone. Aline didn't have to look to know where they were, and she turned suddenly toward them when the first volley cut into the cool, still air.

The loud, threatening soldier held to his word and squeezed off three short bursts from his weapon less than fifteen yards away. It took a second or two before realizing the bullets went wide when I wrongly believed he fired only to warn her a last time. The sound shocked me back to reality from what seemed a distant and vivid dream, but it was too late as he stopped and pulled at the gun's slide mechanism, suspecting a malfunction, and it was the moment I realized he meant to kill Aline.

Time stood still as he suddenly—inexplicably—abandoned his gun. The image was so strange and alien until he began to slap at his own arms and legs, hopping around like an afflicted man in a bizarre St. Vitus' dance moving in fast-forward. I didn't understand what any of it meant until the first swirls of blue flame appeared around him, and in seconds, his body was engulfed by a blinding tornado of fire.

I stared transfixed and speechless until the screams of agony became unbearable. Aline turned and walked quickly left to meet the last two soldiers at the moment they drew their aim and fired, but again, the rounds missed when they collapsed suddenly beside each other, writhing and convulsing like poisoned insects gasping for air. She went at a near run behind us to where the first pair stood motionless with bowed heads, powerless against an enemy without weapons. I watched her inspect them patiently and deliberately like statues in a museum until satisfied they were no longer a danger, but a man was burning alive ten feet from me and I could take no more.

"Aline!" I shouted, but she didn't notice. I screamed at her again when at last she looked at me with an expression I won't forget and hope never to see again. Her mouth was drawn into a clenched-teeth grimace as if captured by a photographer in the middle of a deep, primal growl. In her eyes there was only distance from anything like humanity, and I felt the fear swarming over me like angry hornets. I don't know how to describe the sensation, only that it was visceral—*physical*.

I experienced night terrors as a kid when imagery was secondary to the feeling of darkness and panic when a buzzing started in my ears and the taste of metal invaded my mouth. It was like that, but my shouts made no difference. In a terrifying, single moment I wondered if she *could* stop. Would her power sweep through *my* mind, if only for the mistake of proximity, to leave me writhing in agony in the wetted grass like the others?

"Aline! Stop, goddamn it, stop this now!"

I shouted as loud as I could until finally—mercifully—it began to slow. Her expression eased and returned to what it was before, calm and nearly emotionless. I went quickly to where the second man lay still in the tall grass, his jumpsuit smoldering at its fringes. I knelt quickly, and when I reached to pull the mask from his head, the material was stuck to skin that was badly blistered. I leaned close with a dreadful feeling of helplessness to take his pulse, but he was already gone. Behind him, the others seemed unconscious except for one who appeared to be choking, and I ran to him. As I pulled away his hooded mask, a gush of thick, clear fluid poured from his mouth in a nearly endless stream, and I stood away quickly in a swirl of revulsion and horror as the last of the soldier's life gurgled from his mouth. I bent low again, but his eyes were fixed and there was no pulse.

I looked up in desperation for help to find the second group was motionless and held in a trance that couldn't be broken until Aline decided to release them. It was strange and unlikely to watch, but the four simply sat down in the wet grass, docile and with blank expressions that haunt me still. It was utterly silent, and the air hung heavy as I struggled to grasp all that had happened.

Aline paced slowly in a wide circle, waiting, it would seem, for the next act to begin as we heard the first staccato thump of a helicopter's rotors and its growling engines echoing up the valley from the east. I turned to watch as a dark blue Dauphin with only its registration number along the tail curved neatly past our hill to settle at the bottom of Aline's field. The door slid open and two crewmen leaped from the opening to reach the fallen soldiers where they lay in the weeds.

I felt terror at the prospect it would begin again, but Aline walked quickly toward me, simply pointing at a third shape as Burke stepped through the soaking grass slowly with his arms extended to demonstrate no threat. He said something, and I could see his mouth move, but the helicopter's noise made it impossible to hear until he drew closer. Aline only watched but gone was that otherworldly grimace, and she waited with me until Burke approached.

"Stand down, now," he called out. "There's no need for this."

"I'm not coming with you," Aline shouted suddenly, but Burke only shook his head and waved a hand to signal removing her was not his goal.

"This was a terrible mistake," he replied. "We tried to contact you, but there was no answer."

"*Your* mistake," Aline replied loudly.

"If you'll just give us a moment, we need to see after our people."

"Take them," she said as she moved close, "but never come here again, do you understand?"

He nodded and motioned for the crewmen to help the first group into the helicopter. Aline watched them, but the extraction process went quickly and without a word until Burke walked slowly to us.

"Please be calm," he began, and I noticed the helicopter's engines were spooling down. "This was not our decision, Aline."

"I thought you were head boy!" I shouted. "What the fuck were you thinking?"

"The others," he replied evenly, "far above my level, ordered these soldiers to bring Aline by force; we discovered the plan only a short while ago and commandeered their helicopter on our Minister's authority."

"And you expect us to believe you had nothing to do with this?"

"It was not on my orders, you have my word."

"Hurd?" I asked, and he nodded twice.

"They will not be satisfied with what happened today, and I'm afraid it won't end here; that is not a favorable outcome for either of us."

Burke's usually calm, knowing smile was gone, and Aline knew what it meant before I did.

"If he sends more of these men, I'll kill them, too; is your experiment worth more lives?"

In that moment I felt a nervous twinge up my spine because it was the first and only time I ever heard a threat to kill made with serious intent and the ability to back it up. Hearing it from Aline, no longer restrained by notions of civility, only worsened the feeling of dread I fought against in the silent, foggy air. I know it was a last threshold but not merely from witnessing her fury and six highly trained soldiers incapacitated by only the force of her thoughts. If there were any lingering doubts before those terrible seconds, all had been washed permanently away on that quiet morning when I understood with stunning finality what she could do and how far she was willing to go when pushed beyond her limits.

"I promise you there will be no more of this," Burke said. "They will see and realize its futility, but you must understand as well that we cannot turn away and forget what happened here. Lives were lost and they will expect an account."

"Then you will risk your own life," Aline said firmly. "I don't ask anything from you, Mr. Burke, except to be left alone."

"I understand," he answered, "but we can't do that. They now know what you're capable of at levels much higher than mine, and some would rather destroy you than allow you and Mr. Morgan to go on as if nothing had happened."

He moved slowly toward us and said, "There is still a chance for a better conclusion!"

"What are you offering?" I asked warily, but I saw the relief in Burke's expression as he stopped only feet from us.

"As I said earlier," he began, "our facility is hidden from the public at a very secure RAF base. We alone maintain it, and no one will threaten you again."

"What the hell would make us trust you now?" I demanded.

"We want only to understand, Mr. Morgan; to speak with her in a private and controlled setting where no one can interfere."

"Hurd's assholes have already interfered!" I shouted, but he held up a passive hand.

"Gregory felt her power for himself, and he has turned his fear into anger and a justification for this heavy-handed intrusion. However, I can keep him at a distance if they know Aline will cooperate."

"You call this 'keeping a distance,' Alan?"

"Our Minister will intercede if need be to prevent more of this, but without her influence, Gregory will not hesitate to send assassins and end it. The violence will continue until they finally kill her, and they *will* kill her sooner or later! Please understand, this doesn't have to end in further bloodshed."

"After all this, I wouldn't trust you with a bag of dog shit!"

I could hear my voice rising, and still Burke stood steady. Today, I admire his calm in so hostile and terrifying a position, and I have to say, it must've helped him achieve those things necessary to win and hold so much authority.

"I implore you both to think about this rationally and understand there is no other way I can offer."

I wanted to argue with him, to shout and scream away the fear and frustration, but Aline intercepted a tirade before it began.

"And if I agree," she said suddenly, "what then?"

"We want simply to speak with you and that is all; once our interviews and a handful of harmless tests are complete, I will ensure there is no repeat of this disaster."

Aline listened to Burke through it all, and she moved close so he would hear her clearly.

"I'll consider it," she replied, "but leave me to do it in my own time. I will call you, but do not allow others to come here again or any hope of an understanding between us will die with them."

It was chilling to hear her describe what anyone else would regard as deliberate premeditated murder so coolly and without emotion, but Burke nodded his agreement and said, "You have my word."

He turned and walked briskly to the waiting helicopter, and we watched as its engines and rotors whined to life before lifting clear of the hillside and swinging neatly around toward the south. A few minutes later our valley was silent once more, but I could only stand in numb confusion until she took my arm. I went along beside her on our customary path as we had so many times up the long field where her house waited in the first rays of sunlight. I pretended not to notice the patches of tall grass matted down where Hurd's soldiers lay only minutes before or the obvious "crop circles" made by downblast from the helicopter's powerful rotors.

Inside once more, I waited in silence, suddenly wary of everything I thought I knew. I wished in my solitary misery there were others who might have seen and experienced the event simply to reassure myself I wasn't alone or driven horribly insane. I expected the police to arrive at any moment, but they never did and we later learned Burke's people explained away the gunfire and a helicopter at treetop level as an unannounced "training exercise." Aline sat beside me to dab away sweat from my face I hadn't noticed was there.

"I'm sorry you had to see all that," she said softly, and the image her expression made was not the frightening visage barely half an hour earlier. "I know you have a lot of questions, but please understand, they were going to kill us and it left me with little choice."

I looked at her for a moment. She was back to the old Aline—the gentle girl I fell in love with—and it seemed absurd to think of her doing those things. Still, the terrible events moved us to another place and a new reality. She was calm but the worry in her eyes was obvious.

"Are *you* all right?" I asked.

"I'm fine," she said, and it was clear her concern was for me. "I never wanted you to go through this, Evan; I am so very sorry…"

"It's okay," I said, but she reached for my hands.

"None of this is okay," she replied, "but I won't let them hurt you—I promise."

She climbed suddenly onto my lap, facing me with her arms around my neck, and yet the pained expression on her face betrayed a concern I knew was mirrored in mine. I did have questions, more than I ever thought she could answer, but I simply didn't know where to begin. I thought my adjustment to her power and the gift of an ability I couldn't understand had been a shining success, all things considered, but there was more and I spoke at a whisper.

"Those two men…they were dead, Aline."

"I know," she replied softly. "I wanted to frighten them and make them stop where they were, but when they aimed and fired their guns…"

"Some of those guys were probably SAS commandos."

"I suppose they were."

I remembered the horror that surged through me when the gunfire erupted.

"They were only a few yards away," I said.

"Yes, I know," she replied, and it was clear she understood what I meant.

"Both times, they shot at you and missed completely."

"I was there, Evan; I remember."

"These bastards are some of the deadliest marksmen on the planet, Aline. They missed with machine guns from *that* range? SAS guys don't miss!"

"I know how it must seem," she began, but the answer was always there, waiting and evidence of what I once regarded as impossible.

"You pushed them from inside? Their hands did what *your* mind told them to do."

She nodded, and I sat for a while as the images tore through my thoughts like a slide show running out of control.

"Was it like that with Claude Dumont?"

"No, not really," she answered.

"How was it different?"

"I was young and afraid for my life—acting on instinct alone."

"And this time?"

"Just anger, I suppose," she replied simply. "I could hear their thoughts, and I knew they were going to kill us."

With each answer Aline showed little remorse or regret, and her words described the most horrific thing I've ever seen the way others would recount changing a tire. Her tone had become matter-of-fact and dispassionate because, in the quiet aftermath, that is precisely what it was to her.

THREE DAYS PASSED without incident, and I began to worry if Burke could keep his end of the bargain. Maybe his masters in London learned about those furious, deadly minutes and the next battle with Aline was being planned.

Hour after hour we watched and waited, but no one showed. It seemed surreal as I examined the present and held it up against the past when I was new to the valley and Aline was a mysterious, aloof neighbor with an odd reputation. A year and a half later, a lot of things had changed, but the drama was hardly over.

Early on Wednesday we sat in Aline's kitchen ignoring *Good Morning Britain* on the muted television. Aline said it was fun to watch their mouths move and not have to hear it, and I smiled knowing the program's on-air talent was no less irritating than our version in the States. She was comfortable at last with her decision to go along with Burke's scheme, and after hours of thorough and pained discussion to make sure we were both in agreement, it was time. She waited with her phone once again in speaker mode until Burke answered, and when he did, Aline went straight to it.

"All right, Mr. Burke," she began, "what do you want us to do?"

"Thank you for calling, Aline," he replied. "I very much hope we can find a mutually agreeable solution to this mess without a repeat of the earlier unfortunate events."

"We didn't ask those men to come here," she said.

"I understand, but let's focus on next steps instead, shall we? As I promised, there will be no more invasions and gunfire, but I must be assured you are willing to cooperate with us; can we agree on that simple condition?"

She looked at me and I nodded in silence.

"We agree," she answered, "but you haven't told us exactly how you envision these conversations will be conducted."

"We have an idea or two that might be agreeable, but I would prefer we discussed them in person, hmm?"

"Sorry, Alan," I replied at once, "but that sounds like 'the check's in the mail' to me. We need to know what you have in mind as an endgame, or this conversation will end very quickly."

"There is no purpose in playing tricks or making promises we can't keep," Burke continued. "After the disastrous encounter a few days ago, there are conditions for us to retain our organizational independence, but I can assure you the result must meet with your approval."

We knew at once what he meant by "independence" and the implied threat his words carried.

"If you're talking about Mr. Hurd," Aline said quickly, "that problem is yours alone; I have already told you what will happen if he sends his soldiers here again."

"I understand," Burke replied, "but perhaps we could meet briefly at a neutral site so that I can provide details to consider. Gregory's Minister is worried you may take revenge against us for the ill-advised incident, and she needs to see and understand we have moved on from any further violence."

"I defended myself and Evan," Aline replied evenly.

"Yes, but none of them in London saw the event and how it transpired; they know only the confrontation resulted in the deaths of two extremely skilled commandos and that you are responsible for it; their concern is understandable, surely."

"Go on," she said.

"If we could settle on a place away from your home to exchange ideas and agree to a process, it will help us establish mutual understanding and trust. Is that acceptable?"

"Acceptable," I answered, "but it has to be a public place and during the day; no lonely roads in the middle of the night."

"Your caution is misplaced and perhaps a tiny bit dramatic, Mr. Morgan, but I agree," he said. "May I suggest the airport in Liverpool? There's a facility for private aircraft on the east side of the field; we've landed there once or twice, and they're quite good at leaving us alone."

I waited as Aline searched through her laptop, pointing at last to a general aviation fixed base operator at Lennon Airport. She told him we would be there at noon the following day before disconnecting abruptly, and I sat out an awkward silence until she looked at me with a stern, purposeful expression.

"If Hurd sends them again and Burke can't stop it…"

"We'll deal with it," I replied, but my words were automatic, and I missed her intent. I thought she was only voicing concern but it was something else and the stark, emotionless expression was back.

"I won't go with them, Evan; if this is some stupid trap, more of them are going to die."

Bravado and big talk in the face of fear and danger is one thing, but her simple statement gave me a chill, knowing she would inflict horrors if the meeting proved a setup.

"Let's take it one step at a time, okay?" I offered, and she nodded quietly.

24
AFTERMATH

OUR ride up to Liverpool passed in relative silence, and I wondered about her thoughts with a bit of jealousy because Aline could always hear mine. The rain was light and easily pushed on a steady breeze when she found Hale Road and a turn-in where the FBO waited on our right. It was an old and familiar sight: light piston twins and shining turboprops across the wet ramp with a fuel truck's amber lights blinking out its position beside a snow-white Hawker XP business jet. Most of my excursions to examine a crash site had begun and ended in places very much the same, and suddenly I thought of Tony and my old gang at the NTSB. What would they make of my condition, I wondered silently, and the insane circumstances that had brought us to a stop along a narrow parking strip across the street?

Burke had cautioned us to use his alter ego "Marsden" when approaching the receptionist inside, and when we did, she pointed us toward a Beechcraft King Air where it waited alone. We went slowly until Burke appeared, and with him was another man in a suit too small for his muscular frame. I looked closer and saw Stuart Halliwell positioned beside the airplane's nose. Burke held up a hand immediately and we stopped, unsure of his intent. He moved forward, calling for me to join him, and it was obvious they worried Aline might do something horrible with two RAF pilots in full view.

"Let me try it first," I whispered. "They know what happened in your field."

Aline stood beside my car and kept her hands inside coat pockets, but I think she did so only because they were cold and not for any deliberate symbol of patience.

"Good afternoon, Mr. Morgan," Burke began with that half-smirk I've since come to realize is simply the man's normal expression and not one of overt familiarity.

"Alan," I replied with a bland, indifferent tone.

"I hope she won't be offended, but we hoped you might agree to discuss preliminaries with us alone; the Air Force gentlemen aren't a part of this, and the colonel would rather they stay that way."

"I don't blame him."

He looked away for a moment, squinting against the drizzle.

"I apologize for the surroundings and this dreadful weather," he began, "but we can address matters here without others listening in."

"I would think you're one of the few people who never has to worry about something like that."

"Oh, the eyes and ears belong to many," he replied, "and not all of them are sympathetic to our work."

"Let's get on with it," I said impatiently, but Burke smiled suddenly and looked down at the concrete tarmac as he spoke.

"Can she hear us from this distance?"

"Farther," I answered, and Burke just nodded. Some would see a sign of resignation, but I think he simply admired what she was and felt comfortable enough in his position to look beyond the adversarial divide objectively.

"I believe we can offer a solution that will satisfy both our positions with a minimum of fuss and bother."

"I'm listening."

"As I said, we are only concerned with knowledge and understanding, but to meet our goals it is essential that we have time with her in a private and controlled setting."

"How much time?"

"Three or four days, I should think. This sort of thing can't be accomplished overnight, and I'm sure you can see the intricacies of her unique nature demand thorough examination."

I heard the voice of a faceless government system with process requirements that can't be avoided.

"What kind of examination are we talking about, exactly?" I demanded.

"Interaction will be confined to discussions and conversations only, followed by one or two physiological tests conducted in a strictly controlled environment."

"By 'controlled,' you mean locking us inside."

"It is more precise to say we are locking others *outside*."

"You mentioned tests before."

"It would be helpful if she could provide a small sample of blood and certain tissues, but retrieving both would take only a moment or two to obtain. Beyond that, an ordinary physical examination and perhaps a demonstration of her abilities for video analysis after you've gone."

"I don't know if the blood and tissue thing is going to fly, Alan, but presuming she agrees, what then?"

"It was easy to explain away the gunfire and helicopters your neighbors heard as a military exercise—a training mission—but there are one or two concerns that may cause difficulty in the short-term."

I looked at him and wished Aline could tell me what he meant, but I was on my own for the moment.

"Which concerns, specifically?"

"Ministerial sensitivities will subside over time, but not if Aline remains in full view. Our proposal necessarily included assurances, and part of that agreement calls for a diminution of exposure; we simply need her to move out of sight until interest in London dies down."

When I'd translated the officious language and understanding dawned, I smiled at Burke's dilemma, knowing at last what it meant.

"You need her to go away because you can't explain any of this; what she did to those soldiers is an embarrassment Whitehall can't afford, and the only way to contain it is to deny and point to an empty house."

His smirk was suddenly gone. It was clear I'd hit a nerve, but Burke recovered quickly, just as he always does.

"Your characterization is unfortunately accurate, but…"

"Let's cut away the bullshit," I added quickly. "Somebody has to tell their families how and why those men died in a 'training exercise,' but you can't do that, can you?"

"That is not your concern," he replied evenly.

"Maybe not, but pressure from London is *yours*. What did they say, Alan? I'm guessing this goes deeper; the suits who keep your paychecks coming in heard about Renard from the Belgians, and now they want answers."

"I think we're losing sight of the purpose," Burke said, but I was rolling and simply couldn't stop myself.

"Before he came up here," I continued, "the inspector was clever, and he sent a little package to his pal Gregory just in case things went south with Aline. Hurd has position and considerable authority in the British government so who better, right?"

"Go on," he said, but the ending was already clear.

"We found out he's also family to Renard, even if it's only by marriage, and when poor ol' Andre came back from Wales sobbing like a schoolgirl, Hurd called *you*."

"My compliments, Evan; you managed to find a few connections we didn't expect you to discover all by yourself."

I ignored the veiled insult.

"When we met in Taunton, none of your bastards were prepared when Aline started probing and least of all Hurd. I'm guessing he gave your Minister a bullshit story, assuring her he had things in hand, but then Aline punched him right in the brain and…"

"Is there a point to this?" Burke asked with an impatient tone.

"He had a peek at what she can do, and it shook him pretty bad. Fear makes people stupid, and the next thing we knew he sent those commandos to find Aline and either bring her in or kill her, but everything went south in that field."

"I'm not sure we're getting anywhere…"

"Come on, Alan," I said with a sideways grin. "Hurd is a politician, which means he's a lying, selfish asshole, but *you* saw something more, didn't you?"

"I'm not sure I take your meaning, Evan."

"If some bleeding-heart, Parliament big-shot starts hammering to find out why two soldiers died and no one knows why, Hurd will fold and the debacle in

Aline's field could be exposed. If *that* happens, funding bills stop cold and your shadow agency will be…well, there's no polite way of saying it, is there?"

Burke held out both palms in an absurd gesture of sarcasm like an amateur actor in an empty theater.

"Congratulations; you've exposed us for conniving, evil brigands in one glorious American speech!"

I waited for a moment because it was satisfying to watch as Burke walked very close to the line where his temper could be lost. The events that had changed everything also brought deadly consequences, and I wanted nothing to do with sarcastic indifference.

"Here's the bottom line, Alan: if you're looking for answers and information, I might be able to convince her to play along for a few days, but we need to know what comes after. Those men were likely SAS, but Aline knows they came up here with shoot-to-kill orders if she resisted."

"I've already told you, Evan, that was not my choice nor was it my decision," he replied, "and for the record, they were not SAS; trained to similar standards, perhaps, but Gregory's security staff isn't part of that organization."

"Maybe so, but it changes nothing," I declared quickly. "If Hurd was willing to have Aline killed, what's to stop him from trying it again?"

Burke looked at Halliwell and the colonel saw his cue.

"Gregory walks between several political realities, but all of them carry a responsibility for the safety of the British people."

"And you think Aline is some kind of threat to national security?"

"No, but Mr. Hurd *does* and now, so might his Minister."

Halliwell waited for a second or two until a subtle nod from Burke gave him silent permission to continue.

"We know what she is capable of, Mr. Morgan; we're not fools. After our meeting in Taunton, Mr. Hurd knows it as well, and we're sure he told them all about it in London."

"So?"

"So, this process has been shifted, and there are larger concerns for us to deal with."

"Get to the point, Colonel."

Halliwell's hesitation was obvious, and I could see he waited, unsure and reluctant, to make revelations people like Hurd would never tolerate. Another nod from Burke and Halliwell moved close with a hushed tone as if to underscore the grave importance of his words.

"They believed her ability was limited to eavesdropping on the thoughts of others, Mr. Morgan; they didn't accept those stories from Glasgow *or* Belgium until quite recently."

"Yeah," I said, smiling thinly, "two lethal commandos brought home in body bags can change your perspective."

"Yes, but our point is the *cause* of their condition and what it meant for Mr. Hurd's masters. They looked at the events in Miss Lloyd's field differently, and it is that distinction we are speaking of."

"Which means?" I demanded.

"It means, Mr. Morgan, they've found a useful tool and they mean to exploit it."

I felt the sudden wash of realization when Halliwell's carefully hidden truth broke through at last. My eyes shifted between them, but it was clear he was serious.

"Stop right there," I said with a false smile. "Are you telling me all this has been a scheme to turn her into some kind of secret agent?"

"A dramatic way of putting it," Burke replied, "but after the episode in Aline's meadow, Gregory's superiors are now interested in pursuing a similar objective; the temptation to cultivate a powerful asset was inevitable."

"I wish I could say I'm surprised," I replied.

"It is understandable," Burke countered. "In Gregory's position, you might very well do the same. Can you imagine how valuable Aline would be in an interrogation scenario, for example, capable of looking inside the mind of a terrorist and exposing plans for something horrible? A person with her ability could save dozens or even hundreds of lives."

They waited and watched as I stumbled toward my own conclusion, knowing they were correct: anyone with equivalent responsibilities to their nameless Minister would be compelled by duty to at least investigate the possibility. Burke knew it, too, and he stepped closer still.

"We may not care for the method, Evan, but I don't have the luxury of ignoring those possibilities simply because they're distasteful."

"She won't agree to this, Alan," I said flatly.

There was no longer any reason for her to remain at a distance. I turned to motion for her to join us, and when she stood beside me, Halliwell continued.

"You now understand why Mr. Hurd's interest in you has become something more than mere curiosity?" he asked.

"I've always understood, Colonel," she answered.

"Yes, I suppose you have," he replied with a sad, knowing smile.

Burke waited another moment or two.

"Then you can surely understand the Minister's colleagues, particularly those in close cooperation with our intelligence branch, have a vision for the future and your potential help reaching it."

"Of course," she said. "After everything that has happened, they are more determined than ever."

I looked at her with a confused expression but Burke knew and he offered a translation so that I would as well.

"They call it 'wet work' in some circles, particularly among our colleagues on your side of the Atlantic, but it's all the same thing."

"Does the British Government now condone murder?" I asked bluntly.

"Our Minister's friends prefer to call it the pejorative elimination of an enemy actor as a last and final option."

I shook my head in what might seem to others as disgust and revulsion, but it was mostly resignation and surrender to the obvious. I wanted to turn and walk away—to run and not look back, but that option was long expired, and I waited through those first moments when you suddenly realize you're in over your head. The true endgame was one with life-or-death consequences, and I hated knowing I was out of my depth so badly.

"He wants the ultimate assassin," I said with a crooked smile. "Somebody who can kill without lifting a finger. There are no weapons or tangible evidence, and without either she could never be caught or even suspected."

"I suppose so, yes."

I wasn't finished, and it was my turn to move closer.

"It's nice and tidy because phantom assassins no one can find shield politicians from having to explain or justify what some might call ordinary murder."

"We are engaged in a perpetual war, Evan," Burke replied. "I should say wars *plural* because there are always so very many of them being waged in one part of the world or another. Killing an enemy who is trying to kill you first hardly qualifies as murder, wouldn't you agree?"

"You approve of this?"

"I did not say I approve," he answered, "but I do understand the expedience. After those horrific events in New York City years ago, so should you."

Aline listened through it all and still she seemed almost bored with a distant conversation between strangers. I didn't wonder if she knew what Burke's blunt descriptions meant because she had all along.

"Evan was right, Mr. Burke," she said at last. "I won't give away my future for the sake of Mr. Hurd's career."

"No indeed," he replied, "but that is not our purpose."

"What *is* your purpose?"

"What it has always been: investigation of those things no one else can explain."

"None of which matters if he sends out another squad to find and eliminate her," I added.

"The Ministers are intrigued by the prospect of molding Aline into a security implement, and I don't deny it," Burke replied, "but they are also reasonable men and women who like winning. If she agrees to help our investigations along, they will prevent further interference from Gregory."

"You can't guarantee that, Alan," I said.

"Yes, I can," he said. "If they mounted another stupid blunder, any hope of cultivating her abilities another time will forever disappear."

"What makes you so sure?"

"Gregory has been ordered, and he has reluctantly agreed, to transfer all security authority to another officer. There are benefits to taking a longer view…"

I looked at Halliwell where he waited with his hands clasped behind his back—scowling and determined—as Burke finished his sentence.

"Stuart is in command of our armed detachment now."

I turned to Aline where she waited, and she looked away as she spoke.

"May we have a few moments to talk about this in private, Mr. Burke?"

He nodded his agreement and said, "Take as much time as you need; we'll remain here."

I followed her across the wet surface of the ramp toward the FBO offices until we were safely distant from Burke and Halliwell. I knew the answer but my question came out anyway.

"Did you get all of the earlier conversation?" I asked.

"Yes," she replied, "but he still hasn't told you what they intend to do once these meetings he wants to conduct are finished."

"I wanted him to tell you directly; he won't lie because he knows you'll hear it in his thoughts."

Aline held my arm for a moment and said, "Are you comfortable with this man Halliwell?"

"I think so," I replied. "My friend Andy says he's okay and that's a pretty solid recommendation."

She looked at them from around my shoulder, but I couldn't resist asking.

"Can you hear them right now?"

"Of course," she said with a smile.

"What are they saying?"

"Halliwell is explaining how he knows your friend; he's telling Burke about the Gulf War and…"

"Aline?"

"I think it will be all right if we talk to them, Evan."

"Are you sure?"

"Yes; Burke is furious with Hurd for the incident in my field, and he wants Halliwell to ensure it doesn't happen again."

"What about the blood samples? I didn't know if you'd be willing to do that."

"I don't mind," she said, and it was surprising to me how indifferent she seemed. "I'm not sure what they hope to discover inside my blood, but if they want to look, I have no objections."

"And the demonstrations? Burke seemed a little hesitant when he asked, as if he worried it might be a deal-breaker."

"It's not surprising; in their place I would ask for them, too."

"I'm sure they'll be relieved to hear it," I said with a sudden, sideways grin.

"This isn't going away, Evan; we may as well give them what they want and be done with it."

"They want *you* to go away, remember…"

"Only for a while," she replied.

"How do you know what…"

I stopped myself in mid-sentence.

"Burke?"

"He's already discussed this with their Minister, who's called Kate, by the way."

"And?"

"He envisions several months, but no more."

"We'll let him make his pitch, but are you okay with it?"

"I'm okay, so long as we're together, Evan."

I smiled and nodded as we returned slowly to Burke's plane, and I watched Halliwell to gauge his reaction. Men like him are designed and built in different ways than the rest of us, and the reality hiding inside Aline's mind was a threat he couldn't ignore. He waited and watched carefully when Burke stepped forward.

"May we consider the matter settled?"

She nodded, and Burke began.

"Quarters have been prepared at our facility, and you should find them quite comfortable as we proceed through…"

"No," Aline interrupted. "I agree to speak with you, and your people can conduct their tests, but we will go home at the end of each day."

"I don't understand," Burke replied. "You will be provided with anything you need and…"

"Staying on-site is out of the question, Mr. Burke; if you don't trust us to return until this is finished, then we have nothing more to discuss."

I could feel the anxiety filtering through, but it wasn't clear if the tension came from Burke or Halliwell. Aline let me inside just enough so that I could feel and hear, but the effect was powerful.

"Trust is a crucial part of this exercise," Burke said suddenly. "I agree, and we will make appropriate arrangements."

At once the air seemed to calm, and a swirl of uneasiness drifted from my thoughts. I nodded involuntarily at Burke's surprising position, but it was clear, even to me, he didn't hide sinister intent or a trap to be sprung when we were safely inside their compound.

"Where is this place of yours?" I asked.

"We are maintained at RAF Waddington, Lincolnshire," Burke replied. "They remodeled a special annex for us a few years ago, and it has been our home away from home. The security is rather excessive, and sometimes bothersome, but it is comfortable and private."

"The base commander knows about this?"

"Good lord no!" Burke said, smirking. "The Royal Air Force has been a very accommodating host, but they are not cleared for access to our activities nor will they be. I'm not sure they would *want* to know, frankly; we keep to ourselves and the RAF allows us to remain at a discreet distance."

"Go on, Mr. Burke," Aline said.

"As I told Evan, the process shouldn't take more than a week at the very most."

Aline waited another moment to consider before she moved close, and I thought Halliwell might spring into action but he held his position.

"We will be here at eight o'clock every other morning."

Burke cocked his head to one side and said, "It's at least 130 miles; a long drive from Llangollen to Lincolnshire, Aline."

She nodded toward Burke's airplane.

"Your pilots obviously know how to find their way to Liverpool. Oh, and understand this: if you or Gregory Hurd send watchers to keep an eye on us between sessions, I'll hear them. When I do, our agreement ends then and there."

"As you say," Burke replied.

I was in no position to challenge Aline's decision, but I needed more.

"You'll get what you want, Alan, but you haven't told us what happens when this is finished."

"The result of those unfortunate events at Aline's farm demands a slightly unorthodox treatment. While I understand defending herself, and you as well, it ended with the deaths of two security officers."

"That's on Hurd!" I said at once.

"It is, but there is more. The ill-advised assault on your weed field left two men dead, and *that* has invited scrutiny from quarters we would rather avoid."

"Which means?" I asked.

"It means we must ask that you leave the UK for a suitable period until people in high places lose interest."

"What does she get in return, Alan? Everything you've described so far is only beneficial to you and your group; what's in it for her?"

"No one will approach her on this subject ever again," he said simply. "After interest fades, you and Aline can return and continue as before. It will be as if none of this happened, and she will not hear from us unless and until she initiates it."

"How long do we have to stay away?" Aline asked, merely to keep the pretense that we didn't already know.

"Six months ought to be sufficient," he answered. "In this way, we will have enough time to deflect unwanted interest permanently. We have made the proposal to our Minister, but the final decision is hers; if she agrees, we proceed with this bargain."

"If she doesn't?" I asked slowly.

"Gregory is disappointed with the arrangement, and he has urged in favor of a less inviting solution. The Minister knows his argument is more likely resentment after the incident in the meadow, but she cannot dismiss his position completely."

Aline smiled as she moved suddenly closer to Burke.

"Where are they now?" she asked. "The others who were here before me?"

"Most simply returned to their normal lives," he answered. "One or two moved away to other countries. We have occasional interaction with them, but it is rare; we leave them alone, just as we will with you and Evan."

"Very well, Mr. Burke," she said at last.

He handed Aline a new phone number, and it was at least comforting to know her approval took us past an uncomfortable discussion of what would happen if she *didn't* agree. I knew we would have to go away regardless but doing so under a mutual understanding and the effort to cooperate suggested Burke's proposal had been made with sincere intent. They all knew what she'd do to them if they busted the deal, and short of assassinating her, his group's compliance was likely a matter of course all along.

Aline drove us home, and we spent the time discussing conditions and processes from Burke's proposal. I made myself let go of the persistent anger with Hurd and his poisonous influence that ended the lives of two soldiers, but the tragedy left questions. I asked about them before he boarded his plane, but Burke's answer was given with a sober expression of regret.

The life of the first commando who raised his gun to shoot was ended in a searing vortex of fire that consumed the oxygen around him and destroyed his lungs. Gruesome, but not unexpected. The second soldier's fate was no better, and I cringed to hear he suffered from what Burke's medical staff reported as "liquid respiratory impairment." A detached, clinical way of putting it to the rest of us he choked and drowned in a river of saliva Aline compelled his body to produce. I didn't need to recount the details because she already knew.

At home there was no more talk of separating so that I would be spared the ordeal, but we had work to do when the last phase of the process became clear. Once complete, the interviews, tests, and demonstration experiments would send Burke and his team off to analyze and do whatever it is they did after such a strange and indescribable event, but we needed to prepare.

Jeremy would have to be told at least some of the facts, we knew, but not enough to get him into trouble if Hurd's people ever came sniffing around. We decided to tell him only that we were off on a romantic worldwide tour, and I made arrangements for a monthly administration fee to be paid into his account to hire a property management firm. In this way, our homes would see regular activity and maintenance to keep up the grounds and check things inside so that nothing would change while we were away.

It was a sudden, sad experience knowing it would be a while before we saw home again. Burke asked that we not delay more than a few weeks and a month at most; an obligation to update his Minister (and Hurd) when the interviews were finished meant questions about Aline's location. It made me feel better when she decided we should treat our extended absence as a new and grand adventure instead of forced exile. I suppose you could say it was both, but she looked at me and said, "It doesn't matter where we go or what we do when we get there; we'll look the world over a bit, and then we'll come home."

25
SHALL WE GATHER AT THE RIVER?

ONCE more at Lennon Airport, we stood beside the apron watching a student and his instructor preflight a Piper Aztec. Aline sipped slowly at a cup of tea as we waited, and she seemed no different than a passenger about to board a train for her morning commute. A Citation business jet was idling when we arrived, and I watched with detached interest the shimmering heat distortion swirling out from its engine exhausts as it pivoted and trundled slowly for the taxiway. Aline wondered where it would land at the end of its journey, and the parallel to our own condition made her look at me and smile. When Burke's King Air appeared minutes later, the strange week ahead of us was finally underway.

Barely an hour later, after a bumpy descent through heavy clouds, our pilots taxied to an empty corner of the ramp at RAF Waddington. A tiny staff member from Burke's team called Mairead Murphy met and steered us quickly toward an idling van, and after a short ride across the flight line, we walked past air police guards who behaved as if we were somebody important. I watched them for signs of caution or stern readiness, but it was clear they had no idea who we were or why we were there. Unburdened by details about Hurd's dead commandos and the truth of Aline's nature, the guards saw only two more credentialed civilian visitors among many.

A narrow, brightly lit corridor led to another and another again until Mairead ushered us into an open area manned by two men in civilian clothes we guessed correctly to be part of Halliwell's security contingent. Beyond them, three doors led to private quarters and one was set aside for us to rest during breaks. Burke arrived at last, signaling to one of the attending officers to arrange for refreshments, and when I wondered to myself when the session would begin, he answered before I could ask.

"If you're up to it," Burke began, "perhaps we could start in ten minutes' time?"

Aline nodded her agreement and asked if we could wait outside on the grass. Burke nodded with a polite smile and Mairead pointed us toward a door between the bathrooms. It was chilly but the sun felt good on my face as we loitered near an inner fence. I know she could feel it, but my relief at her calm invited another more troubling question, and I leaned close to whisper.

"You're not going to say anything about Tegwen or the other lives, right?"

"Not in a million years," she said, snorting.

"I just wanted to make sure."

"And anyway," she continued softly, "I don't think it would matter even if they *did* believe."

"I wouldn't be so sure," I replied. "This is a place built to study the supernatural, and I can't think of anything in the category that tops reincarnation."

"Burke's thoughts are easy to read; there's nothing more interesting to him than my ability to hear or project thoughts."

"To *him*," I noted softly, "but what about Hurd and the Whitehall crowd?"

"They are one and the same, Evan; Mr. Burke is simply more polite about it."

I nodded at the image, but we agreed the mandate had been created and given for no more important purpose than keeping the United Kingdom safe. Beyond his polish and smarm, Burke's goal—and Halliwell's, too—was at least honorable and proper. Hurd, on the other hand, remained far beyond the borders of my trust zone.

"Burke didn't seem distraught over the deaths of those two commandos," I said softly.

"I know," she replied.

"They died in agony, Aline."

She looked at me with narrowed eyes, and I could feel her disappointment at once.

"It wasn't a hollow threat, Evan; they were going to kill us both."

"When did you know for certain?"

"I heard it before we got out of bed; thoughts like that are hard to miss."

There was nothing I could say; she was right, and the sobering truth of our near-death experience washed away my lingering concern for what became of two faceless mercenaries who crossed the line and paid for the mistake with their lives. I nodded, but Aline's expression was changed again, that odd transformation I learned to recognize when she seems to become somebody else. I know it's Tegwen's influence, when circumstance demands, but the phenomenon takes some getting used to, even now.

After a few more minutes Halliwell led us to a standard conference room, positioning us on one side of a long table. On the other, four or five chairs we presumed were reserved for the various members of the investigation teams waited empty. One of Halliwell's lieutenants, a rugby-player-looking brute called Terence, appeared first. He motioned for two armed guards to lock the door on their way out, and it occurred to me he wanted us to understand what could happen if things went wrong. I wanted to remind *him* what happened the last time they pointed guns at Aline, but it was certainly possible he didn't know, so I left it alone.

"Can we bring you something while we're waiting for Alan and the colonel?" His voice was nothing like his image: a higher pitch, plagued also by a slight but noticeable lisp.

"We're fine," Aline replied.

Terence moved to a corner and stood in polite silence with his hands clasped before him. I hate awkward pauses, but Aline made herself comfortable as though we were alone. A minute or two passed until the door lock clicked twice as Halliwell made his grand entrance, nodding for Terence to get lost.

"Before we begin," he said, "I wanted to cover some basic assumptions and operating rules so that nothing is missed, and you will be at ease here."

Halliwell presented a confident face, but all the while Aline was inside his head and measuring him moment by moment. He seemed unaffected by our meeting in Somerset (and the knifing agony she'd swept through his head) but this time, she was only listening and Halliwell might've misinterpreted the pain-free condition as a sign Aline was at rest. I wondered if Burke had cautioned the colonel to avoid needless subterfuge, knowing Aline would see through it in a second. When he continued, the answer was obvious.

"First, let me reassure you both there will be no more of the unfortunate circumstances that ended so badly in your field; it was not our choice, and we will not allow anyone to threaten you here."

"Thank you, Colonel."

"There is one other matter I think we should address, however."

"Go on," she said with a nod.

"I believe Alan mentioned something about blood and tissue samples, but we hoped to get that part out of the way sooner rather than later. May we proceed?"

"Yes."

Halliwell nodded and two female technicians, both of whom looked like librarians in rubber gloves, appeared with a yellow case filled with medical equipment. They worked quickly and efficiently until four small vials of Aline's blood went into an aluminum box with gray Styrofoam separators. A moment later, another person walked in whom Halliwell introduced as an RAF flight physician called "Doctor Stafford." She asked Aline for permission to administer a local anesthetic, followed by a small incision halfway up her left forearm to remove a tissue sample, and five minutes later, it was done. With only a butterfly stitch and a bandage no larger than a Post-it to show for the procedure, Aline returned to her seat beside me as Halliwell motioned for the others waiting outside after the medical team withdrew.

He seemed pleasant enough, considering the mother of all headaches Aline had given him at the Marine camp in Taunton, watching over the shuffling feet and movement until Burke led in two others we hadn't seen before—a slight man and a severe-looking Indian woman—and they took their seats across the table. Burke waited until everyone was settled.

"This is Dr. Mohini Kambhampati and Gilbert Berezan; Mo heads up our life sciences section, and Gilbert is observing on behalf of your government, Evan."

There was no need to introduce Aline, and it made me wonder how much Berezan knew and when he became involved. I watched him for a while and still he said nothing when Halliwell decided to get administrative details out of the way.

"After our previous encounter," he began and looking only at Aline, "there is some concern for overall safety I'd like to address with you."

"Safety?" Aline said.

Halliwell glanced toward the heavy door.

"We cannot have participants in the room who are not cleared for this sort of process, but I'm sure you already know they are maintaining position just outside in the unlikely event order must be restored."

"Why do you believe order will be lost?" she asked. "We came here willingly and with the understanding there would be only conversation between us."

"A mere precaution," Halliwell answered confidently, but Aline wasn't buying it.

"Your precaution is insulting and it tells us the trust Mr. Burke was so careful to mention yesterday is meaningless after all."

It was all I could do to keep from giving her a high five, but the tension was rising and Halliwell leaned forward awkwardly in his chair while he thought of something to say. In a single moment, a thin pretense of cooperation had been washed away before the meeting even started, and it was fun watching the fierce warrior scramble for answers. I wondered if all of it would unravel completely, but Burke waited so that we would see the proper degree of good faith interaction.

"As Stuart said," he began, "this is only a procedural demand and the normal method of conducting these conversations; there is no need for concern."

"If that's true," she replied, "why are *you* concerned?"

Burke's eyes closed slowly, and everyone noticed him nod very slightly when she continued.

"Or perhaps…"

They looked at her as she paused because everyone knew Aline was probing again. Before Burke could protest, she smiled and said, "Your guards are here at Mr. Hurd's request; the demand is *his*."

Burke returned his own grin to acknowledge the brief, effective scan, and it seemed he was privately delighted. I didn't understand until Halliwell looked only at Berezan, and the weedy little man's frown made it obvious Hurd's clumsy play and show of power was a secret now exposed.

"Very nicely done, Aline," Burke said with a smile, "but I'm sure you can understand Gregory's worry after experiencing your abilities in Taunton?"

Berezan stood and approached from around the table with a finger to his lips and an elbow supported in his palm the way haughty people do when considering options dramatically in front of others. It was harmless enough, and he looked at us for a moment before taking a deep breath.

"So how does it work, exactly?" he asked, and it was obvious even to me his interest was being led by a sarcastic tone to let Aline know he wasn't convinced. "Does the target always feel it when you're starting to worm inside, or what? Is there some sort of…"

Before he could finish the question, Berezan reached for his forehead, cradling it in his palms with a loud moan when it began. I heard the same tone in my own ears, growing to a high-pitched screech as Berezan turned slowly in place until the pain was more than he could endure.

"Okay, okay!" he cried out. "I got it!"

Aline released, and he braced against the table to steady himself before sitting slowly while the intense ache subsided. My ears popped, one after the other, and I hoped they wouldn't notice the invisible needles jabbed at me as well. There was no pain, but I promised myself to stay out of range the next time she opened fire.

"When I'm only listening," Aline said softly, "they never know; when I *want* them to know, that is how it feels."

Mo went to Berezan immediately and examined his eyes with one hand as she took his pulse with the other, and it occurred to me it was the first time Berezan had spoken. Halliwell stood, too.

"We hoped you might suspend your abilities for a while so that normal conversations can proceed."

"He wanted to understand," Aline replied.

"That is not for you to decide," Burke interjected quickly.

"I didn't decide," she answered. "*He* did."

Berezan waved Mo away and nodded.

"She's right," he said suddenly. "I asked, and she answered."

"His heart rate is elevated," Mo declared, but Berezan insisted her examination wasn't necessary. When he looked again at Aline, his indifferent expression was gone: another message delivered.

"That's what Greg felt the first time down in Taunton?" he asked.

Aline nodded, and Burke positioned himself in a corner.

"Now we've gotten the first demonstration out of the way…"

Halliwell returned to his seat and clasped his hands together on the table's surface.

"There will be ample opportunity for the physical element later on, but we must have your word and assurance no repeat of this will occur if and when we find ourselves in dispute."

"All right," she replied simply.

I couldn't recognize it in all the excitement, but when it dawned on me at last, it was obvious my discomfort was unintended and a by-product of Aline's demonstration for Berezan. She'd never mentioned the possibility (or likelihood) before, but I was simply too close when her thoughts reached out and with them was enough of the mysterious power she projects that I, too, felt its terrifying effect.

"May we proceed?" Burke asked at last.

Aline didn't respond, but he was already moving and we knew the cameras would index the moment as our starting point.

THEY HAD A prescribed interview structure and a long list of questions, but following Aline's answers, and an obvious need to keep her talking, any information she could offer was more important than a chronological process ladder to be climbed. I listened, and the focus Burke had demanded at the outset dissolved in the moment with an opportunity to learn what they could never get from others. Aside from blind tests with playing cards and numbers moving through a random generator at a slow, predictable rate, none of the earlier participants had come close to Aline and what she could do.

Halliwell and Berezan were subordinate to Burke's authority, but they were given wide latitude and both wasted little time going straight to those most interesting aspects.

"How long have you been aware of these unique abilities?" Halliwell asked. I looked at her and waited with my own interest to hear the answer; there was no chance she could tell them the whole truth, so she simply replied from her present perspective.

"During my transition from adolescence to adulthood."

Mo perked up and interjected a secondary question.

"Was your awareness gradual or sudden?"

"Gradual."

"Did it coincide with your first menstrual experience?"

"No."

In less than a minute they heard a predictable cadence to her answers, and I wondered if they would complain and ask her to expand. Brevity is valuable, but watching their patience slipping into frustration was amusing to me, and I said nothing when Halliwell asked her if *she* experiences physical discomfort when the mental probes become more purposeful and intense. I must admit it was a good question and seemed to catch Aline a little flat-footed, if only because she hadn't considered it before. She looked away for just a second or two and said, "It's never uncomfortable for me."

Mo decided the question didn't go far enough, and she muscled past Halliwell so that the events in Brugge would become the first point of focus. In her mind, there was no better place to begin, and since no one thought to challenge her, Burke nodded his approval. It was at this very moment I must've smirked because he wondered what I found amusing about the process. Aline glared at me, but I simply couldn't stop myself and I said with gentle sarcasm, "Miss Persimmon takes control!"

No one found my remark amusing, and Aline least of all, so I apologized through a chuckle and the "conversation" resumed. Mo recovered enough to ask about parameters and limits to Aline's "range" so that identifiable distances could be matched with obstructions and those barriers through which her thoughts could or could not be projected. Halliwell found the concept more interesting when Aline described one or two occasions when she could "hear" from a moving train, and a theory she had to be stationary was eliminated.

I sat on the periphery while she took them through the details, but it seemed to blend into one run-on sentence after another. In a spectacular display of multitasking, I heard Aline inside me again with a silent, stern warning for me to stop acting like a bored child. All the while, she spoke to Halliwell without pause, and it was stunning to find her thoughts could be divided to work individual tasks and all of them enjoyed a disturbing level of autonomy.

I went to a side table and found some bottled water, if only for a chance to stretch my legs. While I fiddled with its cap, Berezan stood as well, but he leaned on both hands and looked straight at me.

"Have you approached a representative in any of our embassies?"

"No," I replied. "Why would I?"

He waited and drew in a deep, dramatic breath as if to suggest I'd failed to meet a solemn responsibility, and that was when my dislike of the man took flight.

"Without Alan's considerate alert, neither I nor anyone in our government would know about this and *your* involvement."

"I didn't realize I was under an obligation to tell you," I countered.

"You're a citizen of the United States, Mr. Morgan, regardless of where you happen to live."

"Oh," I said with as much false concern as I could manage. "In that case, I guess I should tell you my girlfriend has these really cool powers, see, and Mr. Burke here, well, his team is going to study them to figure out how it all works. Friends again?"

I felt her hand on my arm gently pulling me back to my chair, but Berezan's dismissive smirk remained.

"We can discuss it later," he continued. "There are interests beyond this gathering that will have to be addressed."

"Thank you, Gilbert," Burke said quickly.

I wanted Berezan to be in a pout, particularly after Burke's skillful shift back to business, but he jotted a few notes on a pad with an indifferent expression as he waited for Mo to resume. Whatever he wanted to discuss "later" was unimportant to me, and I waited for a chance to tell him so.

They went back to the playbook and a seemingly endless list of questions designed to establish the history of Aline's abilities, but most of it was focused on her unique gift of hearing inside another's thoughts. Burke was obviously interested in the passive aspect, but after an hour Halliwell's patience was thinning.

"Could we just divert for a moment?" he asked. "I'd like to understand more about thought projection and the process specifically for the intent of causing pain or discomfort."

"All right," Aline said blandly.

"You showed us an example," he continued, "but I'm interested in the degree; was my or Gilbert's example a low-level demonstration or was it the full extent?"

"Quite low," she answered.

Aline's speech slowed considerably, and I looked at her closely. Again, she was changing, and I know Burke could see it, too.

"I see," Halliwell replied. "If you decided, on the other hand, to turn it up a notch or two, what would a recipient expect to find?"

Mo leaned forward in her chair as the colonel's question went quickly to the physiological manifestation of Aline's ability in tangible terms.

"How far would you like me to take it?" Aline asked.

"How far does it go?" Berezan said suddenly and with a demanding tone.

I waited to see if she would retaliate, but instead Aline's eyes darted between Halliwell and Burke and I felt the uneasiness return. Her toe began to tap in nervous anticipation when the first waves made their way through in my mind, and I sat sideways quickly to offer a clarification. It wasn't needed, I suppose, but each second that ticked by brought Halliwell and Berezan closer to another painful demonstration, so I spoke.

"I think the colonel means something more than what he experienced in Taunton but less than Brugge."

She looked at me, and I felt myself teetering on the edge; had it worked, I wondered?

When she took a deep breath and looked away, the strange, pulsing sensation in my ears stopped and her toe-tapping also ceased.

"It would depend," she answered coolly. "If I want to warn somebody off, it would feel like a very severe headache. If they continue the pain increases and unpleasant images appear."

"If they're not dissuaded after all?" Halliwell asked and the room fell utterly silent.

They knew the answer could be found in a coroner's report and the fatal damage to Claude Dumont's brain at the very least, and two dead soldiers removed from her field in a helicopter when the full powers were released. Still, Halliwell waited to hear it from Aline.

"You have seen the answer to that question for yourself."

"We know you can kill," Halliwell continued without a pause, "but I am speaking of those levels that fall short of fatal intrusion; the images you referred to just now."

"It varies according to the person," she replied simply. "I listen and find those things that frighten them most and if they cannot be warned away, it begins and there is no place for them to hide."

"It?" Berezan asked quickly.

"Sometimes," Aline answered, "your own imagination is more effective than physical discomfort; I give them a glimpse, and a warning that things will become far worse if they persist."

Halliwell nodded and that was that. He wanted to establish threat-to-response ratios, and Aline's description made it clear her abilities could be meted out in distinct increments. He would never say it outright, but I think the colonel was looking ahead to a time when she might still be enlisted to a darker, more purposeful role inside Britain's security apparatus.

Silence is often hardest to maintain in those moments when it must be, and I squirmed in my chair with a powerful urge to tell them who and what Aline really is. I wanted to tell them if only to watch their world crumble, but a cool breeze of understanding moved past me. Burke announced a brief pause to rest, and they shuffled from the room in silence. I hoped the exchange with Halliwell was fresh enough in Aline's mind to distract her, but the image of Claude Dumont sprawled on a sidewalk made me wonder if there was a difference when Tegwen's influence was in control. She was ahead of me, and when we stepped outside to stroll around their abbreviated compound's fence line, she smiled and said, "I wondered when you would come back to this."

As it had always been, she waited like a patient mother with outstretched hands to encourage and entice a toddler waddling along in a park.

"I really wish you wouldn't do that," I protested. "It would be nice to have a private thought now and again."

"When you're dwelling that way, it's impossible for me to miss."

"Good job pointing the blame back at me, Aline."

"You know what I meant."

"Yeah, yeah, I know, but it's still hard to get my head around this," I replied. "How can you be two people at the same time?"

"We've already been through this, Evan," she answered.

"Each time there are two halves that make a whole—I remember. But one of those halves is always Tegwen; every life, every identity was lived as…I don't know, a *hybrid* person?"

"An odd way of putting it, but I suppose so."

"She emerges when your emotions run high?"

"Tegwen and Aline are always here and one is never gone from the other."

I waited with caution to continue, but the questions were piling up.

"When something makes you angry, Tegwen's personality is prominent."

"Not always," she replied with emphasis. "When I lose my temper and shout at you, for example, Aline is often the one you hear, but it was *Tegwen* who wept when they opened Rhian's time capsule."

"Aline doesn't invade some poor bastard's mind and rip it to shreds!" I complained. "That process belongs to Tegwen."

She looked at me with a barely concealed scowl and said, "You speak of Tegwen as if she's not here, and I wish you would stop. I am right here, for Christ's sake, and so is Aline!"

"Damn it, this is confusing!" I said in desperation, but she looped her arm inside mine and pulled it close.

"You're making this harder than it needs to be. Others might find my ability a useful ally, not frightening or dangerous; have you ever considered *that*?"

"I'm just trying to keep up, Aline; the last thing I want to do is become reliant on bizarre, supernatural shit I can't even understand!"

"It's just *new* to you. When enough time has passed, you'll know without being told—you will feel it and the influence of one or the other will be obvious. You will adjust to this, Evan, I promise."

Her arguments were reasonable and so I accepted them. And anyway, it's not always easy discerning Aline's reaction to the things we discuss; what might seem a signal of rising anger is just as often injured feelings and sadness. When she hears my thoughts, they're unfiltered and raw because I am never given time to sort through and refine them. Aline cuts out the middleman and goes straight to the source, making it all the more interesting when she doesn't like what she finds.

WE HAD TIME, and the late morning air was warming in a mostly clear sky, so I decided to wash out a few nagging questions we hadn't covered. The first was made by my weird trip to Sweden and the short visit with Birgit Nyström.

"Before Damon bought the property, Jeremy says there were three other owners since you came down from Stornoway."

"Yes," she replied as though we were speaking in hypotheticals. "Why do you mention it?"

"Three owners in four years?"

"What of it?"

"Did you..."

She turned away quickly, and I couldn't see her face.

"Some of them were assholes, Evan, rude and thoughtless assholes."

The answer hovered above me and Jeremy's very mild description seemed a lot more plausible when I saw the scenarios and how it must've played out when they ended up on the wrong side of Aline Lloyd.

"How bad?"

"Them or me?"

"You."

She looked away again but not fast enough to hide a sheepish grin. It was precocious and perversely endearing to me, but it also meant the turnover rate really *was* her doing.

"I may have sent a suggestion or two from time to time."

"I see. Did they know where it was coming from?"

"Maybe," she answered through a coy smile, and I couldn't stop myself from laughing.

AFTER WE SETTLED, they continued to chisel away at their list, and Aline sat patiently through it all. Mo succeeded in convincing Burke to allow a preliminary physical exam ahead of schedule, but it left me isolated with the "inquisitors" and a battery of associated questions meant to gauge *my* emotional reaction, knowing Aline could chew me up and spit me out on a whim. Mo's colleagues wanted to know if I felt my masculine identity was diminished because my position at home was made secondary by Aline's extraordinary abilities.

When I asked them "what man's position at home *isn't* secondary," their frowns (and reaction to a deliberate insult) became my silent reward.

I tried an honest description, mostly to satisfy Mo's curiosity, but also to correct an obvious misperception. There was no doubt, I told them, Aline would win any real fight between us before it could start. However, you could say the same about an ordinary man attached to a karate black belt, or maybe a girl who practices mixed martial arts at a high level. It doesn't mean we're sissies or "metro boys" temperamentally suited to a submissive role. The distinction in our house is never at the forefront and Aline hasn't asked me to surrender my manhood to avoid conflict. When I finished, Mo just smiled and nodded. To this day I can't decide if her response was a sign of understanding, or if she thought I was only blowing smoke to save face.

Midway through the afternoon session, Aline decided she was done for the day, and Burke disappeared to arrange our plane ride back to Liverpool. The RAF guys were waiting on a noisy ramp while a gray Boeing E-3 Sentry jet, with the disc of its huge rotodome perched above, taxied past us. We crawled into our King Air's seats feeling better about the first full "discussion" than we had that morning, knowing the second pass would be interesting at the least.

26
THAT TIME WHEN A SPIRIT BRUSHED DAMON'S EAR

BY an agreement with Burke, our day off the next morning was spent sorting through the things that could be left as-is and those valuables to be removed and secured at a storage facility while we were away. Regular visits by Jeremy's people watching over both properties (and the occasional check-in by Margaret) bought peace of mind, but it didn't stop Aline from inspecting with painful diligence, "Just for in case," she said.

The weather was quiet and dry, inviting us for a walk in the trees we knew would be missed all too soon when our grand "tour" began, so we strolled the length of it in our mismatched Wellies as the sun climbed beyond the distant ridge. What to take along was a good question, and we talked about it all the way around to where the tiny brook at the far side of Aline's field gurgled like an old friend. I was working my way through a mental list of things not to forget when she stopped and turned to me.

"When we leave his laboratory for the last time, Burke is going to warn you," she said. Aline's expression reminded me of the face we sometimes wear when hearing sad news from a casual acquaintance: we don't feel its impact as they do, but we still need them to see a gesture of kindness and support. She had heard his thoughts, and the silent eavesdropping revealed something new.

"Warn me about what?"

"He believes I'm manipulating you—controlling what you think and how you feel, especially about me."

"Are you?"

"Not in the way he thinks."

"What the hell does *that* mean?"

"I *have* shaped your thoughts once or twice, but that was a long time ago and I simply wanted to learn about you."

It wasn't betrayal or even disappointment I felt because I'd moved past such useless emotions after enough of the subtle "reminders" she lobs at me from time to time. Instead, I heard a rare and direct admission that her influence is something greater and focused at me for a deliberate purpose. I remembered her earlier words and held them up like a badge.

"When I asked, you said influencing my thoughts would make our relationship worthless if they weren't natural and made without external forces."

"That was only in the beginning, Evan," she said quickly. "After we met, I wanted to see how you would react, so I provoked a response and watched; it is not the same thing and certainly *not* what Burke is afraid of."

There were times when I could feel her inside and recognize what it was, but Aline's description pointed to something altogether different and my curiosity became more important than any notions of hurt feelings.

"Okay, I'll bite; how *did* I react?"

She steered me back toward her house, and it was clear the answer wasn't going to be simple.

"Our first time, after we met in the glen, you asked if I couldn't sleep," she continued.

"I remember."

"I told you I knew you were there but not the reason *why*."

"I didn't understand at the time, but I figured later on it was just your ability to hear my thoughts that brought you out."

"It was, but there's more," she replied softly. I waited for her to finish, and it was easy to see a struggle within—a hesitation—to show me what I couldn't know.

"You came to me that night because days before, I sent something while you slept; vivid thoughts of us alone together."

I felt my face run red when the images returned, just as they had on that first night when I saw the powerful, raw images of a sexual encounter beyond any I could imagine on my own. Aline saw it and moved close.

"That wasn't a dream, Evan; I gave you those sensations and images but only to see what you would do. I wanted to know if your desire for me was already there and waiting or if you would recoil from it. When you walked to where I stood in my field, the answer was very clear."

"So, all that work was…priming the pump?"

"You never told me about those images because you didn't want me to know about a sex dream so vivid and extreme. It was much more than that, but there was no way for you to describe it to a person you'd only just met a few weeks before."

The truth behind another mystery emerged, and with it, a more important question called out and I spoke the words with no hesitation.

"That first time…it was different from most of the other times when we're in bed."

"Yes, it was."

She heard my thoughts and finished the question for me.

"You wondered if our first time together was different because of Tegwen's influence, and now you know that it was."

"When you spoke, I couldn't understand some of the words. That was Tegwen coming through?"

She nodded and said, "It was a very emotional moment, Evan."

I smiled because I understood better her first life's unique and fundamental part in it all. She followed her own nature, unfettered by modern-day notions of morality or societal judgment because they didn't apply to a girl born in 460. In fleeting memories trickling one by one into my thoughts, the weird, conspicuous shifts when she seemed to drift away or transform into somebody else offered a clue I had missed completely.

"Emotional for Tegwen, but not for Aline?" I asked.

"For both," she answered. "Sometimes, when things become intense the way they did on that night, my…*Tegwen's* influence and personality becomes prominent. Aline is always there, and she enjoys every bit as much. Not as loud, perhaps…"

In our most intimate moments, the swirling sensations of singular passion were more than expressions of a powerful physical attraction, and the hidden meaning was finally exposed for me to see. Each time we grasped at each other through an erotic dance in the dark, it was not only Aline in our bed; the change in her voice and language, the narrowed eyes nearly malevolent with ancient primal desire and even the occasional bite that drew blood were always Tegwen's presence and spirit whether I saw it or not.

Had I evolved to a place where disbelief was no longer relevant? Our relationship became a true partnership long before, and I felt an odd sense of accomplishment figuring out at last her answers were not revelations but rather a confirmation of things I already knew. It was quiet in the trees, and I gathered myself to test the theory.

"The day I arrived from London, when I was sitting with Jeremy in his office…"

"You saw me walking on a windy afternoon in Stornoway."

"How the hell did you…all the way from here?"

"No," she said with a broad smile. "I saw you leave the Royal Hotel and I followed. The girl at the desk told me Damon's brother came up the day before, so I waited and listened; it wasn't difficult to hear some of your conversation from the street."

"You've been inside ever since," I said sadly, and she could feel the resignation tugging at me.

"I listen when I need to, but that does not mean I control or direct your thoughts!"

"And you can't let Burke inside to prove you're not a lunatic, or he would see your other lives—he'd see it all."

"It's always been that way, Evan."

"You could hear his thoughts about warning me?"

"His plan was to tell you about his fears before we go; he feels…obligated."

"What *are* his fears?"

Aline stood beside me just as she had on the day we first met, looking into the distance that represented our future and life together.

"Burke is afraid I'll hurt you someday or maybe even kill you in an angry moment."

"He's thinking about Claude Dumont?"

"The two men in Glasgow; he knows how close it was for both of them."

It sounds so normal today: a conversation like any other with the exception its topic was murder—*my* murder—and yet we spoke of Burke's misperceptions in casual terms. Her words pulled me back to the present and Burke's disturbing belief Aline would one day be my destroyer. It was clear she'd heard in his mind enough to know he still regarded her as borderline insane and perhaps criminally deranged regardless of her unique abilities. For Burke, the distinction was meaningless and pointed to an eventual conflict that could end my life if I ever wound up on her wrong side.

"It's a no-win prospect, isn't it?" I asked. "You can't show him why he's mistaken, and he'll brief his masters after we go with the cautionary note and a warning that I may not come home alive."

"He will always suspect," she replied simply. "Months will pass, and long after we return it will remain a 'matter of time' in his mind. I can't help what Alan Burke thinks, but the burden to worry for nothing is his."

We finished our walk and sat in her kitchen to map out a plan. Since we were compelled to take a lengthy vacation on the far side of the world, Aline said, we might as well pick destinations we'd always wanted to visit and check them off an unspoken list. I voted for places where palm trees grow, and we laughed at the absurd, antithetical images of a Siberian steppe or the far reaches of Alaska's North Slope, simply for the sake of variety.

The idea was shifting from a forced exile to a shared adventure and excuse to waste a few months with aimless pursuits without concern for cost or reason. I regarded the change as a natural coping mechanism for making the best of a bad situation, but as we examined unusual sites on the internet, even I had to admit to a sense of excitement. The cost was obviously irrelevant, thanks to Damon's generosity, but I wasn't about to spend my own money to get booted out of the country for six months. Aline grinned and nodded when I told Burke to transfer "appropriate funding" to my London account, but the thought reminded me of Damon and another need to see beyond the veil.

"Now that I understand how easily you can influence others, it makes me wonder again about Damon's sudden change in the way he did business."

I waited for her to reply because she could surely hear my thoughts, and yet she said nothing. There are times when she makes me drag out an entire concept instead of intercepting it with an answer, and this was obviously one of them. It's irritating when she does that, if only for the sake of brevity and the time we could save, but Aline doesn't always function along predictable or convenient lines.

"How far did you go?" I asked.

She smiled at me, and I was at least grateful for not having to plod through an explanation she didn't really need.

"Far enough," she replied.

"Directly, or did these suggestions filter through when he was within range?"

"I didn't say anything directly, but they were taking advantage of him, Evan; I don't like people who do that, and Damon didn't deserve to be cheated."

I nearly shuddered at the thought of somebody pushing her to act, but the answer demanded clarity.

"Who are 'they' and how were they cheating Damon?"

"Three people came to see him," she replied, "two men and a woman. I was visiting with Damon because he wanted to see our catalogue and ask for help selecting a birthday gift for Isolda."

"Let me guess: you heard their thoughts and didn't like what you found."

"Something like that, yes."

"Okay, give me the story," I replied with a knowing nod.

"They were brokers who represent collectors—extremely wealthy collectors. Damon had an exclusive arrangement with them, and five unique collections were being discussed."

"They came all the way up here to see him?"

"An idea of adding pieces to one of the collections he was asked to appraise was on the table, but that's when I heard her thoughts—the woman, I mean…"

"And?"

"She was nervous that Damon would understand the resale value and see how grossly underpaid he would be when they settled."

"Were you just standing there listening?"

"I was in his backyard, waiting for them to finish so they would have privacy."

"But still close enough to hear," I said with a knowing smile.

"She was lying to him and the two men were part of it; they were all edgy, and it was obvious they wanted him to agree quickly so they could go."

"Wait," I said, "this woman…was she Birgit Nyström?"

"Not likely," Aline answered. "She was Chinese—from Hong Kong, I believe."

"Okay, so what happened next?"

"They had photos of the collection, and while he was waiting for them to lay each copy on a table…"

"What did you do, Aline?" I asked, almost afraid to hear her answer.

"I sent a thought—a suggestion—so that he would feel a need for caution. It was subtle, at least from your experience, but it was enough."

"That couldn't have been good," I said with a grin.

"It surprised them when Damon said suddenly he would only *consider* the job, and it made each of them react privately with frustration and anger—they suspected another broker had already spoken with him and their plan had been compromised."

"Did they say as much?"

"No, but they pretended there was no problem and they left rather abruptly. The impulse I gave to Damon was confusing for him, but there was no other way."

"Is that where you left it?"

Aline shook her head slowly, and I knew the rest of the story was going to be interesting at the very least.

"Over the next week or two," she continued, "I passed more thoughts and considerations through to his mind. Mostly, I wanted him to see for himself and understand the kinds of people he was dealing with."

"He never said anything to you?"

"Not directly, but I'm afraid I may have taken things a bit far; he became agitated and withdrawn."

"I'm guessing that was when he changed his mind about fee structures."

"Damon went to Spain quite suddenly. He told me it was time for him to speak with Isolda, but I knew he was lying. I could hear the resentment in his thoughts, and I know he began to take steps; the fee increases followed, and after a few months, he moved quite abruptly back to Malaga. We heard of his death months later, and…"

She let me see the images and feel the thoughts from her memory so I would understand. There was a distinct sensation of regret, and it took a while before I realized Aline hadn't intended so dire a reaction when Damon decided to fight back against sharks who always swim in waters filled with money. Her intentions were honorable, but even she couldn't foresee the effect, and it left her wondering if her good deed had backfired. When she learned Damon passed away, there was nothing more to do.

I considered the chronology and a fruitless adventure to Karlstad where Birgit met my questions with enough of her own to make clear the visitors to Damon's farm were not acting with her sanction or even her knowledge. It meant, at the very least, Birgit's business dealings with Damon were honest, and I wondered if her sphere of influence didn't extend to the unnamed trio pushing for his agreement. Either way, Damon's sudden "awakening" regarding his finances told a different tale.

The image forming in my mind was all too familiar and made worse by my own experience and what it means when Aline launches her mental invasions. I don't wish to speak ill of the dead, and least of all my own brother, but I am a much stronger emotional package than Damon ever was, and his reaction could only have been shock and dismay. Sudden, unexplained thoughts can be passed off as intuition, perhaps, but Aline's powerful influence is something else and compelling in the extreme. In his place, I would have no more explanation or defense against the storm driving me to reverse established business practices, and its result doubtless surprised and disappointed clients he'd known for years.

"You got Damon all spooled up," I declared at last. "He saw the darker side and understood they were working him. Maybe he panicked and went overboard in leveling the playing field, but that was the effect and it stuck until he died."

"They were cheating him, Evan," she replied evenly.

"I'm not complaining, Aline, but it does explain a few things. Vienne and I both worried Damon's sudden behavior change was something worse—that he went off the rails completely. Birgit worried, too, but now we know better."

She stood in front of me and leveled her eyes.

"You mustn't ever tell Birgit Nyström about this; you understand that, too, don't you?"

Her caution was as correct as it was understandable but also delivered with a different tone and one, others might argue, that carried an implied threat. I knew better, but the thought did cross my mind.

"Of course!" I replied in protest to the veiled insult, but there was another hidden meaning lurking inside when I noticed she didn't include my sister in her warning. Aline heard that thought, too.

"We may tell Vienne at some point but not today."

"I know."

She said nothing for a few tense seconds, likely to ensure her point had been made clear, and then it was done. Aline returned to evaluating destinations for our grand tour, and I notched another useful lesson in the way she thinks and those pieces of a puzzle she considers more important than others. I wonder today what Burke would offer in exchange for that understanding.

27
A PLACE WHERE INNOCENCE WAS BURIED

WHEN we made our fourth and final trip to RAF Waddington, it seemed like the bustle when a college kid prepares for graduation day, except there would be no commencement speeches, all-night parties, or heaving into the nearest toilet after repeated keg stands. For a week, they poured out questions and attached them to scenarios designed to establish triggers and responses. Mo wanted to find the bridge between thoughtful, deliberate action and a near-autonomic system that comes to life of its own accord. She seemed more satisfied when Aline's answers associated those extraordinary things she can do with deliberate choices.

They prepared a shielded room and asked her to repeat one or two of the more extreme examples of her power, but observers were restricted mostly to Burke, Colonel Halliwell, and Berezan. She obliged to a fair degree, but repeated lockouts of the fire suppression system invited disaster, so the more flammable demonstrations were discontinued and the carnival sideshow's appeal was replaced by a sober examination of thought projection.

Several lab assistants and technicians were enlisted to sit in an empty room and follow a prescribed menu of mental tasks to measure Aline's ability to "hear" inside their thoughts. Halliwell was keenly interested in that part, particularly the effective range of her passive eavesdropping skills, until it became clear there were no secrets they could keep from her. When she emphasized the point by writing details from a conversation two rooms away between Burke and Mo *while* monitoring the thoughts of her test subject, Halliwell gave up and moved on to the last phase.

For those few (including me) who have been a target of Aline's outbound "thought artillery," there is no equivalent experience. When it begins, she gives no warning, no subtle buildup to a crescendo to be met and endured. Instead, her invisible knives stab and slice one after another so abruptly a recipient is consumed as much by confusion and fear as real, tangible pain. They always referred to the process by the antiseptic, detached name, and when Halliwell asked if Aline was ready to conclude the "defensive cognition" tests, she walked straight to him as though he would be her target. She knew he was not, but I think she pretended otherwise for her own amusement as he stood quickly aside to signal he wanted nothing more to do with personal demonstrations.

At the end of a long hallway, a lone figure waited in a chair, and it was clear he had no idea why he was there. Of course, that meant neither Burke nor Halliwell had briefed him beforehand. A necessary detail in order to avoid predisposing him to what would follow? Probably, but when Aline arrived down the hall, it took only seconds until the subject stood quickly with both hands to his forehead. Once more, she aimed her thoughts at an unwitting person, and this time it was Berezan who paid close attention. The best conclusion I could reach was the likelihood Aline's ability to injure or even kill had been his focus all along, and when the lone figure cried out and stumbled to his knees at last, the little runt just smiled and nodded.

I asked Burke who the man was but he refused to tell me. I reminded him Aline could quickly contravene that determined silence, but he would only say "one of our security chaps." The man's true identity was of no use to me, but the test revealed Burke's unwillingness to budge whenever I asked questions he'd rather not answer. I think he simply enjoyed the novel ability of keeping a secret simply because he *could*. After days with Aline, and his mind forever open to her, I can't blame him for the indulgence.

Aline released the unnamed subject and his painful moment was finished as quickly as it began. He stood straight and looked at Halliwell for an explanation, but there would be no such thing and they gave him something to drink Doctor Stafford insisted would help. Mo told Burke potential swelling of a subject's brain was an unnecessary risk, demanding that Aline refrain from going too far.

At last, Aline decided to end it. They had enough data to study, she declared, and it was time to wrap things up. I remember the expression on Burke's face that changed quickly from astonished outrage to serene acceptance. She was always in control, and I think he found her blatant reminder strangely satisfying. Maybe because they'd succeeded in conducting detailed studies of a live subject but also for the private admiration he holds for that tiny minority of people who are not like the rest of us.

Halliwell suggested a twenty-minute break, and we went outside to follow our customary path along the perimeter to stretch our legs and unwind until the word from Burke's Minister came up from London. We stopped and leaned against the fence, watching as a flight of training jets executed touch-and-go routines under a fair sky. My mind drifted to the points along our bizarre journey until it fixed on the time capsule sitting in a crate at the back corner of Aline's garage.

"Assuming this politician goes along with Burke's plan, should we get that glass monstrosity some place safer while we're away?"

"I thought of that, too," she said with a smile. "Margaret has a spot in her mum and dad's garage picked out already."

It was one less detail to worry about, but the capsule pointed my thoughts at the one life she hadn't yet described.

"It's obvious why Rhian Pryce was so important to all this, but you never gave me the backstory on who you were in that life. I know when and where you were born, but nothing more."

Aline turned a bit so that the prevailing wind came directly at us, relieving her of the constant swipes with a hand to pull the strands of hair from her face.

"It was a normal life, I suppose you'd say," she began. "We weren't poor, so I was tutored and grew up much as I did in Jane's life. When I was nineteen, I went with my mother and a cousin to Cardiff for the wedding of another cousin. During a party for the couple, I met a young man called Owen Thomas; he was a junior manager for the Great Western Railway in Bristol."

"You sound different when you describe Rhian's life," I noted. "Happier, I guess."

"It wasn't a life of adventure," she said, "but it passed by the way it does for most people, and I have few negative moments from it now."

"So, you met Owen Thomas and…"

"He was full of fun and we spent a lot of time laughing," she continued. "So, it was no surprise when he came to Aberystwyth a month later. The courtship was brief, at least by standards of the day, and we were married in the spring."

"He moved up from Bristol?"

"*I* moved," she corrected, "and we took a small house near the channel where the ships pass by. Our children were born there, and we stayed in Bristol until he was transferred, first to Chepstow and finally to Pembroke after he was promoted. That's where we lived until…"

"When?" I asked softly.

"1932," she replied with a sad smile. "I was fifty-three, and that's where the moments end. I found my obituary in a local Pembrokeshire historical archive of news and events a few years ago."

"That's pretty young, Aline."

She looked at me and nodded.

"Pneumonia."

"And your children?"

"William and Charlotte," she answered. "Willie was wounded at the Somme in 1916, but they couldn't stop the bleeding; he died in a field hospital."

Aline's voice was low and deliberate as she recounted the death of another son. I waited in silence until she recovered and told me about her remaining child.

"Charlotte met and married the son of Owen's colleague on the railway—Glyn Jones—and they lived in Swansea the rest of their days. She had two kids as well, Anne and Anthony. They moved away to England and volunteered during World War II."

"Did *they* have children?"

She shook her head slowly, and the predictable end brought a tear from her eye.

"Anthony was killed in North Africa in the battle for Tobruk; Annie died when her building collapsed during the London Blitz. Charlotte lived into her eighties, and they buried her beside Glyn. It's a bit of an irony," she said through a sudden smile, "but their cemetery isn't far from where the hospital I was born in this life stands today."

At last, she finished the on-again-off-again process of acquainting me with each of her six previous lives. It still sounds strange to speak of "previous lives" with so nonchalant a tone, but I've learned to shift my perspective to what *is* instead of dwelling on what I once believed cannot be. As we huddled beside each other against a growing wind, there was only her life as Aline still standing, and the decision from a faceless bureaucrat in London would steer us toward that next path together.

We returned to the conference room to find Burke nodding and smiling into his cell phone. He disconnected and waited as Berezan followed Halliwell to their places opposite ours. Mo and the life sciences crowd were gone (on Burke's instructions, we presumed), and he clasped his hands together dramatically.

"It would appear our Minister has rejected Gregory's fervent plea for regaining control, and she has authorized us to continue with the original agreement."

"What are the conditions, Alan?" I asked. "We need the specifics so there won't be any misunderstandings."

He knew I meant the disaster in Aline's meadow, but his wave of assurance made it clear he and Halliwell had won the battle and Hurd was out of the picture.

"Gregory is prone to rash decisions, but he is also a shrewd politician; there is far more to lose by further intrusions than by leaving it alone, and he is most certainly aware of that cost. There will be other challenges, and his interest in our enterprise will return to the corner where it belongs."

"There are administrative details to arrange," Aline noted suddenly. "Evan and I will need some time to prepare before we go."

"I understand," Burke replied. "The Minister's expectation is that you will be off on your extended tour within a month and also that your return will necessarily include perhaps a brief, discreet conversation with myself or the colonel."

"You have our numbers," Aline answered, "but you told Evan there would be no more contact between us."

"A mere operational detail, Aline," Burke said with his customary smirk. "And only so that we can assure you the coast is clear, shall we say?"

"Then it is time for us to say goodbye," she replied.

"Your plane will be ready shortly, but I believe Mo would like to make a final inspection to satisfy herself your health has not been compromised by this interview series."

"I feel fine," Aline answered.

"It would make things easier for Mo if she could check off the item from her collection of process checklists; it shouldn't take more than fifteen minutes."

I watched Aline closely with the hope Burke's request was genuine and not contrived to a darker purpose. She watched Burke, too, but finally she nodded and Halliwell led her to the medical lab.

It felt awkward as hell, standing between Burke and Berezan in silence. After a moment or two, Berezan tossed a leather folio he carries everywhere onto the desktop.

"We can provide you all the contact information for our embassies and consular offices in the event you need help at some point."

I didn't need Aline's special abilities to recognize the dismissive tone in his voice.

"I'm sure we'll be fine," I said in reflex.

"You are still a citizen of the United States, remember."

"I never forgot, but it makes me wonder why you think I need to be reminded?"

"This isn't a frivolous romp with your girlfriend, Mr. Morgan; your actions can have consequences."

"They'll call if they need us," Burke interjected quickly, and Berezan aimed one final glare at me as he walked from the room with the purpose and stride of one late to a meeting. Burke sat on the table and looked at me for a moment. I thought we might return to the painful silence, but he removed his pocket handkerchief to refold while he made a final point.

"She is quite mad, you know."

Just as Aline knew he would, Burke held me back to warn me away from what he could see as only a looming disaster.

"We're all mad, Alan."

"Perhaps we are," he continued without a pause, "but we don't face the horrors Aline can inflict so intimately as you."

"I think I'll be okay, but thanks."

Burke stood, and I noticed his usual smirk was gone.

"She is the most dangerous person I have ever met, and after you go, there will be no one who understands that ability; there aren't any doctors who can look at what's left of you and diagnose the real cause of death."

I listened, but it was obvious the words would never be enough. Burke offered a last caution and warning that Aline would be my downfall if I didn't separate from her and soon. I know he truly was acting in what he thought was my best interest, but he did so without knowledge of who and what Aline really is.

"I'm not leaving her, Alan."

He closed his eyes and smiled in resignation and the matter was closed. A moment later Mo returned with Aline, and we gathered our things. There were no speeches or offerings of gratitude; Burke and Halliwell shook our hands and handed each of us their cards with a standing invitation to call should the need arise.

We nodded and followed to the usual RAF van and a short ride to the transit line where our blue-and-white King Air waited in its chocks.

AFTER A DAY or two to recover, we went into Llangollen and sat with Jeremy for a while. Our sudden departure was a surprise, but he knew enough to understand our circumstance was created the day Andre Renard came to town, and I was grateful he thought enough not to ask about it. In the morning on the following day, contacting Vienne became the final task to be accomplished. I couldn't tell her why and I felt the grinding, persistent guilt of knowing whatever excuse I made would be an outright lie. There would be time, Aline reminded me, and one day we might be able to tell and show her all the things she couldn't know—the things no one *should* know.

Burke made it clear contacting friends or family would be a mistake since it was likely his colleague agencies could be called upon to monitor our movements and perhaps pry their way into our phone or e-mail conversations to ensure compliance. Maybe after a month or two at the very least, he said, when distance and deniability would make the whole story sound absurd, but certainly not before.

We wasted no time finishing up the preparatory work because, Aline insisted, the last days before departure should be spent enjoying our time in the trees and the fondness of where and how we first met. Jeremy gave us a checklist the property management people had sent, and we followed it to box up our things and remove any chance of fire by clearing away loose items, leaving electrical outlets unused, and tidying up the way anyone does when they leave home for a while. I wondered if it was like that for Damon when he went across the world to one lonely dig or another, but the likelihood did little to slow the clock as our moment edged closer. Aline used it as a good excuse to shed unwanted junk, and when we finished barely a week later, it was time to make the calls to our friends and family.

The shop was left in Margaret's charge and Aline signed over temporary power of attorney so she could run the place as she saw fit. It was amusing to see her reaction, moved by a sense of romance in the belief Aline and I were going away only to cement our relationship and see the world together. It had never occurred to me before, but there was something of the truth in what she said, and I decided to borrow the notion when I called Vienne.

We chatted for a while about ordinary things, but she had a fit when I told her our route wouldn't pass through Montreal for a while. It wasn't possible, at least in the short term, but Aline bailed me out by assuring Vienne our path would bring us through North America on the way home. Vienne was satisfied with it, but mostly she envied our spirit of adventure and dizzy abandon to do what most would never consider when held back by careers and kids.

The illusion was suitable, and we left her with a cautionary note the places we intended to visit were far enough off the beaten path that regular contact was unlikely. But suddenly, and for no reason I could think of, Aline told her we intended to stay a while "where the freeze-dried mummies live." Vienne laughed at the cryptic message because she knew we meant the coastal Chilean city of Antofagasta where Damon spent time unearthing artifacts, but at least she had one place on the map where we could be found.

We spent more time walking through the trees to get in all we could before it was time to go. The melancholy and sentimental tug wasn't as bad as I thought it might be, and Aline's notion of adventure in faraway places gave us a new and positive reason. With the interviews behind us, she said, it would be just us and the world so we might as well enjoy it.

I don't worry one of the underlings will be instructed to track and report our movements because those same officials—the "suits"—want us to go away; they *need* us to disappear for a while and stay hidden until time has passed and the turmoil has been forgotten. People who oversee Burke and the things his section does, including those who visit Downing Street without an invitation, can never know about this. And anyway, Burke, Halliwell, and even Hurd know better than to plan otherwise because their own failures and two dead soldiers would be exposed to the scrutiny of their masters and oblige uncomfortable explanations.

Our extended absence will be filed away with similar stories of others who went temporarily off-grid in search of a simple life; two more who shunned the modern—or became fed up with it—looking only for privacy and a chance at the quiet calm of anonymity. After we go the truth will stay hidden, there won't be further violence, and Burke's team will have the information they think will give them an edge in an increasingly dangerous world. We'll return after interest fades and the Minister's colleagues move on, having never been fully briefed and happy in their ignorance. Both sides win and our long vacation on the other side of the world will shut off the valve and let the bad dream end.

Mob snitches have witness protection programs to give them second lives. Corporate burnouts find counterculture havens in northern California or Vermont to help them deny who and what they tried so hard to become. Neither scenario applies to us because we're not escaping the twenty-first century to a smoke-filled teepee or thatched hut on a Micronesian island. The reasons most people disappear willingly have nothing to do with this, but it brings another problem: with few exceptions, we can never tell family and friends the truth and the reason why we went away.

Burke made another fervent plea that we reveal none of it to anyone for the rest of our lives, but I think he knows better. We did agree to make up suitable lies that no one will think to challenge—a desire to travel and spend time with only each other, for example. They approved, but for Burke and Halliwell, it's more important the secret will hold long enough for them to get enough distance from us so that plausible deniability can take root and grow.

In the evening before our first flight among many to places we'd always wanted to see, Aline and I walked to the spot where two birds had drawn my attention where she stood alone in the trees in those first days. We didn't say much as the wash of memories that belong only to us wandered by in a parade of fond images. She was so quiet, and I thought it was only sentiment and the emotions of our departure holding her in silence.

"Did you hear Burke's play?" I asked, only to spark a conversation. "He gave me the warning speech, just like you said he would."

"I didn't have to hear it," she answered.

"No, I guess not."

She turned to face me, pulling me close for just a moment.

"After all this, and the things you know today, would you leave?"

"What would you do if I did?"

"I wouldn't permit it," she answered bluntly.

I felt the tingle up the back of my neck once again. Despite my commitment to her, Aline made it brutally clear there would be no going back. It sounds strange, but understanding where she stood didn't bother me. I had learned to feel her probes, and I knew they were no longer inside guiding me. Instead, I felt only the quiet satisfaction of knowing our future was secure.

"Burke said I would figure it out someday, and it would open a window to get away from you; he told me to watch for the little signs your control over me is growing. On that day, he said, I will either leave you forever or die suddenly, never knowing the reason why."

"Do you believe him?" she asked.

"Can't you hear my thoughts?"

"I want you to tell me."

"I think *he* believes."

"I asked if *you* believe him."

Aline's voice was changing again, softer but with a subtle change in pitch.

"I know it's hard for you to say or even to think it, but Burke understands; he knows I'm not the good and proper girl, Evan. He looks at me and sees a corrupted mind—disconnected, perhaps, but willing to kill."

"I know you're not insane, but he's right about the rest of it."

"And yet you will stay," she said evenly and without emotion; "that is something *you* have decided and with no help from me."

"So it would seem, but we both know it was never that simple," I replied. "Still, love is a weird thing, isn't it?"

"It's not weird," she said, and I could hear the odd echo behind her voice return.

"How would *you* characterize all this?" I asked.

"Love is just a pleasant word to describe the calmer parts of our animal desires and needs, don't you see? Love means there is no one else for me…and no one else for you. Not *ever*."

She placed her hand very gently against my cheek, and I bathed in the blue of her eyes—the sound of her voice.

"We belong only to each other now, Evan; we do because we cannot stand to be apart and *that* is why you stay—it is why I will never have to force you."

"Is this Aline speaking, or is it Tegwen?"

"Yes."

ADDENDUM

IT'S been a while since I dredged this up from the "double-secret probation" folder in my laptop, but this morning's news demands it. We left home in the middle of November last year, and today is June 10, which puts us right at the seven-month point. It wasn't a huge surprise when Burke finally called this morning. We thought he might last month, but it wasn't a disappointment when he didn't.

We've been in Bunbury on the southwestern coast for three weeks, which pretty much wraps up our two-month Australian experience. For the record, our luxury exile started with a week-long visit with Aline's cousin in Windhoek (long plane ride). We went from there to Durban and a brief tour of South Africa because I've always been fascinated by the Boer Wars, and I just wanted to see where all that history and turmoil happened—Kitchener and a very young Winston Churchill. Cape Town was nice, but we didn't care for Pretoria or Joburg.

Aline wanted to meet up with her parents in Trieste, and then goof around in the eastern Mediterranean. We agreed the lack of political stability makes it a needless risk and so we bypassed it all and decided to confine most of the time to south of the equator and catch up with her mom and dad on the way back. We flew from Johannesburg to Sao Paulo then on to Buenos Aires, and it became our temporary base of operations while we wandered around coastal Argentina and a bit of Patagonia. There's a sizeable Welsh population there, which was surprising to me, but it made Aline happy. We tried a few days in Rio, but the charm wore off quickly when we discovered how violent the place is after dark. Aline declared it a bust because "any place that cordons itself into battle zones when the sun goes down is a waste of time and money."

A hop across the Andes took us to Chile and the fulfillment of a silent promise to visit Antofagasta I'd made to myself after learning of the place when Vienne and I discovered how far ranging Damon's work really was. It's a lovely town right on the ocean, and beyond it, the incredibly dry and inhospitable Atacama Desert. You'll have to look hard to find a city of greater geographic contrasts, and the bulk of our time on this trip was spent there. I'm looking at Aline right now with a smile because our weirdo neighbor, a very lively and kinetic hairdresser called Lali Peña, finally convinced Aline to have a go and change her look. The result was dramatic, to say the least, and I'm still trying to get used to her new, very short style. I was too polite to tell her Lali's expert touch left Aline looking a bit like a platinum blonde cockatoo.

We did fairly well arranging for temporary working visas because the Chilean government doesn't seem to mind as much as others, so long as you already have enough dough lying around to prevent them from having to carry you. There's a significant British population in Anto, and Aline spent some time helping out as a purchasing agent for a specialty store that imports various items to satisfy expats longing for a touch of home. I had no interest in doing anything beyond the borders of cultural investigation or polishing my tan on the beach, so I spent most of my days people watching and editing this narrative.

Aline has read all of it, by the way, and I wondered if my characterization of events might be met with a different perspective. Okay, I really meant to say I thought she might get pissed off about it and another brawl would ensue, but when I asked her what she thought, she just smiled and said it was fun to hear my take on things and know we're still very much aligned.

In the evenings, when there isn't anything more pressing, Aline takes me back for more excursions through the moments in her previous lives. She returned to Tegwen's time, of course, and I've gotten pretty good at feeling her influence in each of the other lives, including this one, which she says makes her proud of me. I'll take the kudos, but at least I've learned that what I don't know still dwarfs what I *do*, and that's probably as it should be.

The last phase, now that our journey is nearing its end, has been spent in Australia. Aline wanted to see New Zealand, but we blew it off in favor of another try sometime next year when we have more time. Farther west, the Barrier Reef really is as amazing as they say, and we loitered up and down the coast between Brisbane and Melbourne for almost a month. We didn't get down to Tasmania, but Aline was determined to see Alice Springs and Uluru. I wasted our time by insisting on a side trip to Coober Pedy because scenes from *Mad Max Beyond Thunderdome* were filmed near there and I always loved that movie. Mel Gibson and Tina Turner moved on to other projects, and Aline just shakes her head at my impersonation of Edwin Hodgeman's splendid *Dr. Dealgood* character.

We moved on through remote sheep stations to Western Australia (they're not kidding when they say the Outback is a huge, desolate place) and didn't stop much until we ran into the Indian Ocean at Perth. We love that city, and it will be a repeated destination at some point, but we made forays south to Fremantle and ended up here in Bunbury. The next leg we had planned was the Maldives and the Seychelles, but obviously those stops will have to wait for another time because the signal was given this morning, and everything has changed.

Burke called Aline's phone, and when she answered, I could feel her thoughts seeping into mine in a second. I know it wasn't intentional, but I've become much better at sensing those mild intrusions than I was a few years ago.

She put her phone on speaker, and Burke's voice seemed strange somehow—alien to us and not recognizable as it once was. He didn't begin with some grand announcement or deliberate speech to tell us it was time. Mostly, it was an oddly satisfying ramble about current events and the gossip coming up from London. Gregory Hurd, he noted with obvious amusement, had dug himself a hole with the Minister he couldn't get out of when the reports confirmed nothing out of the way or unusual had marred our agreement. The Whitehall crowd, at least those few who even knew about us, were given to understand a disaster was coming their way at any moment, and when that proved false, they needed somebody to blame. Hurd's proclamations made with his usual bombast and arrogance did him no good, and now he's fighting to win his way back into the Minister's good graces by overseeing the investigation of finance activities between British subjects and one or two Turkish nationals with dubious connections and a history of arms peddling.

Colonel Halliwell fared better, and he moonlights as a special consultant to the Home Office's liaison to major media outlets in the UK. Burke says Halliwell acts as an intermediary between legitimate information the British public is entitled to know and "deliberate fabrications made by the shitty damned BBC because they simply can't help themselves." Aline asked him bluntly if there was a point to the call, so Burke recounted a visit to London the previous week and a conversation with his Minister. During the discussion, he said, a recent debate in the Commons referred to the inherent risks associated with anything resembling enhanced interrogation techniques when the practice becomes known to an outraged public. He mentioned Aline's unique skills, and the Minister responded with near indifference and a distant, "Oh yes; the Welsh girl and her American gent." In that moment, Burke understood the events that led to our disappearance were forgotten, right on schedule.

This afternoon has been spent sending e-mails to friends and family to let them know our world tour is at an end. Quite a few have already replied with excited anticipation, and Jeremy made a point of assuring us all's well and my landscaping will look better than it did the day we left. Vienne asked…no, that's not correct, she *demanded* to know when we land in Montreal, and it's clear our return to Denbighshire will be delayed by a week or two in Canada. She thinks we should make our relationship "official," but that is due to her sense of romance and an inexplicable enjoyment from going to weddings. Aline didn't come right out and say it, but I think she's waiting for me to take charge on that issue. I told them both the future is an interesting place, but it didn't help much.

Aline wondered if I would be comfortable letting my sister in on the big secret, but I wasn't sure how far it should go. We've agreed to show her the thought-reading stuff at some point, but the jury is still out on the six previous lives part. We hesitate mostly because it would require the same levels of immersion I've endured over nearly two years for her to understand it wasn't a clever trick.

Aline tried to contact her parents an hour ago, but they're obviously offshore and headed who knows where. She spoke with her dad a few weeks ago when they stopped for a while on Ibiza, and our cover story seems to have held; her mom and dad believe we're doing pretty much the same thing they're doing, but we're getting to it before our retirement years.

I'm going to leave it here because there's nothing more to say, and we have a big job ahead getting things boxed for shipment to Wales. Aline is checking online right now, stubbornly researching travel options to the Seychelles because, she insists, it's on the way (it isn't) and one of the alternate "always wanted to go there" places on her list. I thought she would zero in on the most direct flights to Heathrow available, but Aline is never in a hurry, and I'm learning to embrace the journey instead of watching the clock. I'll remind her Montreal is an eastward journey and that will put the Seychelles on a temporary back burner.

We're going home; time to pack.

ACKNOWLEDGMENTS

Chet Benson, Editor

Rebecca Rue, Editor

Erik Johnson, technical and IT support, musical director

Phil Bourassa, webmaster and creative consultant

John Jorgensen, geographic and cultural support

Vern and Joni Firestone, biznis enablers

Warren Kovach, historical perspective

Heather Rose Jones, onomastics in absentia

INSPIRATORS

Ian Anderson

Alan Parsons

Evángelos Odysséas Papathanassíou

Jeff Beck

Robin Trower

Stanley Clarke

Jack Wall/Sam Hulick

Jimmy Hinson/David Kates

Chris Velasco/Sascha Dikiciyan

Anthony Banks/Michael Rutherford

Earl Klugh

Noddy Holder

Avigdor "Spoofy" Avidan

ABOUT THE AUTHOR

Robert Davies is a born-and-raised Michigan kid with an overactive imagination and love of literature that eventually became a disease, curable only through the odd, frustrating therapy of writing fiction. A Navy veteran, musician, private pilot and erstwhile traveler, he crossed oceans and countless borders to find and understand Earth, only to leave it behind in the pages of his first novel. Released from the University of Portland with a Bachelor's in Journalism, Rob has spent the last twenty years as a contract manager in the information technology and telecommunications industries. He currently lives in southwest Washington with his wife Stephanie, daughter Natalie and four mildly overbearing female tabbies.